One

Kensington, London

November

'Duncan, not that awful disco ball of your mother's again! Please, I beg of you. Last year it gave Lydia Mumford some sort of aura migraine before I'd even served the Waitrose arancini,' Lizzie Andrews said, raising her eyes and glaring at her husband who was stood precariously at the top of a stepladder. He was about to fix the large revolving silver sphere to a hook above the kitchen island where, on the hob, something containing cranberries was simmering.

Twenty-six-year-old Keeley hid her face in her mug of super-hot, extra-strong coffee and tried to stop a laugh from escaping her lips. Her parents' conversation over her long-since-passed-away gran's festive regalia had been treading the same path since the decorations had been left to them in the will. Her mum had always insisted it was because the old lady never liked her.

Joan loathed me. Loathed me, Duncan. Right from the get-go. Ever since the first time I came to your house with peonies for her and she shoved them in an empty tin of Heinz beans as a vase. That was when the die was cast.

But Keeley liked the decorations. None of them matched together – there were vibrant purples and emerald-greens alongside 1980s-style robots swinging on bunting and Chinese paper lanterns that probably should have caught alight long ago. At first glance, they might not *seem* to correlate, but somehow they worked. Her sister, Bea, had loved them too. Bea would always be fighting their dad for use of the ladder, having somehow actually worked out complicated things about balance, or the optimum angle to enable the globe to spin in a completely symmetrical way that would please Lizzie's need for order. Bea had always plunged into things with full-on gusto but never without the knowhow to back it up.

Thoughts of her little sister made Keeley's heart squeeze and she took another sip of the coffee before the toaster popped with the crumpet she was cooking.

Lizzie shook her brown curly hair and sniffed, nose in the air like a prized perfumier. She dropped the pinecones she was painting to the newspaper-covered work surface. 'What's that smell?'

'Is that one of those giant crumpets I bought yesterday?' Duncan asked, grinning down from the ladder, both hands still holding the whole giant reflective world in his hands.

'Yes, it is,' Keeley replied, trying to wiggle the large crumpet out of the sleeve of the toaster. She had got it in without too much effort, but now it seemed it was impossible to remove.

A Perfect Paris Christmas

Mandy Baggot

An Aria Book

This edition first published in the United Kingdom in 2020 by Aria,
an imprint of Head of Zeus Ltd

9 7 5 3 1 2 4 6 8

A CIP catalogue record for this book is available from the
British Library.

ISBN (PBO): 9781838933456

ISBN (E): 9781838933449

Typeset by Siliconchips Services Ltd UK

Cover design © Cherie Chapman

Printed and bound in Great Britain by
CPI Group (UK) Ltd, Croydon CR0 4YY

Aria
5–8 Hardwick Street
London EC1R 4RG

www.ariafiction.com

For my much-missed pets…

Sleep well Truffle, Stripey and Kravitz xxx

'Keeley!' Lizzie exclaimed in horror. 'A giant crumpet!'

'Would you like one, Mum?' Keeley asked. The crumpet still wasn't moving and with every pull she was shaving the outer crust away from the body of it. It wasn't going to stay 'giant' for long if it kept this up.

'What you putting on it, Keeley?' Duncan asked, tongue sticking out of his mouth, eyes concentrating hard on the hook on the ceiling. 'Bit of peanut butter? Or... how about that wild blueberry jam? That's nice, that is.'

'Duncan!' Lizzie said. 'That wild blueberry jam was meant for the scones for the advent afternoon tea with the Forresters! I can't believe you've opened it!'

'Sorry,' Duncan answered. 'Perhaps you should stick labels on things you don't want opened by the mere mortals of your family.'

'Well,' Lizzie continued, still sounding exasperated, 'it should be obvious that it isn't for *you*. When have I ever bought wild blueberry jam for *you*?!'

'A change is as good as a rest though, so they say,' Duncan replied. 'I thought it might have been one of your "new opportunities" like the yoga and the... Crap Gaga.'

Keeley really couldn't stop the laugh this time as she opened the drawer for a fork. Her fingertips were not going to move this sucker, so it was time for reinforcements. 'It's Krav Maga, Dad.'

'He knows!' Lizzie said, taking her glasses off and putting fingers to the bridge of her nose like she was getting a headache. 'I've invited him to join me,' she carried on. 'Except he'd rather spend his time playing darts than doing something that's classed as *real* cardiovascular exercise.'

'Are we going to have the "darts isn't a real sport"

discussion again?' Duncan asked, taking one foot off the ladder in a bid to reach out further. 'Because, if we are, I'll find that article from *The Telegraph*.'

Keeley lowered the fork towards the crumpet in the toaster. And it was then that Lizzie screamed. Running like someone might again be about to infiltrate the coveted blueberry jam, before Keeley could even take another breath, her mum arrived at her side and plucked the fork from her fingers.

'What are you doing?! Keeley! For heaven's sake!'

'What?' Keeley asked. Her heart was thumping now and she put a hand to her chest in case she needed to push it back in. 'What have I done?'

Lizzie brandished the fork like it was a light sabre and she knew exactly how to use it. 'Do you know how many people die each year from toaster accidents?'

'Er... no,' Keeley answered. She had a feeling her mum was just about to tell her though.

'Seven hundred,' Lizzie said. 'Seven hundred idiots who should know better. *You* know better!'

Keeley could see her mum was getting emotional, and not simply the kind of emotional she usually got when she started making festive wares for afternoon teas, Christmas fairs and fundraising afternoons. This was almost the kind of emotional she got when she talked about Bea.

'Sorry,' Keeley offered.

Lizzie put the fork down on the worktop with a bang, then shifted past Keeley to tackle the toaster herself. 'Why are you toasting a crumpet anyway? There's low-sugar muesli in the cupboard or there's fresh fruit – clementines and a Galia melon – or...'

'Blueberry jam,' Duncan offered. 'The Forresters won't be able to have it now the seal's broken.' He let out a grunt as finally the globe was hooked in place. 'There we go! Perfectomundo!'

Keeley watched her mother deftly, somehow, pull the crumpet from the toaster. It was dark brown, slightly burned around the edges, just as she liked it. She could almost taste it. A thick layer of butter melting into the fluffy inside...

'I'll leave it out for the birds,' Lizzie said, taking it towards the patio doors and their small patch of decking, leading to grass and then her dad's man-cave where he kept his dart board and homebrew kits.

'What? Wait!' Keeley said. 'That's my breakfast!'

Lizzie stopped, crumpet between thumb and forefinger like it was a land mine she had unearthed from the kitchen tiles and she needed to keep *really* still in case it exploded in her face. 'Keeley, come on, don't be difficult, darling.'

Difficult? Keeley pushed her tongue to the roof of her mouth and pressed hard into her palate. She could already feel where this was going. It would start out as caring, then move swiftly on to running down a tick list for those people living a heavily monitored life. It would end up with Keeley feeling incredibly guilty.

'Lizzie, love...' Duncan began, slowly descending the ladder, the ball above his head turning the kitchen into something akin to a Eurovision stage. Keeley wasn't sure it was rotating as evenly as it would have if Bea were still here.

'No, Duncan, don't you get involved now. You never usually *want* to be involved. It's always me who has to do the tough love while you stand behind me encouraging our daughter to put her health in jeopardy.' Lizzie made a face, crumpet still dangling. '"Nothing wrong with Dominos in moderation as long as you avoid the stuffed crust". "You are what you eat… and no one ever wanted to be a guava". It's not funny! None of this is funny! I've lost one daughter. I don't want to lose another one!'

The crumpet crumbled and Lizzie crumpled, folding her body in on itself like she was an origami swan someone was making very badly.

'Mum,' Keeley said, rushing forward and putting her arms around Lizzie's slender frame, drawing her close. 'It's OK. I'm fine.'

'You're not fine,' Lizzie said, the words rushing out through the tears, voice muffled against Keeley's bright red festive jumper. 'And you definitely won't be fine if you eat giant crumpets and sugary jam.'

'Is the jam *that* sugary?' Duncan asked. 'Because if that's the case I'm not sure Tommy Forrester needs the boost. He's stopped playing squash completely now, you know. Something to do with a frozen calf.' He put a finger to his temple. 'At least I think that was his injury. Although, thinking about it, it might have been what he had planned for Christmas dinner…'

'Mum,' Keeley said softly. 'I *do* watch what I eat. All the time.' She caught a look from her dad then and rephrased. 'Most of the time.' She sighed. 'More often than not. But… it's Christmas.'

'It's November,' Lizzie countered, raising her head from Keeley's shoulder. 'People who say "it's Christmas" the moment Halloween is over should be… tied to a chair and made to listen to… Piers Morgan.'

'Lizzie!' Duncan exclaimed.

'Well!' Lizzie remarked. 'This is Keeley's life we're talking about. And she's ready to play chicken sticking steel into electrical appliances and gorging on food stuffs that are going to stick to her arteries like... like...'

'If you say Piers Morgan again I'll have to tell your father,' Duncan warned. 'He has a framed photo of him in his study.'

'Like...' Lizzie continued.

'Like the chocolate cake Bea used to make.'

Keeley finished the sentence, tears filling her eyes. Someone had to actually say her sister's name instead of skirting around it like the word 'Bea' would curse them for the rest of the decade. Still now, just over a year on from the devastating traffic accident that had taken Bea from them, the pain was still so raw. This was the second Christmas without her. During the first Christmas without her everyone was reeling from the trauma and Keeley was still in hospital.

Everything was suddenly quiet. A tear snaked down Keeley's face and she dashed it away with the back of her hand. She couldn't chance getting any kind of dampness on her newly coloured hair. Her best friend Rach said the 'light brown with copper highlights' was legit from a subsidiary company of L'Oréal, but Keeley suspected she had got a whole pallet of them from Adie at Price Squash. She apparently wasn't allowed to shower until at least tomorrow.

'That cake,' Duncan said, finally on ground level and licking his lips. 'It *was* good. We should make it again. As a family.' He paused briefly before adding, 'Bea would like that.'

'It wouldn't be the same,' Lizzie remarked.

'We don't know that,' Duncan replied. 'Until we try it.'

'It might be nice,' Keeley suggested. 'My kidney and I promise not to actually absorb any.'

Lizzie sucked a breath in through pursed lips. 'Oh, that's right, make fun of me!'

'Mum, I wasn't. I...' Keeley started. But it was too late. Lizzie had turned away and was marching from the kitchen, loose-fitting yoga pants creating a breeze.

'Can you smell burning?' Duncan asked, sniffing.

'Dad, I don't really smell anything,' Keeley answered.

Duncan dashed forward, taking hold of the pan on the hob. Keeley leaned over his shoulder, looking inside. The red cranberries had done more than reduce. They now resembled hard black rabbit droppings and the sauce was less coulis and much more tar.

'Oh dear,' Duncan said, also looking into the pan. 'Your mother's not going to be happy. That was meant to be turning into a cranberry and jalapeno salsa to pep up her book club's nibbles this afternoon.'

'Dad,' Keeley breathed, as her dad put the pan down on a ring that wasn't hot. 'Is Mum OK?'

Duncan put a hand to his short grey beard and mused for a moment. 'Your mum hasn't ever really done "OK",' he answered. 'She generally ranges from "pallbearer" to "Elton John in his heyday" and nothing in between.'

'I know,' Keeley answered. 'But she's more "pallbearer" at the moment, isn't she?'

'Well,' Duncan said, 'it's the time of year, isn't it? The anniversary... of losing Bea... and you... getting up on your feet and getting your strength back… and… Christmas coming and…'

'And?' Keeley asked. She sensed her dad was holding back on her amid the fumes of cranberry and whatever possibly lethal lung-burning gold spray her mother had been trying to coat the fir cones with. She could feel her throat furring up.

'Well,' Duncan said again, 'I think, as much as she does seem to love all these festive coffee mornings and nibbles with the neighbours, it's all a bit of a… time filler.' He looked directly at Keeley. 'If you want my opinion, which your mother makes very clear she rarely does want… she keeps herself busy so she doesn't have time to think.'

Keeley nodded. She knew exactly what her dad meant. Since Bea had died Lizzie had more hobbies than *I'm a Celebrity* had witchetty grubs. If it wasn't Krav Maga, it was yoga. If it wasn't yoga, it was fundraising. If it wasn't fundraising, it was dinner or tea parties with people who had never had much to do with the Andrews family until Lizzie needed them to fill a blank diary…

'Listen,' Duncan said, putting a hand on Keeley's shoulder. 'This isn't your worry to bear. It's mine. And, as her husband, the one that's meant to know her best, I'm keeping a close eye and—'

'Hiding in the man-cave any chance you get?' Keeley suggested.

'No,' Duncan said. 'I'm just… hoping it will all run its course. It's not been that long and she can't keep this pace of hobbies up forever.'

'Mum has always been very determined,' Keeley reminded.

'It could really actually last forever.' Particularly when no one could predict exactly how long you got with forever…

'Have a crumpet,' Duncan whispered. 'Just take some fruit and seeds to go with your lunch. I'll go and check on Mum. Give her the bad news about the cranberries.' He smiled. 'Wish me luck.' He drew the side of his hand across his throat like it was a knife.

Luck. Yes, everyone needed a little bit of luck in their life, didn't they?

Two

House 2 Home, Kensington, London

'Well, Brandon, tell me, what can your favourite estate agent do for you today?'

Rach was already at her desk when Keeley arrived at the estate agency only a fifteen-minute stroll from her family home. Feet up on her desk, taking advantage of every tilt the chair had to offer, a Santa hat complete with bell over her wavy blonde hair and a green dress that looked straight out of Father Christmas's workshop, Rach nestled the phone under her face and held up her coffee mug mouthing the words 'it's a two-sugar morning'. Then the mug dropped a little.

'I beg your pardon!' Rach exclaimed. Her expression was belying the tone and there was a definite spark in her eyes. 'I was expecting you to ask me about the three-bedroom mews house, not say something that would put you straight to the top of Santa's naughty list.' She gave a smutty giggle as Keeley took the mug from her hands and headed through the office towards the kitchen at the rear.

Rach was an estate agent. Keeley wasn't. Keeley wasn't anything really. Since the night the taxi had crashed, everything had fallen away, in slow motion, like a snowy nightmare sequence in a film. One moment she was set to start a new life – leaving her job as an assistant to an interior designer and starting her very own business – the next she was in an operating theatre fighting for her life while her sister tragically lost hers. *Everything* had changed that night. Bea gone. Her career finished before it had even begun. And now, here she was, living back at home and working as a 'house doctor' for House 2 Home. It wasn't exactly how she thought she would be using her artistic eye. She had envisaged her working day to involve the careful designing of a bespoke wallpaper as opposed to deciding what cactus looked best on what Ikea sideboard. But it was a job and it paid OK and there *was* that short commute. Plus, to ease her mum's anxiety further, the business belonged to a friend of the family, Roland Krantz, so you could guarantee if she ran a temperature, had a headache or was in any way not one hundred per cent feeling top notch, Lizzie would know about it by lunchtime...

Keeley put the kettle on and leaned back against the worktop, studying the advent calendar Rach had stuck up at least two weeks ago. Only November and doors open already. Surely that was bad luck. She sighed. What was it with the word 'luck' today?

Rach marched into the kitchen. 'Bloody Randy Brandon is up for it already and it's not even eight-thirty.' She looked at her watch as if to clarify her statement. 'It's not even eight-thirty. What are you doing here already?'

'My mum accused me of dicing with death by trying to

get a giant crumpet out of the toaster with a fork,' Keeley answered. 'And then I ate the crumpet... with some blueberry jam none of us were supposed to be eating and, before I left, she hit my dad over the head with an artisan multigrain baguette because some cranberries got burned.'

'Shit,' Rach replied. 'And here I was complaining about being offered a shag before my second coffee.'

'Yes, well, I definitely have the best excuse for having two sugars in my coffee,' Keeley said with a smile.

'Yeah and hold that thought,' Rach said. 'Because you might want to make it three sugars when I tell you what Roland has in store for you today.' She pulled at the hem of her very short costume.

'Oh God,' Keeley said, closing her eyes, taking a deep breath and then opening them again, watching as Rach ripped at another door on the advent calendar. 'It's nothing to do with the radio station, is it?'

Last year Roland had sent her down there to record a jingle for the new festive advertising he had planned for House 2 Home. It was the last time she had ever joined in with singing in the office. One chorus of 'It's Beginning To Look A Lot Like Christmas' and Roland had turned all Louis Walsh and said she was 'through to the next round' – of which there was *one* round, the final, having to sing words that were Christmassy and all rhymed with 'en suite'. She had felt the furthest from festive last year and had only joined the team a week prior to that appointment with Kensington FM and, back then, even a heavy laugh pained both sides of her abdomen. But Roland always took the angle that what didn't kill you made you successful. Rach said he had once had that phrase printed on compliments slips and a tote bag...

'No,' Rach said, laughing as she stuffed a chocolate in her mouth and opened a second advent door.

'The school? Because, last time I went there, one girl attacked me with an ancient, heavy Bible and three glue sticks.'

'Shall I put you out of your misery?'

'Please. I won't tell my mother it was you.' Keeley held her breath.

'Mr Peterson's put his house on the market again. Roland wants you to get back in there and do your re-styling stuff.'

Keeley carried on holding her breath. She could feel just about everything getting tighter. The waistband of her skirt. Her long socks inside her boots that had definitely shrunk in the tumble drier. Her heart...

'No,' Keeley finally said through shaky lips. 'No, you're winding me up. Roland said, six months ago, that even if Mr Peterson bought him all the scotch in Scotland he would never *ever* take him on as a client again.'

'We-e-e-ell,' Rach said, drawing the word out, her eyebrows going up under the rim of her Santa hat. 'Let's just say it could be a very dry Christmas in the Highlands.'

'No!' Keeley said, putting her hands into her hair and squeezing. 'No, no, no! I can't do it! I cannot do it!'

She really *couldn't* do it. It had been too short a time to even think about stepping over the threshold of Mr Peterson's house again. Mr Peterson's two-bedroomed terrace, albeit on an illustrious street in the heart of Chelsea, was crammed with taxidermy animals that had all been hand-stuffed by Mr Peterson in a very dark, windowless basement room that looked more 'torture chamber' than it did the 'family-room with annexe potential' that Roland had described it as in the particulars. Six months ago, when Keeley had had to restyle it ready for viewings, she had said all the animals had to go, as did some of his rather dated (and blood-spattered) furniture. The house was professionally cleaned, contemporary furnishings were hired, but on the second viewing – a family with three-year-old twins – two beady-eyed pheasants and a mole had fallen out of the wardrobe in the master bedroom and scared everyone half to death. It seemed Mr Peterson's commitment to selling his property didn't stretch to giving up his dead creatures even for a few weeks. And the client was the kind of stubborn Keeley knew couldn't be changed.

'I'm not sure it's up for debate if you want to get your Christmas bonus,' Rach said, patting her shoulder.

'I'll forego the bonus.' It couldn't be that much. Roland was more frugal than Martin Lewis.

'He's promised no animal surprises,' Rach added.

'I don't believe him.'

'Keeley, that isn't like you.'

'What isn't like me?'

'You're usually peace and goodwill to all men – and women – and non-binary – all year round.'

'I'm fine,' Keeley answered. She took her hands out of her hair and picked up the now-boiled kettle, pouring water into the mugs. She wasn't quite fine. Her mum making such a stance about a crumpet had got to her. And the last thing she wanted over the festive period was Mr Peterson's stinky abattoir of an abode to fix again…

'Well, thinking of positives, your hair looks awesome,'

Rach remarked. 'You haven't got it wet yet though, have you?'

'No,' Keeley said, mixing in the coffee granules. 'I *do* listen to you.'

'So, it's just your mum and her thinking you're the poster girl for the *Final Destination* film franchise?'

Keeley couldn't help the smile at her friend's joke. Rach was about the only person who didn't treat her any differently to how she had before. When she'd got out of hospital everyone else seemed to tiptoe around her as if one wrong word or a too-tight cuddle might alter her sinus rhythm.

'She's got more Christmas drinks and nibbles events lined up than Michael Bublé has records played on Kensington FM this time of year,' Keeley admitted with a sigh. 'My dad says she's burying her head in tinsel-wrapped festivities and hobbies so she doesn't have to think. You know, about Bea and everything. Well, mainly about Bea.'

'And what do you think?' Rach asked.

'I think if I don't move out of home soon I'm probably going to go mad... or set fire to something... or go mad... or eat something really *really* bad but really *really* delicious in front of her... like a Walls Viennetta... with my fingers.'

Keeley stirred a spoon in the coffee mugs and handed Rach's over to her. 'Christmas isn't the right time to think about moving though, is it?' she breathed. But when would be the right time? Currently, she knew deep down, she was staying at home because her parents needed her to... or Lizzie did, at least. Their whole lives had been turned upside down after Bea's death and, as well as managing the loss of a child, they had put everything on hold to nurse Keeley back to health. Lizzie had even taken early retirement. Hence the need for all those hobbies…

'Are there two sugars in here?' Rach queried, holding her mug aloft.

'Yes, to go with those chocolates you've eaten from the advent calendar.' Keeley took a sip of her drink. 'You do know it isn't even December yet.'

'You do know it's not my advent calendar,' Rach replied, grinning. 'It's Oz's. I told him the cleaner's daughter is nicking them.'

'Rach!'

'Oh God,' Rach said, leaping forward and putting her coffee down on the worktop. 'Have we got any kitchen roll?'

'I… don't know.'

'Don't panic,' Rach said. 'It'll be fine.' She removed Keeley's mug from her hands and set that down too. 'I'm sure it won't stain.'

'What?' Keeley looked down at her hands to discover they were both coated in dark brown. 'Rach! Is this hair colour?'

'Well, you went all hair-grabby when I told you about Mr Peterson. You probably had palm-sweat and I said don't get it moist. Come on, we'll go to the loo and I'll sort it out. Just don't touch anything on the way.' She took Keeley's arm.

'What do you mean you're sure it won't stain? It's stained my hair! It has all the capabilities of staining! Staining is its sole USP!'

'Take a deep breath,' Rach ordered. 'Think of that Viennetta. I might even buy it for you.'

Three

The Resting Hospice, Kensington, London

'You've changed your hair. Man, it looks terrible.'

Keeley watched twenty-two-year-old Erica devouring Celebration chocolates by the handful. It seemed she had already removed all the wrappers to make the scoffing easier. Some of them were now covered in fluff from the hospice blanket wrapped over her shrinking frame. Erica didn't seem to care. And, frankly, why should she? It wasn't the polyester that was going to kill her. It was the Stage IV cancer.

'Thank you,' Keeley answered with a smile.

'I know my hair looks shit too, by the way. But I'm dying. I'm allowed to look shit. What's your excuse?'

'Rach dyed it last night with some substandard product we've since found out is illegal in the Ukraine. Apparently I'm lucky I haven't been blinded by the fumes or made sterile by the chemicals contained in it. I guess time will tell on that last one.'

Erica's face exploded into a whole feast of expressions.

Her deep, dark brown eyes crinkled up, her cheeks briefly turning from hollowed out to fattened and her mouth opened wide, chocolate pieces spraying all over the bed covers. 'Shit, man, you've made me waste all that chocolate!'

Keeley grabbed the box of tissues on Erica's bedside unit and began to mop up the damage. 'I'll get you another blanket.'

'Don't bother,' Erica insisted. 'It's only chocolate and I can lick the crumbs up when they starve me later.' She lowered her voice. 'That's what they do when they want to get rid of you here. If you're not dead within a couple of weeks, they do anything they can to get you out of here and back into a care home, including bringing down the quality of the nosh.'

'Oh, well, I'm not sure that's true.'

Keeley was just a volunteer here. After the accident, she had wanted to do something to give back. In the weeks after her operation, when she had stopped feeling like she had been pummelled wrestling style by The Rock, as soon as she had learned to walk again without wanting to vomit, she had started volunteering at the hospital. And it had somehow turned out to be as much for her as it was for the patients. It was surprising how much you could get out of a few games of Monopoly, Sudoku and the latest real-life stories from *That's Life!* when you had nothing better to do than mope and miss your sister.

But the very best thing Keeley had got from her afternoons at the hospital was her friendship with Erica. They'd first met on the cancer ward when Erica had started going through treatment. On suggesting that Erica might like to play Scrabble, Keeley had been subjected to all the sass until Erica had decided it 'might be cool, man' if they turned it into a drinking game. Thankfully, as Erica was having radiotherapy *and* chemotherapy, it hadn't involved shots of alcohol. But the forfeit had been that the loser was made to shell out on the expensive hot chocolates from the canteen. Their friendship had – surprisingly in some respects, when neither of them were in the most ordinary of situations – blossomed. There was something about Erica's gung-ho spirit that reminded Keeley of Bea. There Erica had been, with the worst prognosis being levelled at her with every new check-up, still believing in recovery, still full of fight and endless determination.

Week after week, Erica was back in for more treatment – sometimes too sick to even sit up in bed let alone play board games – but in between times, Keeley continued their relationship outside the hospital walls, making sure Erica had everything she needed for home and a professional support package at hand if she needed it. But now, only months down the line, here they were. The hospice. Keeley was now volunteering at the place that had cared for her Grandma Joan and it was now going to be the place where her life-loving friend Erica, at just twenty-two was going to spend the last of her days. But, despite that truth, Erica still had that streak of badass. Keeley felt it was the mark of true bravery – not the winning of the battle, but the knowing how hard you fought.

'Trust me, man. I'm holding out. But if they serve me another meal of liquidised cat food, I might have to give in. At least at the care home you can nick a meal from the person next to you if you don't like the smell of yours. In a room on your own here it's a bit like solitary in jail or, you know, self-isolating.'

'Have you been in solitary in jail?' Keeley asked with a wry grin. 'Because if you have you've neglected to tell me a thing about it.'

'I've got a TV, man! I watch all the shows about all the things that aren't this place!' Erica began to cough, her breaths raspy and mucus-filled. Keeley put a hand on her back and gently rubbed until the coughing subsided and Erica's frail body eased back onto the pillows.

'That wasn't the fucking cancer,' Erica insisted. 'That was the fucking caramel.'

Keeley smiled. 'How are you feeling today? Apart from being short-changed on meals?'

'Dying, aren't I?' Erica shrugged. 'The church came in today. They all looked at me like they were sizing me up for my coffin.'

'Erica, I'm sure they didn't.'

'They didn't look at me like I was Erica,' she answered. 'They looked at me like I was just a worn-out body waiting to fade out the exit door. They looked at me like the "me" was gone already.'

Keeley reached for her hand, but Erica drew hers away. In some ways she knew exactly how Erica felt. Some days it felt like some of the original Keeley had disappeared along with Bea. Like the broken parts of her that had been supposed to heal, mend or be replaced, hadn't quite grown new skin, or weren't working properly.

'Don't give me none of that sympathy handholding bollocks, man. You know I hate that. Don't be as bad as them.'

'Sorry,' Keeley replied.

'You're the only one that doesn't treat me like a corpse round here. Even back when we first met, you would come in with your stories about your shitty life and, I still don't know if you're making them up for my benefit or not, but they made me laugh and they made me *feel*... and when you're stuck in a bed all day every day that's about the best you can hope for.'

'Who bought you the chocolates?'

'Someone called Mary bought them for Miss Phipps, but she died last night so...'

The circle of life. It carried on. One person's gift benefitting another. And didn't Keeley know all about that.

'Want one?' Erica asked, holding out something that looked like a mini-Milky Way. It was hard to tell without a wrapper.

Keeley shook her head. She shouldn't. She had eaten three advent chocolates when Rach eventually managed to get most of the dye off her palms. She had already decided to opt for something with spring greens for dinner later and go home via the gym.

'No offence, but you look like *you're* the one who's dying,' Erica told her. 'I thought you were meant to come in here and cheer people up.'

'You're right,' Keeley agreed.

'Well, tell your face,' Erica replied. 'You're living! You might have made a bad hair decision, but you have time to change it. Me, I'm stuck with me until the Grim Reaper turns up.'

'I could get someone in to style your hair if that's what you want,' Keeley said. There was access to essentials as well as treats here. The hospice worked with all sorts of companies to try and make last wishes come true. Last week Mr Davidson was reunited with a vulture he used to take care of in his days working at the bird conservancy. With a wingspan of almost two metres, it had been quite a challenge getting Little Buddy into Mr Davidson's room when the animal got completely excited by the biscuits on the tea-trolley and decided to unleash and flap. But the tears in the old man's eyes and the tremble of his lips at their reunion had moved everyone who had witnessed it. Who knew that vultures liked to be tickled under the beak?

'I don't want my hair done by Rach! I'm not going to the grave looking like someone painted it with creosote.'

'You're exaggerating,' Keeley said, putting her hand to her hair. 'It doesn't look that bad.' Rach had promised her it didn't.

'No,' Erica said sighing. 'You're right. It's alright. I'm just being a bitch. Dying woman's free pass to say what she thinks without worrying about the consequences. Who cares if anyone's at my funeral anyway? I'll be in a box... well, hopefully one of those rattan baskets if I can afford one of them.'

'You don't need to think about that yet,' Keeley said, swallowing a lump in her throat. But they did. Both of them knew what was coming. Keeley was going to lose someone else close to her yet again. Someone who reminded her so much of her little sister. How was any of it fair?

'Well, what should I think about then?' Erica asked, big eyes studying Keeley so intently. 'Because from where I'm lying there's only so much interest you can pay to the crap surroundings. Like that terrible painting over there.'

Keeley's gaze went to the oil painting of two poodles on their hind legs dancing with each other. One of them had a beard like Charles I. It was pretty terrible. 'Well,' she said, turning back to Erica, 'what would you like to look at while you're here?' Perhaps she could get Erica one of the rooms with a large window a little bit earlier. Those rooms were usually reserved for patients at the very bitter end of their journey. They all had a fantastic view over parkland and, even now, at the end of November, when the trees were bare of leaves, the sight of the boughs bright and sparkling with frost was something to behold.

'One of the Jonas Brothers? I'm not fussy which one… actually, Nick… no, Joe… nah, definitely Nick.'

Keeley laughed. It wouldn't be that hard to arrange a poster… or a cardboard cut-out… or a body pillow. She would have a look on Amazon later.

'Nothing Christmassy though,' Erica continued, now looking a little wistful. 'I can cope with the chocolates, but the decorations are mocking me.' She sighed. 'Because, chances are, I won't be here for turkey this year. And that's just cruel, man. I love turkey.'

'Turkey and the Jonas Brothers… *Nick* Jonas,' Keeley said, counting on her fingers. 'I'm sure Christmas can come a little early.'

'What are you doing for Christmas?' Erica asked, smoothing her blanket out with her skinny fingers and picking up a tiny fragment of chocolate.

'Oh,' Keeley began. 'Well, I'll be at home on Christmas Day. My mum will be cooking a feast I won't be allowed too much of and Dad will probably have my share of the things I shouldn't eat. And, after we've eaten all the turkey dinner – sorry – we'll all eat low-fat cheese, pickles and chocolates we don't need and then probably fall asleep in front of the wood burner that my dad has stoked so much it's made the living room the temperature of the inside of a volcano.'

Erica snorted. 'Love it, man.' She sniffed. 'Apart from the not-eating-what-you-want bit. They don't go into that in films where the characters have had transplants, do they?'

Keeley shrugged her shoulders. 'Those scriptwriters are kidney-ing themselves.' She smiled at her transplant humour. She had a kidney joke for most occasions.

Because that was why she had to proceed with caution in life. Her ultimate gift last year had been a new kidney from a donor she knew nothing about. A priceless present that had saved her life and stopped the Andrews family losing both their children in the same accident. It had been nothing short of a miracle, but it had also been a complete game-changer where normal life was concerned. Nothing was ever going to be quite the same again. But, at least she was here.

'That's better,' Erica stated with a grin. 'Your face has cheered up now.'

'So, shall I get you a cup of tea? Or shall I see if I can make it a hot chocolate? I can't guarantee the ones here are as good as the hospital's though,' Keeley offered.

'Carlsberg?' Erica asked, ever hopeful.

'I might be able to find some mulled wine.'

'Make it a double. My kidneys are already as done as the rest of me.'

Four

The Andrews' Home, Kensington, London

Keeley pulled her boots off by the front door and closed her eyes as she took a second to rest up against the wall of the hallway. Opening her eyes again, she saw there was tinsel around the plants that hadn't been there this morning and a poinsettia in a pot on the telephone table. Her mum really was kicking early festivities up a notch this year and it was possibly because Lizzie was an emotional purchaser. Their confrontation this morning over Warburton's finest had probably prompted a trip to John Lewis...

Stifling a yawn, Keeley picked up her boots and padded down the hall. She was tired today. First she had planned out a house-doctoring project in Lambeth and then she had tried to persuade Roland that if he made her enter Mr Peterson's house again she would most probably voluntarily succumb to the formaldehyde or, if that somehow didn't work, she would quit. Remarkably, neither of those vaguely veiled threats had stopped Roland from putting an appointment for a visit into her online diary...

And then there was Erica. Her gorgeous friend wasn't doing at all well, despite all the bullishness. She really wasn't expected to last until Christmas and that thought cut Keeley to the quick. She knew Erica was in pain – despite the heavy medication she was on – and that her leaving was inevitable now, but the thought of her slipping into a final sleep was unthinkable.

Keeley took a breath and put a hand to her middle, just above one of her scars. It still ached sometimes and it had been aching so much today she'd skipped a visit to the gym. She just wasn't in the right frame of mind.

She put her hand to the door of the kitchen/diner ready to be faced with whoever her mum had round that evening for Baileys and a charcuterie board. But the conversation she could clearly hear wasn't about who had done what to who at the last Wives Association meeting, but her parents discussing something that sounded important. She paused. And kept listening...

'Lizzie, we're going to have to tell her. How can we not?' Duncan's voice said.

'Oh, I'll tell you how we cannot. We can pretend that the email never arrived. We can send it to junk like you do with all my discount codes from Wallis. I'm quite happy to forget I saw it. What I'm not happy about is that I decided to share it with you,' Lizzie said in reply.

'You didn't share it with me. And I'm not sure you *would* have shared it with me if I hadn't snuck up behind you and seen it. I think it would have been deleted already if I'd played another game of darts before I came back into the house.'

What was going on? Was *she* the 'her' that needed to be

told something? Was it something awful? Bad news from the hospital? The doctor had said at her last check-up that everything was fine...

'How can this be a good thing?' Lizzie asked. 'You tell me that!'

'Well,' Duncan began in soft tones he usually reserved for placating her mother when a new recipe hadn't turned out quite how it should. 'We did agree, after it happened, that should the other party want to connect, then we would be open to that.'

'We were grieving!' Lizzie exclaimed. 'They shoved so many pieces of paper at us I felt like I was... trapped in the paper bank at the recycling centre!'

A shiver of some sort of recognition that this *did* involve her ran over Keeley's shoulders. She didn't wait any longer. She pushed down the handle and stepped into the room.

Immediately, her mum bounced towards her, dressed in tight Lycra leggings and a fluorescent pink vest, with a sweatband around her forehead, curls springing over it.

'Keeley! You're back! Lovely! Lovely! Isn't it lovely, Duncan?'

Lizzie repetition of words was a trait that always appeared when she was backed into a corner. Last Christmas Lizzie had said the words 'frightfully festive' so many times during an awkward soiree with her newly formed crochet society that it had ended up turning into 'festively frightful' which meant her canapes were scrutinised a lot more thoroughly than usual.

Lizzie caught Keeley up in a hug that definitely could have expired a gerbil.

'I told Dad I would be back for dinner,' Keeley said.

She stepped back from her mum and clutched her bag to herself like it was a comfort pillow or maybe a shield to what she was about to find out. 'But if there isn't enough I can always—'

'Of course there's enough!' Lizzie said with a snort. 'There's always enough.' She trotted back to the hob on the island where pots were steaming and lifted some lids. 'It's my chickpea shakshuka with cauliflower rice.'

Chickpeas. Again. Chickpeas were the princes of protein in this house since red meat was almost abolished completely. Lizzie had made a bold statement about their carbon footprint but Keeley knew it was really about her diet.

Keeley stood still, watching her mum faffing about with a sieve and a wooden spoon as her dad avoided looking at her at all. He seemed to be spending a great deal of time polishing spoons for the table setting, eyes down.

'What were you talking about before?' Keeley asked, still cuddling her bag. 'I heard you... from the hall... and it sounded like—'

'It sounded like your father was trying to spend the whole of Twixmas at The Rabbit Hole. Some silly darts tournament he wants us to go and watch. I mean,' Lizzie said, finally drawing breath, 'a Kensington pub isn't exactly the World Championships at Lakeside, is it?'

'Lizzie,' Duncan said, finally putting a now shiny spoon down on the table. 'We weren't talking about the darts competition. You have to tell Keeley.'

'Tell me what?' Keeley asked. She was suddenly nervous. As if whatever her parents were going to tell her was somehow going to really change things again. She didn't want things to change *again*. Things changing had been her life's plotline for over twelve months now and she wasn't sure how much more she could cope with. She was still very much getting used to how her life was now, without Bea, without two kidneys, with all these tablets to take to keep the new kidney going…

'Let's sit down and have some food together,' Lizzie said, clattering pans as she became hidden behind a veil of steam under the glitter ball.

'Shall we open a bottle of wine?' Duncan suggested.

'There's a *non*-alcoholic cabernet sauvignon in the wine rack. After all, it *is* a Thursday, Duncan.'

Keeley pushed a forkful of her meal into her mouth but tasted nothing. However, she knew, if she didn't keep eating, if she didn't wait for her mum to 'settle' she might not find out what was at the bottom of all this slightly tight and nervous sitcom behaviour. And she needed to know *tonight*, at this dinner table, before all her imaginings of more visits to the hospital grew into giant grotesque Grinch-like gargoyles and swallowed her entire thought process.

'How's your food, Keeley?' Lizzie asked. Her mum was still wearing the sweatband and had already told them an entire story of one woman's fight against the Sh'Bam trainer's dodgy sound system and her even dodgier inferior quality Spandex.

'It's nice,' Keeley replied. 'The chickpeas have… a nice texture today.'

'Crushed soggy nuts, they always remind me of,' Duncan

piped up. 'Terry at the pub dropped a whole bag of Planters into his pint once. Refused to fish them out and, once he'd finished the beer, he ate them. I had a couple and they tasted just like this. Nice.'

'Fascinating,' Lizzie remarked, shaking her head.

'OK,' Keeley said. 'I think we've done all the necessary small-talk now.' She put down her fork and looked at each of them in turn. 'What's going on?'

'I can't,' Lizzie breathed immediately. 'I just can't.' There were tears in her mum's eyes and Keeley watched as Duncan reached for his wife's hand. This *was* serious. Was her body somehow rejecting the kidney and she didn't know? Surely she would know. She'd be ill, wouldn't she? She was sure the doctor said she would be ill if that happened.

She swallowed, then ploughed on. 'Dad?'

'Duncan,' Lizzie bleated. She seemed to be pleading with her eyes.

'Keeley, love, we've had an email today,' Duncan began, squeezing Lizzie's hand in his. 'It was from a lady called Silvie Durand.'

The name rang no bells with Keeley. Should it? Her dad was looking at her now like Silvie Durand might be the keeper of the secrets of the universe or the real mastermind behind Oreos. Lizzie let out a whimper.

'Who is she?' Keeley asked, her tone a little tentative. If this woman was making her mum cry then she didn't like the prospect of what came next. *Shit... was she adopted?* That was the tone of this conversation. She held her breath. Was this Silvie Durand her birth mother? She shuddered. No, that only happened in books... didn't it?

Duncan cleared his throat and picked up his glass,

downing the contents of the alcohol-free wine like he was hoping for a hit akin to Jack Daniels.

'She's... the mother... of your kidney donor,' Duncan said, the words forced out. 'Her daughter. She was called Ferne. She was the girl... the woman... whose kidney you received after the accident.'

Not adopted then. But it was ground-breaking, life-shifting stuff and she wasn't prepared. Keeley held her breath, as the shock rose up from her chest to her head, her eyes prickling as she tried to keep looking at her parents. Her donor now had a name. A woman. A woman who had passed away on the same night Bea had. A woman who had chosen to give life to others after she died. A woman who had saved her. Her name was Ferne.

'What did she say?' Keeley whispered. 'In the email.' For some reason the one thing at the forefront of her mind was the possibility of someone asking for the kidney back like it was a present they regretted giving and now wanted to return to the shop for a refund or give to someone else. Someone more worthy maybe. She tried to shake those thoughts out of her head. The counsellor hadn't suggested that action would work with regard to clarity of thought process, but Keeley always felt a little better after she had done it.

'This Silvie wants to take you away from us,' Lizzie jumped in. 'She will think, that because you've got a bit from her daughter, that you're partly *her* daughter now and, if you go, you'll like it better there and then you'll leave here and then you'll... you'll divorce us... because we haven't coped well with losing Bea and we've jumped between being overprotective, to being dismissive, and all the things in between. And I don't ask you enough about what's going on in your life because I'm always too busy filling *my* life with things so I don't have to think. Because if I think then… I hurt.'

Keeley watched her mum burst into a flood of tears that could have washed over the Thames Barrier and sent the city whirlpooling to the bottom of the riverbed. She didn't know what to do. *Why* didn't she know what to do? Because she was in shock. Both from this news of her donor's mother making contact and her own mother breaking down and being open for the very first time.

'There's a lot to take in there,' Duncan said, breaking the sobbing with words. 'A lot to take in.' And Keeley still didn't know what to say. She'd asked what the email had said and no one had answered her question.

'What did she say?' Keeley asked again. 'Please.'

Lizzie was still eyes down towards the contents of her concoction, hair almost touching the plate. Keeley wasn't sure she was going to get any more conversation from her mum at the moment. She moved her gaze to her dad.

'Well,' Duncan said softly, pouring himself another glass of wine, 'she sounds very nice. She said… that over the past year, after her grieving, she had done a lot of thinking. And, she has decided, that she would really, really like to meet you.'

Lizzie tried to muffle her sobbing with a tissue she had plucked from her sleeve, but Keeley could still hear. Her donor's mother wanted to meet her.

'I…' Keeley began. 'I don't know what to say.'

'She wants you to visit her… in France,' Duncan carried on. 'Paris, actually.'

'Paris,' Keeley said, nothing really sinking in.

'That's where she lives,' Duncan said. 'That's where… Ferne was from.'

Keeley shook her head. This was all too much. *She* now wished the wine was alcoholic. She reached for her glass anyway and took a sip. Her donor was from France? She had never known any details of who had donated her kidney. Her mum hadn't been able to donate after a small brush with cancer some years ago and although her dad was willing and able, the match wasn't as perfect as it might have been. Then, almost magically, someone on life support at the very same hospital Keeley had been admitted to, someone who was not going to recover, had provided a lifeline. Amazingly, they were a high marker match in blood type, tissue type *and* cross-matching. Keeley had got incredibly lucky that one night while someone else's world was splitting at the seams.

Lizzie raised her head a little. Her eyes were red and still leaking tears, the serviette pressed hard to her nose.

'Keeley, it's completely your decision what happens next,' Duncan told her.

'I don't know,' Keeley said. A shiver ran over her and she felt a pull from inside of her. That also happened now and then. It wasn't like the ache or the pain, it was almost like an acknowledgement. Some sort of internal ripple effect when she thought about how her life had altered from the night of the crash.

'You don't have to decide anything, Keeley,' Lizzie said, voice a little robotic. 'Nothing at all. It's too fresh and it's nearly Christmas and…'

'Lizzie,' Duncan interrupted. 'Come on, that isn't fair.'

'I'm just saying,' Lizzie continued, battling her emotions. 'This kind of pressure might be too much for Keeley right now.'

'I think that decision is Keeley's to make, Lizzie,' Duncan said, making direct eye contact with his wife. 'Don't *you* think?'

Keeley watched her mum again. She looked about ready to crumble like breadcrumbs into stuffing mixture. This moment wasn't *the* moment to be making *any* decisions. Keeley took a breath and reached for the tureen on the table. The only thing to do *right* now was to do the very British thing and keep calm and carry on.

'Can I have some more cauliflower rice?'

Five

L'Hotel Paris Parfait, Opera District, Paris

'The red or the green? Or the… green swirls on the red? Or… the red swirls on the green? Or, I know it is a little out there, but maybe, perhaps for something a little different, we could think of… electric-blue and silver?'

Ethan Bouchard popped another sugared almond into his mouth from the glass bowl he had drawn nearer and nearer to him throughout this meeting with his assistant, Noel. Then he placed a finger on his top lip and his thumb to his chin in a pose he hoped showed 'thoughtful'. As Noel had shown him swatch after swatch of fabric, Ethan had sucked in a sugar high to stop his eyes from glazing over. Filling his mouth with hard-boiled goodness was to stop him being sick or immediately reacting with the disdain he usually felt when Noel was trying to get him to make a decision about something Ethan considered mundane. And what constituted 'mundane'? Literally everything in his life since his best friend and business partner, Ferne, had died. He sucked on this latest sweet and finally cast a glance at the fabric books Noel was proffering at him. Why was he doing this again? What was the point? Life was mean and it was cruel and everyone died in the end.

'What exactly is this for again?' Ethan asked, moving the sweet from one cheek to the other. He was bored and he was hungover. He could feel the alcohol floating from his system with every glitterised suggestion Noel was making. And his assistant should be capable of making a decision about whatever this was without requesting his presence first thing in the morning when he had other more important things to do. Right now he needed to... drink coffee and... smell other people's cigarettes and dream about smoking them himself and... eat more sweets. He was a very busy man. He brushed a hand back through his dark hair and adjusted himself in the seat. He should try to look interested.

'This is for the whole, grand, 2020 Christmas theme for all the hotels!' Noel reminded, rather loudly in Ethan's opinion. 'It is very important! It is one of the most important decisions we make every year!'

Ethan could tell Noel was getting flustered. His perfectly gelled-back black hair was starting to shift out of sculpted in places and his cheeks were reddening like the fat breast of a seasonal robin. And *that* was Ethan's issue here...

'It is November,' Ethan reminded.

'Monsieur Bouchard, with respect, it is *late* November. We are behind schedule this year already. We need to make a decision as soon as possible. Our guests will be expecting a Perfect Paris Christmas any day now.'

What would Ferne choose? Before Ethan could stop it, the thought had arrived and the day's not completely dour manner started to disappear quicker than the contents of the candy bowl. None of this was the same without Ferne. And how could it be? Ferne had *made* Perfect Paris. It was all her vision. He had helped her, yes, but whether she had actually *needed* his input to succeed... well, he knew what most people's answer would be to that. That age-old feeling of not being good enough rode over his shoulders and he leaned back into the chair.

'What do *you* think, Noel?' He looked through the floor-to-ceiling windows to the cityscape outside.

Paris was alive. Paris was *always* alive. Here in the Opera Quarter, the former Parisian cloth manufacturing district, Ethan was constantly surrounded by all the things Ferne had loved most. The *Place des Victoires* with its nineteenth-century shopping arcades, designer names amid the covered shopping centres still resplendent with brass and wood panelling, was like a step back in time. Ferne had adored the boutiques, often spending hours and hours searching for something original, a dress she could make a new classic or a pair of shoes or a hat. To anyone else some of her purchases might seem a little 'out there' but the way Ferne saw things, the way his best friend had always worn things, was always unique. Somehow, Ferne could manage to make anything look like the new latest trend. Ethan had always teased her that of course this was the location she wanted their flagship hotel. How easy would it be for her to take a long lunch and stroll under the glass-topped roofs of *Galerie Vivienne*? He blew out a breath, making eye contact with a pigeon perched on a ledge just outside the window. That was where he liked to think of Ferne now, meandering through heaven's shopping malls, picking out must-haves to adorn her, light on her feet, floating just above him, still somehow connected...

'I think I could do a lot with blue and silver,' Noel said, his enthusiasm for dressing the hotels emanating from his every pore as Ethan looked back to him. And then his assistant seemed to rein the passion in a little as he spoke again. 'Although, traditionally, we have always gone for red and green...'

Ethan didn't care. He *really* didn't care. He wanted to scream 'what difference does it make?' Because what difference *did* it make? Green? Red? Blue? If he chose badly would a dislike to the décor for Christmas pull down reviews on Trivago? *What to say?* Would Ferne have liked a change? He couldn't remember who had come up with the red and green concept from the outset. Had it been Ferne? Or had it been the team of colour experts she'd employed? The only thing Ethan knew was it hadn't been him.

'Blue and silver speaks of luxury and opulence and... fine dining and impeccable taste and...' Noel continued. He was wafting his arms around now like he might be a ballet dancer from *The Nutcracker*.

'If I sign off on blue and silver will this conversation be over?' Ethan asked, popping another sweet into his mouth. Maybe he needed more alcohol and not coffee...

'Absolutely,' Noel replied, already beaming at his triumph. 'Not one more word on the topic. I will handle everything. You will not even have to think another thought about Christmas.'

And that last sentence was music to Ethan's ears. 'Fine,' he told his assistant. 'Blue and silver it is. Make it so.'

Six

The Hour Glass Pub, Kensington

Keeley drank three quarters of the pint of cider before even stopping for a breath. It tasted so refreshing. It was exactly what she needed. She might have skipped the gym last night, but today was a new day. She had spent an hour working out there earlier, pushing her body to its limits, unconcerned for her rapid heart rate or the pinch of a stitch, she had carried on running through. Yes, more water might have been healthier than alcohol, but she needed the hit. She was alive. She wasn't adopted. She had an invitation to Paris…

'Christ! You know it's barely lunchtime, right?' Rach remarked, jaw dropping with an expression somewhere between admiration and astonishment.

'Cheers,' Keeley said, gesturing the glass towards her friend and taking another mouthful. It was Saturday. Keeley had suggested lunch. She needed to talk to someone other than family about the email from Silvie Durand. She needed to say words, out loud, rather than rolling them all around her brain and having them form knots even the best Scout leader wouldn't be able to undo. She'd suggested here because she was also going to coat her stomach with the pub's homemade steak and Guinness pie...

'Something's happened, hasn't it?' Rach guessed. She sat forward in her chair, festive snowmen earrings hanging from her ears, leaning an elbow against the snow-sprayed windowpane next to their table. 'Is Roland forcing the issue on Mr Peterson? Because, if you really don't want to do it, even for a big bonus, then we can say the feathers... or the fur... is detrimental to your health.' Rach took a swig of her flavoured gin and tonic. 'I know I said you should stop playing the Little Miss Transplant card but, when it comes to stuffed carcasses, I'd be inclined to let it slide just this once.'

Little Miss Transplant. Yes, that was her. She was the keeper of someone else's precious organ. A walking, talking, living mausoleum. And that was one of the reasons she shouldn't be considering this offer to meet with her donor's mother. What good could it do for either of them? More than a year had passed. What was there to say? No, she should email back, type that it was so nice to hear from her, that she would be forever grateful for the gift of life but... Keeley took another swig of her drink. Except no matter how she worded a 'thanks, but no thanks' it sounded like a 'sorry, not sorry'. And this woman had lost her daughter. *Ferne*. Now her donor had a name it seemed to make things even harder.

'Keeley?' Rach said. It sounded as if her friend was asking for clarification to a previous question and Keeley had zoned out.

'Yes?'

'What's wrong? Because I know there's something wrong.'

Now that pint was fizzing back up into her throat and Keeley was regretting the speed in which she'd swallowed it.

'The mother of my kidney donor wants to meet me,' she started. 'She's offered Eurostar tickets and a stay in Paris in exchange for a chance to get to know me… a bit… I guess however much you can get to know someone in… a couple of weeks or so.' The words were in the air and the look on Rach's face said it all. Her friend downed her gin and tonic and looked like she wanted to give head to the ice cubes to get every last millilitre of booze from the glass.

'Is that allowed?' Rach asked suddenly. Her cheeks were now as red as the ones on the snowmen dangling from her earlobes.

'Is what allowed?'

'Mothers of donors being able to jump into your life like that without warning.' She picked up her glass and swirled the ice cubes around. 'Do they tell you about that before you go through with the operation?'

It hadn't been a case of deep consultation on anything to do with the operation from what little Keeley could remember. She had been more-or-less unconscious, in and out, not knowing what was going on at all and calling out for Bea. She had learned later that Bea had never made it to a hospital bed. Bea had died in the taxi, the paramedics having to gently separate their joined hands so they could cut Keeley free…

'My dad said that, at the time, after it happened, we

agreed that if the donor's family wanted to get in contact we were happy for our details to be passed on.' Keeley took a breath. 'I think, my parents were so grateful, so happy that I was alive… that they would have agreed to pretty much anything.' Not that it wasn't a good thing. She swallowed as that thought went across her mind. *Was* it a good thing? She wasn't sure, if her mum had the time over again, that she would agree to contact.

'And who is she? Is she *really* the mother of your donor? I mean, there are hundreds of people emailing other people telling them they know they're entitled to compensation from an accident they never had.' Rach sniffed. 'So, how do you know she is who she says she is?'

There had been many things that had crossed Keeley's mind since she had read the email from Silvie Durand, but the woman being an imposter wasn't one of them. What would there be to gain?

'You don't think I should go,' Keeley translated.

'I don't think someone sending you an email inviting you to Paris is a normal, everyday thing, that's all.'

'I know,' Keeley breathed. 'But my whole life isn't a normal every day thing, is it?'

'What does your mum say?' Rach asked.

Keeley curled a hand around her glass, fingers tightening. Rach knew very well how Lizzie would have reacted. Rach was well aware of Lizzie's overprotective bent.

'She thinks Silvie Durand is going to imprison me in a Perspex, soundproof box in a storage facility and start calling me Beck… or, you know, Ferne,' Keeley sighed. Why had this situation arisen? Why now? When the Andrews family were just, somehow, beginning to mend.

'Ferne?' Rach queried, snowmen still jangling.

Rach obviously had no idea who Ferne was. And the name hadn't meant anything until the email. But now her donor had a name and a mother, Ferne was becoming one of the most important names in Keeley's world.

'That's the name of my donor. Ferne Durand. She's French. *Was* French. Hence the invitation to Paris and—'

'French?' Rach queried, brow furrowing. 'How does that work?'

'Um, what do you mean?'

'Well, what was she doing here in England when you had your accident? Was she sick? Did she have an accident too? Or did they fly in the body part from France? Isn't there some sort of use-by date with a kidney?'

'I...' Keeley didn't know where to start. She only had some of the puzzle pieces. Which was maybe why she *needed* to speak to Silvie Durand. But was it *speak* to her? Or *meet* with her? She took a breath. 'Rach, I wanted your take on it. Because you're my best friend and because you're not my mum and because you don't always take the safe option.'

'What's that supposed to mean?' Rach asked, sniffing as if offended. 'You've somehow just made me sound super-slutty.'

Keeley sat a little taller in her chair, taking a glance outside at London life on the street below. There were workmen on ladders, attaching festive signage to lampposts, swarths of thick green fake fir swags under their arms. What would Paris feel like at this time of year? What did Paris feel like at *any* time of the year? She focused back to Rach and steadied her nerve. 'I want to go.'

'You want to go?' Rach exclaimed.

Keeley hadn't known she *actually* wanted to go until the words were out of her mouth and she felt them in her soul. How could she *not* go? How could she not want to meet the mother of her donor? She was only here because of this woman's daughter's selfless act. She nodded at Rach.

'You want to go,' Rach repeated, softer this time, as if saying the words again, more slowly would help them feel more agreeable.

'She sounds normal in her email. It's not pushy. It's a request. It doesn't sound like any kind of demand. She simply wants to meet me and—'

'And she's paying for tickets on the Eurostar to make it happen.' Rach still looked suss. But Rach looked suss a lot. Particularly when designer goods were marked down in a Boxing Day sale and she thought they *had* to be counterfeit. Counterfeits she could get even cheaper from someone she knew...

'I think,' Keeley started, putting a hand through her hair and pushing it off her shoulders, 'she's offered that because she's in France and I'm here and... it just makes sense.'

'Does it though?' Rach asked. 'Why isn't she offering to come to London?'

'Well,' Keeley began again, 'if I was her, I might think that coming into my space – into my *family's* space – would be more intrusive. I mean, she hasn't just suddenly turned up at our front door, she's emailed. She even said that if it was all too painful, or I didn't want to, then I never had to hear from her again and she wished me all the best for the future.'

Rach plucked a drinks menu from the table and dropped her eyes to it. 'I'm going to have another one. You?'

'Rach,' Keeley said softly. 'I don't want to be afraid of what's happened to me anymore.' She inhaled. 'Sometimes, being here, being inside the same world but feeling completely disconnected with everything that's gone before is really *really* hard. And I know you think I should "woman up" and you're right in a lot of respects, but I think doing this, meeting Silvie, might be a way to really move on, you know, properly.' She pulled the drinks menu down, trying to get Rach to engage with her gaze.

'I don't know what you want me to say,' Rach admitted, looking a little unsure of herself.

Keeley took ownership of the menu and put it back on the table. 'I was hoping, if the dates work, if we can swing it with Roland… that you might come with me.'

'What?' Now Rach's gaze was connected.

Keeley smiled at her friend's obvious new enthusiasm. Yes, she might have her concerns about the true purpose of the trip, but Paris was Paris and Paris at nearly Christmas time was even better according to the googling Keeley had done already. She had to admit, the escape factor was a draw too. It was all a little claustrophobic at home, life revolving underneath Grandma Joan's Christmas ball. This time of year always brought up so many memories – good and bad. And Keeley hadn't really had any time apart from her parents since Bea's death. At twenty-six, that couldn't be healthy.

'Come with me. You can meet Silvie Durand too. If nothing else it would reassure my mother that I'm not going to be made the centrepiece of a creepy shrine.'

'Paris,' Rach whispered. A dreamy sigh ensued that, if

visible, Keeley was sure would have been dripping with the gorgeous gooey inside of a *pain au chocolat*.

'Will you come with me? If we can arrange it?' Keeley asked her.

'I don't feel good about the set-up. I mean, Silvie Durand – it just sounds like a name from one of my mum's Danielle Steele novels.'

'Please, Rach,' Keeley said. 'I think I need this.' She didn't actually think. She knew.

Rach blew out a breath and then said, 'I'll come. On one condition.' She fixed her best 'no messing' face on.

'What?'

'If this is really going to be the start of your new beginning you have to not be Kidney Girl.'

'Rach, I'm going to meet the mother of my donor. There will be kidney talk.'

'I don't mean with her,' Rach clarified. 'Obviously the *offal* subject will be raised then. I mean… with the Parisian men. Because,' she grinned, the snowmen earrings wiggling like they were taking part in a twerk-off, 'if I'm coming along there *will be* Parisian men.'

'I—'

'Do we have a deal?' Rach asked, striking out her hand ready for a fist-bump. 'No tragic undertones to introductions anymore.'

Keeley drew in a breath. It wasn't her fault she got tongue-tied on first meetings. Her transplant was always somehow an instant go-to for a conservational topic. But Rach had a point, she *had* made the last guy at the Wool and Goose cry…

'Deal,' Keeley agreed, connecting fists with her friend. 'But I have a condition too.'

Rach looked suddenly suspicious. 'Is it my Christmas dress you're always telling me is too short? Because I *have* to take it to Paris!

'No!' Keeley exclaimed. 'I want you to do something to stop this dye coming out of my hair!' She presented her hands forward, streaked with brown again.

'Is that all?' Rach said, relaxing back into her seat again. 'Phew.'

'Can you do it?' Keeley inquired.

'I've no idea,' Rach admitted. 'But I'll have a look on the internet. Someone somewhere has always had a similar experience. Even if your experience is... "what to do if you've got your left foot trapped between a fire extinguisher and man called Joey."' Rach picked the menu off the table again. 'Can we order lunch now? I really fancy the lentils and nuts Haggis.'

Keeley smiled. Now all she had to do was reply to Silvie Durand and accept her offer... and break the news to her parents. And then there was Erica. She wasn't quite sure who was going to take it better but there was only one person whose time was really running out.

Seven

Bistrot Vivienne, Galerie Vivienne, Paris

Ethan was late. Deliberately so. He would not be coming here at all if he had the choice. He stood stock-still, a few metres away from his destination, looking at the person waiting to dine with him. He supposed he *did* have a choice, but he had cancelled a few times too often lately and his conscience was prickling him about that. Plus, being absent would have hurt Ferne and still, even in death, he didn't ever want to think about hurting Ferne.

He pulled his coat around him, fastening the buttons, and continued to look at the woman waiting for him to arrive. Her hair was that silver colour people choose when the greys begin to appear. It looked good and the soft fall of the cut, following the curve of her jaw, suited her. She had always reminded Ethan a little of Dame Helen Mirren. Sitting underneath the glass ceiling of the arcade, at an outside table, the mosaic tiles beneath feet clad in boots with a flatter heel than she used to wear, she definitely looked a little older. Ethan sighed. Everyone had been aged by circumstance and loss. No one came out of tragedy unscathed. He watched her pour a little *vin rouge*, then bring the glass to her nose. Was this her first glass? He shook his head. Why was he judging? Wasn't alcohol one of the first thoughts in his head every morning, even after a heavy night before? Or rather, the thinking was more about the feeling alcohol gave him. It wasn't pleasure, it wasn't the high from the intoxication, it was simply the knowing it was going to bring on a numbing of his senses and a switching off from reality. He stepped out from the doorway that was shielding him and paced forward.

'Ethan!'

She leapt from her seat the second he must have met her sightline and her voice was that slightly too loud version of itself – the kind that might be attributed to someone who *had* indulged in *vin rouge* already. He waved a hand and hurried to reach the table.

'Silvie,' he greeted. He leaned in, expecting the usual two-kiss greeting that was customary. Instead, Silvie Durand embraced him, hard, her arms coming around his body and drawing him in close. It was a determined hug, more than strong, and as the moment ended, Ethan realised that Silvie did feel a little more slender. The very last time she had held him that way was at Ferne's funeral. He swallowed. That day had been soaked with emotion, with everyone who had attended trying to console each other and make some sense of Ferne's loss. He stepped back. 'You are well?'

'I am well,' Silvie responded, taking her seat. 'And you are late.' She passed him the menu. 'I have ordered a bottle of Saint Joseph.'

'So, I see,' Ethan answered. He sat down.

'Ah, you disapprove.' Silvie smiled. 'Good.'

He went to reply, but decided against it. What could he say? He had been the master of day-drinking this past year and today he had only not had alcohol already because Noel had kept him in the hotel talking about the Christmas décor. Currently his assistant was walking around like the happiest orchestra conductor with a choir of hotel employees ready to play the tune of Christmas on his command.

'I have ordered the pink shrimps to start. Enough for us both.'

Ethan felt a tug on his heartstrings. *Ma crevette*. From the moment his friendship with Ferne had begun he had called her that nickname. It meant 'my shrimp' and was a light-hearted reference to the fact that he had always dwarfed Ferne as far as height went. The pink shrimp dish here was Ferne's favourite. His best friend wouldn't have shared the meal though. She was always able to happily devour an entire portion on her own and still have room for profiteroles to finish. Again, he went to say something and then reconsidered. Silvie had already made the decision on their food choices. He should let her have this gastronomic reverie.

'You look tired,' Silvie remarked. 'Are you sleeping?' She poured some *vin rouge* into his glass.

'Of course,' he lied. In truth, he couldn't remember the last time he had slept for a whole night. Since Ferne had passed, the most he had ever slept was three hours and that had been when he had slipped into an unconscious drunken coma after an evening spent regaling a group of Australian tourists with *La Marseillaise* from inside the *Fontaine Saint-Sulpice*.

'Then you need to start taking supplements for your grey skin,' Silvie informed him. 'You have the pallor of a street artiste mimicking Pierrot.'

He chewed the inside of his lip. So apparently he looked worse than her. He had almost forgotten Ferne's mother's straight talking ways. Ferne hadn't been like that. Ferne used to say what she thought, yes, but with a lot more tact and diplomacy. Ethan took a sip of the wine. That was better. That first warming trickle of alcohol coating his throat and trailing its way to his stomach lined only with nut-based sweets. He definitely needed to eat some of the shrimps if he wanted to continue with the *vin rouge*.

'Ethan!' Silvie barked.

He almost dropped his glass of wine at the volume of Silvie's shout. He cupped his hand around it quickly, desperate not to spill a drop on the table. Silvie always had the ability to make him feel that he had done something wrong. Or perhaps that feeling was inbuilt in him. The feeling that someone calling his name was going to lead to an accusation. 'OK,' he said. 'I promise, I will drink more orange juice.'

'You are not listening to me,' Silvie accused. 'You have never listened to me.'

'I have *always* listened to you,' Ethan disagreed.

'How about the time that you hid a dog in my living room when I expressly said no animals?'

He didn't know whether to be amused or concerned. The dog incident had been fifteen years ago. And it had been Ferne's idea not his. He had also told Ferne that the thin, yet tall, whippet would not fit in the spherically shaped bottom of the family drinks cabinet.

'Silvie...' he began.

'I can see that you are not looking after yourself. Everyone can see it.' She spoke hard and direct.

Ethan really wished he had made more of an effort this morning. He should have chosen one of the silk ties Silvie had bought him for Christmas a few years ago, or perhaps shaved, or eaten more than candy... He should say that Silvie wasn't looking her best self either. Retaliation. Always better to put someone else under the microscope so they were distracted from looking at you. But what would that achieve?

'*You* are the face of Perfect Paris,' Silvie continued.

He felt himself shrink into his seat. So, this wasn't a simple catch-up lunch or touching base, this was about the business. The business he felt he was failing at. Perhaps this was a good thing. Maybe he could confess his difficulties with feeling love for the hotel franchise and perhaps Silvie could offer a solution.

'I am not the face of Perfect Paris,' he responded. 'That was Ferne.'

Silvie didn't seem to miss a beat. 'And Ferne is gone.'

Ethan met her eyes with his. There was nothing but a formidable look. This was the very first time that Silvie hadn't dissolved into tears at the mere mention of her daughter's name. Usually, particularly when she came into the flagship hotel, her face was a leaking palette of eyeshadow and mascara whenever someone said the 'F' word. What had changed?

'Ethan,' Silvie began again, her tone a little lighter as she topped up her wine glass, 'what plans do you have for the Christmas period at the hotels this year?'

He swallowed, having the most intense feeling that telling Silvie about the silver and blue decision for the décor wasn't going to cut it. But what did she expect? Events weren't his strong point. He wasn't sure what his actual strong point with this hotel chain had ever been. He had just supported Ferne in this venture, like she had supported him when he needed it most. He hadn't ever really looked beyond that, hadn't needed to. He had worked hard. He had done whatever needed to be done. But Ferne had been the one with all the ideas.

'I... thought we would go for... "simplicity" as a theme this year.' He cleared his throat and reached not for the wine but the water. 'Strip things right back and lead with light piano music in the lobby, then exquisite and festive artisan meals in the restaurant.'

Even before he had finished, Silvie was shaking her head. Ethan wasn't sure whether to keep talking or to cut his losses and stop. Perhaps he should have paid more serious attention to Noel earlier.

'Ethan,' Silvie said with a heavy sigh. 'The way you speak. It is like you think you are telling me what it is that I want to hear. Except what I am hearing makes me feel like you do not care about the hotels any longer.'

He *didn't* care. He had only cared about Ferne. What did it all matter now she was gone? She had been his one true friend. She had never let him down... until she had, by leaving him. And in a dark, twisted and selfish way, he hated her for that! He could not count the number of nights of not sleeping he had spent cursing her name for not being around, for abandoning him. She had been his one constant and he had adored her. Why couldn't she have held on a little longer? Fought a little harder? He swallowed. He couldn't admit these feelings to Silvie, to anyone. Silvie would have him under the scrutiny of a shrink before he could say 'brain drain'. But he needed to say something and fast...

'I thought maybe ballet,' he said tentatively. '*Sleeping Beauty*. The hotels could embody the story somehow. We could have a princess and a prince to greet customers, a small ballet performance after dinner on some evenings.' He truly had no idea why he had said that. It was madness. 'It is festive, but it is also different.' What he did know was it wasn't really leaning towards blue and silver...

'Ferne loved *Sleeping Beauty*,' Silvie breathed. There was definite reverie now, but still there was control.

'I know,' Ethan admitted.

Silvie then seemed to straighten in her seat, adjusting the scarf at her neck and taking him in anew. 'But I do not think we should be looking at the past.' She took a breath. 'I think we should be looking at how to shape the future. The future of the Perfect Paris hotels and *your* future, Ethan.'

An uncomfortable feeling stirred in his stomach now. Suddenly all those calorific nut products were doing the dance of the Sugar Plum Fairy, pirouetting amid the wine and water and the fear about what Silvie was going to say next. What exactly did the emphasis on 'your' future mean? Except he did know. Deep down he knew exactly what it meant. It meant what it always meant when it came from a figure in authority. *Stupid boy. Idiot. Useless. Good for nothing*. You couldn't change the hand of destiny you had been dealt. And his cards had been marked from the very beginning. Here was the moment when the hotels were going to be stripped from him. And it wasn't the financial implications of that that bothered him. It was the idea of losing another part of Ferne.

'I am thinking of stepping back from... things,' Silvie told him.

'Things?' He felt the need to repeat the word to seek some sort clarification.

'Louis is coming back from America.'

Now Ethan's hackles were really rising. Louis Durand. Ferne's older brother. His nemesis. If you were allowed to have a nemesis within the family who had practically raised you. Ethan had never been able to put an actual finger on the reason he had always disliked Louis as much as he had always adored Ferne. Perhaps it was Louis's entitled attitude and the fact that he was good at pretty much everything. He worked for a big corporation in the US as a head-hunter. Paris and Ferne's hotels had always been small-time to him, like tiny Monopoly properties on a small-scale board.

'Is he staying long?' He couldn't think of anything better to say, but he hoped he had managed not to weave too much animosity around the four words...

'Perhaps,' Silvie replied, pouring herself another glass of wine. 'It depends.'

'On what?'

'On how you feel about working with Louis instead of with me.'

Ethan's chest tightened. He hated the idea. He hated the idea of the idea. He loathed it! He wanted to stamp all over the idea and set fire to it! Whatever Silvie was about to tell him, he was sure he wasn't ready to hear it.

'I am getting old, Ethan,' Silvie explained, sighing.

'I am too old to be concerned with profit and loss and accountability. I did not envisage taking this role. I did not foresee losing my daughter and…'

'I know,' Ethan said. 'You were not the only one who lost her.' Inside his mouth he pushed his front teeth into his tongue until the burn was enough to make him stop.

Silvie sighed again and there was much more weight to this particular sigh. It was a sound of discomfort. It told Ethan that there was a little more to this.

'I need to be sure, Ethan, for the future of the Perfect Paris chain, for Ferne's legacy, that the right person is leading the way. Preparing for the future, coming up with new ideas and aspirational themes to ensure we always offer that perfect Parisian experience we are known for, but, also, not to limit ourselves to what has gone before.' She was looking directly at him now. 'Do you understand what I am trying to say?'

Yes, he understood. He understood that Silvie was most probably going to gift her shares in Perfect Paris to Louis and put her son in charge of the organisation. Silvie didn't need him. Didn't want him. Louis was coming back and Ethan was being asked whether he could take a step back, let Louis in to Perfect Paris, work *for* him… He was rage-ridden now. He could feel it manifesting, starting to tip the scales heavily towards making a knee-jerk reaction. He had to try and calm. He bit down on his tongue again and when he spoke he tried to make it even and balanced.

'Louis will take over your shares,' Ethan said, managing a nonchalant shrug that defied completely how he was *really* feeling. 'He will be the CEO and the face of Perfect Paris hotels. Your problem with my lack of forward-thinking will be solved. It will keep things in the Durand family.'

'Ethan, *you* are part of the Durand family,' Silvie insisted as a waitress arrived with their order of shrimps.

Ethan shook his head. '*Ferne* made me feel I was part of the family. You made me feel like I was… a stray you had to put up with to keep your daughter happy.' He downed his glass of wine. 'Like the dog that would not fit in the drinks cabinet.' He shook his head again, this time more forcefully. His cheeks were heating up. He wanted to hit something. He clenched his fists under the tablecloth.

'Ethan, I… do not know what to say,' Silvie breathed. Now the older woman was showing some emotion. Now her eyes were blurring with tears. 'I do not think of you that way. I have never thought of you that way.'

'You do not have to say any more. I understand what's going to happen. I think I always knew it was going to happen one day.' He stood up, buttoning his coat as swiftly as he could. 'But you should know,' he began again, 'the hotels, they belonged to Ferne and a large part of them still belongs to me. And I will not stand by and let her be forgotten. I will not let Louis come over here and turn Perfect Paris into… Las Vegas!'

'Ethan, please,' Silvie began. 'No one would do that. And of course your position will not be undermined, I just thought…'

White-hot anger was bubbling through his veins now as he leaned over the table and addressed his best friend's mother. 'You just thought you would remind me of my place,' he spat. 'Well, bravo, Silvie. As if I could ever forget!'

'Ethan,' Silvie said firmly. 'That is just not true.'

'Is it not?'

'No, of course not. You have always been part of the

family and… that is why… there is something else you should know.' She waited a beat before carrying on. 'There is another reason Louis is coming home.'

Something in Silvie's tone now made him hold still, taper the anger for a moment. Whatever it was, it was even more serious than business…

'I have… made contact with the person who received Ferne's kidney.'

Now Ethan's stomach turned upside down and threatened to banish the contents of last night's drinking session. 'I… do not want to hear this.'

'Ethan, this is a good thing that has come from Ferne's death. A life continuing because of Ferne's generous heart.'

'No.' Ethan said, shaking his head as the lights and the sounds of the arcade all began to spin in his vision. He felt drunk all over again. Dizzy and hot and nauseous. He unfastened a button of his coat.

'I would like the family to get together and—'

'I said no,' Ethan started. 'How could you…? *Why* would you…? It's not right.'

'Ethan,' Silvie said, getting to her feet.

'No,' Ethan said again. 'I want nothing to do with… that. Nothing.'

Fury forging him on, he turned away, tears making his eyelashes bristle. He was heading to the nearest bar. He might even smoke.

Eight

The Resting Hospice, Kensington, London

A week later – December

Keeley had Eurostar tickets for her and Rach, dated tomorrow, paid for by Silvie Durand. She had told her parents her decision and afterwards she had watched her mum eat wild blueberry jam straight from the jar with a dessert spoon. Her dad had comforted Lizzie and said all the good and positive things to ease his wife's concerns but Keeley knew it was also to reassure *her* that she was doing the right thing. She still wasn't *completely* positive she was, but she really felt that *not* taking the opportunity would be much worse. Not accepting would have meant a lifetime of wondering 'what if'. This was a once only opportunity to find out exactly who her donor was and maybe feel a little more at peace with what had happened that one night.

She paused outside Erica's room and felt inside her bag for the turkey-flavoured crisps she'd bought plus the framed Nick Jonas photo. She was hoping it was going to soften the blow of her leaving for a while. She also prayed it would give Erica a small boost to keep her spirits up. The very last thing she wanted to happen was for her leaving for France to be a cue for Erica to give up. Keeley swallowed. She didn't want to think about the possibility that when she got back Erica might be gone...

Positivity. Seasonal cheer. She couldn't let any other thoughts appear on her face or manifest in her disposition. It was all about Erica today. She knocked on the door and got ready for all the sass and shade. She waited a beat for a response but, when one wasn't forthcoming, she opened the door and stepped into the room.

Breath left her, almost audibly so, and Keeley was caught both trying to retract it and put a smile on her face at the same time. The mixed motion didn't work and she coughed, almost choking on the dryness of her mouth. Erica looked terrible. Her Caribbean colouring was significantly depleted, her deep dark-brown eyes a lot more sunken into their sockets. Her eyes were barely open at all. Was she sleeping? Had the nurses upped her pain relief making her slip in and out of consciousness? No one had said anything when she had checked in at the desk. Then Erica turned her head, just a little, as if acknowledging Keeley was there.

'Are... you sitting down... or what?' It was pure Erica just on a much lesser level.

'Yes,' Keeley said quickly, stepping forward. She slipped the crisps back into her bag. She wasn't sure something so sharp and spiky was quite the right food source for someone in Erica's condition. 'And I have a surprise.' She brandished the photo of Nick Jonas in the glitzy frame Rach had given her. Rach had actually given her a pack of five that Adie was selling at the discount shop and Keeley hadn't had the energy to refuse the bulk buy.

'Sweet,' Erica mouthed, drawing fragile fingers up to clutch the picture, a small smile on her lips. 'Man, he looks hot in that photo.'

'Shall I put it on your dresser?' Keeley offered, about to take the frame back.

'Not until I've held him a bit longer and... you know... imagined all the dirty.'

Keeley smiled as she remembered a similar interaction with Bea over Timothée Chalamet. They had planned to watch *Little Women* together. 'How are you today?' She settled into the chair.

'Still dying,' Erica replied.

'Still living actually,' Keeley reminded, upbeat.

'If living is puking into a cardboard bowl, sucking water off a lollipop sponge and talking to a shitty painting of a poodle.'

'See!' Keeley announced. 'I've cheered you up already.'

'I've called the big one Henry by the way,' Erica announced, taking a long slow breath as if summoning up stores of strength from a back-up life generator.

'Who?' Keeley asked.

'The big shitty dog in the painting! Keep with it!'

'Oh,' Keeley replied, looking to the awful picture. Perhaps she should take it down and put the Nick Jonas one there instead. Except Erica seemed to be hugging that one to her like it might be the man himself...

'Thought it might as well have a name seeing as it's the only thing that listens to me when you're not around.'

Keeley felt a prick of guilt in her chest like someone

had stabbed her with an extra sharp and spiky bough of a spruce tree. And here she was about to tell Erica she wouldn't be coming to visit for a while. The train ticket was currently open-ended and Silvie had booked a room at a hotel called Perfect Paris near the Eiffel Tower. It sounded so quintessentially French that Keeley had allowed herself to get a little excited for the holiday element of the trip. It was a country she'd never visited before and she was going with her best friend.

'The fat nurse came in this morning to wash me,' Erica carried on, trying to sit up a little, but flailing. Keeley leaned in to help her, supporting her shoulders and adjusting her pillows. 'She smells so bad, man. Even *I* can smell her!'

'Oh, well...' What did you say to that?

'I told her,' Erica carried on. 'I said "has anyone introduced you to Lynx Africa? Because it ain't just for men, it's for man-sized issues in the armpit region no matter what your gender and you... you are holding on to the perspiration problems of *all* the continents".'

'You didn't!' Keeley remarked, suppressing a laugh.

'Just because the nearly-dead might stink a bit, doesn't mean everyone here should let their standards slip, man. Before all this I never left my flat without Lynx under my pits and large-arse spray of eau-de-toilette.'

'I remember,' Keeley said. 'But... what was it called again?'

'Bronze Goddess. Like me.'

'Do you have it now?' Keeley asked. 'I could get it out and we could spray some on your blankets.'

Erica shook her head, vigorously at first, and then less so, as if the exertion had suddenly got the better of her. 'I can't... it doesn't... it doesn't smell the same anymore.'

Keeley swallowed a lump in her throat. 'I'm sorry.' She knew a little of what it was like to have that aroma familiarity begin to slowly fade away. Her impaired sense of smell was another thing she had had to adapt to since the transplant.

There was no easy way to tell Erica she was leaving, but delaying the news wasn't going to make it any better. She needed to say something right now.

'Erica…' Keeley began.

Erica turned her head, those large eyes surveying her now. 'That's your serious and concerned voice. What's going on, man? The last time you had that voice was when you were softening me up because they said I was too wobbly to take showers anymore.'

Keeley remembered. She also knew how much Erica loved to shower. Erica had said the joy was the combination of searing hot water, her favourite lemon shower gel and the chance to sing at the top of her voice. Bathrooms had acoustics to rival the best concert halls according to Erica. Keeley took a breath. 'I'm going away for a bit. To Paris.' She didn't want to stop talking. She wanted to get it all out before Erica had any chance to react. She would deal with any fallout when she was finished. 'The mother of my kidney donor contacted me and she's offered me the chance to go to Paris and meet her. I didn't want to say no. I thought it was the right thing to do to go and see her. To maybe find out a bit about who my donor was.' She checked Erica's expression, but her friend wasn't giving anything at all away. 'I'll be away a week or so. But I'll be back before Christmas and I'll… send you some postcards and I'll FaceTime.'

'Paris,' Erica finally said, the word hanging a moment too long on her dry, cracked lips. 'The home of the Eiffel Tower... and cheese... and all the good coffee.'

'Yes,' Keeley said. And Erica was never going to experience it. She felt terrible. 'I'm sorry I'm going now. I replied to Madame Durand and then it all happened so quickly and Rach had to make sure her clients were introduced to Jamie and I had to shift a few things around with my schedule and... we both had to shunt Mr Peterson on to Oz and—'

'Stop,' Erica begged. 'You've got "Desperate not to piss off the girl on her death bed" written all over your face.'

'Well,' Keeley began sadly, 'I am... desperate not to piss off my friend.'

'The clues were right there,' Erica said with a sniff. 'Girl. Death bed. It's not like I'm gonna come back and haunt you.' She managed a smile. 'Or am I?'

Keeley took Erica's fragile hand in hers then, not worried for showing sentimentality Erica usually shied away from. 'You are going to be strong,' she said firmly. 'You are not going to go anywhere until I'm back here holding your hand again. You and... Nick Jonas and Henry... you're going to find the strength to hang on and I'm going to keep you posted on every single thing I get up to in France.' She gave Erica's hand a gentle squeeze. 'OK?'

'Whatever,' Erica answered with a sigh.

'Don't make me call the smelly nurse back in here,' Keeley warned. She watched Erica's lips turn into a small grin.

'Take me with you,' Erica ordered.

'What? I...' Was she serious? Erica couldn't get out of bed anymore. She didn't really think she could manage travel, did she? And it wasn't as if she really could.

'Not like that, man!' she said with a bit more fierceness than she had shown earlier. 'I mean... do it for me too. Your trip. Imagine I'm there with you, inhaling all the coffee and trying all the perfumes and eating all the cheese. Even though neither of us can smell anything.'

'I will,' Keeley said positively. 'I absolutely will.' She'd try to go a little easy on the cheese...

'OK then,' Erica replied, eyes brightening considerably. 'I'll hang on to Nick Jonas and ugly poodles, craving turkey dinners, while you hang out with all the hot French dudes and suckle souffle.'

Keeley laughed. 'Suckle souffle?'

'I'm glad you questioned *that* rather than the French dudes. I want action on this trip of yours. One of us has to be getting some.'

Keeley let go of Erica's hand and picked her handbag up off the floor. 'I got you something else. I don't know whether you'll be able to eat them but...' She produced the packet of turkey crisps.

Erica's eyes lit up and there really was a visible injection of vigour about her now. 'Open them up. Now. If I can't manage to swallow I'll just enjoying the licking.' She grinned. 'But, you know, in France, you make sure you swallow. I mean it. All in, remember? Every time.'

'I promise,' Keeley answered. 'All in. Every time.'

Nine

La Barbouquin, Rue Denoyez, Paris

Ethan bit into his breakfast sandwich and simultaneously forked up a portion of pancakes and put that into his mouth too. This was what a hangover needed. Houmous and salsa with fresh vegetables and a tomato confit, plus pancakes covered in deliciously sweet fruit. And coffee. Lots of coffee. He shucked back his head, inhaling all the goodness of the ingredients, willing the restorative powers to the internal organs that he was sure had taken the hardest of hammerings.

The last few nights were a little sketchy in his mind, in so far as he wasn't really sure what events were part of which evening or when and where he had landed at what time. Everything was changing and he was standing still watching it happen. It was like he was the lone audience to a horror movie and that film was his life. Silvie was going to rinse Ferne out of Perfect Paris and someone who now owned one of Ferne's body parts was going to come over and act all grateful and grief-stricken. They might even try and exploit Silvie's grief once they found out about the hotel chain or the money her husband, Pierre, had left her when he died. Ethan tried to focus again on the enjoyment of his meal. He didn't even know whether this person was a man or a woman. But, really, who cared? Whoever it was meant nothing to him and he wasn't about to play a part in this creepy My Long-Lost Transplant Family scenario.

Louis Durand was arriving today. Silvie had sent Ethan an email. Not a text. An email. Business-like and professional. Definitely not the same way you would message a so-called family member. Even a family member who had lost their temper before they had finished pink shrimps. The Durand with the Devil's horns was due to fly in later today. And Ethan's priority today was preparing. He checked his watch. Noel was late. But, as that thought unsettled him for a moment, his gaze met the door of the café and his assistant was right there. Seeming to be fighting with the wind at the glass door, Noel finally pushed his way into the premises, his entry bringing a gust of icy draught to the comforting warmth. Noel's usually perfectly tamed hair was everywhere and his bright purple scarf had come out from the confines of his wool coat and was only just clinging on to his neck, its length trailing to the floor. Ethan waved a hand before shovelling in more pancakes.

'It is eight in the morning,' Noel greeted, peeling off his scarf and coat and sinking down into the banquette seat opposite Ethan. 'I should be at the hotel. I have four tours arranged this morning. Then there is Francois, he is having so much of a crisis about his latest quiche creation he telephoned me at 3 a.m. talking about the consistency of his onion ganache. *And* we are down three chambermaids. Three.'

Ethan smiled at him. 'Relax, Noel. Take a breath. Have some pancakes. I will get another fork.' He had to blot out everything else and maintain a little bit of upbeat.

Noel raised an eyebrow. 'What has happened? Are you sick?'

'No,' Ethan replied. 'I am invigorated.' It was more like single-mindedly determined for Ferne's brainchild to continue to honour everything she had been.

'That is why you came here? To a café that looks like an ancient bookshop with graffiti on the walls outside?' Noel indicated the bookshelves that lined the interior of the café.

Ethan felt insulted on the café's behalf for Noel's words. They were here because Ethan loved this place. La Barbouquin was almost his fantasy of what a home should look like. From the bright graffiti art on the outside of the building, to the eclectic style inside. The café was a hodgepodge mix of mismatched chairs and tables with an assortment of different styles of lampshades hanging from the ceiling. There was a multitude of reading material – hardbacks, paperbacks and magazines – most dogeared and pre-loved. There was retro wallpaper and *papier mâché* heads, jars and plants, teapots and art. You could imagine it as the living space of a close-knit family with every decoration and ornament there for a reason. Nothing went together, except somehow maybe it actually did.

'I like it here,' Ethan said, picking up his sandwich and taking a bite.

'I do not,' Noel answered. 'And I almost lost a shoe sliding on the cobbles.' Ethan noticed then that his assistant was not fully sitting on his seat. His weight was balanced as if in the hope not to catch anything – dust motes, germs, history – from the slightly worn fabric. 'Plus, this place feels like it holds the breath of a thousand forefathers.'

Ethan smiled. Yes, Noel was right. But he liked that. The café felt like it had origins, a tale attached to every piece of furniture. Ethan had somehow always felt comforted by the age as well as the well-worn state of the things here. It was relaxed. It did not conform. No one asked questions of it. He drew his focus back to Noel. 'I want you to tell me who does Christmas the best here in Paris.'

Noel looked at him a little strangely. 'You know that our biggest competitor is Marriott.'

'That was not what I asked,' Ethan said. 'I want to know who you think does Christmas the best.' He thought about his own question. 'I do not mean only hotels. I mean, think of everywhere. The stores… the markets… restaurants.'

Noel seemed to then muse on the question, staring into the mid-distance and moving his head a little to the left, then a little to the right, then back to centre again.

'Well,' Noel began, his voice even and thoughtful, '*Galeries Lafayette* is always the most exuberant. In my humble opinion, they have all of the bright and ostentatious, with that giant Christmas tree decorated like they have piled up hundreds and hundreds of multicoloured macarons and sprinkled them with stardust. Or, one year, the tree was made to look like a gigantic cupcake version of Candy Crush, with doughnuts and lollipops and pretzels…'

'Do you think something like that would work for Perfect Paris?' Ethan asked. 'A large centrepiece that will immediately catch the eye?' Ferne would have approved of that, wouldn't she? Something the press would talk about.

Something different and flamboyant. Something others would follow in the wake of...

'No,' Noel said crushingly. 'Where would we put it in the Opera hotel? Last year we removed the flower display in the foyer because it was not amenable to wheelchair users.'

'What else then?' Ethan asked. The sweet taste in his mouth was starting to sour a little, his enthusiasm waning. Why was this so difficult? He needed the hotel to have *something* in the works before Devil Durand arrived. At the moment there wasn't even any of the blue and silver Noel had waxed so lyrical about a few days ago. For someone who had demanded that Christmas needed to start *now* it felt like an oversight.

'I have ordered the blue and silver reindeer for the dining room,' Noel said, allowing his bottom to make actual contact with the seat. 'The smaller lead reindeer is animatronic. It will turn its face to the open room and engage its mouth to the tune of "Walking In A Winter Wonderland".'

Was Noel serious? Ethan looked at his assistant's expression hoping to detect some kind of hint of a joke. It sounded the very worst of tacky.

'There will be delightful swags for the reception desk including real blue fir and crystals, plus floor to ceiling diamante icicle curtains framing all the doors to the common places – the toilets, the restaurant and bar, the luggage room...'

Noel continued to talk but Ethan was starting to zone out. None of what his assistant was saying felt right to him. And he instinctively knew Ferne would have hated all these ideas. He picked up his coffee mug and filled his mouth with the dark, bitter blackness. He knew he couldn't wholly rely on what Ferne would have done going forward. He also knew he hadn't wanted any part in the Christmas decoration at Noel's meeting last week. But his lunch with Silvie had changed things. Once he had processed – and processing consisted of drowning his insides with fine wine, not so fine wine and calvados – he realised two things. Hell would freeze over before he let Louis Durand ruin the business he and Ferne had worked night and day to make a success. And he was having absolutely nothing to do with this visitor with part of his best friend inside them.

'... and there will be someone dressed as a decadent swirl of chocolate praline from *Maison Paradis du Chocolat* handing out small treats I have managed to secure for a good price. Then, as we enter the middle of December there will be...'

'Noel, stop,' Ethan begged. 'I... you... are hurting my ears.' He wanted back into the bubble containing the comforting sounds of the coffee machine, the jazz playing from the radio and the condensation on the windows.

'You do not like my advent of activities?' Noel asked, his voice full of concern. 'You said you wished me to go ahead and make things happen. You said you did not want to think about the arrangements.'

He had definitely said that, there was no getting away from it. He had also said something very similar in response to every new suggestion Noel had made to try to improve things throughout the year.

'I know,' Ethan answered, putting down his coffee mug. 'I did say that.'

'And you did not answer any of my calls over the past three days.'

That was true too. In between the calvados and the not fine wine there had been a flat phone battery and a stripper called Celine…

'I know,' he repeated. 'But now I would like to help.' No, that wasn't quite right. He didn't want to help. He wanted to *lead*. Like the CEO he was. Like the head of a small hotel chain Ferne had tried to teach him how to be. But, from buying him his first business suit, to sending him on a training course he had never fully understood, she had been by his side and now he just felt… incomplete. Ferne had represented the only good thing in his life. Without that connection he was back to being Ethan Bouchard, the orphan again.

Noel folded his arms across his chest and set his expression to 'quite agitated'. Noel did a good line in degrees of agitated. This one probably hit about medium on the scale.

'Louis Durand is coming back,' Ethan said in a rush. It was like the man's name had the ability to scorch his lips if he hung on to the syllables too long.

Straightaway, Noel's expression flipped from 'quite agitated' to 'full-on terrified'. 'What?'

Ethan nodded his head, pushing away his plate of half-finished pancakes for something to keep his fingers busy. He drew in a breath and continued. 'You did not know.' Although Ethan had wondered if Louis would take up residence in one of the hotel's suites rather than the Durand family home on the outskirts of the city so he could be at the centre of operations. If Silvie had made a reservation it definitely wouldn't have gone unnoticed by Noel.

'Is he staying long?' Noel asked, his words clipped.

'Not if I have anything to do with it.' He checked himself quickly. Noel was his closest confidante at the hotel, but was he a friend to be trusted? Ethan swallowed. Friends weren't something he made very easily. And he didn't want to blur the lines between employer and employee. 'What I meant to say was... Madame Durand has invited him and he will be visiting the hotels, no doubt. I just want to make sure that we are ready.'

'He will inspect everything,' Noel said, sounding like his life essence was slowly draining out of him. 'The last time he was here he checked for dust behind the picture frames. *Behind* them. As if there was going to be the contents of a vacuum cleaner on the wallpaper. What kind of individual does that?'

And now for the harder blow. Ethan looked directly at Noel. 'He's arriving this afternoon.'

Noel made a sound like someone who had caught their finger in the car door but had taken a vow of silence. It was high-pitched, slightly muted, but still sounded of the whole world's pain and suffering.

'I need something in place before he gets here,' Ethan admitted. 'Something great. Something that speaks of the luxurious brand Perfect Paris is meant to be.'

Noel had clicked on his pen and it was now hovering above his portfolio pad as if he was waiting for the starting pistol at the beginning of a race. 'In all the hotels?'

'Opera for today,' Ethan decided. 'Then we think about the others.'

'That is why we are meeting at 8 a.m.,' Noel deduced.

'That is *exactly* why we are meeting at 8 a.m.' Ethan sighed, his gaze going over Noel's shoulder as he looked to the outside where this area was starting to wake up. Here on this street where the graffiti art was a new type of tour for a city usually obsessed with museums and relics, the vibrant street culture was a treat to behold. People were already stopping to take photos for Instagram, admiring the shop fronts that acted like canvasses and the planters decorated with mosaic tiles. One spray-can-painted effigy caught Ethan's eye, evoking a memory from the past…

'Noel,' he said, a glint in his grey eyes. 'Do you think, before this afternoon, you could procure a penguin?'

Ten

L'Hotel Paris Parfait, Tour Eiffel, Paris

'Wow! I mean, W-O-W!'

Rach had scrambled out of the car first, before their driver – yes, they had a driver – could get out from behind the wheel to open the door for them. It was freezing and Keeley quickly did up the zip on her new, bright red, three-quarter-length padded coat her mum had insisted on buying her before she 'ventured into the unknown'. Keeley thought it resembled a sleeping bag or perhaps a survival tent for those seeking shelter after an avalanche. Yes, Lizzie was still insisting this trip was somewhere between a hostage situation and an invitation to a cult, but at least the front door back in Kensington hadn't been barricaded or reinforced with steel to prevent Keeley leaving at all. She had promised to text as soon as she arrived in Paris but, in front of this scene, she wasn't going to start dipping her head to her phone screen right now.

'Look at it, Keeley!' Rach exclaimed. 'Look. At. It.'

Keeley linked her arm through Rach's as they admired

the Parisian skyline laid out before them. It might be close-to-zero temperatures coupled with a keen wind, but there was a bright, crisp blue sky as a backdrop to this city's – if not this country's – most famous landmark. Paris life was going on around them, cars and mopeds zipped up the street, tooting horns, revving engines. Pedestrians, the inhabitants of Paris, rushed – coffees in hand – from A towards B. Tourists moved slower, focusing cameras at the impressive sight before them, taking their time and letting the French capital sink in...

'The Eiffel Tower,' Keeley breathed, her eyes drawn in and captivated by the iron structure that, she had read in a magazine on the Eurostar, had been standing strong since 1889. She swallowed. This icon was the first thing she had thought of when she had found out her donor had been French. Now, standing here, so close, it was a little overwhelming.

'Wonder when we're going to see an onion seller with a thin curly moustache in a blue and white T-shirt, riding a bike?' Rach asked, nudging Keeley's ribs.

Keeley smiled. She had Rach for all the clichés. But Keeley was determined to look deeper, not second guess – experience everything, all in – exactly like she had promised Erica.

'*Madames*,' the driver said, indicating their trolley cases on the pavement.

'Do we have to tip him?' Rach asked quite loudly.

The driver smiled and touched the peak of his cap. 'Please, this is not necessary. Madame Durand has taken care of everything.'

Rach looked at Keeley and raised her eyes. 'It's like being

a royal… you know… the ones who are still active… and *not* Prince Andrew.'

'Thank you so much, Sebastian,' Keeley replied to the tall, slim twenty-something who wasn't exactly uneasy on the eye. He had greeted them at the *Gare du Nord*, no cheap cardboard sign with her name written with a Sharpie, but an iPad, the words 'Keeley Andrews' in large font, blinking on and off. And she had managed to introduce herself without saying something like 'I only have one kidney so drinking games are like Russian Roulette'. Yes, she had said that once. No one had laughed.

'You are welcome,' Sebastian answered. 'And Madame Durand asked for me to tell you that she invites you to take afternoon tea in the hotel restaurant at 3 p.m. With her compliments, of course.'

Afternoon tea with the mother of her donor. Keeley felt a dart of panic prick her chest. It felt too soon. Yes, the principal reason she had travelled here, the whole point of the trip, was to meet with Silvie Durand, but she hadn't really thought it would happen this quickly. Keeley had half-hoped she and Rach could settle in, have a night to themselves, a chance to get grounded and comfortable with this winter escape. But, on the other hand, she hadn't paid for the train tickets. And she wasn't paying for the hotel so…

'Afternoon tea! I love a scone or six,' Rach admitted. 'How about you, Sebastian? Or are you more of a cream horn kind of a guy?'

Keeley pulled Rach away from the black town car, catching the handle of her trolley case too. 'Let's go and unpack.'

'I'm thinking of *you* here, Keels,' Rach whispered. 'He's quite cute.'

'And he's not deaf,' Keeley replied, desperate to get Rach away. 'And he can speak perfect English.'

'What?'

'He can hear you! Come on!' Keeley sent a soft smile back to the driver before hauling Rach and her case forward towards a revolving front door.

Paris Parfait the sign read. It looked a little like the branding for Hotel Chocolat. Succinct, without too much detail. Keeley didn't know what to expect from the inside. Was this a large hotel or something more boutique? It was hard to tell from the exterior that spoke of days gone by with its ornate pillars and worn stonework. Rach was first in the revolving door, immediately going too fast and halting the motion. Keeley stepped into the pod behind.

'Don't touch it,' Keeley said through the glass, trying to keep her case from knocking into the moving door too. 'It just slows it down.'

'What?' Rach asked, turning her head slightly, but still pushing.

'The door,' Keeley continued. 'It moves at its own pace. You can't make it move faster.' Surely Rach had been in a revolving door before? Keeley jolted a little as Rach's eagerness stopped the glass panels yet again and they were stationary once more. There had been a revolving door at the hospital back in 2019. After being inside for eight weeks, coming through that and out into the chill of a London winter had been the best breath of fresh air Keeley had ever had fill her lungs.

'Ow! Ow! Keels! Keeley! My hair is stuck! My hair!'

Keeley came out of her reverie pretty quickly at that shout. Rach was pushing at the glass again, but this time Keeley could see that her friend's hair was caught somehow in between the glass and the rubber seal. Was there an emergency button? Not that was immediately obvious and this was a door not a lift. It should have been a case of walking into reception with ease, not high drama.

'Keeley! It's pulling my hair out and my head is getting closer to the glass! Keeley!'

Rach was really, fully panicking now and Keeley didn't know what to do. If she pushed one way it would make things worse. If she pushed the other then would it make things better? What happened if two people got trapped in a revolving door? Then, suddenly, before she could think about moving at all, a man appeared. Next, the revolution of the glass panels stopped immediately. In a flurry of manual pushing, Keeley watched as Rach's hair was delicately released and her best friend stepped out into the foyer, conversing brightly and flicking around her blonde hair in a way that was not at all like someone who had potential scalp chafing. And Keeley was still in here. She pushed the glass and let it swing around until the welcome opening appeared.

'I'm Rach, by the way, and this is Keeley.'

Keeley observed their door saviour. He was over six feet tall with neat, short, blonde hair and the build of someone who went to the gym or played sports – maybe basketball given his height. He was wearing smart black trousers and a cream-coloured thin-knit jumper.

'*Bonjour*,' Keeley greeted. Instantly, as the French word came out of her mouth she regretted it. She didn't even know if this man was French and, if he was, all the French she had left to use were the other nineteen top phrases in that Eurostar magazine...

'*Bonjour*,' he answered. '*Ça va*?'

Keeley could feel her cheeks warming to being-able-to-cook-steak levels. 'Yes,' she replied. 'I... think so.'

The man smiled at her, a small laugh escaping his lips. But it didn't sound like it was a laugh meant to embarrass her any more than she was already embarrassed. She had only been here minutes...

'It was nice to meet you both,' the man said, ducking a little like he was paying reverence in a bow.

'Thank you,' Rach said, smiling widely. 'For being the prince to my Rapunzel.' Keeley watched Rach boost up her hair and shake her shoulders a little.

'*À bientôt*,' the man replied, heading for the door.

He'd barely gone before Rach made a sound someone might make in the middle of a booty call.

'What is it with this country? Sebastian was hot. Mystery-Hair-Hero is hot. Are all French men hot?' Rach asked.

'Excuse me!'

It was another male French voice that seemed to be directed at them and it was coming from the lips of a slim black man stood behind the reception desk. He was wearing a pristine dark suit with a red silk tie resting on a bright white shirt. He was beckoning them now, with all the finesse of someone experienced in semaphore.

'Hello,' Keeley greeted, walking over the marble tiles towards him. This area was all high sheen on the floor and antique decadence making up the rest of it. Parisian scenes in thick acrylics were framed in regal gold, the wallpaper was pale with small golden trees in its pattern and rich oak sideboards held the tourist information material. The reception desk was bare of everything except one highly polished chrome bell. 'My name's Keeley Andrews and we have a room booked. It's possibly in the name of—'

Rach banged her fingers on the bell and giggled as it chimed. She hit it a second time.

'Why are you pressing the bell?' the receptionist asked very stiffly. He was actually looking at Rach like lasers were going to shoot out of his eyes and carve her down the middle.

'It sounds nice,' Rach replied with a smile. 'Old-fashioned.' She rang the bell again.

'The bell,' the man told them, 'is to attract my attention.'

'Thank you,' Keeley answered. 'Sorry.'

Rach rang the bell a fourth time.

'What is your problem?' the man exclaimed, looking as exasperated as he sounded. 'At first you cannot manage to get in through the door and I have to stop the operation of it. Then you think it is amusing to ring my bell.'

Keeley looked at Rach. 'We're sorry and...' She saw Rach's fingers flex like she was going to chime the bell again, but before she could make a move to stop her, the receptionist had swept the bell off the desk and onto his workspace below. Gone and now completely out of reach.

'The bell,' he said again, seeming barely able to hold his temper, 'is to attract my attention... when I am *not here*!' The final part of the sentence was barked like an angry Royal Marine commander.

'Alright... Antonie,' Rach said, reading the man's name badge on his jacket. 'Take a chill pill. It's nearly Christmas.'

'It's ANTOINE! Not Antonie!'

Keeley shifted a little, making sure *she* was in the man's line of sight and Rach… wasn't. 'I apologise, Antoine. Let me start again. My name is—'

'I know who you are,' Antoine told her. He began clicking with his mouse, eyes dropping to the screen of his computer. 'You are guests of Madame Durand.'

'Yes,' Keeley answered. 'That's right.'

'You are in one of our best suites on the top floor. Here are your room cards and all the information you need for your stay will be in your room.' He placed two key cards on the desk.

'Is there a bell in our room?' Rach asked with a grin.

Keeley poked her in the ribs with her elbow. 'Thank you,' she answered Antoine, picking up the cards.

'The lifts are over there.' He pointed with flair. 'I will arrange for someone to bring up your luggage. Madame Durand has booked you in for our world-renowned afternoon tea at 3 p.m. Do not be late. It is *very* popular.' He set his expression to deeply serious and Keeley prayed that Rach didn't laugh. 'Breakfast is from 6 a.m. until 10 a.m. on weekdays and from 7 a.m. until 11 a.m. at the weekends. Dinner is 6.30 p.m. until 9.30 p.m. every day. I hope you enjoy your stay.'

'Oh, we will,' Keeley replied. 'Thank you.'

'Thanks, Antonie,' Rach said.

'Come on,' Keeley ordered, grabbing Rach's arm. 'Let's get to our room before you upset anyone else or get your hair caught on something.'

'Like on Antonie's stiff upper Poirot moustache?' Rach whispered.

'It's ANTOINE!'

Eleven

'This isn't a hotel room,' Rach announced, throwing open the balcony doors and letting in a blast of frosty air. 'This is like an apartment!'

Keeley couldn't deny it. This suite was as palatial as it got. Not that she was one to judge hotel suites as she hadn't actually ever stayed in one before. The hotels she had stayed in were usually either something cheap and cheerful her dad had managed to get at an even cheaper price thanks to collecting tokens from the newspaper, or they were not really thought about as destinations themselves, more for practical purposes. Like when she had travelled up to Birmingham to an expo on home design. Bea had gone with her. They had eaten all the free biscuits in their room and Bea had encouraged the drinking wine out of the hotel mugs. And they had eaten pizza and chips at midnight, watching *Naked Attraction* and being horribly judgemental about the contestants' body parts while mozzarella grease got all over the duvet covers. Bea had always gone with her to shows when she wasn't working – which wasn't often when you were someone in charge of designing bridges and roads. Her sister had been clever and brilliant and often Keeley had felt pride oozing from her when Bea talked about her career.

Those weekends with Bea were the ones Keeley had looked forward to the most. Arriving at an exhibition, Keeley would always look at everything from a home interiors angle – smooth arches and fluffy cushions – whereas Bea would be there eyeing up a standard lamp and telling Keeley how bright a wattage you could get away with before the shade would catch fire. Bea had always been as practical as Keeley was creative. Not that Bea wasn't creative, they just went at things from different perspectives… and Keeley missed that. She shivered, in the midst of her unpacking.

'Rach, could you close the doors? It's not really the weather for letting the air in.'

'We've got a balcony though! With the most amazing view of the Eiffel Tower!' Rach was shouting *from* the balcony where she seemed to be leaning out over the railings and embracing the Paris skyline. Keeley put down a burgundy jumper she didn't even remember packing and stepped towards the outside.

And the vista blew her away. There was that grand lady of Paris, a little to their right, its feet planted just behind two buildings ahead of it. It wasn't quite close enough to touch, but it was near enough for Keeley to feel even more awestruck from this position outside. She was already wondering exactly how much more spectacular it was going to look at night.

'Brilliant, right?' Rach asked, nudging Keeley. 'I've already taken a million photos. You can help me pick the best one for Instagram. I'll tag Roland and the firm in it, try and get him a bit of attention so he isn't pissy with us when we get back.'

'He *was* pissy, wasn't he?' Keeley said with a sigh. 'Maybe coming here now *was* completely the wrong timing.' Maybe she wouldn't have a job to go back to because of this surprise holiday...

'Until your mum spoke to him,' Rach piped up. 'Then he wasn't too bad.'

'What?'

'Didn't you know?' Rach asked. 'Your mum came in when you were at the house belonging to that Serbian couple with all the houseplants and the dog that pukes the moment anyone comes through the front door. She was in his office for about half an hour – *Roland* even made the coffees – and when she left he was in a much better mood and that's when I got the signed holiday form back.'

Keeley shook her head. Her mum interfering again – but also going against all the 'please, don't gos' and 'Paris is full of beggars and wannabe Monets' she had been spouting since Keeley had replied to Silvie Durand's email. This was a shock.

'And while we're on the subject of your mum... I have to tell you... she gave me a whole load of your tablets for my bag in case you fall off the wagon with them.'

'She didn't!' Keeley gasped, hands going to her face. *That* was definitely a step too far. Her pills. The pills were something she had been taking for over a year now to stop her body rejecting the kidney. After her last check-up the consultant had said everything was working brilliantly, even better than anyone could have expected, and that when she hit the twelve-month anniversary of the transplant they could significantly reduce the medication. Except Lizzie hadn't wanted to hear the word 'reduce'. And the very first thing her mum had said when they got back to the car park was, 'it would be silly to reduce the tablets before Christmas, wouldn't it? Because, you know, everywhere winds down for Christmas, and, if something happens and we have to call the doctor, we don't want him turning up more soaked in brandy than a Christmas pudding and his mind around the Bendicks.'

'She told me not to tell you,' Rach admitted. 'You're not pissed with me, are you?'

'No,' Keeley exhaled, her breath as visible in the air as the thin vapours of smoke rising from the chimney pots on frost-glazed rooftops. 'I'm annoyed with *her*. Every time I think she's releasing a little control, like by not commenting on my consumption of food with a higher fat content than celeriac, then behind the scenes she's doing something else. I'm twenty-six! I should have moved out. I should be running my own business.'

'You *do* run your own business, Keels,' Rach said, turning away from her photo-snapping for a moment.

'I work for Roland. I basically desk share with Jamie who overspills the second he has more than two files on his desk and a takeout from Subway.' Keeley sighed. It wasn't in the same league as the small office overlooking lush green parkland she had put a deposit on that had made her feel all the *feng shui* realness from the moment she set foot on the deep pile cream carpet. That had been her dream. Her own interior design business – not working for someone else – somewhere with her own professional premises. She'd picked up a couple of jobs right off the bat through word of mouth recommendations after successes at Ulterior Interior. She had ordered a desk and a sofa and had bought the comfiest armchair at a flea market in Camden Passage. But she'd never got to move in. After the accident, somewhere in-between the vomiting, the exhaustion and the trying to walk again, Lizzie had sent back the sofa and the desk. But the armchair had survived the cull and it was in Keeley's bedroom, reminding her of what obviously hadn't meant to be...

'Jamie's a dick,' Rach remarked. 'I'll speak to him.'

'No,' Keeley said in a rush. 'Don't.' She softened her tone a little. 'You don't need to fight my battles for me. I don't need two people trying to control me.'

'I wasn't trying to...' Rach began.

'Sorry,' Keeley said, annoyed by this conversation but knowing her friend wasn't at all to blame. 'Sorry... I didn't mean that. It's just, I want being here to be different and, with my mum at home and me being away for the first time, I didn't expect her to be so... present.'

'I should have kept my mouth shut about the pills. Binned them or something,' Rach said.

'No,' Keeley said. 'It's fine. It's not your fault.' It wasn't really anyone's fault. And that made it even harder. The accident – the lorry skidding on ice and crushing the side of the taxi Keeley and Bea were travelling in – was just that: an accident. There was nothing anyone could have done. There was no one to blame. And Keeley couldn't blame her mum for being overprotective really. Keeley losing her sister had been unbearable – was *still* unbearable – but she couldn't imagine how much worse it must have been to lose a child. Lizzie and Silvie had that awful, awful thing in common.

'You could move out though,' Rach suddenly said. 'You mentioned it before we left. I mean, Lizzie would probably go ape-shit for a bit, but she's not going to be able to *make* you stay.'

No, Rach was right. But was it *really* Lizzie making her stay? Or was it somehow her own guilt? Her guilt about being here. Surviving. Not being Bea…

'I… don't know.' Keeley swallowed, a breeze whipping her hair around her face. 'Places are expensive and… I didn't get my deposit back on the office and…'

'And Ken Jeong might one day know *exactly* who *The Masked Singer* is.' Rach put a hand on her shoulder. 'You could make excuses all day long. If you want something you have to go for it. That shouldn't change just because you're packing someone else's piece.'

Rach was right *again*. And why did Keeley really need telling what she already knew. She had to start living life for herself and not for her parents. It wasn't like she was going to move to the other side of the world. Although Lizzie did once say that a Tube ride to Tottenham had been like being aboard a Cambodian bamboo train she had no desire to revisit…

'I mean, if you were looking to move, I could be persuaded to shift out of my tiny room in the tiny apartment with chain-smoker Bertram and look for something a bit bigger and more conducive with trying to get a proper boyfriend, not just one who eats, shoots and leaves.'

'Is that what you want?' Keeley asked, turning her attention to her friend.

'What?' Rach asked, suddenly looking like she wanted to retract her last words.

'A proper boyfriend,' Keeley said. 'Someone long-term.'

'I...'

'Rach.'

'I just want someone to look at me and see *me*,' Rach admitted in a rush. 'You know, not just the blonde hair and the big smile and the even bigger...' She stopped then sniffed. 'Someone who would... love me even if I was in my pyjamas.'

Keeley put an arm around her friend's shoulders and squeezed. 'You know I love you in your pyjamas.'

'Which is why we need a place together. I've been thinking about leaving Bertram's for ages. I just don't have enough money to manage it on my own and I guess I thought you were settled at home, or I would have mentioned it before now.'

'OK,' Keeley said, excited by the sudden potential of change. 'Obviously it wouldn't be sensible to think about anything before Christmas but... after New Year... shall we look at some options?'

'Yes!' Rach said, turning and getting closer to Keeley to snap a selfie. 'Yes, let's do it. God, why didn't we think of this before? It's going to be brilliant. We can eat takeaway together and we'll find a place with a pub on the corner we can walk to together and we'll... get a dog... or a cat... or a giant African land snail.'

Keeley didn't have the heart to tell Rach she was running away with herself a little. Moving out of home was going to be expensive. It was likely there wasn't going to be spare cash for drinks at the pub or Just Eat or pets. But she wasn't going to dampen Rach's happiness now and it felt really good to make plans. Maybe this chance in Paris was going to be the start of something much more than finding out about her donor, maybe it was going to be the beginning of everything.

Twelve

L'Hotel Paris Parfait, Opera District, Paris

Ethan picked a sugared almond from the bowl now on the reception desk and popped it into his mouth. It was either keep eating the sweets or start biting his nails again. Except his nails were already down to the quick from an earlier nibbling session when the Christmas décor began to arrive. He checked his phone again. Nothing. Desperate to know what time he should expect Louis to turn up, he had sent an email *and* a text to Silvie. There had been no reply. Was it so hard to respond? He couldn't help feeling, after his last meeting with Silvie, that mother and son were both working to catch him by surprise. It was as if they *wanted* to find him or the hotels lacking somehow.

'Please!' Noel directed, red-faced and a little sweaty despite the winter temperatures that swept in every time someone opened the door. 'You are not listening to me.' He stepped towards the two men who were currently trying to position a slightly too large Christmas tree. Despite Noel saying that going all-out *Galeries Lafayette* wouldn't work for Perfect Paris, here they were with a spruce whose tallest branches were scratching the ornate ceiling. 'The tree, it needs to be perfectly straight. Do you know what perfectly straight means?'

Surely it wasn't too much to ask to know when Devil Durand was descending on his hotels? Or was the not telling the shape of things to come when Louis got himself back behind the boardroom table? Ethan swallowed, the taste of last night's Calvados on his tongue.

'*Straight!*' Noel said again, putting his arms out like he was a 747 lining up with the runway. 'Like... my teeth!' He opened his mouth, gurning at the men, two rows of pearls in perfect white rows shining an example.

The door of the hotel opened and Milo, their head chauffeur entered, dodging the goings-on with the tree and heading into the bowels of the hotel. Ethan hurried forward to catch him.

'Milo,' he greeted.

'Oh, Monsieur Bouchard, good morning.' Milo straightened his hat as if he was about to be pulled up on his appearance.

'Milo...' Ethan stopped. He shouldn't be asking this. He hated himself for asking it. 'Do you... have you... been asked to collect Monsieur Durand from the airport?' He swallowed, feeling a little like someone collecting covert information to sell on the dark web.

'Yes,' Milo responded immediately. 'I went this morning. I dropped him at the hotel at a little after nine.'

Ethan felt the nervous tension drop away, replaced quickly by fear and a sheen of ice-cold perspiration on the back of his neck. 'The hotel?' he queried. 'Not the house.'

'No,' Milo replied. The driver looked a little unsure now, almost as if he had made a mistake. 'Madame Durand said... did I do the wrong thing?'

'No,' Ethan said quickly, his thoughts now speeding like the fastest TGV. 'No, I...' He tried to inject some professionalism into his demeanour. 'I was expecting him here, that is all. Which hotel?'

'The Tour Eiffel hotel,' Milo replied. 'Should I go to collect him? Bring him here?'

'No, no, no, it is fine. Fine.' It wasn't fine. There were no Christmas decorations at the Tour Eiffel hotel yet. He had been convinced Silvie and Louis would visit the flagship branch here at Opera first. It wasn't like Louis was a tourist who needed a view of the tower to make his Paris trip complete. But was he actually *staying* at the hotel? And, if that was the case, could Ethan get Noel to arrange for the temporary ice rink and other festive touches to instead go to the other Perfect Paris branch? His mind was conflicted. What should he do? *Make a decision. You are in charge.* Except he wasn't in charge in his heart. Ferne had always led. She wouldn't have left anything to the last minute. Everything would have been precisely planned out and actioned without encountering any hitch.

'Can I do anything for you, Monsieur Bouchard?' Milo asked.

The driver was looking at Ethan as if gauging what the right course of action was. He needed to immediately play this down. Because it was nothing. Ethan was going to *ensure* it was nothing. Louis was not going to come here and take over. Louis was all about chasing the money. He had never understood his sister the way Ethan had.

Ethan shook his head. 'No, Milo, thank you. Everything is… perfect.' Just like their brand. He nodded then, like he was decreeing it so and ended the conversation.

The second the driver was gone, Ethan skidded back across the tiles to Noel.

'We need to move the tree,' Ethan hissed.

'What?' Noel exclaimed, eyes bulging, sweat running down his nose.

'The tree,' Ethan said again. 'It needs to go to the Tour Eiffel hotel. Now.'

'But…' Noel began.

'You said it was not straight,' Ethan remarked, trying not to give out all the harried he was feeling. 'We can… get it moved.' He smiled at the delivery men who looked less than pleased that none of this was going to end for them soon.

'Monsieur Bouchard…' Noel started.

'Noel,' Ethan countered quickly, lowering his voice slightly as guests approached the reception desk to be greeted by Monique and Annika. 'I need your help. Louis Durand is at the Tour Eiffel hotel. We need to make *there* the priority today. Now.' He took a decisive breath. 'Deal with the tree, then call the company about the ice rink.'

'Monsieur Bouchard, this is—' Noel began, the bead of sweat now on the very tip of his nose and threatening to drip down onto his tie.

'Possible,' Ethan interrupted, pointing a finger and keeping a smile on his lips. 'Only tell me it is possible.' He let his sentence hang in the air and then he rushed towards the door knowing exactly where he was going next.

Thirteen

The Eiffel Tower, Paris

It was breath-taking. Absolutely breath-taking. Keeley held onto the railings, her gloved fingers clinging tight as a very keen wind whipped around her ears and tried to sneak under the knitted hat she hoped wouldn't be covered in hair dye when she took it off again. She hadn't imagined coming to the famous tower on the very first day they arrived in Paris, but Rach had insisted they *had* to. And, after a glass-walled lift ride, they had arrived at the uppermost section, choosing to brave the elements for the outside vistas. And what a view it was! Stretching out before them was Paris in all its glory. The cream-coloured buildings in contrast to the oblongs of green set around the grey roads, traffic like tiny insects but still visible even from this height. Then there was the river. The Seine and its bridges delicately winding its way through the city like a slick silvery ribbon. It was incredible to think that they were actually here. It felt like a world away from Kensington.

'This is so much better than sizing up Victorian terraces,

right?' Rach said with a contented sigh of approval at what they were seeing.

'It's better than everything,' Keeley replied wistfully.

'You can't say *that*,' Rach replied, looking away from the view and towards her friend. 'You haven't seen "everything" yet.' Rach sighed again. 'Tunisia is cool. I rode a camel into the Sahara dressed as a Sheik and ate bread straight out of a hole in the earth.' She sniffed. 'Ryan was a bit nonplussed about the bread thing. I think that was when I realised we weren't going to be a long-term match.' She sighed. 'Still, as discussed, it's better to know than to not know, isn't it?'

'Yes,' Keeley answered. Except there hadn't really been a man on *her* scene since well before she got her new kidney. And even then there hadn't been any dates that had lasted past the first few – her choice. She had always preferred to be head down in work-related activities or spending time at the weekends with Rach and Bea. The expos or, in the summer, music festivals where Bea was always the first to complete putting up the tent. It was Keeley's thought that if someone *was* her Mr Right then it would happen just like that, bam! A string quartet would play and fireworks would crackle and fizz. Or, at least, work would automatically start to slip a little down the list to make room for him. But, as yet, it hadn't happened. And, of course, everyone she met now was greeted with a transplant story before they'd drunk the first drink. She had promised Rach not to do that here though. Except until they had met any men she didn't have the chance to try that out. Although, there had been Sebastian, their driver, and then the guy who had saved them in the revolving door and Antoine, the receptionist.

And absolutely no 'I'm a two litre of water a day, limited caffeine kind of a girl' faux pas had occurred.

'It's two-thirty,' Rach informed, checking her watch.

'Is it?' Keeley answered. She shivered. They had thirty minutes until they met Silvie for afternoon tea. Another involuntary shudder rocked her and she pretended to herself it was the bite of the breeze.

'How are you feeling about it?' Rach asked.

'Terrified,' Keeley admitted. 'I feel like... I don't know... like I don't want to be a disappointment to her.'

'What?' Rach laughed.

'It's not funny,' Keeley said, a smile reaching her lips. 'I feel more responsible for the upkeep of this body part than I did before when it was just *my* mum with the vested interest.'

'You can't think like that. It's yours now,' Rach reminded. 'Your body. Your kidney. Your life.'

'I know.'

'You don't get a used car and have the old owner telling you how to drive it, do you?'

'I guess not.' Keeley didn't know how she felt about being compared to a second-hand vehicle.

'And why would she be disappointed? You're amazing.'

Keeley smiled again. It was nice of Rach to say so, but she kept thinking that her real shot at amazing had been pre-accident with her eye on the home design prize career. Now, with her job at Roland's estate agency, it all felt a little bit second best. But maybe that's what you had to be happy with after a transplant. She was lucky to be here at all and no one knew how long this degree of normal was actually going to last. Her forever was likely going to be a lot shorter than the average twenty-six-year-old.

'Anyway,' Rach said again, snapping more pictures through the fence as they moved along it, taking in different aspects of the view. 'What about *her*? You might not think much of Silvie Durand when you meet her. *And* her daughter might have been a horrible person.'

'I'm not sure *anyone* who has signed up to be an organ donor could be a horrible person.'

'O-K,' Rach said, seemingly thwarted on that line of conversation. 'Well… she might… not like… burned toast. I mean, total heathen if she didn't like that. Or, she might not… do any charity work like you do with the hospice.'

Straightaway Keeley thought about Erica, her lovely friend who was so special to her, getting weaker every day. She drew her phone from the pocket of her coat and began to take photos. 'Most people don't have time for charity work. It isn't that they don't want to.'

'Well,' Rach said, 'all I'm saying is, without sounding too ungrateful about the trip… you are awesome and don't let this swaggy French woman with her free Eurostar tickets and our presidential-style suite make you feel inadequate. Because you're not.'

Somehow, amid this pep talk, Keeley couldn't help but feel more inadequate than ever. She focused her phone camera on the view, zooming in to get a closer look at L'Arc de Triomphe. She had to make sure that she enjoyed the experiences for Erica too and shared as much as she could with her. She should do a video so Erica could hopefully feel a little like she was there too.

'God,' Rach breathed. 'Don't look now but I think that

guy is going to propose.' She put one hand to her chest and the other on Keeley's shoulder, turning her to the scene.

Keeley watched, expectant, fully invested already as the young man wearing dark jeans and a padded jacket dropped to his knee next to his female companion. Rach let out a squeal… and then they both sighed heavily in unison.

'Bloody hell!' Rach said with a grunt.

'Oh,' Keeley said, in disappointment.

'Who does up their shoelace at the top of the Eiffel Tower? *Who*, I ask you?!'

'Come on,' Keeley said, putting her arm through Rach's and leading her towards the inside. 'We have sandwiches and cakes to get to.'

Fourteen

L'Hotel Paris Parfait, Tour Eiffel, Paris

The afternoon tea spread was glorious. Four tiers of food ranging from rectangular-cut sandwiches – egg mayonnaise, salmon and cucumber, a soft cheese with chives, thick ham with a bright yellow chutney – to scones with pots of fresh cream and strawberry jam, then cakes (chocolate eclairs, *tarte citron*, *Paris-Brest* and macarons). Keeley could see that Rach was ready to dig in. Her friend had furled and unfurled her napkin several times and had carefully turned the display a full three-sixty twice, her fingers grazing the edge of the scones as if trying to 'accidentally' loosen a crumb or six... Keeley looked at her watch again. It was ten past three. It was official. Silvie was late.

'She's probably stuck in traffic,' Rach said, doing her best-friend mindreading again.

'Yes,' Keeley said. She lifted herself off the chair a little and flattened down her taupe-coloured woollen skirt. She had quickly changed out of her jeans before they came down to the dining room, feeling as if she wanted to be a touch smarter for the meeting, even after everything she and Rach had discussed over that Parisian view from the top of the tower. Making an effort didn't have to mean her everyday was ordinary, just that she regarded this meeting as important. It was kind of momentous really.

'The traffic *is* mental here,' Rach continued, fingers tracing the rim of one of the elegant plates. 'More than the Blackwall Tunnel kind of mental.'

'Yes,' Keeley replied. She looked towards the door again. She had already decided exactly what Silvie was going to look like. She would be tall. She would be one of those French women who oozed confidence from the balls of their designer-boots-clad feet to the crown of their thick, luscious hair. She would have dark hair, long but well-managed. She would carry a large handbag full of expensive make-up products with a purse containing business cards for all the best boutiques. Somehow Keeley sensed Silvie would give off all the strong and successful.

'You're not listening, are you?' Rach said, interjecting into Keeley's thought process.

'Sorry… I was… it's just…'

'I know,' Rach said. 'It's gone three and she's late and you're worried she's not coming.'

It was exactly that. Surely Keeley wasn't going to have come all this way, having been invited here, to be stood up. It had to be traffic, didn't it?

'*Excusez-moi*, there is something wrong with your food?'

'Bloody hell, Antonie! You scared the shite out of me!' Rach exclaimed.

'It is An*toine*,' the concierge replied through gritted

teeth yet still with a smile on his face. 'You do not like the afternoon tea selection?'

'No,' Keeley answered, patting an imaginary crease out of her skirt. 'That is, yes, I'm sure it's delicious but—'

'We are waiting for someone,' Rach told the man. 'In England it's rude to start eating before everyone's arrived… unless you're *really really* hungry and haven't eaten anything since breakfast… hours ago.'

'You are waiting for another guest?' Antoine pulled a face like this was news to him and removed a small electronic device from the pocket of his trousers. He started to tap at it with his long, slim fingers, eyes visibly flitting from side to side as he checked out the screen.

'Yes,' Keeley answered. 'Mrs… I mean, *Madame* Durand? She booked the afternoon tea with you?' Keeley's mouth felt arid. Never mind eating, she really did need to drink something soon. Could you get dehydrated in close-to-freezing temperatures?

'Ah! My apologies,' Antoine said, eyes coming away from the device. 'Maybe I was not clear. *Madame* Durand made the booking for only two people. You, Ms Andrews and…' He looked at Rach. 'Your guest.'

'It's Rach,' Rach answered huffily, pulling down her micro-mini.

'Oh,' Keeley said, disappointment taking hold of her insides and shaking them like a tambourine. 'I assumed she would be joining us.'

'Antoine!'

'Excuse me, Ms Andrews… *Rash*…' He left their table.

'Did he just call me Rash?!' Rach exclaimed, infuriated. 'Bloody nerve of him!'

Keeley felt completely deflated. The moment the afternoon tea had been mentioned on their arrival she had imagined meeting Silvie and starting to get to know more about Ferne. Initially, she might have thought it was too soon, but now she had all that anticipation followed by… nothing.

'Let's look on the bright side,' Rach said, fingers already crawling towards the sandwiches. 'At least we can start on the food.'

Except there was no bright side right at this moment. It had been a whole giant sizzling bonfire of emotions and expectations and now it was as if someone had hosed the whole thing down with everything a fire hydrant had to offer. Keeley rose from her chair again, but this time she wasn't going to untuck her skirt.

'I… need to get some fresh air.'

'Keels,' Rach said, seeming to be caught between getting up too and stuffing a salmon sandwich in her mouth.

'It's OK. I… just need some air and… a minute. I need a minute.' Suddenly it felt like the ultra-contemporary and sumptuous surroundings in the restaurant were crowding her. It was all different and… foreign and currently Keeley was feeling a little misled. She ignored Rach's second attempt to get her to stop and instead, grabbed her coat and hurried from the room. Removal men were attempting to install a very large Christmas tree in reception and pine needles were scattering all over the floor. Baubles slipped off boughs and dropped to the tiles. It was chaos she didn't need. She headed to the exit.

Maybe her mum had been right. Was it better not to know anything about her donor and her family? Keep a distance?

Had Silvie perhaps also had second thoughts about the whole thing? Keeley ignored the revolving door and instead opted to push at the smaller door next to it. She needed that rush of real air and she needed it now. Barrelling through, she waited for the icy temperatures to hit her cheeks…

'Ow!'

Instead something hit *her* – and not just on her cheeks. It was full-on body contact with something hard and firm and she was currently spiralling her way down to the pavement.

Fifteen

'*Non!*' a voice ordered. '*Non! Non! Non!*'

There was a loud clatter and for a millisecond, Keeley thought it was her body meeting the cobbles, but it wasn't her bones that were breaking, it was her fall. Two strong arms were underneath her and she was suspended, gazing upwards, the strong winter sunlight refracting and making it almost impossible to see anything. Although... Focusing, her breath catching in her chest, Keeley made out the features of the person who was holding her. Dark wavy hair, a little tousled, angular features including a not unattractive nose, and rather appealing grey eyes...

The man said something else in French and Keeley couldn't reply. She wasn't sure whether it was because she didn't have the local vocabulary or because she was winded.

'Can you stand?' the man asked, tipping her upright almost in a move like he was trying to rid her of vertigo.

'I... yes...' She was on her feet again now and he hadn't given her much choice in the matter.

'Where the hell is it?' The man was spinning around now, looking up and down the street outside the hotel. He picked up a plastic carrying box, its metal gate swinging loose at the front and peered inside. 'Fuck!' That word wasn't French.

'Was there... something in there?' Keeley found herself asking.

'Yes!' he snapped a reply. 'And it wasn't mine! I borrowed it and I have to take it back in a couple of hours before anyone notices it is missing.'

'O-K,' Keeley replied. Was this man sane? Or was this some sort of avant-garde street entertainment the French were keen on?

'Can you look behind the bags?'

He was pointing now at a collection of refuse sacks to the left of the hotel. This was so bizarre. But Keeley found herself stepping towards the pile of bin bags... Was it a cat or a dog that had escaped?

'What am I looking for and does it have a name?'

'Pepe,' the man replied.

'OK,' Keeley said. She picked up a bin bag and looked beneath, but how this man thought an animal could have got under it without them seeing was a bit mad in itself. She shook another bin bag to make sure. 'Is Pepe a cat or a dog?'

There was no reply and, when Keeley turned around, the man had disappeared. Where was he? She sighed. Why did she care? She had come outside to try and quell the irritation of being stood up and maybe regroup. Suddenly, she gasped as the man appeared from behind a giant green recycling bin. He still looked harried. He still looked attractive...

Keeley swallowed. 'Is Pepe a cat?' she repeated. 'Or a dog?'

'A penguin,' the man replied almost nonchalantly. 'Not something I can easily pick up a replacement for.'

'What?' Keeley exclaimed. 'Did you say *penguin*?!'

He couldn't have said 'penguin'. That was craziness of the highest order. Who carried around a penguin on the streets of Paris? Who carried around a penguin at any time? Unless you were... heading for a zoo. Keeley side-eyed the man as he mounted a large bin on wheels and the top half of his torso disappeared completely inside. He didn't look like a zookeeper. He was wearing a three-piece suit underneath his dark, expensive-looking woollen coat, smart brown shoes... She shook herself. She should retreat now. This penguin business wasn't *her* business. She was here on the street to get her head together. She should focus on the festive lights being strung up across the street and a stall of shabby chic Santas and star ornaments doing a roaring trade...

The man popped back up, a piece of orange peel in his hair. 'Have you seen him?' he asked her.

'No, I... don't know where else to look.' And helping strangers recover animals who should be living in the Antarctic wasn't her remit.

'There!' the man shouted, pointing a finger to a bright red fire hydrant. 'Pick up the box!' He took off in hot pursuit.

Before Keeley knew it, she was doing as he'd asked, snatching up the carrier and charging down the street after him... and it. She could just see Pepe the penguin, running at quite a pace, weaving in and around passers-by making a hideous squawking noise and flapping its flippers like it intended to defy everything known about its species and its lack of taking-to-the-air ability.

Who knew penguins could run so fast? Or that a creature usually known for being cute could terrify the crap out of the citizens of the French capital? Yapping dogs were fear-whining and retreating as it flashed past them, grown businessmen were clutching their iPhones to their ears and leaping out of its path... and now Pepe was heading for the road.

'*Excusez-moi! Excusez-moi! Bouge toi!*

The man was getting caught up in a group of people who were coming together in an attempt to take a selfie with the Eiffel Tower in the background. Pepe was about to sprint off the pavement and into traffic. Mopeds gathered pace beeping their horns, taxis continued to buzz along and now there was a van revving its engine as a pod from its roof extended out and up, a man in its basket ready to hang Christmas garlands. Keeley couldn't wait. Dropping the carrier down, she stepped up her pace. Then, praying it wasn't going to hurt too much, she launched herself forward, hands outstretched, focusing on her black and white feathered target...

The pavement rose up to meet her and its cold, hard concrete impacted through the thick padding of her coat. But her fingers had definitely met small and fuzzy and she clung on, ignoring the ache in her ribs and concentrating on establishing her connection with the animal, dragging it towards her and out of the gutter. A bicycle rang its bell in warning and then suddenly Keeley found herself propelled backwards.

Ethan caught his breath as he sat on the ground. There was now a woman and the penguin between his legs, only a few inches away from the roaring of the Paris traffic. He felt sick, as if the sweets he had consumed were going to make a reappearance. He was also completely out of breath. He really did need to get back to the gym.

'I'm... not sure how long I can hold it for.'

Ethan shifted then, gently moving the woman's weight from his body and shuffling around her to grab Pepe who was squawking like he could front a heavy metal band.

'I did not know it was going to be so... crazy,' Ethan admitted to her. 'But that might pay off later.' He watched as the woman gingerly got to her feet, travelling back a few paces to where she had abandoned the carrier. She brought it over and Ethan managed to place the bird inside before ensuring it was securely locked this time. He turned away from the animal to the woman, noticing she hadn't quite caught her breath yet and seemed to be holding the side of her body.

'You are hurt?' he asked her.

She shook her head. 'I'm fine.'

'No,' he said. 'You spoke the words like you are not fine at all.'

'I'll be OK,' she answered. 'I've been through much worse.'

'I can call a doctor,' Ethan said. She looked pale, her skin in contrast to the brown waves of her hair. She was a little shorter than his five feet ten, lean, but not too skinny. Pretty.

'No,' she answered. 'I don't need a doctor. I... probably just need a cup of tea and some of the cakes I held off from.' She took another deep breath, closing her eyes for a second. She opened them again.

'Are you certain?' he asked. She had the most beguiling eyes. A mix of not-quite-blue-yet-not-quite-green. 'I can easily call someone.'

'I think you would be better off taking care of your penguin.'

Ethan glanced down at the carrier. Pepe had his beak sticking out of the gate, half a sardine in its mouth. Was this a madness brought on by all his insecurities relating to the hotel? Should he take the penguin back to where it belonged and stop with the childish desperation?

'I should get back,' the woman said, about to turn away.

'Wait,' Ethan said, reaching out and catching her arm. 'I...'

He found himself rendered a little speechless when she turned back to face him. She really wasn't pretty. Pretty did not cover it at all. She was uniquely stunning and he couldn't quite quantify it. All he knew for now was her eyes definitely had something to do with it...

'Let me,' Ethan began, his voice a little broken. 'Um... let me, as an apology, suggest some places for you to visit while you are in Paris.' He couldn't stop looking at her. 'You are visiting, yes?' What was he saying? Had he lost all his brain cells the moment inspiration had whispered 'penguin'.

'Yes, but...' the woman began, obviously about to tell him there were countless guidebooks available to purchase, plus the internet.

'Places that are... not on the tourist trail.' He smiled. 'Hidden Paris.'

'I don't know...'

'Where do you stay?'

'I'm at the Perfect Paris hotel.' She smiled a little then. 'I know. Straightaway a tourist cliché.'

She was staying at one of his hotels... and she hated the name of his brand. Disappointment wrapped around him like gift paper and the tightest of bows. He quickly regrouped. 'Allow me to leave a map in reception for you. Places to see. Restaurants to try. The sights you should not miss. A thank you for helping me with Pepe.'

She smiled and Ethan felt its warmth sink through his skin and into his bones. This wasn't normal. This was completely unsettling.

'OK,' she replied.

'OK,' he parroted. *Stupide*. He cleared his throat. 'So, your name? To leave the map for your attention?' He was eagerly waiting to find out exactly what this enchanting woman was called.

'Oh... um... Keeley,' she answered. 'My name's Keeley.'

'Ethan,' he replied, holding out his hand. '*Enchanté*.'

She placed her fingers in his and gave his hand a firm shake. It wasn't the skin-on-skin contact that rocked him, it was again the meeting of their gaze. He found his heart caught somewhere between stopping and pounding out the national anthem.

'It's nice to meet you,' she responded. Then she dipped her head to the animal carrier. 'And you, Pepe.'

He wanted to offer to walk with her. To say he was going to the hotel himself. But something was holding him back. Perhaps his subconscious reminding him that caring about anyone wasn't on his agenda...

'I'd better get back,' the woman told him. 'Bye.'

Ethan watched her turn away, walking with still a little fragility back towards the hotel.

'*Au revoir*,' he whispered. But the sentence was lost in the air.

Sixteen

L'Hotel Paris Parfait, Tour Eiffel, Paris

Keeley's ribs were on fire, but she wasn't going to give in to the pain on the street in front of the whole world, a penguin and a gorgeous guy who already wanted to put her in front of a doctor. Still, the throbbing sensation in her torso, was taking her mind away from the irritation that she obviously wasn't going to meet with Silvie today.

This day! She just needed to sit down for a bit, in the warmth of the restaurant and see if she could make herself feel better with scones and tea. She took a deep breath and willed her legs into further action.

'Oh! Keeley! Come and sit down! Come and meet Louis!'

It was Rach up and out of her seat, waving like she was the lone party sending off a packed-out cruise ship. And who was Louis?

Steeling herself for more movement, Keeley offered a weak smile and made her way across the restaurant and back to the table. When she got there a tall, fair-haired man got to his feet and extended his hand. He looked immediately familiar.

'Louis,' he said. 'It's a pleasure to meet you... again.'

His accent was a cross between French and American and it was then Keeley fully recognised him. 'You're the man who helped with the revolving door earlier.'

'Yes!' Rach said, all wide eyes and excited. 'Our real-life French hero.'

'Believe it or not,' Louis said, 'you are not the first people to become trapped in that door. And I suspect, sadly, you will not be the last.'

Keeley tentatively sat down and preceded to try and find the position that eased rather than made things worse. 'You have been here before?'

'Yes,' Louis answered. 'My sister is... that is, she *was*, working here.' He picked up his cup of tea. 'I am visiting family.'

'From America,' Rach added, sending Keeley some sort of conspiratorial wink like 'America' had a whole double-meaning that could involve squirty cream.

'Are you OK?' Louis asked. He was looking at her rather intently and Keeley wondered whether she might have ripped her new coat or that she might have something hanging from her like the orange peel Ethan had had in his hair from the Pepe pursuit...

'Yes, I—'

'Shit! Keels!' Rach exclaimed, leaping from her seat. 'Your nose is bleeding!'

Keeley put a finger to her nose then drew it away, a thin bright red trickle on the pad. 'Oh... I...'

Rach practically vaulted a chair to get to her, swiping

up serviettes from the afternoon tea and pressing them to Keeley's nose like she was trying to stop a dam from bursting. It wasn't the blood flow she could feel now, it was the weight of dozens of gazes resting on her and her drama.

'Shall I get someone?' Louis asked, standing and hovering like he was at a complete loss as to what to do. Not quite so heroic when confronted with bleeding rather than the mechanics of entry and exit apparently.

'Yes,' Rach responded.

'No!' Keeley retorted immediately. 'It's a nosebleed. I… might have knocked it when I…' She stopped talking then. It was quite hard to talk when your nose was being clamped with Kleenex and you were using only your mouth to breath. And she couldn't possibly admit that she had got injured running after a penguin. The only doctor they would be calling for then would be a psychiatrist.

'Is this because you're not taking your tablets?' Rach whispered, eyes a little frightened.

'I *am* taking my tablets,' Keeley answered. 'Forever. Just at a reduced dosage.'

'But could it be…'

Keeley shook her head. 'No, Rach. It's just a nosebleed.'

'Are you sure?'

'Yes!' She shrugged off Rach's attentions, putting her own hand to the wad of tissue and easing herself back into the chair.

'I should make a move,' Louis announced, looking at his watch. 'If you are sure that I cannot do anything and that everything is OK.'

'Oh, do you have to go?' Rach asked, finally moving her

attention from Keeley. 'You haven't even had a cake and there's plenty.'

'The cakes are excellent here,' Louis responded. 'World-renowned.' He smiled at them both. 'I am sure I will see you again. I am here for a few weeks.' He waved a hand. '*À bientôt*.'

'I'll try not to get trapped in any doors again,' Rach began. 'But if I do…'

Louis smiled and left the table, heading in the direction of the lobby. Rach's attention seemed to go with him and Keeley just watched her friend while she attempted to thwart the bleeding.

'He was nice,' Rach said with a sigh.

'You think he's hot,' Keeley replied, her h's coming out as d's, her nostrils still held closed.

'Don't you?'

No, she didn't. She could see that Louis was an attractive man but he wasn't attractive to her. *Unlike Ethan*. Even that name was sexy. Not quintessentially French, perhaps, but sexy all the same. She shivered then, probably in reaction to the blood loss…

'Where did you go?' Rach asked, suddenly cramming an éclair in her mouth.

'I told you,' Keeley said. 'For some fresh air.' She swallowed. She might have had a little cry if she hadn't had her feet taken from under her right outside the entrance. It only went to prove that she was hanging a lot on this connection with Silvie Durand, maybe more than she should. Why was finding out about Ferne feeling almost crucial? Should it be?

'Listen, we both need to chill,' Rach said through her

mouthful of pastry and cream. 'We've had a big day and we're train-lagged. Your woman probably thought she'd give us a treat with this tea and let you settle in before she meets you. I'm sure she'll make contact tomorrow.'

Keeley nodded. What else could she do? She was the visitor here. What happened next was up to Silvie.

'Have a cake,' Rach urged. 'And a sandwich. And tell me what my best outfit will be for loitering around a hotel looking romance-ready.'

'The elf costume,' Keeley said, finally feeling able to take the tissue away from her nose. 'Or, if we're testing your "looking for a long-term boyfriend" theory, maybe your pyjamas.'

'Did you see they're setting up some kind of Christmas-themed ice rink in the bar area?'

Keeley shook her head. Her body had been aching so much when she got back inside she hadn't really seen anything.

'Antonie was there and another guy who looks like a slightly chubbier version of him. They were both being all stiff and French and telling children not to touch anything.'

Keeley tried to stifle a yawn. She *was* tired. She hadn't been sleeping that well lately and she had been taking out her frustrations with Lizzie's overprotectiveness at the gym, maybe deliberately pushing things too hard.

'Listen, Keels, you can tell me if there's anything wrong, you know, with your health.' Rach had leaned forward now, her sleeve dropping into the jam pot.

'You said I wasn't allowed to mention my kidney,' Keeley reminded.

'Out loud,' Rach said. 'In company. You know, as a meet-and-greet.'

Keeley smiled and picked up a delicious-looking egg sandwich from the silver platter. 'I'm fine, honestly. Nothing to see here.' Except a little part of her was wondering if there would be a map for hidden Paris waiting for her at reception later…

Seventeen

L'Hotel Paris Parfait, Opera District, Paris

It was morning. A cold frost had coated the streets of Paris overnight, but, despite the plummeting temperatures, a bright blue cloudless sky spelled wintry sunshine to come.

Ethan had skipped into the restaurant half an hour ago and was delighted to see the festiveness coming together in the flagship hotel. There were wreaths of blue and silver flowers hanging from every available space that wasn't taken up by their traditional artwork, there were ornate posies of icy branches and royal blue pearls in small glass vases on every table and there was a decorated tree in reception, thankfully slightly smaller than the one he had removed to the *Tour Eiffel* hotel.

Sitting at a table for four, he took a sip of his black coffee almost giddy with excitement. He was back in control. Thanks to a penguin. Laughing quietly to himself, he replayed in his mind the video he had filmed of the chaos ensuing after Louis had found Pepe in his bedroom last night. He supposed some might think it juvenile to pay one of the maids to let the animal in, then capture Louis's distress for Ethan's personal viewing pleasure but… it felt good. Whatever scheme Louis and Silvie had cooked up between them with regard to the hotels, it would not hurt to have his nemesis feeling wrong-footed from the outset. And, Ethan would get to see just how out-of-sorts Louis was this morning, as Silvie had arranged this breakfast get-together.

'*Bonjour*, Monsieur Bouchard.'

Ethan looked up from his croissant and coffee and smiled at Noel.

'*Bonjour*, Noel. It is a beautiful day to be alive, *non*?'

Noel looked a little confused as if he was trying to decide if Ethan's words were a sarcastic prelude to an official warning.

Ethan laughed. 'What is wrong? This hotel is looking great! The *Tour Eiffel* hotel is looking great! The others all have plans to implement this week…'

'You are too full of cheer,' Noel admitted. 'It makes me uneasy.'

'Well, my friend,' Ethan said, raising his coffee cup in the air, 'perhaps it is something for you to get used to. I intend to fully embrace the season this year and that is to begin with smiles on the faces of all Perfect Paris employees. But, as with every good business, the management shall take the lead.' Ethan cleared his throat, then, adjusting the lapels of his suit jacket, he smiled wide, holding it then elongating it until he felt like he was impersonating The Joker.

'If you were not my boss, I would tell you that that was terrifying,' Noel replied, deadpan.

'You can tell me,' Ethan said, taking a drink of his coffee. 'I will take it only as a compliment.' He watched Noel wrap another brightly coloured scarf around his neck and fasten his coat as if he was leaving. 'What are you doing? Are you going somewhere?'

'That is why I am here. To tell you I have been drawn away on other business this morning.'

Drawn away on other business? 'What?' Ethan asked. 'Drawn away by who?'

'Madame Durand. She has VIP guests staying at *Tour Eiffel* she wants me to take on a tour today.'

Ethan felt the first turn in his good humour. *He* was the manager. What his staff did – particularly his right-hand man – was down to him, not Silvie. And who were these VIP guests? Could it be someone they were bringing in to replace him. A hotel manager out of the family who would be only too willing to obey Louis's orders? Ferne had never wanted the hotels to be without family management overseeing the core of the chain. Yet again, his best friend's ethos was being challenged now she was out of the picture.

'Was there something you needed me to do?' Noel asked.

'I wanted to go through the accounts with you.' Ethan hadn't *exactly* planned for that, but it would be a good idea to get Noel's take on where they could be saving a little more or spending a little less.

'Well, I told Madame Durand, quite politely, how much I had on my list of things to achieve today, but she was insistent that I do this instead. *Very* insistent, in fact,' Noel elaborated.

The coffee on Ethan's tongue felt completely bitter now. Again, it felt like he was being played.

'I should go,' Noel said. 'You can call me if you require anything urgent, but I would prefer it if you did not.

Sometimes I can completely lose my flow on a tour when that happens and if these guests are important to the hotel then…'

'You go,' Ethan replied, more than a little put out. 'I will ring the accountant if I need to.' He watched Noel leave the restaurant and then pushed his croissant away from him. His appetite was completely lost.

He didn't have long to mope however as Silvie and Louis were being greeted by the maître d' at the door. He sat a little taller in his chair and tried to resurrect some of the simple triumph he had felt after watching the video of Pepe. His two guests were walking swiftly. There were no smiles on their faces. Ethan quickly got to his feet, not liking the feel of this approach.

'*Bonjour*, Silvie. *Bonjour*, Louis. Welcome back to Paris!' Ethan stuck his hand out to Ferne's brother.

'Sit down, Ethan,' Silvie ordered.

He hesitated, wondering whether to obey or not. He remained standing but retracted his arm now the handshake wasn't forthcoming.

'Is something wrong?' Ethan asked. It was then, as the words left his mouth that he took a better look at Louis. The man's complexion was covered in harsh red welts, his eyes glazed, one of them a little closed like he had done a few rounds with Anthony Joshua. What had happened to him?

'Of course there is something wrong!' Silvie snapped. 'Look at Louis.'

Ethan didn't want to look at Louis. He'd rather Louis was where he should be – on the other side of a very large body of water. He carried on with his visual inspection though, his brain desperately attempting to come up with something to say that would sound concerned and completely innocent. Because this – whatever it was – couldn't be because of a penguin, could it?

'*Mon Dieu*! Pickpockets are getting more and more violent these days,' Ethan said in sober tones. 'Did they get away with anything?'

'Ethan, this is not—' Silvie started.

'No,' Louis interrupted, his face a picture of fury. 'They did not get away with anything. Nor will they while I am here.'

The man couldn't have been clearer. Louis *knew* what he had done. Ethan couldn't explain the state of the guy's face, but Louis knew that the penguin arriving in his suite had been down to him. Ethan continued quickly. 'We thought about putting notices up to warn the customers but you do not want to scare people. Customers in fear of having their valuables taken are not customers who will linger and relax over the cocktail menu.'

'This is an allergic reaction,' Silvie said, finally sinking into a dining chair as if the weight of the world was hanging from the beaded pearls at her neck. 'A severe allergic reaction.'

'Oh?' Ethan exclaimed in his best slightly surprised voice. He didn't want to ham it up too much. He settled for 'faintly astonished' rather than 'reaction to a shock pregnancy'.

'Someone put a penguin in Louis's room.'

'A what?' Maybe pretending he didn't even know what a penguin was a little over the top.

'You know exactly what my mother is talking about.'

Louis's face was reddening even more considerably now,

but Ethan suspected that was down to anger rather than a second strain of the reaction.

'Sit down, Louis,' Ethan urged. 'Take the weight off your feet. Ease your…' He paused briefly. 'Boils.'

'This was you!' Louis said. 'I know it was you!' He wasn't sitting down and he was pointing now. Ethan stood his ground, trying to look a little overwhelmed by the reaction.

'You knew that I was allergic to penguins,' Louis continued, 'So you arranged for one as a welcome committee.'

Ethan put a hand to his throat and set his face to aggrieved. 'I do not know what you mean.'

'You came,' Louis said. 'Back then, that day we all went to the zoo as a *family*. We fed the penguins and then…' He stopped talking like the topic of conversation was becoming too much for him.

'Then?' Ethan urged. He didn't remember Louis being allergic to the creatures, only that he had run away from them, slipping and sliding on the ice, his gloved hands over his ears. Ethan had laughed. Ferne had laughed too. Until Silvie had told them both to stop. That had been a little after Monsieur Durand had died. At that time, the laughs were few and far between. Pierre Durand had been tough but fair. The man had a hard exterior that was instantly off-putting, but when someone had earned his trust he had slowly let himself ease open like an obedient clam. Ethan couldn't say, even now, looking back, that Pierre had ever welcomed him, but the man had seemed to accept his presence – and Ferne's desire for it – in a way Louis never had. Ferne's father had been motivated by money, exactly like his son. Retiring from his fast-paced career running his executive chauffeur service hadn't suited him and the moment he tried to relax, switch off, embrace this slower pace of life, a heart attack had claimed him.

'You did this,' Louis repeated. 'I know you did.'

Ethan scoffed, shaking his head. 'Come on, Louis. I am twenty-eight years old. You speak of such childish things.'

'Childish things that you would commit! Like you always have! You are like… Peter Pan!' Louis snapped.

'OK,' Silvie broke in. 'That is enough. Quite enough.' She raised a hand, taking the fabric of Louis's coat between her fingers and encouraging him to sit down.

'Well,' Ethan began, dropping into a chair too, 'I had no idea the meeting was to begin this way. Compared to a fairy-tale character. How very grown up.' He straightened his waistcoat. 'I was thinking we were getting together to establish plans for Christmas at the hotels. You will see I have made a start and—'

'We *are* here for that,' Silvie agreed.

'But it is more,' Louis piped up, reaching for the coffee pot and squinting his good eye in an attempt to focus on the pouring.

'Louis,' Silvie said. 'Let us order some breakfast and have a little coffee first.'

'So sentimental,' Louis whispered, shaking his head. 'That has always been to your detriment, Mother. Father always said that business must be done with the brain and the brain should never be connected to the heart.'

Ethan felt like he was watching rather than participating now. That Silvie and Louis were privy to something he did not know about. And he did not like that. 'What is going on?' He looked from Silvie to Louis then back again. Silvie opened her lips, but it was Louis who voiced the next words.

'I told my mother that I am here to help shape the future of Perfect Paris but, well, I lied,' Louis said, full of nonchalance.

'Louis,' Silvie attempted to interrupt. 'We need to talk about this a lot more before anything is firmly decided.'

'No, *Mother*, we need to make decisions to secure your comfortable retirement.'

Now Ethan *really* disliked this turn in conversation and, again, he felt like the bystander, the fly on the wall, the child at the top of the stairs at the orphanage listening to the beatings. He pushed his teeth into his tongue and willed the iron taste of blood on his taste buds. How much damage to Louis would *two* penguins have done?

'We touched on this at our lunch last week, Ethan,' Silvie said softly, leaning forward a little as if to draw his attention away from Louis for a second. 'If you had stayed I would have explained further but—'

'You told me at lunch,' Ethan began, the blood rushing through him powering every word, 'that you were meeting the person who has Ferne's kidney.' He could barely bring himself to say the sentence, rage threatening to consume him. 'After that announcement, I am afraid that there was nothing else I wanted to hear.'

'Ethan, I—' Silvie started.

'We're going to be selling the brand, Ethan,' Louis said bluntly. 'By the beginning of next year, I want all the hotels gone.'

Eighteen

Arc De Triomphe, Paris

'Your fat finger is over the lens, man!'

Keeley quickly adjusted her grip on her phone and tried to hold it still, over the view, as the wind swirled around her. It was freezing, but the chill wasn't quite getting deep into her bones because they had climbed up all the steps to the very top of the Arc de Triomphe. The vista was phenomenal though. The highly sculpted stone archway depicting French battles – with all the wide-eyed horses and battle-weary soldiers – was basically the ornate centre piece of a roundabout. Paris cars were circling quickly, then stopping still as traffic built up, horns blaring. Tree-lined roads led off from the circle including what seemed the longest and widest, the *Champs-Élysées*. Rach had already told their tour guide, Noel, that no matter what tourist hotspots he had planned for the rest of their morning they definitely wanted time to look in the designer stores.

'Is that better, Erica?' Keeley asked. There was no immediate answer from the FaceTime in the UK and she wondered if the connection might have been lost. She didn't want to move the phone to disturb the view if not though.

'Erica?' Keeley queried. She hadn't collapsed or anything, had she?

'I… can't believe you've done this for me.'

Erica's voice sounded so emotional it caught Keeley in a tender spot that straightaway caused her eyes to tear up. She swallowed the emotion back and took a glance over her shoulder. Rach was busy snapping pics and Noel had some kind of iPad he was tapping away at.

'I said I would,' Keeley said, moving the phone a little to capture as much of the ambience as possible. And she had said she would because this was her chance to be there. To hold Erica as she fell.

'I know you *said* you would. But I told you, my whole life, people have said shit like that to me all the time and they haven't meant it.'

'I mean it,' Keeley said, tears pricking her eyes.

She could admit it to herself that when she first met Erica at the hospital she had seen taking her under her wing and supporting her through her treatment as trying to make up for feeling there was more she could have done for Bea. That fateful Saturday night out – a few bars, a band, the taxi that never reached home – it had all been Keeley's idea. And she did blame herself. What if they hadn't gone out? What if they had gone somewhere else? Why hadn't they got the Tube? It didn't matter how many times Keeley told herself – or the counsellor reassured her – that those thoughts weren't logical and were in fact unhelpful in terms of her recovery – it didn't stop the mindset arriving now and then. Erica, she had a spark about her, just like Bea had. Both women had a complete and content vision of their place in the world and a fierce nature that everyone else should accept it. But Erica was Erica. A one off. Not Bea. Instead, Erica was someone who had saved Keeley. With her uncomplicated friendship even amid her medical struggles, Erica had been there when everyone else in Keeley's life thought perhaps the path to recovery had already been fully travelled.

Keeley took a breath and smiled to herself. 'All in, remember? Every time.'

'OK, so, flip the view around, I want to see your face.'

'The Paris scenery is much better than my face,' Keeley insisted. 'It's cold here and windy and my hair is still leaking. I think the dye might have even stained the tiles of the shower in the plush bathroom we have at the hotel.'

'Let me see you, man!'

Keeley pressed the screen of her phone and greeted a smiling Erica. She didn't look too bad today. Yes, her skin had taken on a bit of a waxy sheen, but her eyes were animated, focused. She looked better than when Keeley had last seen her just before she travelled here.

'You look different,' Erica announced.

'What?'

'You don't look weighted down and you're smiling.'

'I... don't know what to say to that,' Keeley answered.

'Meeting that woman whose kid gave you the kidney has worked a makeover miracle.'

'Well,' Keeley began, 'I haven't actually met her yet.'

'What?'

Keeley drew in a breath and walked slowly to another section of the rooftop. There were other tourists here, all wrapped in thick coats, taking pictures, some on fully guided tours. Noel had given them lots of information of the history of the landmark while they admired the Tomb of the Unknown Soldier at ground level until Rach had said he was overdoing the dates and details a little. Rach's idea of a tour was more finger-pointing and finding out what celebrity had visited than it was delving into the archives of yesteryear.

'I thought we were meeting her yesterday, for afternoon tea, but that was apparently a treat for us on our arrival. And then this morning, when we were at breakfast, this tour guide turns up and says that Madame Durand has asked him to show us some of the Paris sights today.'

'That's weird as shit,' Erica offered.

'It is, isn't it?' Keeley sighed. 'She brought me here. She said she wanted to meet me and now... it's a little bit like she's hiding from me.'

'Maybe she is,' Erica suggested.

'Well, why would she do that? She was the one who wanted this.'

'I don't know. Because, like, she's scared? Because she's got you in France and now she's wondering whether meeting you is gonna be too hard. It's gotta be hard. Bringing it all back that she lost her kid.'

Stupidly, Keeley hadn't really thought about that. She had presumed the email exchange they had shared meant Silvie was definite about her intentions. That smart, strong and sassy power-woman she had envisaged wouldn't be fazed by anything. Surely, if Silvie had had doubts, was *having* doubts, she would have called or messaged, said something. Keeley, if she was truthful, had the jitters about it too, but she *was* going to meet her. She had done all her pros and cons before she got on the Eurostar.

'*You* could call her,' Erica said. 'Arrange a time to meet.'

'No,' Keeley said swiftly. She couldn't, could she? Take control of this situation herself and drive things? It somehow seemed safer if someone else was calling the shots. She hadn't really done taking ownership of much lately.

'Well, if you don't do that then you have to play to her rules and she can take her own sweet time about things.'

'OK,' Keeley replied. She looked sincerely at Erica and nodded. 'You're right. I need to stop worrying. She might be taking her time because she feels a little unsettled about it all. Or she might think I'm feeling a little unsettled about it all and—'

'And now you can tell me what's really got the colour into your cheeks if it isn't the donor-mum.'

It was as if Erica had got hold of a window into Keeley's time here and *knew* there was something she wasn't telling her about. Except it wasn't anything really, was it? A chance meeting with a hot guy she had chased a penguin for. Everyday stuff…

'I… met a penguin called Pepe,' Keeley blurted out, turning her back on the area Rach was standing in. She hadn't told Rach about Ethan yet. She didn't know why. Probably because there wasn't *really* anything to tell. Or the fact Rach would latch on to this potential mating opportunity and order fireworks and cheerleaders or perhaps courier over discount party poppers from Price Squash.

'Right…'

'And… Pepe's *owner* was quite, you know… good-looking.' She could feel herself blushing. Did anyone say 'good-looking' anymore? She sounded like Grandma Joan referring to Monty Don as 'dishy'.

'*How* good-looking?' Erica asked, eyes serious now.

'Better than Nick Jonas,' Keeley suggested.

'Shut *up*!'

Keeley laughed at Erica's reaction. He had been *terribly* handsome. Almost too handsome. But somehow different. Quirky. A little rough around the edges despite his smart attire...

'Well, what's his name? Where's he from? And is he single?'

'Ethan,' Keeley whispered. 'I don't know anything about him. We just... met on the street and I helped him and...' She paused before carrying on. 'He said he would give me a map of Paris with undiscovered gems on. Things tourists might miss because they don't know they exist.' And there had been precisely nothing waiting for her at reception this morning. He *hadn't* made a map. Meaning, she probably hadn't made an impression on him at all. Perhaps he offered off-the-beaten-track Paris to everyone he bumped into.

'But he hasn't left me anything so it's unlikely I'm ever going to see him again.'

'Love your confidence for someone promising to be all in.' Erica's tone was pure scalding. It sounded just like the time when Keeley told Erica she was never going to be able to eat popcorn again because it reminded her too much of Bea. Erica had ordered her to 'take a look herself' and the next time they saw each other Erica was accompanied by half a dozen multi-flavoured bags of popcorn and a Blu-Ray of *Boyz n the Hood*. Popcorn still reminded her of Bea but now it also reminded her of gangsters, Erica's celebrity crushes before Nick Jonas and feeling sick to her stomach.

'I'm working on "all in",' Keeley answered. 'Slowly.'

'Why didn't you ask for his number, man?'

'I… don't do that.'

'What d'you mean you don't do that?! How do you and Rach meet men?'

'At the pub. Badly.'

The last time Rach had struck up conversation with two guys in the pub and plonked one of them down in front of Keeley, the very first thing Keeley had said after a weak 'hello' was 'nice nuts'. Not even pushing the small bowl of pistachios towards him helped with the shame factor…

'So, you're gonna let a sexier-than-a-Jonas-brother walk out of your life?' Erica queried *really really* loudly.

Keeley turned around, checking to see if Rach had heard anything. Rach *was* looking at her now, distracted from the view. Keeley waved a hand at her friend, then pressed at the volume keys on her phone.

'Are you turning the volume down?'

'No.'

'Maybe Rach *should* hear me. I'll call her. Rach! Rach!'

'Erica! Stop it!' Keeley begged. 'Please!' She really didn't want to have to mute her completely. And apparently her brain was still telling her she didn't want Rach to know about her street-meet…

'I'll stop if you promise to start,' Erica demanded. There was heaps of determination in her friend's eyes now, despite her frailty.

'Start what?' Keeley asked.

'Start living,' Erica ordered. 'Someone gave you a second chance, remember? You need to take it.'

Keeley swallowed. She really should start embracing the world a little harder.

'Go after this guy! Chase him! Hunt him down! Nail his arse to the floor and—'

Keeley did mute Erica then and waved a goodbye to the screen as Rach stepped across the roof towards her.

'Everything OK?' Rach asked. 'That wasn't Roland, was it? I had a missed called from him this morning and I ignored it.'

'Everything's fine,' Keeley insisted, linking her arm through her friend's.

'Good. So, I was thinking we'd get Mr Dates and Times over there to show us the best place to find hot chocolate and then hit the shops.'

'That sounds good,' Keeley agreed. 'Watch out, Morgan and Gucci.'

Rach smiled, squeezing Keeley's arm. 'Now I know you're invested! You've researched.'

'Maybe a little.'

'Well then, I'll let you break it to the guiding guru again that the next stop is definitely going to be fashion and not… ancient and Agincourt.'

Nineteen

Canal Saint-Martin, Paris

At this moment, Ethan felt a little like he had right after he had lost Ferne. It was as if he was caught in a riptide, struggling to surface, the water dragging him down deeper and further away from solid ground. He could hear her, talking to him, telling him over the phone all about the things she had seen in London, filling his mind with the sights and sounds of the English capital preparing for December. Ferne had wanted to branch out from Paris. But not into other cities in France, no, Ferne had never wanted to do things in half measures, she always wanted to go big. Her idea, the first seed of a new arm to their small empire, was 'Luxe London'. A boutique, high-spec, contemporary hotel in the centre of the city. He remembered her words, the energy in her eyes, the thrill of a new challenge rippling through her, the way she tossed her blonde hair around when she got too excited. *Why stop at Paris, Ethan? Why not London too? Why not the world?*

Ethan still didn't know hotels. But he had known Ferne.

So he had done what he had always done. He had supported the dream and promised not to breathe a word about the purpose of the trip to Silvie. Silvie didn't even know now and Ethan wanted to keep it that way. What good would it do to tell her that her daughter had been thinking about leaving France?

Blinking over his half-filled glass of Calvados, the only voice he could hear was Louis's, repeating what it had said earlier. *We're going to be selling the brand, Ethan. By the beginning of next year, I want all the hotels gone.*

He shuddered. It wasn't from the wind as more patrons swept inside the café-cum-*tabac* he was sitting in, turning once more to alcohol as a coping mechanism, it was from that feeling people described as someone walking over their grave. Except it wasn't his grave he felt Louis was stomping on, it was Ferne's. How could Silvie be letting this happen?

Ethan slugged back a mouthful of drink and glanced around the high-ceilinged low-lit establishment where groups of people were happily drinking and dining, some wearing festive jumpers, others unwrapping gifts. It was December. It was the Christmas season. But in Ethan's mind there was nothing to celebrate. How could Silvie and Louis try and make a decision about Perfect Paris *now*? Now when it was only a little over a year since Ferne had died. Now when they had also decided to engage with the person living because of his best friend. *Instead* of his best friend.

Although, it was also true, when Ethan had been caught not knowing the direction the chain should go in, when Noel had been talking 'confetti canons' and 'giant baubles as big as the moon', getting out of the business *had* crossed his mind. So why now was he thinking the sale was completely outrageous? Why was his brain saying a definite 'no way'? Because he hadn't raised the subject first? Because it was *Louis's* plan? No, it was simply and definitely because the idea that Ferne's hard work, her dream, was going to be handed to the highest bidder and that was simply too much to take.

He picked up his pen and made another dot on the map he had laid out on the table in front of him. Why he was doing this he didn't really know. Except he had half a dozen places marked already. Places that were special and held memories. Most of them he had visited with Ferne. He marked the page then dropped the pen with an audible groan. Quickly he realised that the noise hadn't gone unnoticed over the party atmosphere of some of the other patrons and they were now looking at the loner drinking brandy from Normandy. Why did everything still come back to Ferne?

Ethan shook his head. As much as he loved and missed her, he had thoughts of his own. Ideas of his own. He *hadn't* simply been the extension to his best friend everyone thought he was. He needed to find himself again. And raging against Louis was going to help. They couldn't sell the brand without him. He was certain of that. Well, he would be wholly certain of that once he had checked in with his lawyer. It was time for action.

He dotted another location on the map then looked out of the window onto the darkening street. It was starting to snow.

Twenty

Palais-Royal, Paris

Welcome to Paris. I hope you enjoyed the afternoon tea and Noel's guided tour yesterday and I hope everything is satisfactory with your room. I would very much like you to join me for lunch today. I have booked a table at Café Marly for 1 p.m. The concierge, Antoine, can give you directions. I am so looking forward to meeting with you.

'It's not going to change you know,' Rach said, nudging Keeley's arm. 'Messages don't mysteriously alter their meaning on an hour by hour basis.'

Keeley's eyes still tracked over the words again. This text from Silvie had come in while they were eating breakfast earlier. And it was about lunch. *Today.* She checked her watch. It was 11 a.m. now and she and Rach were visiting Palais-Royal and the apparently controversial *Colonnes de Buren* – black and white striped pillars of varying heights that were described as 'a striking show of modern architecture amid the historic' in one guidebook they had looked at. Antoine had described them as 'grotesque cylinders that mocked the city'. Even Rach had laughed at that.

'I know,' Keeley breathed. 'I'm just nervous that's all.' She lifted her head from her phone screen and stepped forward, her boots crunching on the fine layer of snow that had fallen last night.

'I'd be more nervous about the fact some stranger knows your name and left you a map at reception,' Rach said.

'Oh, well, about that, Rach. Actually...'

'Shit, that's my phone ringing again!' Rach said, dipping her fingers down into her bag and pulling out her mobile. 'It's Roland. The third time he's called so I'd better...' She answered and stepped a little away from Keeley, turning her back to the wind. 'Hello.'

Keeley now had the promised map. Somewhen between their going up to their suite last night and coming down to breakfast this morning, the mysterious penguin-carrier – Ethan – had left the map for her attention. She really must tell her friend that the map-giver wasn't a *complete* stranger. They had shared a tumble to the pavement after all...

Palais-Royal and the *colonnes* were one of the places marked on that map. Not exactly a hidden attraction but, admittedly, it wasn't as Top Ten as the Louvre or Versailles. Except, with this impending lunch, Keeley didn't really have the capacity in her mind to think about the hot guy she knew Erica would have told her to nail to the floor if she'd been allowed to finish her sentence on FaceTime yesterday.

Keeley looked up at the building with its many windows – some arched, some oblong and leaded, column-lined walkways making it reminiscent of ancient Rome. As she approached the black and white structures all over the large courtyard she was struck by a thought. Had Ferne Durand been here? Had she once stood in this very spot and admired it all? It felt a little strange to be standing here in Paris, Keeley's reason for being in Paris and stood here, entirely down to someone else. She drew in a breath, kicking a little of the snow that was already starting to decrease as the temperature rose just a little. And then her phone began to ring. Straightaway she wondered whether it was Silvie, cancelling their lunch. Then she worried it was Erica or, worse still, one of the nurses with news of Erica. She grabbed her phone from her bag and checked the screen…

Mum

She answered. 'Hi, Mum.'

'Oh, hello darling! Or, should I say, "bonjour"? What time is it there?'

'It's an hour later than with you. Just after eleven.'

'Are you wrapped up warm?' Lizzie asked. 'Your father's been checking the forecast and it said snow for today. Is there snow? Are you wearing a hat? And gloves. Do you have gloves?'

'Yes, Mum,' Keeley replied. She wasn't wearing a hat or gloves. She was still worried the hair dye would stain anything she put in close contact of it. There was definitely a taint on her pillow this morning completely like there had been the one and only time Bea had got her to try fake tan…

'Yes, you're wrapped up or yes, there's snow? Are you outside? It sounds like you're outside.'

'I am outside,' Keeley replied, taking a breath of the cold

air and appreciating her surroundings with a little bit more awareness. 'Rach and I are sightseeing this morning. And there is snow, but only a little bit.' But it was fresh and white and crisp and was currently making Keeley feel a little Christmassy.

'So... what's she like?' Lizzie blurted out. 'I don't want to crowd you, or interfere, or say or do any of the things I always get condemned for, but... you're in France and I'm not and I... need to know!' There was harried breathing then that sounded like someone on a bike. Except Lizzie didn't do exercise unless it involved making shapes with her body or full-contact combat.

'Where are you, Mum?'

'Me? Oh, I'm... you know... just on errands.' There was a spit of laughter. 'Your father wants me to do something ludicrous with his darts at the sports shop. Sharpening the flights... or was it the tips? I don't know. Phil Taylor issues.'

'Mum—'

'Anyway,' Lizzie butted in again. 'Don't change the subject. Tell me... what this Silvie is like. Is she glamourous? Because I've been imagining her glamourous.'

Keeley glanced at her watch. Time seemed to be going super slowly today when she was both anxious and excited about the meeting later. 'Well... I haven't actually met Silvie yet.'

'What?! What d'you mean you haven't met her yet? You've been there for days! On her invitation! What's going on? Keeley, you tell me now, what's going on?!'

She was surprised other visitors to the *colonnes* weren't able to hear her mum's ranting. She spoke a little softer herself. 'Nothing's going on. We arrived, we've settled in and I told you we have the most amazing room with a view of the Eiffel Tower…'

'But she's not met you yet? I knew this would happen! I said to your father, I said it's all splashing out on Eurostar tickets here and sleek hotels there and it's all very generous and attractive but now we know, don't we?'

What did her mum know? 'I don't—'

'She's playing with you, Keeley. Toying with your emotions. In my book club we all read this story about this rich, perfect woman who we all imagined looked like Susan Sarandon and really it was all a façade. In reality "Susan" was a penniless whore who prayed on the vulnerable.'

'Mum, it's not like that. I'm actually meeting her for lunch today. Near the Louvre.'

'*If* she shows up.' There was an exasperated sigh. 'In this book, "Susan" had a whole host of excuses why she couldn't be one place or another. Of course really she's burying bodies of the people that crossed her and—'

'Mum, why did you give Rach a load of my medication to bring here?'

Keeley had pounced into the conversation with the only ammunition against this mad book club analogy she had. The fact her mum had pushed her anti-rejection drugs on her friend. Apparently, because she had to take tablets for the rest of her life and look after her well-being more than most, her mum had gone back to treating her like she was six.

'I… didn't know if you would remember so I was, covering all the bases… ow! Ooo! You're alive!'

Keeley baulked, taking the phone away from her ear for a moment and looking at the screen. Had she been cut off? What was her mother doing? 'Mum? What's happening there?'

'Nothing. Nothing. I'm just... opening a few windows and...'

'Windows? It's December. And you said you were out on errands.'

'I'm on my way to *do* errands. In a minute. And a house still needs airing even in the winter and... your father unleashed his festive shallots last night. You remember the festive shallots? Bea always...'

Immediately Lizzie stopped talking and Keeley could feel the shard of grief coming down through the connection. Some of the Andrews family still seemed to be at the stage where the memories were still too painful to reminisce about.

'Everything here is fine, Mum,' Keeley told her. 'I'm going to meet Silvie later today and I will call you and tell you how it went.' She could see that Rach had finished her phone call and was heading back towards her, inappropriate-for-walking-heeled boots stabbing at the snow.

'You promise?' Lizzie asked.

'Yes, of course. Now... tell me where you are because I don't think you're at home and you don't sound quite like yourself.' She had a sudden thought. 'You're not doing that circus skills course are you? Because you said you'd gone off that idea.'

'Oops!' Lizzie interjected. 'There goes the dinger on the microwave. I'll speak to you later, darling. Stay warm! Bye!'

And with that, the call was over. Keeley pocketed her phone and smiled at Rach. 'How was Roland?'

'Surprisingly calm for someone having to deal with a complaint,' Rach said, sucking in a breath as she put her phone away.

'It wasn't the flat with the dog with two sets of teeth was it? I thought he wasn't allowed to be left on his own anymore.'

'No, it was Mr Peterson's place,' Rach replied as they walked forward across the square. 'Jamie only went and showed an elderly couple around before Roland had got someone in to give it a once over.'

Keeley opened her mouth in horror. 'Oh God.'

'Yeah,' Rach said. 'Think a not-yet-dead badger pouncing from the breakfast bar and nabbing dentures.'

'I can see it. I can actually visualise it.'

'So,' Rach said with a confident nod, 'you might be a little apprehensive about this lunch later, but things could definitely be worse. You could be poor Mr and Mrs Ackroyd.'

'OK,' Keeley breathed. 'A little perspective was exactly what I needed.'

Rach sniffed and stood in front of one of the black and white striped columns, regarding it like it was a still life model. 'What do you think of these then? And why did some random mark them on a map for your attention? I think they look a little bit creepy.'

'I think maybe them looking out of place is what makes them special. It's the contrast. They're different to everything else here.' Keeley splayed her arms. 'See?'

'They're totally ugly in my opinion,' Rach said. 'Look like a stick of rock. Or some trousers Miley Cyrus once wore.' She smiled. 'Come on, let's go and try and see the Mona Lisa before lunch. Now *there's* a woman with never-aging class. Sorry, Miley.'

Twenty-One

Café Marly, Paris

'Are you sure this is the place?'

Keeley whispered the question through juddering teeth. It wasn't the cold. There was actually the brightest of winter sunshine now and a cloudless blue sky, the wind had also dropped away. It meant the snow on the pavements was starting to melt even further, a lot of the cobbles and concrete now only containing the faintest smudges of white. No, Keeley's lips were quivering with nerves, and coupling that with the fact they were standing at the edge of an eatery that looked very much like it had been placed inside a holy building, she had never felt more out of place. Tables lined the cream-stone arcades as if they were intruding into reverential cloisters. Outside of the colonnade was the impressive *Pyramide du Louvre* – all sharp edges of glass and metal compared to this stoa of soft granite and age.

Rach didn't immediately answer and Keeley saw her friend was tapping on the screen of her phone. 'Rach, are you sure this is the place?'

'Yes!' Rach said, not even looking up. 'We followed the directions Antonie gave us *and* we set Google Maps. Sorry, I've just got to reply to this email a minute.'

'Aren't you supposed to be on holiday?' As soon as the words were out, Keeley felt immediately guilty for saying them. She had asked Rach here and Rach had said yes almost straightaway. A free vacation or not, there were many other things Rach could be doing with her precious time off from the estate agency...

Keeley put her hands in the pockets of her coat and tried to look natural. Easier said than done when your heart was thumping as if someone was bashing it like a Scottish pipe band drummer. Was Silvie here already? She scanned the diners for the vibrant fifty-something with a glossy handbag to match her hair she had conjured up in her mind.

There were quite a number of people enjoying the winter sunshine and the food. Others had simple coffees and an accompanying biscuit. Was there a woman sitting on her own? Would Silvie actually *be* on her own? What about Ferne's father? She hadn't thought to ask. Maybe this meeting wasn't going to be just the three of them...

Then her breath caught in her throat as her eyes met with a woman seated in the middle of the arcade. She was wearing a taupe-coloured coat and had her fingers entwined in front of her on the table. She was nothing like the stylish icon of fashion Keeley had made up in her head. This woman had silver hair, smartly kept, modern, simple and her face was subtly made-up, a sheen of apricot colour on her lips.

Keeley didn't know how she knew but she knew. This was Silvie. This was Ferne's mother.

'Rach,' she whispered. 'That's her.'

'What?' Rach said, looking up from her phone.

'The lady over there, halfway down... I don't know why... I just... that's Silvie.'

Keeley looked to Rach then and watched her friend narrow her eyes, as if tuning in to the potential Silvie with a truth-finding glance. Before Keeley could say anything else, Rach had taken a waiter by the arm.

'*Excusez-moi*,' Rach greeted. 'We are here to meet Madame Silvie Durand.'

'*Oui, Mademoiselle*. Just this way.'

And now it was happening. Before she had a chance to process further, Keeley felt her knee joints lock together as every step she took down through the rows of tables and chairs under this elaborate and regal ceiling led her towards the decision she'd made to do this. Her face flushing, her eyes almost too scared to leave the stone of the floor, she shrunk into Rach's shadow letting her friend lead the way and take the initial impact of discovery.

It seemed to be taking such a long time to traverse mere metres. And she remembered the last time life had slowed like that. One moment she had been singing along to Dua Lipa, the next there was a horrendous squeal of brakes, glass shattering and shards of it were flying through the air along with her handbag, the contents of her handbag and her unsecured sister...

'*Bonjour*.'

It *was* her. It *was* the woman Keeley had locked eyes with and she was standing up now, her expression warm and welcoming, her eyes kind.

'I...' Keeley began. She didn't know what to say. It was like she had lost her ability to form any kind of sensible speech. How hard was it to say a simple 'hello'? Just start with a smile and maybe the 'h'. 'I'm... Heeley.' She shook her head, embarrassment painting its red hue all over her face. 'I'm sorry, I... I'm Keeley.' Her eyes were smarting with tears all of a sudden.

'And I'm Rach,' Rach said quickly. 'It's nice to meet you.'

'It is OK,' Silvie said gently. 'This is a very... unusual situation, I realise. Please, both of you, sit down. Let us order some more coffees or perhaps something stronger.'

Keeley had to gather herself together. Except when you were about to sit opposite the woman whose daughter had saved your life as she left hers, it wasn't quite so simple.

'I could murder a beer,' Rach informed, taking the seat on the edge of the table for three, almost between Keeley and Silvie.

For this, Keeley was grateful. It meant there was a little distance, the table between them and, for now, that felt right.

'Keeley, would you like a little *vin rouge*?' Silvie asked her.

'I probably shouldn't, but thank you.'

'She definitely should,' Rach replied before turning to Keeley. 'You definitely should.'

'You can order anything you want,' Silvie assured her. 'I am so glad you came all this way.' She took a long, languid breath. 'It really is so wonderful to meet you.'

Keeley felt herself calm a little bit, and as she moved her chair a touch closer to the table, her insides twitched in that way they sometimes did, as if in acknowledgement that this was a big deal.

'I'll have a glass of red wine,' Keeley agreed with a small smile. 'If you will have one with me.'

Silvie smiled back and gave a laugh. 'But of course. And we will order some water too, *non*?'

'And a beer,' Rach added, unbuttoning her coat. '*Une pinte*.'

'*Bon*,' Silvie said, raising a hand to beckon back the waiter.

They had got their drinks, they had ordered food, then discussed the weather and the fact that Christmas would soon be here. But everyone knew there was a topic they couldn't avoid much longer. It was, after all, their whole reason for being here. Keeley took a sip of her wine as easy conversation that had bubbled up with no effort at all suddenly dried up like a very poor comedian.

Keeley offered a smile to Silvie, mentally willing her to break the ice. But then she watched the woman draw an expensive-looking handbag up from the floor, propping it onto her knee. Perhaps *Keeley* should take the lead...

But, before she could, Silvie began. 'I... was not sure what exactly to say when I met you, Keeley. I have thought for a long time, perhaps for *all* the time Ferne has been gone, that I would like to meet you. But it took me many many months to think about it with logic.' She took a breath. 'Do you understand what I say?'

Keeley nodded. 'Yes. Yes I do.'

'To begin with I would think that to want to know you... to want to know how you are... that it would be selfish of me. And maybe it still is. But...'

Keeley could see Silvie was becoming emotional and she had so many feelings too. 'I understand.'

'I am not putting all this very well, am I?' Silvie asked. 'Keeley, my reason for wanting to meet you is to thank you.'

'Thank *me*?'

Silvie nodded. 'Just to know that there was someone out there, living their life, enjoying fresh air and… the red wine.' She smiled. 'And experiencing all the colour that life has… it gave me hope through the very darkest of times. But then, most recently, it became something else. My wish changed. Now, I would like to get to know *you*.' Silvie smiled again. 'I wish for you not to be a stranger. If that is acceptable to you, of course.'

Keeley felt her tension ease a little and then she spoke. 'Well, Madame Durand, I am here because… I want to thank you… to thank your daughter… for giving me that chance to keep on living.'

Tears were glistening in Silvie's eyes then. 'Well,' she started. 'This…' She paused. 'This is Ferne.'

From the handbag on her lap, Silvie pulled out a small oblong photograph and placed it in the centre of the table next to the glass of festive pinecones, silver swirls and condiments.

Keeley gasped immediately. 'Oh… goodness… she's… so beautiful.'

'*So* beautiful,' Rach agreed. 'Gorgeous hair.'

Keeley lifted her eyes from the picture to meet Silvie's gaze. 'May I… pick it up?'

'But of course,' Silvie said, still smiling. 'Please.'

Keeley took the photo between her fingers and looked into the face of the woman who had saved her. She truly was so pretty and it was the most natural of poses. Ferne was wearing a bit of make-up – not that she needed any at all – her long blonde hair flowing loose like it was caught on a breeze. She had the widest most genuine smile and blue eyes that seemed to be smiling too. She looked so vibrant, so full of life. It was heart-breaking to know that she was no longer here.

'I am so *so* sorry for your loss,' Keeley breathed. 'So sorry.'

Silvie nodded, her bottom lip trembling as she reached back into her handbag for a tissue. 'Thank you.'

Rach swiped up some serviettes from the table and passed them over to her. 'Here, Madame Durand.'

'Oh,' Silvie said. 'Thank you. You are kind. And please, both of you, call me Silvie. Whenever anyone calls me Madame Durand I expect my mother to materialise behind me… and she has been dead for twenty years.' She gave a small laugh as if to belie her true feelings, then she dabbed at her eyes with one of the serviettes.

'I thought about who my donor might be too,' Keeley said. 'But I don't know, this will probably sound really stupid, but when I was recovering I felt so guilty knowing that someone had died but I had survived.' She took a deep breath. 'I almost *didn't* want to know who they were. I think that's why *I* didn't try to find out.'

'You have to remember,' Silvie said, cradling her glass of wine. 'Ferne did not die *because* of you, Keely. Ferne died because she was involved in an accident. You realise, that she had already passed… inside her brain.' Silvie took a breath. 'She spent three days on a machine until all the tests were complete and they told me there was no hope of a recovery.' Silvie stopped and gathered herself before continuing. 'It was Ferne's wish to help others if something like this ever happened.' Silvie shook her head. 'Ferne was *always* helping others. Anyone actually. She had a particular affinity for animals. I cannot count the number of times I had to shoo strays out of our home… after they had stayed the night and eaten some of what was planned for meals during the week of course. I am a terrible cook. It was probably a deterrent to that.'

Keeley laughed then, looking back to the picture of Ferne and trying to imagine this frankly glamourous-looking individual feeding a pack of hungry dogs. It just showed that you couldn't tell that much about a person from that visual first impression. What would Ferne have thought about *her* from a photograph?

'Keeley likes animals,' Rach butted in. She had already almost finished her pint of beer and was obviously drinking Keeley's share of Dutch courage. 'Once she fed a rat some of her kebab on the Underground… you know… when she was allowed to eat kebabs.' Rach hiccupped. 'When she wasn't, you know, looking after someone else's body part.' Rach looked startled then. Like Ant and Dec were in her ear telling her what words to say. 'I didn't mean it quite like that. I don't know why I said that.'

Keeley put a hand on Rach's arm and gave it a squeeze. 'It's OK.' She looked to Silvie. 'I do try and look after myself,' she admitted. 'Second chances are precious. I want to make the most of mine.'

'Feeding rats?' Silvie asked, her eyebrow raising a little.

All three of them laughed out loud then and it was like the unseen barriers gently fell away. Things immediately began to feel a touch more natural to Keeley, the previous slightly palpable nervousness eased by a tale about London vermin. She put the photograph back on the table.

'Thank you for contacting me, Silvie,' Keeley said softly.

'Thank you for agreeing to visit.' Silvie looked to Rach then. 'And you are a good friend, coming all this way with her to meet an old lady.'

'How could I say no to all the free...' Rach cleared her throat. 'Free time to spend with Keeley.' She gulped down the last of her beer.

'Ah!' Silvie said as the waiter arrived, arms filled with plates of steaming meals. 'Here is our food. And I promise you, the monkfish really is exquisite.'

Keeley smiled and settled back into her chair. Everything was going to be OK.

Twenty-Two

L'Hotel Paris Parfait, Tour Eiffel, Paris

'Where is Monsieur Durand today?'

Ethan asked the question of Antoine as he used the reception desk to lean on and write notes. He didn't commit well to iPads or electronic devices, for him it always felt better to write things in ink. Whether it was the definite pressing motion as ballpoint met paper, or the secret thrill in being able to heavily strike out and eradicate that brought him some sense of security he didn't really know. Perhaps it had more to do with his lack of anything but chalk and crayons when he was growing up. But what he definitely *did* know today, was that he was more determined than ever to find a way out of Louis Durand's plan to sell the chain of hotels from under him. From under Ferne's memory. The fact was, the hotels were doing well. OK, they were not doing *exceptionally* well, hence Ferne's idea to branch off, but every business suffered lean times. Even Ethan knew it was moving with those times, keeping up and shoring the ship if necessary, that sorted the winners from the losers. Today there were lots of guests with smiles on their faces in the reception area, passing through to leave on an afternoon of sightseeing, or returning to their rooms for quiet time after lunch. The decorations here looked perfect. Yes, perhaps the tree was a little on the large side, but Noel and the team here had done an excellent job at making it a shining beacon of luxury. From the impressive crystal star at the very top, to the chains of really-able-to-tinkle bells that skirted the lower branches, it was a vision of exuberance.

'You wish me to locate Monsieur Durand?' Antoine asked in loud tones.

'Sshh!' Ethan hissed, looking over his shoulder to the hotel entrance. Why was he cowering in one of his own hotels thinking his adversary was going to sneak up on him and strike him down with fancy speech? 'No,' he told Antoine. 'I do not want you to find him. Is he... here?'

Antoine shook his head. 'No. He left this morning. After breakfast.'

'Where did he go?' He shouldn't be asking but desperate times...

'I do not know.'

'Antoine,' Ethan said, looking at the man and seeing the wavering expression on his face. 'How long have we known each other?'

Antoine stood a little resolutely. 'Is this related to the dates on my employment contract?'

'Antoine!'

'Yes, Monsieur Bouchard.'

'You must know where he is. You asked me if I wanted you to locate him.'

'I did not say I could.'

'Am I not your superior?'

'If you wish to discipline me we will need to have a meeting and I will be entitled to have someone present from my union.'

God! What was this? He couldn't seem to get a simple answer from his own staff members anymore. Had Louis bribed Antoine to keep quiet about his whereabouts? That would be just like Louis, already throwing his weight and money around and trying to take over a business he had never cared about before. Louis would have seen the potential to make money and not seen the love and energy his sister had breathed into the brand. Ethan went to answer Antoine, but his attention was drawn to a small boy loitering near the revolving door. The boy's head was covered in a black beanie hat that was way too big for him and he was wearing jeans with holes – and not the designer meant-to-be-there kind of rips. Over his top half was a very thin and aged sports jacket. However, it was the expression the boy was wearing that stood out to Ethan. He could *feel* that expression. It dug into his soul, bringing back the sharpest of uncomfortable memories. He watched as the boy inched towards the Christmas tree. Ethan knew that slide-cum-walk. The boy was trying to be invisible, blend in somehow, even though everything about him was only sticking out.

'Monsieur Bouchard? I said, we need to deal with the health and safety aspects of the ice rink before we allow members of the public on it. At present we just have Jean and Jacqueline performing routines from a traditional Nutcracker suite, *Sleeping Beauty* and, for the *children*, a number Mickey Mouse skated to in *Disney on Ice*. Although one person has said the head of Jean's outfit looks more like the evil twin of a character called "Cat Noir". I have no idea who Cat Noir is, but we should look into making the face of the costume more joyous.'

Ethan watched as the boy reached out towards the branches of the tree, hiding a little behind two guests who were perusing a gastronomic guide to the city.

'Stop! You!'

Ethan jumped at Antoine's tone and for a second he was blindsided as his concierge leapt out from behind the desk, pacing across the floor.

'Do not think about touching the tree!' Antoine ordered.

He was snarling at the boy now and had all but scared off the couple reading about restaurants who were walking quickly towards the door. Ethan moved towards the scene.

'You are not staying here,' Antoine continued. 'I have not seen you before… hey! Wait!'

Before Antoine could say anything else, the boy grabbed at the tree, then span a hundred and eighty degrees, swivelling towards the exit with all the panache of a seasoned free runner.

'Stop! Thief! He has taken something from the tree!' Antoine yelled.

Ethan didn't waste any time. As the hem of the boy's jacket whipped through the non-revolving door, he followed, shooting from the hotel's entrance lobby and out onto the street. The boy was quick, but Ethan tracked him, running to his left and skirting around a group of pedestrians who had their mobile phones trained on a street artist dressed as a snowman, painted head to boots in glittering white and silver spray.

'Wait! Stop!' Ethan called as the boy continued to sprint ahead. The boy's desperate pace was sending him off course, causing him to knock into people, completely off balance, broken trainers showing sock-covered feet with more than a few holes. Where was he running to? And why was Ethan making it his mission to chase after him? He was out of practice with real street running. The most he could manage these days was a few kilometres in the hotel's gym and it was definitely showing now.

Instead of drawing the pursuit to an end he called out: 'Stop that boy!'

Then, all at once, there were raised voices, cries and a large amount of decorated balls bounced onto the slushy pavement. Ethan tried to avoid them, still running on, until he got to the midst of the chaos. The boy had upended a small stall and its wares were on the ground, being trampled by people-traffic and rolling into the road. The boy was on the floor too, trying to backpedal his way out of trouble, his trainers slipping and sliding on the pavement as he attempted to scoot away at speed.

Ethan grabbed him by the jacket and pulled him onto his feet before he fell into the path of an oncoming cyclist.

'Do not touch me!' the boy hissed.

Something was a little off, but Ethan couldn't quite put his finger on it. He held his hands up. 'You took something from my hotel. And… I think I know what it was.'

'I have nothing,' the boy replied, walking away from the stall and its annoyed owner who was busy trying to pick up what was salvageable from his goods.

'Hey,' Ethan said, still following. 'You are not in trouble. Not with me anyway. It is just… I think you only took chocolate from the tree and… if you need food then… I can get you some food.'

The boy faced him then, fierce attitude in the look. 'Are you the police?'

'No,' Ethan replied, a bit softer. 'I—'

'Then I do not have to talk to you, or do anything you say.' The boy turned away again, Ethan suspected ready to flee.

'You are right,' Ethan answered. 'You do not have to talk to me or do anything you do not want to do. But maybe you would like a warm brioche and a hot chocolate or… anything you like.'

He watched for a tell-tale flicker of acknowledgement in the boy's eyes. There was nothing. Until… there it was. Not in the boy's expression, but instead in a quirk of his body. *Hunger pangs*. The mere mention of food and drink and your instincts gave you away.

'Come on,' Ethan said. 'What have you got to lose?' He knew he couldn't push, just make a suggestion. But his heart rhythm was telling him he wanted the boy to accept his offer so much.

'Hey! You there! You need to come back here and clear up this mess!'

It was the stallholder, the festive hat he was wearing at odds with the fierce look on his face. The expression was all anger and grumpy beard. Ethan knew what was going to happen now if he didn't step in.

'Listen,' he began, addressing the man. 'I will pay for any damage and…'

Out of the corner of his eye he saw the boy turn away and Ethan couldn't help himself. He reached forward, intending to gently halt his progress. Instead, his fingers found the boy's oversized beanie and, before he knew it, the hat had come off in his hands.

Ethan gasped, the stallholder gasped and traffic on the road next to them continued as if nothing had happened. Except something *had* happened. Ethan was holding onto the black woollen hat and he was staring at the small figure whose long dark hair had come tumbling out of its knitted captivity. He was not now looking at a boy… he was looking at a girl.

'You're a…' Ethan said. 'You're a girl.'

'And you,' the girl retorted. '*You* are the real thief!'

She snatched the hat out of Ethan's hands and before he could do or say anything else, she turned and sprinted away up the street into the crowds.

Twenty-Three

Café Marly, Paris

'I have talked too much, I know I have.' Silvie took a sip of her coffee.

Keeley smiled at the woman with real affection. As every moment of the past couple of hours had passed she had grown to like Silvie more and more. There was nothing *not* to like about her. She was kind and warm and she had put Keeley at immediate ease. Perhaps it was because she had been through a similar tragedy, but more maybe it was because they had Ferne as their common denominator. They both seemed to understand how each other was feeling and it hadn't felt at all awkward or uncomfortable. It had been light and undemanding. In fact, it was probably the only undemanding conversation Keeley had had since the accident. With her own mother, every conversation had an underlying theme of well-being…

'No, you haven't,' Keeley answered quickly. 'If anyone's talked too much it's—'

'Me!' Rach interrupted brightly. 'And I've definitely drunk

too much. In the volume sense, not the alcoholic sense. A pint and a jug of water and two coffees. Just popping to the loo.' She put a hand on Keeley's arm. 'That OK?' she whispered.

It was nice that her friend was checking on her. But she really had no qualms about being left on her own with Silvie. 'I'm fine,' she told Rach.

'I won't be long,' Rach said, standing up and moving away from her seat.

'Another coffee, Keeley?' Silvie asked her.

Keeley shook her head. 'No, thank you. I'm completely full too. It was a lovely lunch.'

'It was, wasn't it?' Silvie answered. 'I like it at this place, very much. Yes, it may be in the middle of the touristic area, but I like the… how do you say… the mood.'

'I like the mood too,' Keeley agreed. 'It feels very grand, but at the same time it's also cosy.'

'You have a good feel for places, I can tell,' Silvie said, taking another drink from her coffee cup.

'Well, that's kind of my job,' Keeley admitted.

'Really?' Silvie said, showing surprise. 'You told me that you work for an estate agency.'

'Oh, I do. But I work there in a different capacity to Rach. They call me a "house doctor".' She smiled at what she considered to be a silly title.

'A house doctor? What is this?' Silvie asked. 'When your home has a little rise in temperature do people ask you to visit and… give it medicine? Or maybe a dose of the vacuum?'

Keeley laughed. 'No, not like that. I'm a qualified interior designer but, lately, it's been my job to stage homes before they are put on the market to sell.'

'How fascinating,' Silvie said, seeming truly taken with the idea.

'I do enjoy it,' Keeley said. She picked up her coffee spoon and absentmindedly stirred it around in the cup. 'But I don't think it's quite enough for me.'

'What is it you really want?' Silvie asked her.

Keeley lifted her eyes from the coffee then. 'To rewind the past year.' She sighed, preparing to divulge even truer feelings. 'To have my sister back.'

She swallowed. Perhaps she shouldn't have said that. Regressing in front of the very person who had enabled her to have a future at all wasn't really on.

'Sorry,' Keeley blurted out.

'Your sister?' Silvie queried. 'She has gone away?'

'Oh,' Keeley said, a lump the size of a sugar cube arriving in her throat. 'You don't know. I'm sorry. I mean, why would you know?' She sighed, before starting again. 'I lost my sister in the accident. The accident I was in.' She paused. 'Her name was Bea.'

'Oh, you poor girl.' Straightaway, Silvie had reached across the table and enveloped her hand in hers. It was a reassuring, gentle touch but also firm and supportive. 'I had no idea,' Silvie breathed.

'It's OK.'

'No,' Silvie said, sighing, fingers squeezing Keeley's. 'It is not OK. Here I am, telling you about my grief for Ferne and you are grieving too. Your sister. Your poor, poor parents.'

Keeley nodded, telling her brain to hurry up and batten down the hatches. She could almost hear Bea telling her to stop being such a cry baby and eat the biscuits that had come with their coffees. Bea, the youngest of the family, but the one who'd had an infinite supply of strength and resilience in pretty much the face of anything. Keeley's confidante and hair stylist... the one she had whispered secrets to in the night when they'd shared a bedroom.

Keeley took a breath and spoke again. 'My parents will forever be grateful that they didn't lose *both* their children that night,' Keeley told Silvie. 'And that is what would have happened if it hadn't been for Ferne.'

Silvie shook her head, finally letting go of Keeley and picking up a serviette from the table to dab at her eyes again. 'Look at me,' she said, her voice rich with emotion. 'I am leaking again.'

'I leak too,' Keeley responded, a small smile forming. 'But lately it's mainly from my hair. Cheap products.' She pulled at a section to demonstrate, then instantly regretted it when a smear of brown appeared on her forefinger.

It earned a light laugh from Silvie and she coiled the tissue up in her hand. 'How old was your Bea?'

'She was twenty-four,' Keeley answered. Forever twenty-four. Always that upbeat, focused, funny individual thinking she had all the time in the world. She forced a smile. 'She was living her best life which, when I look back at things now, I am so glad about.'

'What did she do?'

'She was an engineer,' Keeley said proudly. 'She worked for a company designing different components to help repair or maintain bridges. Sometimes she got to design them from scratch. Bea was always the Lego builder of the family.'

'That is such a wonderfully different job for a woman. Am I allowed to say that?'

Keeley nodded. 'She was up against six men for the position and she got it, fresh out of college.' And Keeley still remembered how much they had celebrated the weekend after Bea had received the email. They'd had too much wine and pizza Bea had tried to build a replica Golden Gate bridge out of the crusts. Her little sister had been destined for such great things...

'It is such a waste,' Silvie said, tone regretful. 'All of it. Is it not?'

'Yes,' Keeley agreed. She didn't really know what else to say. 'Tell me what Ferne did. You said she loved music and animals. Did she do either of those passions for a job?'

Silvie shook her head then. 'No. Ferne, she was in hospitality. Apart from the music and the animals there was nothing she liked more than people and parties. Her great gift was being able to communicate at every level. She would always treat people exactly the same, you know. It did not matter to Ferne if you were... say, part of the royal family or... someone who sleeps on the streets. She wanted to know *you*, no matter what *you* you were.'

Her donor was kind. In touch with humanity. It all made perfect sense.

'But Ferne was not without her faults,' Silvie admitted. 'She could have a temper when things did not go her way. She once gave me the silent treatment for a whole week when I did not immediately get on board with a plan she had for a charity summer fiesta.'

'Phew,' Keeley said tongue-in-cheek. 'I was beginning to think she was a saint.'

'*Non*,' Silvie said. 'Not a saint. A normal, ordinary girl who was living her best life too.' She smiled at Keeley. 'That always gives me comfort also. To know she was happy with life and not struggling with sadness, or illness, or the weight of the world.'

'Yes,' Keeley agreed. 'I feel the same with Bea.'

Silvie smiled again. 'In a lot of ways we are lucky to have those perfect memories, no?'

'Yes, you're right.'

'So,' Silvie said, 'you have plans for tonight?'

'I don't know. Rach mentioned maybe taking in a cabaret show one evening while we're here but…'

'Will you do one favour for me?' Silvie asked her. 'My son, Ferne's brother, he is in Paris for Christmas and he has been away for some time. I have two tickets for the ballet tonight, but I need to be elsewhere. Would you go with him? It would be nice for you two to meet and maybe talk about Ferne a little more. To be honest, I think he has struggled with his grief even more than I have, although, he is a man and men can be very inverted. Is that the right word?' She sighed. 'What else can I say? Men tend to hide away things that they feel will show a weakness in them.'

'I…' Keeley didn't know how to reply. It was odd, wasn't it? To accept an invitation to the ballet with someone she didn't know. She barely knew Silvie. And her donor's brother. How would *he* feel about her being here?

'I have asked too much. I am so sorry. Please, ignore me, forget I said anything.'

Keeley was suddenly wracked with guilt. Ferne had saved her life. Silvie was paying for her to be here and she was so nice. What harm would it do to see a show with her son? As long as Rach could keep herself occupied and didn't mind.

'No,' Keeley said. 'You haven't asked too much. But can I… can I think about it?'

'But of course,' Silvie agreed. 'No pressure at all. I will send you the details and you can see what you think.'

Keeley smiled and nodded as she saw Rach making her way back to the table. She took a deep breath. 'OK.'

Twenty-Four

L'Hotel Paris Parfait, Tour Eiffel, Paris

'I can't go.'

Keeley's heart was racing so much it felt like she was still in those first tentative days of recovery, her body battered and bruised from the accident as well as the operation, a cast on her arm and a bandage around her skull, every breath bringing excruciating pain and utter fatigue. She'd got ready, even making a special effort with her outfit. She hadn't been sure what people wore to go to the ballet in Paris, because the nearest she'd got to anything 'theatre' was watching *Hamilton* in the West End. And people didn't tend to dress up for matinee performances at all…

'What?' Rach looked up from her phone.

Keeley shook her head at her friend who was still sitting cross-legged on her bed like she had been since Keeley's 'getting ready' had started an hour ago. It was six o'clock now. She was supposed to be at the theatre at half-past for pre-performance drinks. 'It's… too much.'

Her breathing pattern felt uncomfortable and she put a

hand to her chest, fingers brushing the burgundy corduroy fabric of the Topshop dress she was wearing. It was smart-casual at best, but it was long-sleeved and warm and more snow was predicted that night. She tried to steady the in and out motion, be mindful of her breath like the counsellor had taught her.

'OK,' Rach said, unfurling her legs and getting up. 'You just need to relax. This isn't a big thing.'

'But it *is* a big thing,' Keeley immediately blurted. 'It's a huge thing.'

'It's not a date,' Rach said, making her way over to Keeley. 'This is how you usually get before a date.'

'I don't have dates.'

'OK, wrong choice of words.' Rach started again. 'This is how you get before we go out for drinks where there might be the chance of meeting someone.'

'I shouldn't have said I would go.'

When they'd left Silvie outside Café Marly, Keeley had said again that she would think about it. And then, very quickly – obviously a little too quickly – under the influence of fine food and feeling that the lunch had been a success, she had actually *accepted* the ballet invitation. But now the thought of going and meeting another member of Ferne's family so soon, felt insurmountable.

'It's been a big day already and… you wouldn't be with me and… it's a man and…' Keeley stopped talking when she realised she didn't know what else to say. Was she blowing this out of all proportion?

'And what bit of that sentence is freaking you out the most?' Rach asked. She was stood in front of Keeley now, her eyes locked on hers, soft yet definitely questioning her sanity. There had never been anywhere to hide when it came to her best friend. Rach was honest to a fault and never one for lowering the curtain on things. Sometimes Keeley was really grateful for it. Other times not so much… like right about now.

'It's not him being a man.' Keeley blew out a breath she'd been holding tight, as if someone had knotted her throat like a party balloon.

'Are you sure?' Rach asked, still all scrutiny.

'Yes.' Keeley nodded. 'I'm sure I would feel the same if I was supposed to be meeting a sister instead of a brother.' She wasn't *completely* sure.

'So, it's just the high drama of carrying around one of his sister's internal organs.'

'Just?' Keeley said, letting go of another breath. She moved towards the balcony doors then, needing to look at something other than her best friend. It was dark outside now, Paris lights brightening the cloudy skies, headlights streaming back and forth along the road, cafés all warm and inviting, storefronts glittering with festiveness…

'Well, how about I go with you?' Rach said. 'I'll buy a ticket and I'll come along.'

'Do you think we could do that?' Keeley asked, looking back to Rach.

'No,' Rach said. 'It sounds exclusive and expensive and I probably can't afford it. And there's no way I'd be able to get a ticket anywhere near you. Plus, all my dresses are probably too short for the theatre.'

'What?'

'Never mind.'

Keeley deflated again. She had been anticipating a

pragmatic solution. Even though it shouldn't be up to Rach to bail her out. It was easy. She either went to the ballet or she didn't. A quick text to Silvie saying she didn't feel very well wouldn't be that far from the truth at all.

'So... how did it feel meeting Silvie?' Rach asked, checking her reflection in the glass and preening her hair a little.

'It was actually better than I thought it would be,' Keeley admitted. 'She was nice and... she made things easy and calm, didn't she?'

'But you don't think it can be like that tonight with her son?'

'I don't think I can do it all again this soon. I think that's the issue,' Keeley said, pangs of worry gathering in her stomach again. Silvie had suggested they meet up again in a few days' time and a few days' time was well-needed breathing space. 'I think I'd much rather... go for a walk.'

Looking back to outside, she felt Paris was calling. A quiet stroll along the Seine watching the illuminated boats drift by was what Keeley wanted. But perhaps it shouldn't be about what *she* wanted. Being here was all about meeting Silvie. And Silvie wanted her to meet her son.

'*I* could go,' Rach said, breaking the silence. 'You know... without you.'

'What?'

'Well, if you really feel you can't go, I could take one for the team.' Rach sniffed. 'If they don't have a dress length policy. And I know nothing about ballet. Except that all the dancers are a lot more graceful than me and all the men wear tight tights... OK... actually, thinking about it, maybe it's right up my street.'

'You'd do that?' Keeley said, already feeling a wave of relief flow over her. 'Go in my place?'

Rach shrugged. 'I've come here for you, Keels. This trip is meant to make you feel better and... empowered about getting your second chance, right?'

'Right,' Keeley replied. She felt the total opposite of empowered at the moment if she was honest.

'So, you can either tell Silvie you've changed your mind and we can both head out for a walk and dinner at a nice brasserie...'

'I'd like that,' Keeley said. 'But... I'd feel bad about letting anyone down at late notice.'

'OK then, that's decided.' Rach said with a nod. 'I'll go to the ballet and meet Son of Silvie.'

'God, I feel so much better,' Keeley said, breathing out what felt like a whole tumult of anxiety.

'Good,' Rach said, nodding as she looked back to her reflection in the window of the balcony doors. 'That's settled then. Just promise to keep your mobile on – and not on silent – and let's hope Son of Silvie is at least a little bit hot... and not too young for me.'

Twenty-Five

Dodo Manege, Jardin Des Plantes, Paris

Ethan was blaming tonight on the street girl. After he had emailed his lawyer asking for advice on Louis Durand's plan to try and sell the hotel chain, he had gone out for coffee and ended up standing outside the orphanage he had grown up in. From the exterior it looked like an almost quaint Parisian townhouse – impressive steps to the front door, Juliette balconies – but behind the not-at-first-noticeable bars on the windows, it had been the kind of dwelling depicted in television crime dramas. Ethan had stood there, almost trying to look through the bricks of the building and vividly remembering the deep, rich, coldness he'd endured each and every day. A bone-chilling icy temperature no high tog duvet could ever fix and the kind of wicked, cruelty that carers who should never have been carers had doled out. Was it still going on behind that charade of a façade? Was this the kind of place the street girl came from?

Ethan shook his head now and took a sip from his

take-out cup of coffee. He was thinking too much about the girl. Maybe she wasn't an orphan or even in foster care. Perhaps she was just a thief and his feeling of false kinship was because of what was happening with the hotels right now. He should have guessed this was coming. Without Ferne here, the Durands were always going to revert to type. Rich people liked rich people. They didn't like strays like him. Guttersnipes shouldn't exist in their world. They turned a blind eye and willed extinction.

Endangered species. Ethan watched the menagerie of animals in front of him slowly rotating to music. Drawn to a carousel! Drinking coffee and refreshing his email inbox! What a life! Ferne would be laughing at him now if she were here. As hard as she had worked, she had played equally as much. She had always, somehow, been able to switch off as quickly as she switched on. And this children's ride amid the *Jardin Des Plantes* was a throwback to his youth. The very place he had first met Ferne. These model animals on the ride were all extinct or endangered. Unlike the more familiar fairground horses, this circular whirl comprised of a dodo, a Barbary lion, a horned turtle, a panda and other animals dead, or on the brink of eradication.

A young Ethan hadn't really thought about what these animals were when he had snuck on for a free ride, but Ferne had shown him the guide on a small plaque next to the roundabout. The animals had been as foreign to him as the girl who had ridden next to him. She had been all smart clothes and long words – even at that age – and he had marvelled at her mere existence. Back then, young, knowing nothing about a brighter, lighter world outside the walls of the orphanage, everything about the moments

Ethan achieved when he snuck out felt exotic. The smell of the air, mingling with other scents that invigorated his soul – fresh, rich coffee he had never tasted but longed to, sweet pastries that sang of sugar and syrup, the water of the Seine, its smell a muddied mix of fresh water and for some reason, pigeons. Ferne smelled like a light summer's day wrapped up in a covering of Chanel, a delicate perfume the exact opposite of the clawing brand the manager of the orphanage wore over her body like a second skin. Ferne was joy and hope with a laugh that could have made the sullenest tramp crack a smile at life. From that very first encounter, Ethan had wanted to find out exactly what it was that made someone so in love with being alive.

He swallowed another mouthful of coffee and watched a little boy, holding a snowman-shaped lollipop out into the air as he revolved around squashed into the seat of the turtle. The boy was wearing the purest of smiles on his face. And it was at that moment that Ethan saw her. Walking through the park, hands in the pockets of her red padded winter coat, was the woman he had chased the penguin with. The one he had left the map for. *Keeley*. He adjusted his stance, straightening up on the metal bench. Was that why he was really here? Because he knew he had marked this place on the map? No. That was madness. After all, if he had wanted to see her again, he knew exactly where she was staying. He took a breath, watching her pause, a few metres away. She took something from her pocket and unfolded it. The map. His map. So, she *was* following it...

This was it. Something called *Dodo Menege*. A roundabout.

Cold-looking little children were currently circling around aboard manufactured animals to tinny-sounding music, looking either captivated or frozen in situ. Keeley was surprised this ride was marked down as a part of the hidden Paris she should see while she was here. What was so special about it? Although, maybe her penguin-chasing stranger's X marking the spot wasn't meant to be quite as specific. Perhaps he had simply meant to mark *Jardin Des Plantes*. Keeley had to admit *that* was beautiful even now in the winter when plants were few and far between. The large, ornate greenhouses had frost on their glass panes and the bushes and boughs of trees lining the pathways were jewelled with beads of December sleet. She imagined it would be even more impressive in the spring – lush green bulbs peeping out from beneath the earth – or summer – a riotous carnival of coloured blooms.

'*Bonsoir*.'

Keeley jumped at the sound of a voice so close, jarring her rib cage and reminding herself that she still had bruises from her brush with the pavement. And that voice brought her right back to that moment.

'Oh, it's you.' It *was* him, wasn't it? In the half-light, the only illumination the small bulbs on the carousel, it could be that she had just acknowledged a beggar or a pickpocket as if he were a well-established friend.

'Ethan,' he greeted like it was possible she had forgotten his name. She hadn't. Neither had Erica when they had caught up on the phone just before she ventured out on this walk. Erica had overemphasised the 'e' and said it loudly with a French accent that sounded like it came straight out of Croydon.

'Hello,' Keeley said, pure British.

He smiled. He had a nice smile to add to the other plus points – thick dark hair, grey eyes that somehow gave off both sexy sharp and deeply melty. 'I do not want you to think I gave you that map so I could follow you around Paris.'

That thought hadn't actually crossed Keeley's mind. But *was* that what he had done? Was this statement bravado and bluff about it? How clever! Or frightening! Maybe her hair was still chemically ridden enough for her to use it to defend herself if necessary. He opened his mouth as if to speak again before she could think about how to reply.

'I really did not do that,' he said. 'I can see you are thinking that might exactly be something someone would say if they *had* done that.'

Gosh! He had read her thoughts. That was scarier than the idea of him trailing her around the French capital.

'So,' he continued, delving his hands deep into the pockets of his coat and wavering a little on his feet, 'I am going to stop talking now and you are going to tell me what you think about the carousel.'

'Oh,' Keeley said. It was an impulse 'oh' to buy her a breath of time before answering. 'It's... definitely not something I... would have thought I would see here.'

He laughed then, and it was such a warm, hearty sound, bursting the cold air, it felt like the gentle timbre of it was spiralling itself around her in a whirlwind of a touch that almost seemed to put its arms around her. She moved her feet to break the feeling. It was too intimate to feel that way about a laugh...

'I was a little drunk when I made some of the pinpoints

on the map,' Ethan admitted in a whisper, like it might be a covert secret. 'But it is one of my favourite places.'

'From when you were young?' Keeley queried.

'You do not like it,' he seemed to surmise.

'No... I do think...'

'You do think...'

'That it's...

'It's...'

'Different,' Keeley managed to finish.

'I will not accept only that,' Ethan said, his eyes now giving a flash of challenge. 'Come on.' He held out his hand to her.

'What?' Keeley gave a nervous giggle, the kind she usually thought was ridiculous when displayed by anyone else.

'I do not know of anywhere else in the world you can ride a carousel on animals that have long-since died.' He took her hand then and his skin was so warm compared to hers. She had given the gloves her mum had packed a hard stare before she left the hotel suite and decided to brave the elements without them. Rebelling in all the little ways still felt satisfying.

'But,' Keeley said, moving with him towards the roundabout that had stopped moving. 'It's for children, isn't it?' She looked at the size of the animals. There was no way she would be able to get inside the dodo. She wasn't even sure her bum would fit on the seat of the something that looked half-leopard, half-giraffe.

'Who is it that says children should be the only ones to have fun?'

'But, Ethan, there are *no* adults on it.' Suddenly she felt conspicuous. Like she was doing something really wrong and everyone was watching. Except it wasn't very busy here. It had to be near to closing time and the city had better things to do than watch her spin around on a ride. Was she *actually* going to do it?

'You are frightened to have fun?' Ethan asked, turning to look at her.

'No,' she answered immediately. She wasn't frightened to have fun. Was she?

'Then, take your choice,' Ethan offered, placing out an arm as if he were giving her a personal introduction to the animals.

Keeley eyed them all up. The lion had a flattish space she might be able to sit on without breaking any parts of the roundabout. It seemed the only sensible choice. Apart from obviously getting off the ride completely.

Then there was Ethan's laugh again, followed by a whoop of excitement. 'I have not ridden this one before.'

Keeley turned away from the lion and saw he was already aboard his stead – a large bird that looked a little like a giant ostrich. His legs were dangling over both sides of the beast, almost touching the wooden floor. He looked both ridiculous and yet still so attractive...

'This is really silly,' Keeley remarked, her cheeks reddening as she climbed onto the back of the lion. 'We might be so heavy the ride isn't able to turn.'

'*Bof*!' Ethan scoffed. 'Have you seen the size of some of the children in this day from all the *chocolat*.'

This might not have been the quiet, thought-processing stroll through the city she had envisaged when Rach had left her for the theatre, but it was definitely lightening her mood. Suddenly the ride jerked forward and Keeley had to grab the lion's neck to steady herself. An 'oof' left her mouth and then she laughed as the roundabout settled at slug-pace slow. 'But... we haven't paid!'

Ethan laughed then, looking across at her. 'You English people do worry about everything, do you not?'

'You say that as if it's a bad thing.'

'I read recently that when you panic you buy antibacterial handwash and toilet paper.'

Keeley sat firm, unmoved by his statement. 'We like to be prepared for any eventuality. Some of us stockpile chocolate and wine too.

'What do *you* fill your cupboards with?' she asked. 'Or do the French people not panic about anything?'

'We fill our cupboards with cigarettes, cheese, red wine and baguettes of course.'

Keeley looked at his straight expression, somehow knowing it was going to turn into a smile. Except it didn't.

'What?' he asked, tone brusque. 'You think I am joking with you?'

'I...'

And then his face *did* crack and he laughed. 'Of course I am joking with you! English! So serious!' He put fingers to his eyebrows and, together with a face contortion, he moved them down into a frown. She couldn't help feeling a little bit stupid. She *was* serious by nature. More so now than ever before. And it was going to take more than a pep talk from Erica or riding on a fibreglass lion to shift the layers of caution that had built up over her foundations this past year.

'I was not insulting you,' Ethan said quickly, maybe sensing his try for humour hadn't hit the spot. 'You might be serious as a nation, but you are right – you are organised and methodical in all your approaches. You will live longer. We French take too many risks.'

Keeley swallowed. She was living now, but living as long as a normal-haven't-had-an-organ-transplant person might hope to live, well, that wasn't in any way assured. In fact, it was likely she'd have to have another kidney transplant a few years down the line. But she couldn't bring herself to even think about that yet. Another hurdle to get over when the time came. She was having to learn to be quite the expert in leapfrog…

'I took a risk coming here to Paris,' Keeley found herself replying before she really realised it.

Ethan took his fingers away from the elephant-bird and waggled them in the air. 'Ooo so scary coming to France. Did you fly?' He laughed again.

'We took the train.'

'We?'

'I'm here with a friend.' The friend who was currently at a performance of the ballet where she should be. She hadn't thought through what she was going to say to Silvie Durand about that yet. Would she lie and say she hadn't felt well? Or would she tell the truth about feeling overwhelmed? It felt wrong to think about not being honest.

'Is he organised and capable like you?' Ethan asked.

Keeley smiled as the ride continued to slowly rotate. There were parents watching children from the nearby benches, smiles and waves for their tots, looks of bewilderment every time she and Ethan moved past them. 'It's a she… Rach.'

'And where is Rach tonight?'

'She's at the ballet.'

'Alone?' Ethan asked. 'She did not invite you?' He paused, looking at her as if he was trying to figure her out. She felt his grey-eyed gaze seeping under her skin somehow. 'Or do you not enjoy the ballet?'

What should she say? Remembering her promises to both Rach and Erica she took a breath. She wasn't going to be Kidney Girl. She was going to be all in. He didn't need to know anything about the past year if she didn't want him to. She could be *her* here in this moment with this formerly penguin-toting stranger.

'She met someone. A guy,' Keeley answered. 'On the Metro. He's taken her.' It was only a partial untruth. Anything else would be tip-toeing close to a region where more explanation would be required.

Ethan looked immediately outraged. 'She met a stranger underground and she let him take her out? This friend, she is not British. She is not even French. Is she crazy?'

'She's fine,' Keeley insisted. 'She texted me from the theatre.'

'I understand that sometimes visiting another country makes you leave caution behind but... you should not simply feel that everyone you meet is who they appear to be.' He looked away then, seeming to clamp together like a bad mussel. Was he talking about himself? Or about an experience he had had?

A silence between them grew, the only sound the musical accompaniment from the roundabout. 'Well,' she began, 'I met *you* on the street. And *you* were chasing a penguin.'

He raised his eyes to hers then. 'But I have not taken you out.'

The way he said the words made Keeley's heart beat a

touch faster. She didn't know what to say in response. She was so out of practice. Did she want him to take her out? And then just like that the ride came to a halt. She needed to say something. Take the lead. Own her future.

'Have you had dinner?' Keeley found herself asking, her voice all the shaky and hesitant. 'I mean, I had quite a big meal at lunch time but—'

'*Non*,' Ethan said, getting down from the ostrich-bird. 'I have not had dinner.' He put his hands into his pockets and said no more.

'We could... maybe... get something together?' How old was she? This was not sounding all that smooth and confident like she had hoped. But she knew, no matter what his answer was, Erica was going to be so proud of her. This was a giant step forward!

'*Oui*,' Ethan answered. 'OK. How about we can choose somewhere from the map?'

He had said yes! Her heart grew little butterfly wings as he held his hand out to her.

'I know you have enjoyed it, Keeley,' he whispered as she placed her hand in his. 'But it is time to get down from the lion.'

The way he said her name – all the sultry and all the French accent – made her insides feel like they had been dipped in the fizziest prosecco. She smiled and descended with as much grace as she could, until she was stood beside him. 'I understand why you like it here.'

'You do?' he asked, his warm breath visible in the air between them.

'I do,' Keeley said, nodding. 'It's... I don't know... somewhere they don't make postcards of.'

Ethan nodded. 'They *should* make postcards.'

'They should,' Keeley agreed. 'I would definitely buy one now.'

He smiled at her. 'And, I know exactly where we should go next.'

Twenty-Six

Rue Des Barres, Paris

'This is so beautiful,' Keeley breathed.

Ethan smiled at the pleasure in her tone. This was exactly what he had hoped – almost quietly anticipated – to come from her when they arrived in this thirteenth-century street situated in the 4th Arondissment. It was the soft, peaceful, old-fashioned side of Paris that he loved so much. With its cobbles on the ground, the pretty church of Saint-Gervais and tables still outside under heaters, it was an oasis of winter calm amid the bright lights and bustle of the city. A small touch of Christmas had arrived in the shape of coloured fairy lights adorning the frontage of eateries and apartment balconies. Ivy cascaded down buildings in places – some still green, other leaves red, for the most part dark – and all-weather alpines stood stoic in planters and pots, some decorated with tinsel.

'Would you like to sit inside or outside?' Ethan asked, stopping in front of a bright blue, painted bistro he hadn't been to in quite some time. He was still a little apprehensive about being here now. There was an underlining fear running through him that all the good times he had shared with Ferne at this place might jump out and become the sharpest reminders of her absence rather than sweet treasured memories. But here he was, holding his nerve.

'Outside,' Keeley replied.

He watched her pull her coat a little tighter, shrugging herself down into it. Even under the warmth of a heater it was going to be cold outside and she looked freezing already. 'You are certain?'

Her lips trembled and she let out a laugh then. 'No.'

He laughed too. 'Come. It is nice inside also. Warm. We can find a table by the window.' He pushed open the door and led the way wondering what she was going to think about the interior. The *salon de thé* was anything but contemporary. It was basic and bohemian and definitely not the Paris offered in holiday packages.

'Oh,' she remarked as they stepped inside, feet hitting the tiles.

Even her breath sounded excited and that did something to Ethan. The few women he had lost himself in since Ferne's death would have all turned up their noses at this setting, expecting champagne and five stars from the owner of a hotel chain. But in this moment there was no expectation. This woman only knew his name. He could be anyone he wanted to be – perhaps even himself – the man behind the Perfect Paris brand who didn't know where he had come from and didn't really know what he was going to do with the rest of his life.

'You like it?' Ethan asked, stepping forward to a table by the front windows and pulling a seat out for her.

'It's not at all what I was expecting,' she answered. 'In a good way.'

Her eyes were still roaming around the interior and he watched her taking it all in as if she was standing in one of the city's famous museums, admiring the artwork and statues. But instead of paintings from famous artists, here there were posters – their edges ripped. Old adverts for perfume, pictures of parasols and Chinese characters, music concerts showing performances long since passed. The wooden tables were worn with age and shelves of mismatched glasses of all sizes, cups and condiments lined one corner. He watched her remove her coat and put it over her chair before sitting down. He sat down opposite her feeling something he couldn't quite put his finger on. A connection of sorts, a hidden unable-to-fathom vibe between them.

'In the summer,' he said, 'when it is warm, they open the doors right up.'

'It's so relaxed here,' she said, settling into her seat and smoothing her fingers over the rough scratches on the table, varnish lost through years of use. 'It's like places used to be until someone decided to make everything so chrome you could use every surface as a mirror.'

'You like things more traditional?' he asked her.

'I like things that make me feel comfortable,' she admitted. She seemed to go a little coy then, dropping her eyes to the table and putting her fingers to the ends of her hair. 'I just made myself sound like the most boring person in the world.' She looked up. 'Storing toilet rolls in case of Armageddon and liking things plain.'

'*Non*,' Ethan replied. 'Not at all. Comfortable… it is good.'

'Well,' she started, 'I have two close friends who think "comfortable" says "given up".'

He smiled at her. 'Perhaps they are too scared to embrace "comfortable",' he suggested. 'Admitting you enjoy the simple things can be hard for some people.' He hitched his head to their right indicating a couple sitting a few tables away. 'Technology is good. We keep in touch with everybody we are not close to but at the cost of not connecting with the people we *are* close to.' He whispered. 'How crazy is that?'

'Yes,' she agreed. 'You're completely right.'

'So, tonight we will embrace all the "comfortable",' Ethan said. 'We have ridden on animals that were too small for us and now I propose we shall eat food that will be too big for our stomachs.'

She smiled back at him. 'What do you recommend I try?'

'Wait and see,' he answered, grinning as a waitress approached.

Keeley was chewing on a *brik*. A Tunisian-style *brik* that was making her mouth water with every bite she took. This had been Ethan's suggestion for their meal. Not a traditional French dish of *coq au vin* or omelettes, but apparently this café's speciality. It was perfect filo pastry with potatoes, cheese and onion served with a little harissa, the egg with that soft, running yolk so difficult to get exactly right. It was a little piece of simple food heaven.

'This is so good,' she told Ethan. She looked up from her plate to find he was looking back at her. But the moment their eyes connected he looked away as if her catching him had embarrassed him a little.

'Sorry... I confess... I was watching you eat.' His cheeks were hit with colour then and he put his lips around his glass of beer. He took a sip then continued. 'I admit that sounded weirder than I intended. Forgive me.' He smiled. 'I simply wanted to see how you would react to the dish.'

Keeley put another piece of the *brik* on her fork, slipping it into her mouth and letting all the exotic flavours hit her senses. It wasn't an exaggeration to roll her eyes or try to inhale the scents she knew had to be rising up from her plate, but she was now doing it for Ethan's benefit. To make him laugh. Reluctant to bid farewell to the taste and texture, she finally swallowed the mouthful down. Except Ethan wasn't laughing. She actually couldn't quite read the expression on his face but now she felt awkward. Why had she done that? It was probably because Erica's voice was still echoing in her ears telling her to take all the chances including trying to look seductive while salivating over soft yolks...

'It's so delicious,' Keeley said quickly. 'Really delicious. And so different to the food at my hotel.' Why couldn't she think of something better to say?

'There is something wrong with the food at your hotel?' Ethan asked sitting up a little straighter in his seat.

'No,' Keeley said fast. 'No, it's lovely, it's just... little pretty things. They're really tasty but... I don't know... ignore me.' Why was she now dying on her arse when it came to normal conversation? They'd had this relaxed vibe to their chatting on the Metro here, everything feeling so chilled, but now she was somehow tongue-tied. Was it the cosy and intimate setting of this low-lit café? Or was it the close proximity of him and just how attractive he was?

'It is maybe time the menu was changed,' he suggested.

'Ignore me,' she begged. 'I'm not an expert in cuisine. It's my mum, who likes to experiment. Usually on me. Always with the five-a-day... or six a day if Waitrose has a special offer on organic celery.'

'Five a day,' Ethan said with a sigh, beginning to eat again. 'Who are the people to decide how much of anything a person should have?' He seemed to muse as he chewed his food. 'No cigarettes at all. Only so many units of alcohol. A required amount of exercise.' He shook his head. 'All this information to try to force us to make a decision a certain way.'

'I take it you don't follow all the advice,' Keeley said.

'Do you?' he turned the question around, those grey eyes meeting hers.

'Well...' What did she say? If she wanted to, *this* was the opportunity to tell him she was supposed to be watching her health closely – that sometimes she did have to hold off from having what she really wanted. That she had had a kidney transplant... 'Everything is OK in moderation, isn't it? I mean, I'm sure even if you eat too many vegetables or do too much exercise that would be equally as bad for you, wouldn't it?'

Ethan laughed then, wholeheartedly. 'You are right! All these people who compete in marathons who have never run a marathon in their entire lives become surprised when they have a heart attack.'

'Or... I read about a husband and wife who made a stew out of courgettes their neighbour had given them and the husband died because of some sort of toxin in them.'

'No!' Ethan exclaimed, eyes wide. 'Death by vegetables?'

'I swear it's true.' She smiled. Still not Kidney Girl. Rach would be proud and Erica would be practically buzzing.

'Then,' Ethan said, 'leave room for dessert. The crepes are also very good here.'

Twenty-Seven

The Seine, Paris

Having eaten sweet crepes that were as light as clouds, but a whole lot sweeter and definitely highly calorific, they had got back on the Metro. Now they were walking along the banks of the famous river that flowed through the heart of Paris on the way back to Keeley's hotel. It had been the most unexpected evening and Keeley wasn't sure she wanted it to end. For the first time in so long she was reconnecting with the her she thought had been lost long ago.

'Some people say the river has a smell,' Ethan remarked. He was walking close to her, hands in his pockets, the air chill.

'A good smell or a bad smell?' Keeley answered, eyes looking to the water. There were some boats docked, dark and tied up for the night, others were still floating and carrying diners, bright lights and soft music rising up from the river. A bridge spanned the water, soft arches and piers connecting one bank to the other.

'You decide,' Ethan suggested. 'Take a breath.'

'Oh... well... the thing is... I... don't have the very best sense of smell.' She swallowed. Her taste buds were all still in good order but since her operation she hadn't been able to smell so well. Some people might think it was a small price to pay, but it *was* a loss not to be able to experience the simple pleasure of the scent of freshly cut grass or that rich, indulgent fragrance of a Christmas pudding...

'Come,' Ethan said. He took hold of her shoulders and turned her towards the river. 'The best way to get one of your senses to work more fully is to alienate the others.'

'What?' Keeley asked.

'Close your eyes,' Ethan directed, hands still on her shoulders, breath close to her ear. 'Close your mouth. Close your ears...'

'Close my ears?' She laughed. 'Can I do that?'

'Stop listening. Stop breathing through your mouth. Stop looking. Just... inhale.'

Keeley felt him press a little more on her shoulders and she heard him draw in a long, slow breath. Something about the timbre resonated with her and she found herself doing exactly as he asked, closing off all her other senses and tuning into the rush of air through her nostrils. And then, suddenly, there it was! There was *something*. Ordinarily there was very little at all, maybe only the faintest tinge of a change, but nothing to get excited about. But now, tuning in to Paris, the river, the cold of the night, the presence of this virtual stranger's hands on her shoulders there was...

'Something sweet,' Keeley breathed. 'Caramel maybe.'

'And coffee,' Ethan joined in. 'Definitely coffee.'

'Is it waffles?' She was doubting herself now.

'Yes,' he answered, the pressure of his fingers increasing a little. Even through the-able-to-withstand-minus-fifty-degrees coat, Keeley could feel the warmth of his body. It was nice. It even felt a little bit 'comfortable'. But wasn't that what happened when you clicked with someone? You instantly fell into step with them somehow, like you had always meant to arrive in each other's life.

'And pee,' Ethan blurted out. 'Undernotes of pee, *absolument*.'

Keeley opened her eyes then, snapping back into reality and turning to face him. 'I didn't get pee.'

Ethan smiled. 'Ah, that is good. You are still under the tourist illusion that everything in Paris is fragranced like it was manufactured in a perfumery.' He nudged her arm with his. 'I am Parisian. It is OK for me to admit that my city is only perfect because it embraces its imperfections. We learn to live with the scent of pee. No one knows where it comes from. We clean. We sanitise. After that, no one *wants* to know where it still comes from. It is simply part of the fabric of the city.'

Keeley smiled back at him as they began to walk again. He was the most unusual person she had ever met. Wearing the clothes of a businessman with his dark three-piece suit and his tailored winter coat but displaying the heart and charm of someone you might imagine leading a travelling circus – somehow a little bit of gypsy wanderlust mixed with Hugh Jackman's Barnum.

'London has its smells too,' Keeley told him as they fell into step together. She may not be able to experience them fully anymore, but she could definitely recall them. 'The Tube, that rush of warm, slightly sweetened air as the trains rush past... the parks in the springtime, daffodils, ducks... and different cultures.' She breathed, remembering. 'Crazy weird fruit outside Asian minimarkets and... the food stalls at Lower Marsh Market.'

'It sounds *magnifique*,' he answered her.

She turned her head, their eyes connected and Keeley felt it deep. Her words had resonated with him.

'Have you been to London?' Keeley asked him.

He shook his head. '*Non*.' He seemed to stiffen up a little then, his hands going to the top button of his coat, fastening and unfastening it. 'It is not somewhere I have... had the chance to travel to.'

'You should,' Keeley said, finding herself wanting to see his smile again. 'I mean... it's maybe not thought of as quite as romantic as Paris, but it has a lot going for it.'

He did finally smile then. 'The ducks and the food stalls?'

'Definitely the ducks,' Keeley said. She looked up and saw they had arrived outside her hotel. 'Oh.'

'You do not want to be here?' he asked her.

'Oh, no, I do. I mean, it's a *very* nice hotel. Our room is huge and... the Christmas tree in reception is *definitely* huge and—'

'You say the word "nice" like it is a bad thing. You do not like this hotel?'

'I don't *dis*like it,' Keeley said, checking out the entrance and that revolving door Rach had become trapped in. 'It's just... not really that memorable, you know. It's clean and it's modern and there are many glitzy touches of Christmas now, including an animatronic reindeer... but although it's called "Perfect Paris" it could be... anywhere in the world.'

He was staring at her now. Properly staring and it was a

little unnerving. Those grey eyes were fixed on hers and he wasn't saying anything, simply looking at her and breathing slowly in and out. She couldn't tell if he was absorbed or if what she had said had made him angry somehow.

'Ignore me again,' Keeley said hurriedly. 'I really should be more grateful to even *be* here in Paris in December.'

Finally he spoke. 'No.' He looked like he was gritting his teeth. Maybe it was simply the cold weather. 'I am curious for what you say about... this hotel.'

'Well,' Keeley said, turning to observe the façade again, 'my job in England is to pull together themes to create a look that's universally appealing to buyers looking for their perfect home.' She smiled at him. 'Except I don't like to use the word "themes". I prefer to use the word "feelings". Most people, if they're really honest with themselves, buy things with their emotions, whether it's houses or cars or a new pair of shoes. Even if they might try to convince themselves it's for practicality, you can guarantee the thought process has had a "feeling" attached to it.'

'Shoes?' Ethan asked, the corners of his mouth rising to form a wry smile.

'Honestly,' she told him. 'Shoes you can run in – practical – are usually bought because you still remember the time your feet hurt so much when you wore heels for too long. Therefore, a feeling.'

'This coat?' Ethan offered, arms out, turning in a spin like he was performing on ice.

'You might *think* it's practical,' Keeley told him. 'To keep you warm in the winter but...'

'But?' he asked, sounding intrigued.

'But... I think perhaps you bought it because, when you

put it on, it took away a memory of when you were once bone-chilling cold.'

The breath caught in Ethan's throat and it was all he could do to hold it together. Astute didn't even come close. Somehow this woman had seen inside of him. He vividly remembered buying the coat. He had been with Ferne, browsing at one of her favourite flea markets, when he had spotted the nearly-new garment on a rack. The pure wool had felt good on his fingertips, soft yet also somehow strong. He had shrugged off the cheaper version he had been wearing and pulled the coat around him. Straightaway it felt like some kind of suit of armour. Looking at himself in the stallholder's mirror he had seen two versions of himself. This version in the new coat, the vision of the him he could be, and then the old version. The too-skinny boy who *had* been bone-chilling cold every night of his life at the orphanage. This coat, although second-hand, had been the most expensive item he had bought up until that day. And it still meant the world.

'Sorry,' Keeley spluttered. 'That was stupid and... way too deep and...'

'*Non*,' Ethan said, shaking his head. 'I am sure you are right. About people leading with feelings. I simply thought, with vacations, people would want "luxury".' That's what Ferne had wanted. That's what Ferne had wanted for their clients. And Ethan still very much needed to trust that she had been right. Why wouldn't she have been right? Perfect Paris was a success story after all.

'Well, "luxury" means different things to different people,' Keeley told him. 'Like, "luxury" to my mum means getting all the Waitrose best stuff to impress her friends. Whereas, to me, "luxury" really does mean "comfort".' She drew in another breath as if musing on the subject a little further. 'I always think the best things are the little cosy touches coming together to make up the bigger finished picture.'

Was this true? His heart was thudding in response to what Keeley was saying, but what was it telling him? That his best friend's creation of a sleek, opulent brand was flawed? That Perfect Paris was a little too perfect? He didn't know how to respond. He was so conflicted and he couldn't get his brain to slow down.

'You are free tomorrow?' he asked her. Conflicted or not, something was telling him he wanted to see her again. He wanted to hear what she had to say and get to know more about her 'feelings'.

'I...'

'*Excusez-moi*, you are on holiday. You are busy. I apologise.' What was he thinking? He had enough on his mind with Louis breathing down his neck. He should take her reticence as a sign and back away.

'No,' she said. 'I mean, I *am* here with my friend and I don't know what she has planned but maybe we could—'

'Run,' Ethan suggested quickly. He'd said the first thing in his brain just to get something out there. Apparently backing away wasn't going to happen.

'What?'

'The... exercise we talked about. You said you sometimes like to run. I could... maybe show you hidden Paris this way.'

'Early,' Keeley breathed. 'And, to be completely honest with you, I'm more a 4k person than a 10k person.'

Somehow she was suddenly closer to him now, her body only an inch or two away. 'Early would work for me,' he answered.

God, the overriding feeling he had now was that he wanted to kiss her. Long and slow yet fierce. As that realisation hit, it was all he could do to stop himself sweeping her into his arms. Why was he allowing himself to feel this way? How come he could not stop it?

'Is six too early?' she asked him, wetting her lips a little.

The action sent a shot of adrenaline spiralling around him like lights around the boughs of a Christmas tree.

'Six is... *comfortable*,' he whispered.

His heart was beating hard, and it took every bit of restraint he owned not to simply take her face between his hands and draw it towards his. And then, somehow, her fingers found his or maybe his fingers found hers. Whichever way it was, their hands became entwined, skin on skin, tiny movements, so delicate, but infinitely there. He had absolutely no words for how the connection was making him feel. And he understood it even less.

'I should go,' she said, breaking the contact, albeit slowly, one gentle fingertip at a time.

'*À bientôt*,' Ethan said, watching her as she finally stepped away from him. '*Bonne nuit*.'

'Goodnight.'

Twenty-Eight

L'Hotel Paris Parfait, Tour Eiffel, Paris

I want to see this guy. Take a photo. Find out his last name so I can stalk him on socials. French kiss his face off. I can't sleep. Morphine needs to be stronger man.

The text ended with the emoji of the green pukey face and the smile dropped from Keeley's lips at Erica's message sent an hour ago. It was 5 a.m. and the comment about morphine reminded her again exactly how sick Erica was. There *she* was, texting every nuance of her chance encounter with Ethan and Erica was back in the hospice, clinging to the time she had left. She would FaceTime her again later, show her some more of the sights of the city and attempt to keep her spirits high.

Keeley put one foot out of bed and onto the carpet and straightaway the floorboards underneath let out a creak. She gritted her teeth. It was too early to wake Rach up. Rach was never good in the morning until she'd had at least three strong coffees with two sugars. Plus, Rach would ask her where she was going and Keeley still felt a little odd about telling her she was meeting up with a man she had met on the street. Holding her breath, she planted her second foot on the floor and stood up. This time the floorboard groaned like it was a bit-part monster in *Doctor Who*.

'Who's there?' Rach sat bolt upright in bed, even in the dark a large shadow of blonde bed-hair apparent.

'Sorry,' Keeley whispered. 'I didn't mean to wake you, but this old building's floor had other ideas.' She crept across the room then, heading for the shower. Why she was showering before going for a run she didn't really know. Except she didn't fancy smelling day-old before the real perspiration kicked in. 'Go back to sleep. I'll be quiet.'

Rach's bedside light flicked on and Keeley could see that her friend's make-up was all over her face. *Literally* all over her face.

'Rach, your make-up...'

'Oh, don't worry, I fucking know!' Rach replied, whipping the covers off her body and leaping out of bed to get to the dressing table mirror. There was no concern for the floorboards and the people sleeping below. 'This is *after* I tried to clean it off last night. It's like... like... I'm Pennywise or something. Bloody Adie at Price Squash. This is supposed to be the best you can get in Bulgaria. They even call it Low Re-al.' She put fingers to her lipstick-bleeding lips and rubbed to no avail.

'How was the ballet? You should have woken me up when you got back.' Keeley stepped across the bathroom threshold and looked at herself in the mirror. Not too bad for little sleep. Her eyes went back to Rach when an answer wasn't immediately forthcoming and she watched her friend's demeanour transform. The mascara encrusted, eye-liner ringed eyes turned into something from a soft-focus romance movie and her friend let out a breathy sigh.

'Oh, Keeley, the ballet was… the most wonderful thing I've ever seen.'

'Really?' Keeley answered. This was huge and surprising news coming from someone who didn't often use the word 'wonderful' and, when Rach did use it, it was often about a basement flat that was as far from 'wonderful' as cubic zirconia was from diamonds.

'Really,' Rach insisted. 'It was amazing. *And*, Keels, the big news is… I'd met Silvie's son before. And so have you!'

'What?' Keeley stopped running the tap and paid proper attention.

'Louis Durand is my hair hero Louis.'

Keeley didn't understand.

'Louis!' Rach said again, all bright eyes despite her make-up spread across her face. 'Louis who saved me from the revolving door. Louis who we bumped into at the afternoon tea. Louis who actually looked into my eyes last night instead of just staring at my boobs.'

'Oh my God,' Keeley said, palming her face.

'I know, right?! But, instead of looking all the hotness like he looked over the chocolate eclairs… he actually looked terrible,' Rach carried on.

'What d'you mean?'

'He was covered in blotches. Like seriously huge blotches. I don't know, like he'd been attacked and stung by a thousand bees.'

'Really?'

'Really,' Rach continued. 'The poor guy was obviously a bit embarrassed about it. I don't know whether it was a food allergy or a reaction to washing detergent or something but—'

'Well, didn't you ask him what it was?' Keeley wanted to know. She checked her watch again. She didn't have that long to get ready and those butterflies weren't letting up. So much so, she couldn't really focus on this conversation with Rach.

'I did,' Rach said. 'But I'm pretty sure he made up his answer.'

'What did he say?'

'He said he was allergic to penguins.' Rach scoffed. 'I mean, is that even a thing?' She sighed. 'It was a shame really, because, like I said, he did look me in the eye when we talked... well, the eye he could properly see out of.'

Keeley frowned, her thoughts immediately going to Pepe. Where had the animal ended up? And she had never asked Ethan what he had been doing with the creature in the first place.

'I made the same look that you're making right now,' Rach said, swiping up one of her wipes from the dressing table. 'And then I offered him some concealer.'

'Only you,' Keeley said, shaking her head.

'But, despite the horrible hives, he was really funny and charming and he gave me tissues when I cried.'

'You cried?' Keeley remarked.

'Yup, I cried at the ballet. I told you. It was... I don't know... all kinds of beautiful.'

What *was* Paris doing to them both? Rach – strong, ballsy Rach – was crying over a dance performance and Keeley was riding on a too-small extinct animal on a children's roundabout. And now she was planning to go running...

'And... well... he's actually suggested dinner one night,' Rach blurted out. She rubbed at the make-up on her face like she was scrubbing at a grubby oven tainted by ten years of cooking Christmas turkeys. 'But I didn't know whether to say yes, because we're here together, girls united, and I didn't know if that would be OK with you.'

Keeley smiled. 'Say yes to a dinner. Can you text him?'

Still scrubbing at her face, Rach nodded. 'We swapped numbers and he asked all about you, but I didn't tell him that much because, well, he's going to want to hear it all from Kidney Girl herself, isn't he?'

'I'm not allowed to be Kidney Girl,' Keeley reminded.

'That's right!' Rach said, pointing with her finger as well as her wipe. 'That was a test!' She sniffed. 'But, you know, you'll have to go into it a little with Ferne's fam, won't you?'

'What *did* you say about me?' Keeley asked, checking her reflection again.

'I told him that if there was one person in the whole world who was definitely worthy of one of his sister's body parts, then it was you. I said you were all the kind and conscientious to a fault when it came to respecting your newly acquired organ... except when I led you astray.'

'What did he say to that?'

'He said,' Rach began, one of her eyebrows raising, 'that he could imagine I was very good when it came to leading people astray. Honestly, Keels, it was like an episode of *Heist*, without the Spanish subtitles.'

Now was the perfect time to tell Rach about Ethan. Rach had just told her all about her evening with Louis and now it was Keeley's turn. Her solo walk following the mystery map had led her to a cosy dinner and trying to breathe in the essence of Paris. She took a breath and out came: 'Well, strange things do seem to happen here.'

'Like you being up at early o'clock. What *are* you doing awake at this time?' Rach asked.

'I'm... going for a run.'

'You're what?' Rach turned to face her then, her skin still thick with wayward make-up, but now also red raw from all the attempts to take it off. 'It's a job to get you down the gym at the best of times and you *hate* the running machine.'

'I don't hate it,' Keeley protested. 'I just... like doing anything else a lot more. Besides, I'm not running at the gym, I'm going to run through the streets of Paris, taking in the sights and inhaling all the coffee smells.' Straightaway she was back by the banks of the Seine, Ethan's hands on her shoulders...

'I thought you couldn't smell much anymore.'

'I can *remember* what coffee smells like. I'll pretend.'

'On your own? It's not even light.' Rach's eyes went to their balcony doors and then her fingers were parting the curtains, revealing a few inches of barely light early morning. 'I'm not sure you should be running on your own in the dark somewhere you don't know. Lizzie would have a fit.'

Keeley sighed, turned on the tap again and began splashing water up and over her face. There was no doubt about it, Lizzie would definitely have a fit if she knew she was meeting up with a Frenchman she didn't even know the surname of and had shared a handhold that was still giving her shivers every time she thought about it. But Rach was her best friend. She would *totally* get it. Why was she keeping this from her?

'Get back to bed,' Rach suggested. 'Let's have another hour of sleep, then we can get an early breakfast and ask Noel to take us somewhere. Silvie did say he was ours to call whenever we wanted.' Rach threw the wipe down on the dressing table and clambered back under the covers. 'How about Christmas shopping? I need to get gifts for my mum and my brother… and Roland if I want my plan to become his senior negotiator to pan out. If Jamie goes all out and buys him something from Sloane Street I'm screwed.' Rach took a breath. 'Or how about Notre Dame? I know we can't go in it, but we can have a look at how the reconstruction is going.'

'That sounds like a good idea,' Keeley agreed, sweeping her hair back from her face and tying it into a ponytail. 'After I've been for a run. I'll only be an hour or so.' And she *still* hadn't mentioned she wasn't going alone.

'Ugh, really? You *really* want to run?'

'I really want to run,' Keeley answered.

'Well… do you want me to come with you?' Rach asked, eyes already closed, yawning as if she was going to drop back off to sleep again at any moment. 'I will if you want me to. I don't want your mum blaming me if you get kidnapped by an onion seller on a bicycle.'

'Go to sleep, Rach,' Keeley urged, checking her reflection in the mirror again. She definitely didn't have time for a shower now.

'OK, Paula Radcliffe, just don't do an inappropriate piss and get arrested. And don't get abducted. Text me if you're going to be longer than an hour.'

'Yes, Mum,' Keeley replied.

Twenty-Nine

L'Hotel Paris Parfait, Tour Eiffel, Paris

Ethan checked his watch. What was he doing? When had he last run through the streets of Paris? He never really had the time. What he should be doing was preparing for this meeting with Silvie, Louis and Ferne's solicitor this afternoon. He had received an email late last night with only the vaguest of details, but it had said enough to get him worried. Where exactly did he stand? Was there some loophole he had missed with regard to his part-ownership of Perfect Paris? Had his grief veiled the nuts and bolts of things he should have paid more attention to? Perhaps, while Louis was rushing back across the ocean to get away from the desperate loss felt by pretty much everyone except him, it seemed, Ethan had overlooked details that were going to determine his future here. And, if something had happened to shake his foundations within the company, it might mean he couldn't be at the centre of making sure Ferne's hotels didn't become an anonymous part of a bigger corporation. Who else was going to stand up for Ferne if he didn't?

The door of the hotel revolved and there Keeley was coming out onto the street. This woman who gave him goose bumps simply by being in his orbit. His skin was already reacting underneath the long-sleeved tight-fitting sports top he was wearing. He had gone for joggers instead of shorts as there was frost on the ground and the air was just as cold. She was wearing leggings, trainers and a sweatshirt bearing a picture of a dartboard and, with her hair tied back from her face, she still looked adorable.

'*Bonjour*,' he greeted.

'Good morning,' she answered. 'I'm sorry I'm a bit late. I—'

'Not at all,' Ethan said. 'I… like your sweater.'

'Oh,' she said, looking down at it. 'Yes, well, I didn't bring any running stuff with me so…' She laughed a little. 'It's my dad's. He's part of a darts team back in England.'

'Ah,' Ethan replied. 'In France we prefer to play *petanque*.'

'My dad's never been good with sports involving balls,' she replied. 'He once played cricket in the back garden with one of our neighbours and ended up breaking three windows with the one shot. Not a greenhouse. Don't ask. It involved a budgie.'

He couldn't help but laugh.

'Could we start running now?' she asked him, pulling the hem of the sweater down a little and starting to shiver.

'You are cold?' Ethan said.

'No,' she replied. 'It's just, if we don't start running now I might go off the idea and suggest coffee and a croissant instead.'

He could give in. He could easily swap the frozen streets of the capital for the cosy warmth and early-morning ambience of a coffee shop. But he needed the exercise, the blood pumping around his body to ready himself for whatever the day held. Plus, he really wanted to show her a little more of Paris. *His* Paris.

'OK,' he answered. 'We will go.' He started to jog, checking over his shoulder to see if she was following.

Keeley's ribs were already hurting a little. She had inspected her bruises from the Pepe fall again when she'd got dressed this morning and they were still that initial wondering-what-colour-they were-going-to-grow-up-to-be-blue, lined up alongside the still-red scars from her operation and her ordeal. The running motion was definitely not helping. Not that she was going to let that show on her face. She was also not going to show the fact that street running was very different to running on a treadmill and her knees were partially jarring over every piece of solid pavement.

'This is the best time to run,' Ethan told her. 'No one much around.'

They had passed along by the Seine, a cold mist settling over the water and they were now heading off the tourist beaten track from what Keeley could tell. The Christmas decorations on the buildings had changed a little from garish bright lights and sparkle to more gently traditional and home-made. Garlands of ivy and fir, painted wooden effigies, silver stars that looked well-used. All much swankier than Grandma Joan's stash of Woolworths' finest, as much as she was fond of them.

Ethan's words were coming out level and even. Like

the effort of running was having zero effect. Meanwhile, Keeley's heart felt like it was the prominent bassline in a dance track. 'Yes,' she squeaked. She cleared her throat.

'You are OK?' he asked.

She nodded. 'Yep.' She wasn't. This was such a bad idea. She never looked attractive during or after exercise. Why would she agree to this?

'We can slow down a little if...'

'No... I'm fine.' She let out a raspy cough then hastily sucked in vital air. She wasn't someone who gave in easily. Her still being here was the ultimate testament to that.

'This is Passy,' Ethan informed, keeping pace beside her. 'Personally, I think it is one of the most overlooked areas of Paris.'

'Is it an area for... rich people?' Keeley replied. 'It looks... affluent.'

'*Un peu,*' he answered. 'But that is not why I like it.' He turned his head to look at her. 'Come this way.' He sped up just a little so he was dictating the direction.

Keeley gritted her teeth and willed herself to dig into special reserves. They had run maybe just over a kilometre. She hoped he wasn't going to suggest more than three or four more of them...

They rounded a corner and Keeley let out a gasp. This time it wasn't from the exercise, but because of the view ahead. A cobbled street had appeared like someone had just drawn away a curtain of modern times and revealed a scene from yesteryear. There were thick stone walls and iron gates, lumps of rock attached to the base of houses and old-fashioned gas-style lampposts glistening with frost. This didn't look like the previous rich person's city paradise, it seemed as if something rustic and ancient had been plopped right into the centre of Paris's metropolis.

Keeley slowed her run to take it all in. 'What is this road called?' she asked.

'*Rue Berton*,' Ethan answered. He was back alongside her now, matching her running rhythm. 'Do you like it?'

'It's like nothing I would have imagined finding in the middle of Paris, so close to the Eiffel Tower.'

'I know,' Ethan replied. 'You can imagine how things were years ago, *n'est-ce pas*?'

'Monks,' Keeley answered, continuing to jog, being careful with the sheen on the cobbles here. Slipping for the second time this break wouldn't be ideal.

'*Pardon*?'

'Sorry,' Keeley said. 'I just imagined monks walking down the narrow lanes, whispering in prayer or something. It's so... atmospheric.'

Ethan had always thought it was atmospheric. The place of daydreams. When he was younger, when he used to escape, he'd made his way down here to roam the alleyways and paths imagining he was someone else. Not a monk perhaps, but someone who wasn't a street kid from the orphanage. Someone who could be anyone he wanted to be. And that chance had come... in the shape of Ferne.

'Do you live near here?' Keeley asked him as they picked their way up the street. The road narrowed significantly, until it was all but a pathway. She dropped in behind him.

'I live in the Opera District,' he answered. 'I have a small apartment above a bakery. I rented it simply because of the aromas.' He stalled suddenly, acutely aware he had just said something wrong. 'Oh… I am so sorry. I did not mean to mention the smell. I—'

'It's OK,' she answered. 'I recall the amazing scent of fresh bread.'

'It was a ridiculous thing to say. Thoughtless!'

'It's OK,' she insisted again. 'Honestly.'

He kept running, passing flashes of festive in the windows of the houses not knowing how to pick the conversation back up after that faux pas.

'So, I've been wondering, what you do… as a job I mean.' She cleared her throat. 'Do you work at the zoo?'

'The zoo?' He suddenly wondered if he might smell. He hadn't managed a shower this morning. He had woken irritably at the early alarm call until he remembered who he was meeting for the run. Then it dawned on him. *Pepe.*

'When we met you *were* chasing a penguin,' Keeley reminded.

He wanted the pathway to widen again, so they could jog next to each other. As cute as her bobbing ponytail and rear view was, he really wanted to look into her eyes. 'I was.'

'So, you don't work at the zoo?'

'Not the zoo,' he answered. And he couldn't tell her the truth about why he had acquired Pepe. He didn't want her to think he was juvenile. And it *had* been juvenile. In the end his prank had played right into Louis's hands. 'I… work in…'

Emerging from the narrow street and onto a bigger road there was the sudden sound of squealing brakes followed by a loud wail that sounded very much like a cry for help.

Thirty

For a second, Keeley froze. Those sounds. Metal on metal. A tell-tale crunch. And then she came-to as a cry hit the air.

'*Mon chien! Mon chien*!'

There was a small boy in the middle of the road ahead, his body draped over the prostrate form of a shaggy-coated brown-coloured dog. Keeley's heart was already in her mouth as she powered towards them. It was the dog, not the boy. The boy had shouted out. The dog was not barking.

'What's happened?' she asked.

The boy cried out again, this time so loud and with such anguish that Keeley dropped to her knees onto the ground next to the possibly-ten-year-old. 'It's OK. It's alright.' She had no idea if it was going to be alright. The dog was very still and with the boy lying over it she couldn't ascertain exactly what had occurred. She assumed, given the boy's concern, and the dog's lack of movement that the animal had to be injured.

'*Une voiture*,' the boy simpered, raising his head.

'*Tu*!'

Ethan had arrived and after this single first word that Keeley understood as 'you', he had started talking at speed in French to the child. She didn't understand a word of it, so while the boy got to his feet *she* focused on the dog. It *was* breathing, but it was very slow and shallow, as if each rise and fall of its abdomen was taking it further and further away from this world…

'Keeley,' Ethan said. 'This is a scam.'

'What?' she asked, looking away from the animal for a second then back to it again as if she was missing a vital component of the scene.

'There is nothing wrong with the dog,' Ethan carried on. 'It will possibly not even belong to her. Come on. Let us carry on our run.'

'*Non*!' The boy was down on his knees again, hands in the dog's mottled fur.

Keeley looked up to Ethan. 'I think the dog is really hurt.'

'Impossible. This girl is from the street. Yesterday I thought she was simply looking for food, but now she is trying out one of the oldest tricks. Playing on your sentiments. Make sure your wallet is secure.'

Had he really said 'girl'? Keeley looked again at the now sobbing child who was cradling the dog's slightly floppy head whispering softly in French. Was 'he' a 'she'? It was hard to tell with her head covered by a hat and the rest of her/him dressed in gender neutral jeans and a baggy black jumper. 'Ethan,' she said her eyes now only on the dog, 'I think the dog is genuinely very unwell.'

'What?'

His word was coated in shock and surprise and in a second he had joined her on his knees on the road as the boy/girl cried out again, body trembling.

'Well… we can take it to a vet,' Ethan said immediately.

He made a movement like he was going to try and scoop the animal up from the concrete. Keeley reached out a hand, holding onto his arm and shaking her head. She whispered, 'It's best not to move him. Can you call someone? To come here?'

'To come here?' Ethan asked.

Was that the right course of action? To keep the dog still? Or was Keeley saying that because she remembered the words of the paramedics when she'd been lying half pinned into the back of the taxi, being ordered not to turn her head or move even a centimetre, calling for Bea and reaching to hold her hand.

She watched Ethan pull a mobile phone from the pocket of his joggers and make a call. She put an arm around the child, patting their shoulder. 'Listen,' she whispered. 'You need to tell the dog you love him. Keep telling him so he can hear your voice. Tell him that he is the best dog in the whole world. That everything is going to be OK.' A lump gathered in her throat as she lifted her eyes to Ethan who still had the phone to his ear, call not yet connected. 'Can you… tell him in French.'

'Her,' Ethan repeated. 'It is a girl.' He took a deep breath and said some words in French. This seemed to make the girl cry anew and she buried her face deep into the dog's mottled fur.

Keeley put her hand on the dog's tummy and closed her eyes channelling hopeful, bright thoughts. This dog had to survive. It had to. She had to be able to save *someone*. She began to talk. 'What a lovely, handsome dog you are. So pretty and…'

'He *is* a boy dog.' It was the girl, juddering out the words, shoulders shaking with either cold or emotion or perhaps both. 'His name is Bo-Bo.'

'What a splendid name,' Keeley said. 'A really lovely, lovely name.'

'Is he… going to die?' the girl asked, raising large haunted chocolate brown eyes and looking to Keeley for the answers.

Keeley watched the dog's breathing. It was slower now, his abdomen barely moving at all. How many times had she sat next to someone at the hospice watching them come to the end of existence? She knew the signs in humans, knew humans had a will to hang on as long as they possibly could. Was it the same for animals?

'Keep talking to Bo-Bo,' she said quickly.

'Someone is coming to help,' Ethan said. 'But I cannot sit here and just do nothing. I cannot. There must be something we can do. There must be. Where is it injured? There is no blood we can see… there is nothing. Perhaps it is in shock. Where is the car that has hit it? Did they just drive away?' He reached out to the animal.

'No,' Keeley ordered, her chest tightening in response to the sentiment in his statement. 'Really, Ethan, stop.' She swallowed as he settled next to her again. 'Just stop and… wait and… just be here.'

The street-girl who had taken chocolates from the Christmas tree at his hotel yesterday was crying like she was about to lose a parent rather than a probably flea-ridden mongrel with unravelling rope for a lead. But the sound was scratching at his heart.

'There's a good boy,' Keeley whispered to the dog, her hand gently stroking its fur. 'You're such a good boy.'

'Good boy… Bo-Bo. Be strong. You can do it. I… love you so much.'

The girl wasn't so tough after all and Ethan watched the tears spilling from her eyes like water from a fountain in *Place de la Concorde*. He didn't know where to look. He couldn't look at the girl anymore. He didn't want to look at the ailing dog. So instead he focused on Keeley and the gentle words falling from her lips that were meant to comfort and soothe.

Across the street a few people had gathered and were watching their odd group circled around the pet in the centre of the road. Where was that vet?

Thirty-One

Un Petit Café, Tour Eiffel, Paris

The *boulangerie*-cum-café was a little like Ollivander's shop from *Harry Potter,* but instead of boxes of magic wands, there were baskets and display cases filled with baguettes, croissants, madeleines and other sweet and savoury delights. Steam from the coffee machines and griddles was rising into the warm air misting up the windows that held a menagerie of quaint festive decorations – golden wire balls and small silver fir cones joined together by rustic rope. The eatery was starting to get busy as the morning took hold and Keeley could only imagine what an odd threesome they made to onlookers.

Ethan had taken charge when the vet had arrived. With the girl still sobbing, he had explained what they believed to have happened and the vet administered some medication that sent Bo-Bo to sleep. Unconsciousness and easier breathing. Not death. Although it took a few minutes, after the vet's gentle examination of the pet, for the girl to be convinced that the man's intention was preservation. And now, with Bo-Bo off to the surgery, they had come here to keep warm and wait for more information before deciding what to do next. A large plate of pancakes with bacon and a huge serving of mushrooms was keeping the girl from crying or actually saying anything at all.

'You are OK?' Ethan asked Keeley.

She had already drunk half her cup of coffee, relishing the way it was warming her up. Her ribs were also a little thankful that their jog had been cut short. 'I'm OK.'

'I am sorry that our run did not turn out the way we hoped it might.' He sighed. 'By that, I mean, that I had hoped I could show you a little more of the city and no one would get hurt.'

She looked at him. His hands were cupping his coffee, but he had not taken a sip of it. He still looked a little pale.

'It's OK,' Keeley answered. 'What else could we do but help?' She indicated their café companion who was now squirting tomato ketchup all over everything on her plate.

Ethan leaned forward then. 'What is your name?'

The girl looked up, chewing brutally. 'I do not talk to strangers.'

'How can I be a stranger?' Ethan wanted to know. 'We met yesterday and today I have bought you breakfast. I have also provided your animal with medical assistance.'

'What is *your* name?' the girl asked, shooting him a defiant look.

'That is simple,' Ethan said. 'My name is Ethan Bouchard. Now, it is your turn.'

She paused, fork in mid-air, then said a curt, 'Jeanne.'

'And your last name?'

The girl shrugged her shoulders and carried on eating.

Keeley picked up the conversation, keeping her tone light. 'Where do you live? Won't your parents be worried about you? You were out very early in the morning on your own.'

'Parents?! Ha!' Jeanne laughed loud and nudged Ethan with her elbow. 'She thinks… that people like us have parents.'

Keeley frowned. What did she mean? Did she have some kind of connection to Ethan?

'You have had a shock,' Ethan told her. 'Bo-Bo being hit by a car.'

The mention of her beloved animal's name seemed to pull Jeanne back into a funk and she forked mushrooms between her lips, one of them falling out and dripping down her chin before landing on her plate. Keeley suspected Jeanne was going to clam up again. She watched as Ethan finally took a gulp of his coffee.

'Where did you learn? You know, what you did,' he suddenly asked Keeley as more café patrons headed in through the front door, a chill blast of the outside weather following them.

'What I did?'

'With the dog,' he elaborated.

'He has a name!' Jeanne interrupted gruffly.

'With… Bo-Bo,' Ethan added.

Keeley drew in a breath, gathering her coffee cup in towards her chest and thinking about Erica. 'Well, it's because I used to volunteer at my local hospital and now I help out at the hospice.'

'Wow,' Ethan breathed and then he seemed to reconsider her words. 'Really?'

'Yes,' Keeley answered. 'I mean, it's not much. In my spare

time I spend a few hours every week visiting the patients who don't have family. I read to them sometimes, or I just sit with the very poorly ones and I tell them things that are going on in the world… like, I don't know, the Spice Girls making another comeback or… what Harry Redknapp is currently endorsing.'

'That is Prince Harry's new surname? The red nap?' Ethan asked, looking super-confused. 'I do not understand.'

Keeley couldn't help but smile. 'No… he's… someone else. It doesn't matter.' She wet her lips. 'What I do at the hospice is… I try to make the patients' lives a little bit lighter. I never think that being there is only about dying. I think it should still be about living. I help patients to… get the most out of those last moments.' She smiled. 'At least that's what I try to do.'

'Why do you do that?' Ethan asked, his eyes meeting hers. 'If that is not too much to ask. I would like to understand.'

Jeanne dropped her knife and fork to her plate, sweeping up her glass of orange juice and gulping at it as if she hadn't had a drink in a couple of days. She let out a satisfied gasp then looked at Keeley with a pertinent expression. 'Yes,' she said. 'Why do you do that?'

Both of them were scrutinising her now, waiting for some divine answer she wasn't sure she wanted to give. But it was obvious from the silence and their expressions that they weren't going to let this go.

'I decided to volunteer at the hospital… after my sister died.'

Ethan inhaled and he knew he had failed to stop it being

audible even above the hubbub of the café. He pushed his tongue into his teeth and kept his expression as neutral as he could. She had lost someone close to her, just like he had…

'Was she very old? Or sick?' Jeanne burst out.

'Neither,' Keeley said evenly. 'She had an accident. The paramedics, they did everything they could that night but… she couldn't be saved. And I… didn't get to say the goodbye I wanted to.' Her voice wasn't so even now and Ethan looked to her fingers, clasping hold of the table, nails digging into the wood grain.

She started to talk again. 'I guess I wanted to give something back in memory of my sister and make a small difference. Help those who have the chance to recover and now… I help others through their final battle.' She paused. 'Everyone deserves someone holding their hand when they die.'

Her words hit home hard as she turned her face towards him, their eyes connecting. She was the most special, selfless person and he found himself only wanting to find out even more about her.

The moment was broken by the ringing of a mobile phone. It wasn't his and Jeanne had turned her attention back to eating.

Ethan took another sip of his coffee and watched Keeley stand up and answer.

'Hello, Rach… sorry… no, I'm fine. Honestly. No, I didn't get your messages I was… helping someone and… I forgot the time. Yes, I'll be back for breakfast I promise. OK. Bye.'

Keeley ended the call then retook her seat. 'Sorry, that

was my friend. She'd apparently sent me five texts and was considering calling the *gendarmerie*.'

She smiled but Jeanne didn't react so well. At the mention of the police the girl had shrunk a little into her seat.

'I should go,' Keeley said. 'Unless you need me to wait for news…' Her eyes went from Ethan to Jeanne then back again. 'From the vet.'

He watched Keeley finish her drink, making to leave. There was nothing she could do here. She had places to be. Except he didn't want her to leave without knowing he would see her again.

'If Bo-Bo dies will you come to the funeral?' Jeanne said, all big water-filled eyes now and none of the insolence.

'Funeral?' Ethan balked.

'You have to have faith, Jeanne,' Keeley told her. 'You believe in Bo-Bo, don't you? You told me he is a clever dog.'

'I saw the look on the face of the vet,' Jeanne said, wiping her nose with her sleeve. 'He does not believe he can be fixed.'

'Hey,' Ethan said, drawing the girl's attention to him. 'I believe he can be fixed. And I anticipate I will be paying a great deal of Euro once the fixing is done.'

'A party then?' Jeanne asked, eyes a little brighter. 'If not a funeral then a party for his recovery.'

'Will I be paying for that also?' Ethan wanted to know.

Jeanne's face was turning red now as she hit him with a look that suggested a meltdown was going to ensue if he did not agree.

'A party,' Ethan announced. 'Of course. We will make sure he will have the best survivor party a doggy could wish for.'

'And you will come?' Jeanne asked looking at Keeley.

'Yes,' she answered. 'Of course, I will come.'

'We should… exchange numbers,' Ethan said. 'For… party arrangements.'

'Oh, yes,' Keeley agreed. 'That makes sense.'

'Good,' Ethan answered as he created a contact on screen.

Despite the unusual circumstances, it seemed that their next date was set.

Thirty-Two

Rue Lepic, Montmartre, Paris

'I know I thought Noel's tourist talk was a bit annoying, but his handwriting is worse than his droning on and on about facts and history. I can hardly see where we're meant to be walking to,' Rach moaned, folding and unfolding a tourist map that had lines drawn all over it.

They were strolling through Montmartre, following a walk their guide had set out for them. But Keeley's train of thought was miles away, not on the cobbles, nor in front of the apartment that used to belong to Van Gogh. Instead she was worrying about a scruffy little girl and her sick dog and her friend in the hospice back home who hadn't answered her latest text. She had received a text from Silvie, though. It was an invitation to dinner the following evening at her home. She hadn't mentioned the ballet, but Keeley guessed by now she would have heard from Louis that he had had a different theatre companion than the one Silvie intended. She hoped she wasn't too annoyed.

'Ha!' Rach exclaimed, appearing to read. 'Noel says to

stop at somewhere called *Les Petits Mitrons*. He says, and I quote, "in the window there are tasty tarts for you to try".' She snorted. 'Do you think he meant to write that note about the area around the Moulin Rouge instead?'

Keeley forced a smile and put her hands inside her coat pockets as they continued to walk. They'd passed brightly coloured store fronts, still selling items outside on the street – jumpers, fresh seafood, the ripest-looking tomatoes – the famous Moulin Rouge with its iconic windmill on the roof, and traditional eateries as well as restaurants with flashing lights advertising seasonal twists on pasta and pizza. Now their surroundings had become more subtle and traditional. There were more cobbles, slightly less mopeds and a gentle vibe about it.

'What's up?' Rach asked, coming up alongside her.

'I... was just thinking about Erica,' Keeley answered.

'She's probably snogging that Joe Jonas photo you told me you got her.'

'Nick,' Keeley said. 'It was Nick Jonas.'

'Really?' Rach said with a frown. 'Oh well, I guess we can't all have the same taste in Jonas Brothers.'

Keeley let out a sigh. 'I need to start making decisions about my future, don't I?'

It had been Erica's pep talk the other day. Or maybe it had been earlier this morning with the girl and her beloved dog? Or perhaps it was meeting the mysterious Ethan? All Keeley knew was for the first time in so long, she was starting to think about reaching out towards a future. Yes, she had only made a few tentative steps – coming here to France to meet Silvie, a cosy dinner with a handsome companion, accepting an invitation to jog at sunrise – but they were somehow the largest strides she had made since the accident. It was acknowledgement that she was here and she wanted to embrace the life she had, for however long it lasted. Because no one knew, did they? She might already know that the longevity of the current oldest person in the world might not be hers to grasp but, just like everyone else, she didn't have a date in the calendar to plan to. All anyone had was the here and now and the hope of a later.

'I've almost wasted the last year,' Keeley admitted suddenly. 'Worrying.'

'Well...' Rach began. 'We all do that sometimes. Look at me, worrying about how to trump Jamie in the overtime stakes and the buying Roland gifts stakes, all because I know that bribery and corruption will get me ahead at House 2 Home.'

'Well, I've let everyone tell me what to do. My mum, the woman in Asda who told me burnt-orange was this season's colour... I even asked one of Mr Peterson's dead stoats for advice the last time I was there. What kind of insanity is that?'

'*I've* tried to tell you what to do,' Rach said, somehow seeming affronted. 'And you didn't listen to me. Now you're telling me you favoured a dead stoat over your alive best friend?'

'Why *can't* I start my business over again?' Keeley asked herself as much as Rach. 'Why did I let my mum make me give up that dream?'

'Why don't I just apply for a senior negotiator job at another firm where I might be respected for my skills in negotiating rather than my short skirts and coffee-making?'

'Rach,' Keeley gasped. 'You are appreciated for your skills… aren't you?'

Rach shrugged. 'I want more too. I don't shop at Price Squash because I prefer it to Harrods, you know.'

There was a Christmas tree in a cobbled pedestrian section now, its decorated fronds swaying gently with the breeze and as they approached it, Keeley marvelled at the multi-coloured décor. There were CDs with writing and drawings on them, like the local children had added wishes for Santa. *Wishes and dreams*. She deserved them, didn't she? Rach deserved them too.

Rach stood next to her. 'Talking about you… I think we all just thought you probably wanted to do something simpler now. Not have the worries of a business-owner. Let Roland take care of public liability and all that.'

'But why did I do that?' Now Keeley was almost calling out to the universe for answers. A passer-by gave her an odd look then hurried into an ivy-covered brasserie. 'Bea would have hated the fact that I'd given up on my dream.' Her sister had been her biggest supporter, always giving her opinion on fabric and pattern. Bea might have been all the practical and mechanical by nature, but she had also loved a quirky print and the feel of silk under her fingertips. 'And I hate it too. It's stupid and… ridiculous.'

Wherever this wake-up call was coming from, Keeley was embracing it and being mindful in the moment. She grinned at Rach then, suddenly feeling like she could take on the world.

'Rach, we are going to move in together after Christmas,' she said with utter determination. 'Like we talked about. You don't want to live with Bertram anymore and I don't want to feel like my every decision has a government five-point plan.' She drew in a breath. 'And *I am* going to start my business again. Maybe I'll have to start working out of home to begin with, maybe those clients I had lined up originally will have gone with someone else but... the one guarantee is, people will always want nice things to... make them happy.'

And by nice she really didn't mean expensive. Maybe *that* could be her USP. Most interior designers she had worked with before, had focused on the elite clients, the ones who wanted slightly mad things like a coffee table combined with an aquarium full of lionhead goldfish or curtains made from their children's handprints. Perhaps Keeley could focus on *her* type of 'nice'. The relaxed and comfortable that made her heart sing, but something a step up from rearranging lounge furniture and choosing travel books as props. Practical, yet beautiful solutions for modern day family living...

When Keeley turned away from the Christmas tree and back to Rach, her best friend was looking at her a little differently.

'What?' Keeley asked, following the question up with a nervous swallow. 'Do you think I'm completely mad? To be getting this all off my chest now. When we're supposed to be sightseeing?'

'No, I don't think that,' Rach whispered, darting what looked like tears away from her eyes. 'It's just... I haven't seen you look that way since...'

She didn't need to finish the sentence for Keeley's benefit. She knew. And she could feel it too. Coming here *had* been a kickstart she badly needed. The comfort zone of protection her mum had wrapped around her was understandable, but only when she had broken out of that did she see all the implications of its limitations. She was living but she *wasn't* living. And that had to stop.

Keeley threw her arms around Rach and gathered her close, closing her eyes and trying to isolate her senses from each other like Ethan had got her to do. What had Rach used to smell like when smelling had been so easy to do? Keeley smiled to herself, recalling memories of bags of goodies from Price Squash – half-price Milka chocolate (the one with the strawberry bits in), toothpaste, pork scratchings, this *bloody* hair dye and the tin of red paint they'd first bonded over cleaning up on a bus eight years ago. Rach had been carrying six tins of it and trying to press the button to alert the driver to stop, one had slipped from her grasp and rolled down onto the floor, spilling open on its journey. Within milliseconds the whole of the 328 was filling up with fumes and everyone was coughing. Only Keeley hadn't run for the exit door as soon as the driver ordered everyone off, instead choosing to offer Rach her large pack of handwipes and help remove the mess.

Keeley laughed then. 'Did they ever get that paint off the floor of the bus?'

'What?' Rach asked, stepping back from her friend's embrace and looking like she had no idea what Keeley was talking about.

'The 328 bus. Where we met. The bus covered in… what was the name of that horrible paint again?'

'Hickory Smoke,' Rach said, laughing. 'It never covered

properly either! Apart from the bus floor. My dad did six coats on the lounge wall before he gave up on it. Bloody Adie!' She shook her head. 'Lucky it was cheap.'

Keeley put her arm through her friend's and turned them towards the street and their proposed incline to take in the view of the golden dome of *Les Invalides*. 'You do deserve more, Rach. You are an amazing negotiator.'

'I know,' Rach said with positivity. 'But perhaps I need to think about a change in agency... or at least put the frighteners on Roland. Make him realise he would be lost without me.'

'I'll help you,' Keeley said, giving her arm a squeeze. 'We'll work out a strategy so he can't fail to realise.' She shrugged. 'And if he doesn't, then House 2 Home's loss will be someone else's gain.'

'Right there with you,' Rach said.

'So, shall we do a little more shopping? I ought to make a start on Christmas while I'm here. I need to find something for my mum that she's going to love so much she won't worry when I tell her I'm moving out and giving my business another shot.' Keeley took a deep breath. She wasn't sure even something by Coco Chanel was going to do the trick there. 'And we can discuss Louis. Has he texted you yet?'

Rach hugged Keeley's arm. 'He did but... I don't know.'

'What don't you know?'

'I don't know if he's really my Pyjama Man,' Rach said with a sigh.

'Well,' Keeley said, 'there's only one way to find out.'

Thirty-Three

L'Hotel Paris Parfait, Opera District, Paris

Ethan burst into his office knowing he needed to freshen up before he met with Louis, Silvie and Ferne's solicitor. Somehow, even though he had changed, he smelled of street-kid, dog and coffee. It was the exact combination of things he had once smelled of each and every day up until he had met the Durand family. Except his plan for a quick shower at the hotel was thwarted by the fact that the three of them were already sat in the room adjacent, around the boardroom table and Noel was collating papers on his desk.

'What is going on?' Ethan hissed at his assistant. 'I am not late.'

'*Non*,' Noel agreed. 'They are early. I sent you three messages.'

He'd seen Noel's messages and ignored them. The vet had called and he had rushed to the surgery with Jeanne, expecting the worst but… it *hadn't* been the worst. Bo-Bo was apparently in a deep sense of shock as well as having an injured foot. He was currently sleeping off the medication in the garage of the hotel at Tour Eiffel. It had been all he could do to get Jeanne into a hotel room there rather than have her rest alongside the dog in the loading bay.

He let out a sigh. So, he was a little dishevelled? Who needed to be in an uncreased business suit to exude professionalism? Self-belief came from inside not from power-clothes. At least he wasn't in his running gear…

'Order the coffee Silvie likes,' Ethan said, straightening the collar of his shirt. 'And something American for Louis. A hot dog perhaps?' He smiled. 'Nothing connected to penguins.'

'Monsieur Durand has already ordered. Honeyed coffee and coconut biscuits.'

Ethan scoffed. 'He orders this yet he wants to—' He stopped himself short. He had been about to say that Louis wanted to sell the hotels, but that wasn't the kind of information you should be imparting to your staff, even your closest confidante.

'He wants to…?' Noel inquired.

'Change the menu,' Ethan said.

'He wants to change the menu?' Noel asked, now looking confused.

'*Non*,' Ethan said. '*I* think we should look at changing the menu.' He took the papers from Noel and hoped it was the information he had asked him for. Details of how well the brand was performing despite the global difficulties of earlier that year. 'The menu has not been changed since the hotels were formed.'

'That is because a long time was taken to perfect a core menu that was, if you remember, almost scientifically devised,' Noel said to him.

Ethan knew that. He had listened to Ferne talk about it, plus two experts she had employed to deliver on it. Ferne had wanted the restaurants of the hotels to be in sync with one another and all the dishes had to be a surprise for the palate with delicate nuances taking well-known French cuisine to another level. The science said that diners were seeking 'different' with a touch of 'unexpected'. But did science really know about *everyone*? And shouldn't food be more about a 'feeling'? Ethan held his breath then, thinking about Keeley. What she had said about 'feelings' had really resonated with him.

'I want a new menu before Christmas,' Ethan blurted out. 'I want you to look at what the other hotels have planned for their festive lunches and Christmas party evenings and then I want you to think the complete opposite.'

'I do not understand,' Noel said. 'The other day you tell me to see what other hotels and restaurants are doing with their decorations so we might create something similar. Now you are—'

'Now I am asking you, Noel, to do something else.' Ethan hadn't meant his tone to be so sharp, but it was important for him to be in charge when Silvie and Louis seemed desperate to strip him away from that role. Ferne had trusted his judgement. Always. 'Think… home comforts. Not everyone who comes away for Christmas is doing that because they want to get *away* from home.' He mused on this anew as the words fell into the air. 'Some people will *have* to be away from home, or perhaps they simply cannot be with their loved ones. They may well want reminders of *those* Christmases.'

He took a moment to remember the best Christmas

dinner he had ever eaten. Not in a restaurant. Not even with the Durands. It had been at a shelter where the goose had been cut thick and served with crispy roasted potatoes, hot and fluffy in the centre, a menagerie of vegetables served with a dark, rich gravy. Ethan could recall just how full his stomach had felt after eating that feast next to other people like him. People with nothing and no one. People who relied on the kindness of others.

'Home comforts?' Noel mused, as if the phrase was alien to him.

'Yes,' Ethan answered. 'Like… all the things you think you should not have, but secretly crave because they remind you of… a happier time or… a special place or moment.'

As he spoke he was filled with the most intense feeling. This was exactly what was missing from the Perfect Paris mission statement. There had been nothing wrong with Ferne's quest for luxury, but perhaps the world had changed. And Ethan couldn't help thinking that the other part of his friend – the part who had cared for strays and given money to beggars on the Metro – would have approved of the shift.

Noel was still looking a little out of sorts, like Ethan had shot down his large, glittery, festive balloon with a catapult. But Ethan was buzzing now. He didn't care if his suit was creased or not. He was going to save the hotels and he wasn't going to let Louis stop him.

Thirty-Four

'Bernard,' Silvie started, 'we have had some coffee and you have eaten three coconut biscuits. The time for small talk about what we are all planning for Christmas is over. We want to know why you have asked for this meeting.'

This was a little news to Ethan. He had assumed that Silvie and Louis had requested this meeting with Ferne's solicitor. Her estate was not completely settled. With business interests in France, it was not always so straightforward. Was the idea of a sale of the hotel business causing Bernard some issues in finalising things? Perhaps this could be a good thing…

'Of course, Silvie,' Bernard answered, picking his small glasses out of the pocket of his suit and putting them on his face. He opened the faded leather folio that had been on the table between them all from the moment Ethan had joined the meeting. The solicitor looked down at the paperwork then looked back up again, then down, then up for a second time.

'Bernard!' It was Louis who had exclaimed. 'Please tell us why we are here. We contacted you regarding the finalisation of my sister's affairs as her will directed. Can we cut to the chase on that if we *must* be here in person?'

Although the swelling and bumps on Louis's face had decreased in size, the man was still sporting an unusual colour. Ethan ordered himself not to laugh. It must be so frustrating for Louis to have to be here, away from the management of his minions and his money.

'Very well,' Bernard said. 'Of course.' The solicitor drew in the kind of breath a doctor might take should he be about to deliver horrendous news to a waiting family.

It was the kind of breath Silvie had taken on the telephone when she had told him the heart-breaking news about Ferne. Ethan blinked and blinked again, his heart thumping hard as his memories took him back. Silvie telling him Ferne's brain had no response. That the doctors wanted her to give permission to turn off the machine. His instant reaction had been 'no'. Ferne was young and strong and there was no way she would want anyone to give up on her. But then Silvie had described how Ferne looked, how damaged she was on the outside, what the medics were saying about the inside, and how it was a miracle that she had even made it to hospital to be on the machine that was helping her to breathe. And then there had been the transplant. One kidney. That's what Ferne's life had come down to. One kidney that was taken for someone else before they pulled the plug. He had hated the idea of that. The truth was, Ethan had never got to say a goodbye because, perhaps selfishly, he was too afraid to see Ferne that way. To him she would always remain bright, vibrant and alive. And he never wanted to know of that moment when Silvie had held her hand as she slipped away.

Bernard cleared his throat and Ethan dragged his mind back into the room.

'It is my understanding that you are looking into the sale of Perfect Paris,' Bernard stated.

So Silvie or Louis or both of them *had* told the lawyer their intentions. When, Ethan wondered? *Before* they had mentioned it to him? He gritted his teeth.

'Nothing has been decided yet, Bernard,' Silvie insisted. Was it Ethan's imagination or did she look a little less than comfortable?

'It is a formality, Bernard,' Louis disagreed with his mother. 'We all know that it has to be done.'

Ethan couldn't sit still and say nothing any longer. 'Wait a moment,' he interrupted. 'It is *not* a formality. It does not *have* to be done. Show me how this decision has been reached with regard to logic and projections.'

'Ethan,' Silvie said calmly, casting a look of concern his way. 'Please, let us hear what Bernard has to say with regard to our idea and—'

'And then you will hear what I have to say?' Ethan asked. He was getting frustrated and he knew he had to try and hold it in. No one listened intently to someone who was raging.

'You don't get a say anymore,' Louis told him. 'In fact you should never have had a say in the first place.'

'Louis!' Silvie exclaimed.

Ethan was biting down on his tongue now, focusing on that feeling rather than the fact he wanted to climb across the table and punch Louis in the face. The only thing that gave Louis the right to be here was the fact he was Ferne's brother. He hadn't *ever* been involved with the hotel business. He had shown no interest in the building up of it over the past five years. And now all Louis wanted to do was get rid of it.

'If I may continue—' Bernard tried to break in.

'It is true, Mother,' Louis carried on. 'And I do not know why we have put up with this for so long. For years. I have no idea why you would allow Ferne to form a company and give so much of it to someone who brought nothing to the table.' He threw his hands up. 'I never understood why you and Father would let a ten-year-old girl become friends with someone you knew nothing about. Someone who knows nothing about himself!'

Here it was. Still, after all these years, everything came back to where Ethan had started from. Ethan couldn't deny it. He didn't know who his parents were or where he had come from. But Ferne had not cared. And because Ferne had loved him so much, his arrival in the Durand family – starting with the odd meal and ending with his spending significant time in their home on the outskirts of the city – had been accepted by Silvie and even Pierre to a lesser extent, but not ever by Louis. And here that resentment still was.

'Why do you think I had to leave Paris, Mother?' Louis asked her.

'You left to move on with your career,' Silvie answered. 'To climb the ladder and become the success that you are.'

'No,' Louis said. 'I left because someone had taken my place!'

Ethan felt the look Louis had thrown his way like it was a hot poker in the heart. There was real poison in his expression and Ethan was a little bit taken aback. He had always known Louis was not his biggest fan, that perhaps they would never have the kind of friendship he shared with Ferne, but Ethan hadn't realised it was quite *this* way. He hadn't taken anyone's place. He wasn't even sure he had made his own place in a way that positions in a family were earned by biology or signing official papers. But Louis obviously felt differently about it.

'Well, that is simply ridiculous!' Silvie exclaimed, staring long and hard at her son. 'You sound like a spoilt prince who has had his polo pony taken away.'

Her comment caused an involuntary smirk and Ethan quickly swallowed it away and attempted to focus not on Silvie's comment but on the fact that Silvie was sticking up for him.

'Could I—' Bernard tried again.

'Mother, come on. We are trying to make a decision for the good of the family and we have someone involved who really should not be. Owning a large percentage of a company that—'

Silvie jumped in. 'A company that Ethan helped to create with your sister. You weren't there when they worked long into the night to make the hotel chain a reality.'

Silvie remembers. She was underpinning his contribution here and now. It might not have been monetary, but he *had* given everything. And that was why he didn't want to give up now, even if giving up might be easier. He couldn't live with it if he forced himself to forgot the toil he and Ferne had put in. The sweat and the tears and the shrimp dinners. *Ma crevette*.

'*My* sister didn't have many faults, but her biggest mistake was him!' Louis blasted.

'I will not have you say that, Louis!' Silvie exploded,

getting to her feet, hands on the table, gripping the edge of it while her temper got the better of her.

Ethan stood then, quickly moving around the table to go to Silvie's side of it. She looked quite overcome and he felt the need to console her somehow, whether it was his place to or not.

'Silvie,' Ethan said, putting a hand on her shoulder. 'Please, do not get upset.'

'This whole situation is upsetting,' Silvie said, sounding even more exasperated now. 'How did we end up here? Fighting in front of Bernard! We were all so close once. We *were*. Ferne would not stand for it.'

Silvie's whimper at the end of the sentence made the atmosphere still a little. Ethan looked to Louis and Louis met his gaze, finally seeming a touch more in control of his emotions. Why had they never warmed to each other? Why *had* it always felt like a competition? Had they both not loved Ferne in their own way?

'I am sorry, Mother,' Louis finally responded, reaching out for Silvie's other shoulder. 'You are right.' He looked again at Ethan. 'We should not be fighting…' He looked away. 'In front of Bernard.'

Ethan adjusted Silvie's chair a little as she eased herself back down into it and then he sat too, deciding not to return to his own seat, but to drop down here, all three of them now on the same side, Bernard at the head of the table.

'Am I permitted to continue now?' Bernard asked, brushing crumbs from his chin having obviously devoured another coconut biscuit while the argument was ensuing.

'Yes,' Silvie said, reaching into her handbag and drawing

out a handkerchief. 'Please, Bernard, tell us what is happening with the conclusion of Ferne's estate.'

Bernard cleared his throat and glanced at the open folio again. 'As you are aware, Silvie, you currently own twenty-five per cent of the hotel chain and Ethan, you also own twenty-five per cent. And, Ferne, she owned the other fifty per cent.'

'Cut to the chase, Bernard,' Louis interrupted. 'We know this. We also know that Ferne's fifty per cent was then to be split, thirty per cent to my mother and twenty per cent to Ethan on her death, therefore making my mother the majority shareholder.'

Bernard seemed to hesitate. 'That was how the will was required to be read from the outset, yes.'

'What does that mean?' Louis asked.

'I am afraid that when Ferne drafted this document with me she foresaw the division that might take place if she was no longer here. She did not want to be unfair to anyone and... as much as she loved you all, she was also uncomfortable with what this change in circumstance might lead to.'

'Again, what does that mean?' Louis asked.

Ethan looked at Silvie. She was holding the handkerchief between her thumb and forefinger, moving the material slowly this way and that. He wasn't sure she was tuned in to what Bernard was saying. He wasn't sure she was connected at all.

'There is a proviso in Ferne's will. A clause that she and I specifically designed to come into being if there was to be any mixed direction over the future of Perfect Paris,' Bernard told them.

A proviso? Were you able to do that in a will? Make a clause of a clause with intricate meanings and consequences if one thing was achieved and not another? Ethan didn't know. He didn't have a will. When Ferne had made hers, back when they had formed the company, she had told him life could be unexpected, that they needed to make sure what they built together went to the right people after they passed. And Ethan had laughed. He was sober now, remembering that he had told his friend he had never had anything and as she was the one who had given him the something he did now have, he was only going to give it back to her. He'd promised to get one done. He hadn't. *Stupide.*

'I'll get straight to the point,' Bernard told them.

'I very much wish you would,' Louis said, still agitated.

Bernard cleared his throat, checking the document in front of him again. 'You knew that you were not allowed to seek a sale of the hotels until twelve months after the death, and that no sale would be able to be finalised until after the completion of probate.' He smiled. 'It was Ferne's wish for there to be a period of grace where things could settle and the hotels could carry on being managed exactly as they had been—'

'Yes, but it is past twelve months now,' Louis reminded.

'And after twelve months... this next clause takes effect.' Bernard began to read from the text. 'After the twelve-month period following my death, this clause shall take the place of clause 8.1.2 in relation to my interest in Perfect Paris. My shares will revert to being held as follows...' Bernard took a breath. 'Twenty per cent to my mother, Silvie Durand, twenty per cent to my best friend, Ethan Bouchard and...'

Bernard raised his eyes from the paperwork and Ethan knew this was the moment the game was going to change…

'Ten per cent to the animal shelter in *Rue Mallard*.'

'What?!' Louis blasted jumping to his feet in a fit of rage. 'That is… insane. What was she thinking?! She has given ten per cent of her share in the hotel to… animals.' Louis pointed at Bernard. 'Animals!' he screamed. 'This is unacceptable! It was a fucking cat that caused her accident and now she wants to give them everything else she had too?!' He glared at Bernard. 'Why didn't you stop her?! She cannot have been of sound mind! Who would make a will leaving shares one way and then create a clause doing something else straight afterwards? It makes no sense!'

'It makes perfect sense.'

These words came from Silvie. She was still rubbing her fingers against the cotton of the handkerchief, her eyes seeking the mid-distance. 'It is perhaps the only thing in all this that *does* make sense.'

'Silvie,' Ethan said, putting a hand on her arm, sensing her distress about this whole situation.

'We all of us knew Ferne. Who she was. What she loved. She loved all of us.'

'But apparently not me,' Louis snapped, pacing his way to the window then stopping, looking out at the street, putting his hands to the back of his head.

'Louis,' Silvie said. 'How can you say that? Ferne left you her apartment!'

'And what good is that to me?'

'That is enough!' Ethan roared.

He got to his feet then, incensed by Louis's behaviour. Louis was talking about Ferne and her estate as if they were all meaningless items on a shopping list, not the hard work of someone he cared about. Someone who had worked hard for everything she was leaving them now. Yes, Ferne had had the best start – a good home, wanting for nothing – but that hadn't made her entitled. She had never been complacent. She'd liked the good things in life, but she had achieved them all through dogged determination and taking risks. She had always taken risks and she had always looked out for the underdog. Or, in the case of her bicycle crash in London, the undercat. So determined to save the life of a furry friend, she hadn't seen the bus coming and had ended up sacrificing her own.

Ethan walked towards Louis now. 'You will not talk about Ferne's decisions on death like that.' He got closer, wanting the man to turn away from the window and face him. 'And we will not fight about this. Because where will that get us?'

Louis turned around then, his eyes filled with tears, his blotchy face looking red again. 'You have won,' he breathed.

'Won?' Ethan queried. 'What have I won?'

'You will have the hotels. We cannot sell them now. Not without your say so or the say so of the animal shelter.' Louis shook his head. 'My crazy, *crazy* little sister.'

Ethan's phone ringing broke into the room and he patted himself down, forgetting where he had placed it. It was Antoine at the Tour Eiffel hotel. He looked to Silvie. 'It is Antoine. It might be a problem with the hotel. I should...'

'Take it,' Silvie told him. She was getting up from her seat now and, as Ethan headed to the door of the boardroom, he vowed to make the call short and get back to her. He turned back for a moment, watching Silvie go towards Louis and begin a conversation.

'Hello, Antoine,' he answered, turning his concentration back to the phone.

'Monsieur Bouchard,' the man replied, sounding out of breath. Ethan's stomach tightened. This *did* sound like an emergency. He hoped there was not a burst water main or, heaven forbid, a fire.

'What is it, Antoine. What has happened?'

'The dog you brought to me,' Antoine said, still breathless. 'The one who was unconscious from medication. The one with the foot that does not work.'

'Yes?'

'Well... it is rampaging... completely out of control.'

Ethan took a second to think about what exactly his concierge had just said. 'What?'

'The dog in the box,' Antoine repeated. 'It is awake and it is causing chaos.'

Thirty-Five

Alsatian Christmas Market, Gare de l'Est, Paris

'Erica still not answering?'

Keeley shook her head, looking at another timed-out call on her phone. They were at the most amazing Christmas market, stalls set up outside the beautiful Paris train station that was something to Instagram all on its own. Deciding they needed to up their gift-buying game while they were in one of the meccas of shopping, Rach had found the market online and they had taken a thirty-minute stroll to get here. And it was living up to all the *Time Out* article expectations so far. Beautiful rounds of Munster and Gerome cheeses were piled high, together with hams, jams and lots of gingerbread. It was a foodie's nirvana with every kind of gastronomic delight you could imagine. They had already sampled wines, liqueurs and *eau-de-vie* – the latter, they were told, was a colourless fruit brandy using double distillation. Whatever it was it was very pleasant on the taste buds. But, experiencing the shopping revelry, Keeley had the urge to FaceTime Erica, particular when they had come across Christmas cookies Keeley knew her friend would have enjoyed seeing even if she couldn't taste them.

'She's probably, you know, resting,' Rach said softly.

'Or she's too ill to answer the phone. Or...' She was already thinking it. *Not there at all.*

'She'll be fine,' Rach said, sounding a little too upbeat. Keeley knew this was because *she* was worrying.

'She won't though, will she?' Keeley swallowed, feeling a little guilty about the bright lights and the warmth beneath the marquee filled with goodies. 'That's the only certainty.'

Suddenly Keeley's phone trilled in her hand and it made Keeley jump, almost knocking into a display of charcuterie items including some rather delicious-looking smoked sausages.

'It's Erica,' Keeley breathed, her heart doing a happy bounce at this revelation.

'Well,' Rach said, 'don't just look at her name on the screen! Answer it!'

Keeley did just that, but turned the screen so it was facing the sausage display in all its glory. She knew her friend would appreciate it.

'Hello?' a voice said down the line. 'Who is this?'

Keeley gulped. It wasn't Erica. It was someone else. Now Keeley was back to being concerned about her friend's health. She quickly switched the screen back around and looked at the caller on screen. It was a nurse.

'Hello?' the woman said again.

'Hello... I'm Keeley... Keeley Andrews. I volunteer there, at the hospice and I'm Erica's friend and...'

'I'm Nurse Walters.'

'And you're answering someone else's phone because?' Rach questioned.

'Rach,' Keeley said, trying desperately to keep composed. 'Nurse Walters, is Erica not… there?' There were so many eventualities that could be associated with the word 'there'. She could hardly breathe. She was seeing the looks on her parents faces when they told her Bea was gone. The first thought that had gone through her mind then was she would never hear Bea's annoying humming along to the radio as she made coffee in the morning…

'No,' Nurse Walters replied, the phone screen wobbling as her face moved in and out of shot. She appeared to be dipping in and out of sight busying herself with something. It was hard to see in what looked like a darkened hospital room.

'Well, where is she?' Keeley was internally bracing herself for bad news. She didn't know this nurse, but her matter-of-fact attitude was obvious. Was she about to brazenly impart tragic information over FaceTime? Surely a carer wouldn't do that…

'We're moving her,' she informed, again no-nonsense. 'To another room.'

'What other room?' Her relief that Erica was still alive would only be absolute if this room was one of the ones further up the corridor rather than down it.

'Room nine,' the nurse said, finally stopping with her business and connecting with Keeley's eyes.

'Room nine,' Keeley mouthed.

'Room nine?' Rach asked, none the wiser.

There was only one reason people got moved into room nine.

'You understand?' the nurse asked.

'I don't bloody understand!' Rach exclaimed.

'It's...' Keeley couldn't bring herself to say the words. 'It's...'

'Listen,' the nurse interrupted. 'She's not too bad today, but she's showing signs that things are taking a turn. We thought the view might be appropriate now.'

Tears were leaking out of Keeley's eyes before she even knew about it. They were streaking her face and dropping onto her red coat, Rach still looking oblivious. She attempted to gather herself together and cleared her throat. 'Could you take the awful painting?'

'What?' Nurse Walters asked.

'The painting. In the room there. The poodles. She's called the big one Henry.'

'I will see what I can do.'

'Please,' Keeley begged. 'And... make sure she has Nick Jonas with her.'

'She can still talk at the moment,' Nurse Walters said, her stern demeanour slackening a little. 'She told me in no uncertain terms that I was not to touch that particular photograph. She actually clung on to it like it was a rock face she was climbing and it was the only handhold.'

Erica was still here in spirit. That was some good news. And the thought of her grabbing onto her favourite Jonas brother and being bolshy was comforting. Keeley opened her mouth to say something else but the nurse beat her to it.

'Maybe try her a little later. Once she's settled into the new surroundings. I'll let her know you've called.'

'It's Keeley,' she said. 'Tell her it was Keeley.'

'I will,' Nurse Walters answered.

'Bye,' Keeley said, ending the call and slipping the phone into her pocket.

Rach put an arm around her shoulder and drew her close. 'I'm guessing room nine isn't good.'

Keeley shook her head. 'No.' She took a breath. 'Room nine is where… people go to die.'

Rach drew her closer still and Keeley took a moment to enjoy the comfort of her friend beside her. And then her phone began to ring again. She drew it out.

'Ethan?' Rach exclaimed, eyes on the screen. 'Who is Ethan, Keeley?'

Thirty-Six

La Barbouquin, Rue Denoyez, Paris

'You cannot still be hungry.'

'It is not for me. It is for Bo-Bo.'

Ethan still could not believe that the dog was behaving as if nothing had happened to it. The call from Antoine had been almost as shocking as the news that the ownership of the hotels was now shared with an animal charity. When Ethan had arrived at the hotel it was to find Antoine and members of his housekeeping staff attempting to corral the frightened rampaging canine in the underground carpark with mops, brooms and large cardboard rolls of Christmas gift wrap. The dog remained terrified until Ethan had fetched Jeanne from the hotel room and straightaway, her presence had calmed the dog and turned the violent yapping into uncertain whining. Then Jeanne had managed to launch herself at Bo-Bo and bearhug him to the ground while deftly snapping on a new lead Antoine had acquired from somewhere.

'Bo-Bo should not even be in here,' Ethan reminded.

He had needed to get out of the Tour Eiffel hotel earlier. He didn't want the questions about the dog or Jeanne from anyone and he definitely didn't want Silvie or Louis to find out and make a big issue about it. Louis's shock over Ferne's change in wishes would not last long. Ethan knew how the man responded to things. It was all immediate knee-jerks followed by simmering in the juices of rage, then finally a coming to a boil with renewed vigour. Just like he had when they were children when he would protest about something Ethan and Ferne wanted to do that he didn't agree with. He had lost a man-at-arms when Pierre had passed away but today's Louis would still try to find a way to push his idea through, maybe attempt to coerce the animal shelter somehow. Ethan now had to ensure that Perfect Paris was worth more to the charity going forward and looking at growth, than it would be as one quick financial fix in a sale. And he already had the beginnings of an idea forming...

'Bo-Bo has been through a trauma,' Jeanne responded, dropping a piece of cake into the dog's mouth. 'It is not every day that you almost die and then come to life again. It is like Jesus being reborn.'

Ethan looked at the still-slightly-grubby-looking girl, the beanie hat low on her head, her clothes baggy and loose on what he knew would be the tiniest of frames.

'Is your girlfriend coming to see Bo-Bo?' Jeanne asked then, sneaking another slice of cake from the whole of one Ethan had bought to share.

'My girlfriend?' he asked.

'She promised to come for the Survivor Party,' Jeanne stated. 'Bo-Bo survived. She would want to celebrate with us, no?'

Celebrate with us? What *was* that sentence? There was no 'us', not with him and this scrap of a child and a dog with more lives than it was supposed to have. Not with Keeley. Was there? He had never really ever been part of an 'us'. He had always kept things casual in his relationships, lightweight. He told himself it was living for the moment, but in reality he suspected it was more a case of not living for an undiscernible future. With life taking unexpected turns every single day, it was better not to hold on too tight to anything.

'She is not my girlfriend,' Ethan answered. 'We have only just met.'

'But you like her,' Jeanne said, mouth moving around the cake. 'I can tell.'

'Well, *I* can tell that you have been eating a lot of room service while you were in the room I gave you. There is ketchup on your cheek and cheese souffle down your jacket.'

'You said that I could "be your guest".' She sniffed. 'You look a bit like that grumpy candle thing in *Beauty and the Beast*.'

'Most guests do not binge-eat five or six main meals or stream as many movies.'

'What *do* they do?' Jeanne queried, letting Bo-Bo nibble crumbs from her cakey fingers. 'Look out at the boring Tour Eiffel while they hold hands and kiss and whatever else.' She clamped her hands around herself then, acting an embrace, and began to make the most hideous wet kissing noises with accompanying moans. '*Je t'aime. Oh, je taime.*'

'Jeanne!' Ethan ordered, taking her hands away from her smooching. 'Stop that.'

The girl laughed and picked up her giant mug of hot

chocolate, almost dunking her face in it. He couldn't keep her at the hotel for very long. But where did she belong?

'Where is home for you, Jeanne?' Ethan spoke his mind.

'Is she coming?' Jeanne asked. 'Your not-girlfriend?'

Classic avoiding the question. Something he had been quite the master at in his time. Sometimes he still was.

'She said she would,' he answered. 'I think she is wanting to see this transformation of Bo-Bo with her own eyes.'

'It is a Christmas miracle,' Jeanne agreed, ruffling the dog's ears.

'Jeanne,' Ethan began. 'You cannot stay at my hotel forever.'

Her eyes grew larger still then and even Bo-Bo seemed to turn his head and show interest in something other than the cake. This dog really had made a miraculous recovery. There was no sign of injury on him at all.

'So, it *is* your hotel! You... are a millionaire!'

Jeanne has spoken rather loudly and now there were definitely other customers trying to tune in to their conversation over the gentle Christmas carols coming from a radio.

'I am not a millionaire,' Ethan insisted. He wasn't. But also he rarely took notice of how much money he *did* have. Because, when you had lived on the street, wealth meant something else entirely. It wasn't a bank balance or stocks and shares. It was lukewarm discarded coffee. It was leftover food from bins. It was not feeling too scared to fall asleep for a few hours in the dead of the night...

'*I* would feel like a millionaire if I could give people a room in my hotel and let them sign up to Disney Plus,' Jeanne told him. Bo-Bo barked as if in agreement.

For a second Ethan felt good about her statement, and then he realised exactly what Jeanne had said. 'How have you signed up to Disney Plus?'

She touched her nose with her finger smearing cake crumbs across it.

'Let me get this straight, *once more*, before we go in,' Rach began, halting Keeley outside the eatery. She blew out a breath. 'We are meeting up with some guy you met on the street outside our hotel, who you also rode on a fairground ride with and ate dinner with, and went for a run with – where a dog was half-killed and then somehow got revived – and this is the whole truth and nothing but the truth.'

Keeley nodded. 'Yes.'

'But I still don't know why you didn't tell me,' Rach moaned. 'Would you have told me if I hadn't seen his name flash up on your phone?'

'Of course I would,' Keeley said straightaway. She would have. Probably. Eventually.

'So, who is he?' Rach continued. 'Because you haven't said all that much apart from listing out a lot of really *really* random things that have happened that I didn't know about.'

Rach was right. Who *was* Ethan? Now Keeley felt a little silly. She didn't know anything about him. Except that she thought he was the best-looking guy she had ever seen and he listened to her, intently, with those eyes resting on her, looking as if he were reading her spirit. She *had* asked him what he did, but earlier Bo-Bo had taken priority.

'I... don't know,' Keeley admitted, putting her hands

into the pockets of her coat and bunching up her shoulders against the cold wind. This area was unlike the surroundings around their hotel. There was graffiti on the shopfronts and bright mosaic planters on the pavement giving off a real grungy bohemian vibe. It was definitely another 'hidden Paris' location to mark on the map if it wasn't on there already.

'Keeley!' Rach exclaimed. 'Random men are usually my thing. You usually tell them your full name, your address, your first pet and that you've got a weakened immune system.'

That was all true. Slightly exaggerated, but all true. Keeley jutted her chin out a little. 'I didn't do any of those things.'

'Wow,' Rach said, looking a little impressed. 'Really?'

'Really,' Keeley replied. 'He doesn't even know I have to look out for symptoms of gout. Now, can we get inside because it's turned freezing out here.'

Thirty-Seven

Keeley wasn't sure what she was even doing here, meeting up with this mysterious man, a child who could be a runaway and a dog who had defied all the usual life/death rules of engagement. She also wasn't sure about Rach being here either. Inviting Rach into this odd situation was giving the whole scenario validation and she wasn't sure how she felt about that. It made her slightly odd friendship with Ethan less throwaway and more what-might-this-be-like-if-we-carry-on-meeting-up. And the reason she was supposed to be in Paris was for Silvie *not* for seeing potential mates. She swallowed as she pushed the door to enter. Was that how she saw Ethan? As a potential mate?

Her insides told her yes, that's exactly how she thought of him, particularly now, looking at him sitting in a snug corner of the unconventional café-cum-bakery-cum-bookstore. There were so many books and things pickled in jars amid the books. It was like being part of a fairy-tale, perhaps *Alice in Wonderland,* where items were calling out 'drink me', 'eat me' or 'read me'. And there was Ethan, dressed in that familiar business suit with waistcoat looking smart, but also somehow beatnik *and* avant-garde. He was completely fitting in with his surroundings though, wiping a serviette over Bo-Bo's chin as the revived dog threatened to dribble on the table.

'Is that him?' Rach asked.

'Yes,' Keeley breathed, knowing she was sounding dangerously fangirl.

'Well,' Rach said, no nonsense, 'you'd better introduce me.'

Keeley watched as Rach went striding off towards a table by the counter. It took a second for her to realise what was happening and she scuttered across the floor, reaching out to grab Rach's jacket.

'Rach! No.' Keeley pulled her to a halt.

'What?' Rach asked. 'You can't have second thoughts about me meeting him now. I'm here and I want to see this guy you've hidden from me.'

'I know,' Keeley said. 'But you're going the wrong way.' She turned Rach around a little, pointing her in the direction of Ethan, Jeanne and Bo-Bo. 'They're there.'

'Oh,' Rach said, her tone faltering a little.

What did that 'oh' represent? Keeley suddenly felt extraordinarily protective over Ethan. 'Who were you expecting?' she asked Rach. 'Patrick Dempsey?' She immediately felt guilt for sniping. And Rach wasn't answering straightaway. Until:

'If he was Patrick Dempsey I'd fight you for him,' Rach answered with a sniff. 'Come on then. Introduce me.'

Before either of them could make a move, Bo-Bo jumped down from the chair he was sitting on and came bounding over, leaping up at Keeley, all long limbs and energy, attempting to lick her face.

'Oh! Oh, no, Bo-Bo, don't lick my hair,' Keeley begged,

trying to get the pet to calm down. 'Rach, help me. He's already had one near-death experience, I don't want him poisoned by the traces of hair products.'

'Bo-Bo, down!'

It was Ethan, coming to their rescue, Jeanne rushing up behind him with the lead and a cross look on her face.

'Don't shout at him,' the girl ordered, snapping on the lead and somehow managing to bring him to heel.

'*Bonjour*,' Ethan said, directing the greeting and those incredible eyes at Keeley.

'*Bonjour*,' Keeley answered, her cheeks heating up like a roaring log fire.

'Bo-Bo's alive,' Jeanne announced, all teeth that looked like they were coated in cake.

'I can see that,' Keeley said, smiling and petting the dog's head. Her touch only made Bo-Bo all excited again and she retracted her hand in a bid to stop the jumping that had to be distracting for those customers trying to have a relaxed time.

'*Bonjour*, I'm Rach,' Rach said, sticking her hand out to Ethan.

Jeanne grabbed hold of it first, shaking hard. 'Jeanne.'

'Jeanne,' Ethan said. 'Take Bo-Bo back to the table and give him some more cake.'

'We might need another cake if these two are going to want to eat,' Jeanne suggested. She grinned again and pulled Bo-Bo back towards the table in the corner.

'Ethan Bouchard,' Ethan said, taking Rach's hand in his and giving it a shake.

'Is that your daughter?' Rach queried.

'No,' Ethan said quickly. 'God, no.'

'Then who is she?'

'She's a friend,' Keeley jumped in. 'The daughter of a friend. Did you say there was cake?' She headed into the deeper warmth of the café, enjoying the eclectic mix of items on the shelves. It really was a case of more was more here.

'It is nice to meet you,' Ethan said to Rach. He swallowed. He got the feeling that this woman did not trust him for some reason. She seemed to be inspecting him like she was trying to work out if he was a real person or a waxwork. He also got the impression that if he stood still long enough and led her to think he was indeed fake, she would then expect him to break out of that mould at any second and relieve her of her handbag.

'I'm not going to lie. It's strange to meet you,' Rach answered.

'Strange?' he enquired. He looked to his table, checking that Keeley had got there and that Jeanne wasn't dipping her fingers into anything she shouldn't be.

'Keeley doesn't meet men on the street and start up a relationship with them that she hides from her best friend.'

'A relationship?' Ethan said, unable to stop a laugh from leaking out. 'We—'

'You had dinner with her. That's a date. You went running with her. That's a date too,' Rach carried on. 'Keeley's very particular about who she lets in. Very particular. Get it?'

'I am… getting it,' Ethan answered. He swallowed. He wasn't getting it. Was he being warned off? Warned off from what? He didn't even know he was getting himself involved with anything like a relationship. Except, somehow, he *did* know. The anxiety he was currently trying to batten down was testament to the fact that it was definitely something.

'You screw her around and I will come for you. Do you get that too?' Rach asked, stepping towards him.

'Got that,' he answered.

Then, all at once, Rach's expression altered and she smiled at him. 'Good.'

'May I get you some coffee? Or something stronger?' Ethan offered.

'Stronger coffee will be fine for me. Keeley, she'll have decaf.'

Thirty-Eight

'You were right about believing in Bo-Bo,' Jeanne said, gleefully rubbing the dog's head as Keeley sipped at her coffee.

There was something not quite right about this coffee. Since Keeley had been in Paris she had really enjoyed the French style of coffee, slurping up as many cups of it as she could. But this... she couldn't quite put her finger on why it wasn't quite as satisfying. It tasted a little like the decaf brand Lizzie thought she was still drinking.

'I know,' Keeley answered. 'And I am very glad I was right.'

'He surprised us all,' Ethan added. 'Pretending to be so sick and then arising like a Jack In the Box I am told.'

'I'm sure it's got fleas,' Rach remarked, pulling up her jumper sleeves and scratching.

'Oh, *non*,' Jeanne said merrily. 'That is most likely to be me.' She swirled her straw in a large chocolate milkshake she was now drinking. 'Parasites can actually help a little with the harsh weather in the winter. Keeping you warm.'

'I hope you're joking,' Rach answered. She inched her seat away and focused on Ethan. 'So, Ethan, what do you do for work?'

'Rach!' Keeley exclaimed. It sounded like her friend had turned into an overprotective parent who was sussing out the worthiness of a partner who wanted to propose.

'He owns a hotel,' Jeanne blurted out.

Keeley took a breath. That was not the occupation she was expecting. And a hotel *owner*. Somehow the two things didn't marry up in her mind. Ethan's slightly devil-may-care attitude and the organisational skill set a hotelier would need to succeed.

'I am a part-owner,' Ethan jumped in. 'A very small stake in the business.'

'But he's a big enough deal to give me a room to live in.'

'Jeanne. I—' Ethan started.

'What hotel?' Rach jumped in. 'How many stars?'

'Rach!' Keeley was starting to regret bringing Rach with her. She had actually adopted a very stern expression whenever Ethan had said *anything* and immediately asked a zillion questions like she was a reporter asking ridiculous things at a government briefing.

'No, it is OK,' Ethan reassured. 'It is a hotel I helped to begin with my best friend. I mainly worked in the background, but now they have… left the business… I want to try and ensure the hotel is… how do people say these days?' He smiled then. 'Being the best version of itself.'

'The hotel we're staying in is nice,' Keeley told him. 'But—'

'You told me the menu is a little too elaborate,' he reminded. 'A lot of small things.' He cleared his throat. 'I am interested for this because… I want to improve *my* hotel.'

'It isn't just the food,' Keeley continued. 'It's the way it breathes.'

'I don't know what you're talking about,' Rach scoffed. 'I like the hotel. Except that Antonie on reception. He could do with changing.'

'You are staying at Perfect Paris?' Jeanne asked.

'We are,' Rach answered.

'The way it breathes?' Ethan queried, looking only at Keeley.

'Look at this place,' Keeley said, indicating the café's surroundings. 'This is exactly what I was talking about before. It's like stepping inside someone's private collection of memories. It's almost living. It's almost breathing.'

'It's full of junk really,' Rach remarked, running a finger over a shelf as if expecting to find lint.

'I like it,' Jeanne said with a snotty sniff. 'It reminds me of my aunt's house. Her place was full of… *disques vinyles*.'

'Vinyl records,' Ethan translated. 'To play on a… gramophone.'

'See!' Keeley said excitedly, raising a little in her chair. 'Already it has given Jeanne a feeling and a memory.' She suddenly realised her excitement and tried to taper it down. She could almost sense Rach's lack of understanding.

'She was a terrible cook,' Jeanne added. 'Once she made me chicken livers with so much garlic no one would sit next to me on the bus. When I used to get the bus.' The girl seemed to immediately break out of her reverie when she realised everyone at the table was looking at her.

'Well,' Rach broke in, 'this would never do at House 2 Home. There you always make homes clutter-free before we show potential buyers around. Minimalism, right?'

Keeley bristled slightly. 'Actually, it's a bit more complex than that.' Rach only saw problems and solutions. As brilliant as her best friend was at her own job, Keeley knew she didn't see the full and complicated picture when it came to 'framing' a lounge area or widening a narrow shower room. Keeley put her fingers around the coffee cup, enjoying the heat against her palm, moulding her skin to the porcelain. Right away she was imagining all the other customers who had held it in their hands. 'It's about creating balance,' Keeley said. 'Like making an instant uplifting mood from the moment the potential buyer sees the property. Starting with the kerb appeal outside, then making a welcoming front porch, a spacious entrance hall that beckons people in... and then continuing a positive flow throughout. It's not about how much or how little there is on the shelves. It's about the *kind* of things that are there and how those items might stir people.'

Ethan was absolutely mesmerised. He was hanging on her every word yet again, thinking how, before now, he must have travelled through life with his eyes closed tight shut. Keeley, she saw things other people missed. Here she was, describing one of his favourite eateries, and he had never really known why he liked it so much. He only knew that whatever crazy combinations it was delivering on the décor and ambience front, it always hit his buttons, pressed at his heart. The way Keeley was talking now was making this place's soul sound like a heady mix of science meets kismet. He ached to feel even more deeply what she was selling with her words. He also wanted to know what it would feel like to hold her in his arms and allow the notion of it all to seep slowly inside of him.

'Bleurgh!' Jeanne blurted out, tongue poking out and eyes lolling into the back of her head. 'It sounds like you are writing a card for Valentine's Day.'

Bo-Bo nudged Ethan's chair and he fell out of the spell, almost spilling coffee into the saucer of his cup.

Rach's phone began buzzing on the table and she swiped it up, getting to her feet and moving away. 'Sorry, I'll have to take this.'

'Do you want some more cake?' Jeanne asked Keeley, proffering the plate.

'No, thank you,' Keeley said.

What Ethan really wanted was for Keeley to keep talking about how décor could change the way people felt, but he sensed the moment had gone. Unless, maybe, he could draw it back again...

'Oh! Look!' Jeanne said, standing up, bashing Bo-Bo on the nose with the corner of her jacket as she reached to the bookcase covered with flyers. Below the shelves were posters unevenly pasted to the wall. 'There's a circus.'

He really did need to get rid of the girl. In the nicest possible way. She had to belong somewhere. Except he suspected he already knew the answer. Most likely, she was an inmate of one of the authority-run homes or worse still an orphanage exactly like the one he had existed in. The thought of sending her back to a place like that didn't sit well at all, but what was the alternative? To know that she was going to be curling up in a cardboard box every night? To know that she would be cold, hungry, frightened to close her eyes or even more scared not to close them? Jeanne offered him a flyer now and he felt obliged to take it.

'*Le Cirque Pinder*,' Ethan read.

'Look at the acrobats on the horses!' Jeanne marvelled, face hanging over the flyer in his hands.

'I didn't know there was a circus in Paris at Christmas time,' Keeley remarked.

'This circus… it is on the outside of the city,' Ethan said.

'You've been to it before?' Keeley asked.

'Yes, once.'

It had been one of the first outings with the Durands. One of the orphanage-approved ones before he had made his own decisions about his future. They had picked him up in their fancy car from outside the wicked building. Pierre was driving, Silvie was dressed in a bright red dress with a fur stole around her shoulders, Louis in dark smart trousers, a shirt collar visible under a jumper with garish cartoon character braces Ethan felt he should have laughed at but was secretly a little envious of. And Ferne, she had been alive with excitement that they were going to the circus and that he was being permitted to go with them. She had been dressed smartly too – a pale pink dress with a matching wrap that should have made her look the age of her mother but had instead, in Ethan's eyes, made her look like an advertisement for everything that was good about life. Ferne had chattered all the way from the centre of the city to the big top at *Boir de Vincennes*. *We are going to see ponies who can dance. We will laugh so hard that our stomachs ache and Louis will burst his braces.* And so it had been. Alongside Ferne and Louis in their fancy attire, Ethan in ragged jeans and a jumper that was too small for him, they had eaten hot dogs with the sweetest caramelised onion atop them and watched acrobats, magicians, clowns and daredevils complete amazing tricks of sheer skill.

'Was it as amazing as it looks?' Jeanne wanted to know, her grubby fingers inching over the photographs of horse, ringmaster and tightrope walker. 'Sometimes, in photographs, things look better than they are.' She sniffed. 'Like all the photographs of Big Macs.'

'It was amazing,' Ethan breathed, being transported right back to that night. He could smell the sawdust, the spent gunpowder from the cannonball man, Ferne's bubble-gum…

'Can we go?' Jeanne asked. 'See the circus?'

Ethan passed the flyer back to her quickly. 'No. Don't be crazy.'

'Why is it crazy?' Jeanne wanted to know.

'Because… I am… not… someone who should be taking you to the circus.'

'Do you have to be a certain type of person to be allowed to go to a circus?' Jeanne asked him. 'A president? Like Macron?' She turned up her nose. 'Here. See. There are only prices for "adults" and "children". No price for "presidents".' She raised her eyes to meet his. 'You are an "adult" and I am a "child". So we can go.' Ethan watched Jeanne turn her attention to Keeley then. 'You want to go to the circus, do you not?'

'I should see what Rach wants,' Keeley said, getting up from her seat. Ethan saw then that Rach was waving at Keeley from the doorway of the restaurant, her phone still placed against her ear.

As soon as she was gone, Jeanne jabbed him in the side with her elbow. 'What are you doing? I am providing you with the perfect date night solution and you are not leaping on the opportunity.'

'What are you talking about?' Ethan asked her.

'The circus! Take us to the circus!' Jeanne ordered. 'I want to see it and I will sit quietly, eating hot dogs and candy floss and sweets and we can get the grumpy guy at the hotel to look after Bo-Bo for the night and you can sit next to Keeley and keep staring at her like you have been doing the whole time since she arrived here.'

Ethan sighed. It seemed Jeanne was as astute as they came. 'It is not a good idea.'

'What part of it is not a good idea?'

'All the parts.'

'You do not like her?'

Bo-Bo let out a bark as if he was questioning too.

'This is not a conversation for you and me to have,' Ethan said, pushing his coffee cup away from him. 'We need to talk about one thing only and that is finding you a permanent place to live.'

'No,' Jeanne answered, lifting a defiant chin. 'We need to talk about why you do not want to tell Keeley that you own the very hotel she is staying in.'

Ethan let out a sigh. Why had he not been upfront with Keeley about owning part of Perfect Paris? And trust Jeanne to pick up on it. He well remembered the skill of expertly learning to be alert to anything that might come in useful to gain traction in any given situation.

'Of course,' Jeanne began, 'I could go along with the pretence that you own an inferior establishment with only two stars if you were to say… let me stay in a room at the place with the five stars and take me to the circus.'

He watched Jeanne tilt her head and hit him with what could only be described as the look of someone in prison, their mind set and determined for a last chance at parole. He knew he was caught.

'You will need to make me some assurances,' Ethan told her firmly.

'What assurances?'

'You must promise me that you are not a missing person.'

'I am not.'

'That you are not being actively sought by the police.'

'Not today.' She grinned. 'Sorry, that was a little street joke I was certain you would appreciate.'

'Jeanne, I am being serious. I do not need trouble.'

'No one is looking for me,' Jeanne said in as serious a tone as Ethan had ever heard from her. 'No one is missing me. No one even cares if I exist or not.'

As those words settled on Ethan, Bo-Bo let out a whine and got up onto his hind legs to lick Jeanne's face. Somehow, even though it sounded every kind of crazy, it seemed he had become a temporary guardian to a girl and her death-defying dog. It almost sounded like a circus act itself.

Thirty-Nine

Tour Eiffel, Paris

It had started to snow again and Jeanne and Bo-Bo were currently running around, both trying to catch snowflakes on their tongues, while Keeley walked next to Ethan on the way back to L'Hotel Paris Parfait. Rach had caught a cab back to the hotel a little earlier after the phone call with, what turned out to be, Roland. From what Keeley had gathered from the garbled telephone conversation she could only hear one side of, there had been another 'incident' at Mr Peterson's place. Rach had rushed out something about 'squirrels' and 'rabies' and 'are you OK to get back without me' and after Keeley had affirmed she was OK to do that, Rach had left.

'I apologise if I was picking your professional brains a little earlier,' Ethan said as they continued to stroll along under the darkening skies. 'It is only because you make the dressing of places sound such an uncomplicated thing, yet I do not find this to be the case.'

'Oh,' Keeley said, smiling. 'I didn't realise you were

exactly picking my brain. If I *had* known I would have set out a quote for my services.'

'You absolutely should do that,' Ethan answered. He bent down and picked up a used takeaway coffee cup, popping it into the bin.

'I was kidding,' Keeley said.

'Why kidding?' Ethan asked. 'I am serious. The things you say, about how people behave and what they look for in a place... the things that make them feel comfortable. These are insights and expertise that should be highly paid for.'

'Maybe,' Keeley said, shrugging.

'Completely,' Ethan answered. '*Most* definitely.'

He sounded so sincere. He was walking extremely close alongside her now and she was enjoying it so much. She looked up and observed the snow settling on his thick, wavy dark hair. Every flake was speckling the colour with white that then quickly melted into silver. He was so outwardly handsome yet also inwardly so in tune with his own spirit. That easy self-confidence simply oozed from him. But there was also an air of reticence too that Keeley found sexy as well as curiously endearing.

'My hotels,' he began again, 'they need change.'

He took a long, slow breath and Keeley couldn't help wondering what was running through his mind now. She almost yearned to see inside.

'For quite some time now everything has been at the mercy of familiarity.' He sighed. 'I know how that sounds but, bear with my thoughts for a moment. In this case, familiarity that was once "comfortable" was bred out of being too scared to implement alterations. It is not the kind of "comfortable" you speak of. It is the type of familiarity that ferments and sets firm a certain way because of a lack of ingenuity, or, maybe, because of fear.' He looked directly at her then, his gaze seeming to draw them both to a halt at the iron base of the Eiffel Tower. 'But I do not want to be afraid of change anymore. And, if I want the business to continue, then change, it must happen.'

'Change is always challenging,' Keeley answered straightaway. 'Because sometimes it's change you want, and other times it's change you're dealt.'

'Agreed.'

'But,' Keeley said, watching his breath dance in the air between them, 'the challenge isn't always the "what". Usually it's more the case of the "what if".'

'I am not sure I follow.'

Keeley smiled. 'The difficulty lies in the procrastination that happens once a decision has either been made or has landed in your lap. Like... what if someone's pearlescent-pink is someone else's raspberry-ripple? Or what if someone's promise of a special offer is more than you paid in the first place? Or what if everyone stops going to hotels forever?'

'Do not joke about that. It was a very bad start to 2020 for everybody.' He cracked a smile.

'The "what ifs" are absolutely vital to decision-making. Obviously no one should make a decision without thinking through the consequences but...'

'But?'

'But "what ifs" are just excuses at the end of the day.' Keeley took a breath and looked up at the tower winding its way into the sky above them, lit up now in festive red. She shuddered. 'I've realised that even more since I've been in Paris. I've learned you shouldn't leave things until it's too late. My sister, she always said she would rather regret the things she *had* done than the things she *hadn't* done.' She looked back to Ethan. 'Bea, she was always so wise. And determined. And brave. Always braver than me.'

Keeley wanted to be braver. She had pledged that to herself only this morning. She so much wanted to take this second chance at life and to hold on tight.

'If I was braver,' Ethan whispered. 'I would kiss you right now.'

There was no hesitation in Keeley's reply. 'If I was braver… I would let you.'

Her heart was hammering in her chest as she gazed up at him and he looked down at her. She almost felt like she could pause here with him and let that moment elongate and expand and grow, maybe as far as eternity. Life suddenly felt completely suspended. The sound of the traffic had faded to a faint hum, the Christmas music from stalls around them became merely a gentle backing track to the melody of her heart. This was her time to be all in, like she had promised Erica. She leaned forward a little, holding her breath and saw Ethan do the same…

A loud whistle broke the hush and Keeley backed up, the bubble burst.

'Ethan!' Jeanne called. 'Can we go ice-skating?' The girl was bouncing up and down, pointing at the tower and mimicking gliding around on the pavement as Bo-Bo ran around in circles weaving in and out of her legs.

Keeley laughed, a little embarrassed, but more disappointed than anything else. Perhaps it simply wasn't meant to be.

Ethan put a finger in the air and moved away. 'Just... please... give me a moment.' He shifted a few steps then turned back to her. 'Wait right there.'

Keeley smiled, watching him moving away from her but also seemingly reluctant to turn his eyes away.

Ethan's heart was pounding in his chest. He was out of control and overcome and... he wanted to kiss Keeley. He wanted to hold her in his arms. He wanted to feel her skin with his fingertips. He wanted to press his lips to hers... and Jeanne's presence was the only thing stopping him.

'Can we go ice-skating?' she asked again, making the expression he assumed he was supposed to be rapt by the cuteness of. Ethan almost lost his footing as Bo-Bo jumped around him as if he might be meat on a stick the dog wanted to devour.

Taking his wallet from his pocket, he produced a twenty-Euro note. 'If I trust you with this will you go to find us some food? Or will you run into the night and spend it on alcohol you are too young to be drinking?'

'I do not like alcohol. It tastes like piss,' Jeanne answered, making a gagging noise.

'Pizza?' Ethan suggested.

'You have pizza at the hotel.' She sniffed. 'But... it comes with enough rocket on it to feed a family of rabbits.'

'We are not going to the hotel.'

'We are not?'

He saw her small face crumble then, the façade of bullishness dropping away and the reflection of the real vulnerable child appearing for only a moment before her petite features were once more poker-straight. Did she really think he was already turning her back out into the street?

'You really cannot live in my hotel,' Ethan told her. 'But you can have my spare room. Just... until we think of something else.'

With that said, Jeanne snatched the note from between his fingers and was off, sprinting fast, with Bo-Bo in hot pursuit.

Ethan turned around quickly. He was suddenly scared that Keeley would no longer be there and that all they had shared in that brief moment where life had felt so incredibly heightened would be unable to be recreated. But... there she was, still standing in exactly the same spot. Her hair was gently tickling around her jawline as flakes of snow danced down from the sky. He didn't want to wait a second longer. He *couldn't* wait a second longer. But was this right? Was it OK to feel this way about someone he had only really just met? By pure coincidence. Or was the time for all thinking overrated? *What? Or What if?* Maybe *everything* was *meant* to be not regretting things you should have taken a chance on...

He strode forward then, wanting to close the distance between them as rapidly as he could. He only stopped when he was right in front of her, so close he could feel her delicate breath on his face. She was so beautiful. She was so intelligent. So *real*. He wanted to palm her cheek, feel the weight of her face in his hand...

'I am feeling braver now,' Keeley whispered.

Ethan watched her pupils dilate as the connection of their gaze deepened further still and slowly, but deliberately, he made his move. '*Moi aussi*.'

He touched her hair with his fingers and gently edged

her face towards his. It was, he hoped, subtle, yet left no room for misunderstanding. He wanted this connection, this moment with her, possibly more than he had wanted any other connection he had had in his life before. And then, finally, Keeley's lips met his, *her* intentions completely transparent and he found himself unable to hold back any longer as the depth of his passion took over. This was a kiss he had never known existed. This was every romantic movie scene he had ever watched… and all the ones he had yet to see. He wanted to live this kiss forever.

It was Keeley who broke the connection first, their mouths finally parting. But she kept her body unmoved, it was there so comfortably rested next to his.

'I've… never done that before,' Keeley breathed.

Her eyes were crisp and alive, her lips a little fuller from their kiss perhaps… and he knew exactly how she felt because it was mirrored in him. He went to make a reply but she continued. 'I mean… I have obviously done something *like* that before but—'

'It was not the same,' Ethan interrupted. 'This… was…' He was caught between saying 'different' or 'special'.

'It felt comfortable,' Keeley told him.

The biggest smile erupted on his lips as his heart took flight. Anyone listening in to their conversation, a voyeur to their kiss, might have been mistaken in thinking the moment had just been described as the least exciting, undervalued and boring meeting of mouths that had ever existed. But Ethan knew what 'comfortable' meant to her and his insides were dancing.

'Keeley,' he addressed her. 'Would you like to go to the circus?'

Forty

L'Hotel Paris Parfait, Tour Eiffel, Paris

'They've moved me to the death room.'

Keeley swallowed back the tears as she looked into Erica's eyes on the screen of the FaceTime call. Her friend wasn't looking well at all. Her breathing was slow and laboured and each edged-out word was wrapped in a throaty rasp that told a story all on its own.

Keeley was sitting on one of the little iron chairs on the suite's balcony, wrapped up in her coat, looking out at the Eiffel Tower and feeling a whole mix of emotions. When she'd arrived back at the suite, Rach had been still fully dressed, some bottles from the minibar opened and empty on the nightstand, eyes closed and snoring, lying on top of her bed covers. As much as Keeley wanted to share what had happened with Ethan *and* find out what Roland's call had been about, she also didn't want to disturb her friend. So instead she had decided to step out into the moonlight and try Erica again. The first few moments of their call had been Keeley showing the Parisian cityscape.

She hoped it had been a feast for her friend's senses. Twinkling festive lights strung over rooftops and awnings of brasseries, the sound of mopeds and church bells, the buzz of the metropolis so unlike the quiet of the hospice. But now Erica, at least, seemed ready to talk reality.

'There's no such thing as the death room,' Keeley said quickly.

'Room nine,' Erica answered. 'Everyone knows the death room is room nine.'

'Well, that's not strictly true,' Keeley countered. 'I think, if you compare statistics, you will find that many people have also died in other rooms.' What was she saying? They *all* died. It was a hospice. There was no hope for anyone. The medical team's job was to help make their patients' final journeys as comfortable as possible. Erica had never been under any misconception that she was going to get better. There *had* been hope to begin with, when Erica had started her second round of treatment and had, finally, started to let Keeley in a little. Erica wasn't the type of person to give her heart easily but once you had it, you had it for always.

'Keeley... I know I'm dying,' Erica said bluntly. '*You* know I'm dying. You know I know I'm dying. We both need to face up to the fact it's happening soon.'

'Not soon,' Keeley said. She simply couldn't bring herself to verbalise it. 'Just... someday.'

'Listen,' Erica began. 'I have Henry here with me. And I... named the other poodle in the picture, Sandra.'

'Sandra?'

'What's wrong with the name Sandra?'

'Nothing. Nothing at all. Does the name mean something

special?' She didn't recall Erica mentioning a 'Sandra' being dear to her in all the time they'd known each other.

'It's the name of that Nurse Walters,' Erica responded tartly. 'She's rough with the bath sponge. I did it to spite her.'

'O-K.'

'And I'm holding on to Nick with my left hand by the way.' Erica took a deep breath. 'And I don't care how dirty that sentence sounds.'

Keeley smiled.

'So... why are you calling me now?' Erica asked. 'The view is something else, but was it just to check I wasn't dead already?'

'No,' Keeley said. 'Of course it wasn't that.'

'Then it's... the hot dude,' Erica said, stifling a cough. 'Is it the hot dude?'

Immediately, despite the freezing temperatures, Keeley's cheeks took on a glow and it was as if she was back down on the street below, reliving every heart-thumping second of that kiss with Ethan. It made her shiver all over again. 'It's the hot dude,' she found herself whispering.

'Oh, man!' Erica exclaimed, voice even more breathy. 'You need to start talking.'

How did she even start to explain it? The memory of his mouth on hers wasn't something she could easily begin to define, even to herself. And perhaps it was better to keep the depth of feeling internal and muted. Because being quite this emotional towards someone she had only just met might seem strange to Erica. It was strange to Keeley. Or perhaps 'unexpected' was a better word.

'We spent some time together,' Keeley said, knowing

she was already smiling. 'We bonded over a half-dead dog and—'

'What did you say?' Erica exclaimed. 'A dead dog?!'

'He's fine now. More than fine. He was... stunned somehow... for a few hours... anyway, we met up again and I introduced him to Rach and we... kissed.'

'Hallelujah! There is a God!' Erica shouted. 'He might not have been able to spare *this* sister but he's looking out for you.'

Keeley rested into her coat a little, letting the collar raise up and cosset her like a sleeping bag as she sat back in the chair. 'It was...' Her lips were about to spill the truly insane sentiment about her connection with Ethan whether she was apparently ready for it or not.

'It was what?' Erica asked. 'Don't leave me hanging.' She coughed. 'Not when I'm in the death room here.'

'It was...' The only word Keeley could think of using was the word she'd told Ethan. The word he had understood the meaning of, but Erica definitely wouldn't. 'It was... comfortable.'

'It was what now?' Erica asked, bringing her face really close to the screen.

Keeley could see every blood vessel in her eyes, but she could also see that her gorgeous, flawless complexion had somehow returned even at this lowest point in her health. Keeley had always been a little envious of her friend's perfect skin. She smiled at Erica's confusion.

'It's kind of a thing we have together.' They had a 'thing' with each other. How bizarre was that? But the thought of sharing something like that with this enigmatic man warmed her all the way through. It was almost like somehow they had known each other all along…

'I need to see a photo,' Erica said, her voice a little weaker.

'I will get you a photo,' Keeley promised as Erica's eyes began to close. 'But, Erica, you have to promise me one thing.'

'Sshh… I want to have sweet dreams of Nick Jonas.'

'Promise me you'll hold on a bit longer,' Keeley begged. She knew it wasn't fair to ask this and immediately hated herself for it. She was thinking selfishly, about her fear of losing her friend, not about Erica's pain and her fight.

'Get me a photo,' Erica breathed, the phone screen dropping a little as her grip loosened. 'I want to see who's making you smile that way before I kick the bucket.'

Erica's eyes closed shut, her breathing slowing even more and Keeley knew she had fallen asleep. She ended the call and looked out over the view again. Had more than Silvie Durand brought her here? Could it be that actually the universe had a plan?

Forty-One

L'Hotel Paris Parfait, Opera District, Paris

It was morning and Paris was coming alive. From the inside of the boardroom Ethan could see the light snowfall that had swept over the streets like the pearlescent train of a bridal gown. Last night he had worked on a new menu for the hotels, in between catering for either Jeanne or Bo-Bo. Jeanne needed toiletries. Bo-Bo needed the toilet. Jeanne wanted to sleep with the light on. Bo-Bo wanted to sleep with Ethan. Surprisingly, despite the interruptions, when he had eventually managed to shut his eyes, it had been the best sleep he had had in some time. He had left for the hotel early, leaving croissants for Jeanne, dog biscuits for Bo-Bo and the instruction that the girl was not to sign up for any premium television services in his absence.

Now, Ethan watched Noel's lip curl as his assistant read the email on his tablet out loud.

'*Daube de boeuf Provençale.*' Noel cast his eyes upwards. 'Beef stew.'

'Yes,' Ethan answered, nodding. 'Served with thick fresh bread.'

'*Cassoulet*.' Noel said the word with a scoff. 'With mutton and sausage. Excuse my candour, Monsieur Bouchard, but all these new dishes for the menu, the cuts of meat you are suggesting... they are...'

'Yes?' Ethan knew what was coming but he wanted to hear his assistant say the words aloud. He was relishing the feeling that would come when the word he was expecting floated into the boardroom atmosphere.

'Food of the... *poor*,' Noel stated.

Ethan grabbed his own chest in a theatrical play, leaning back in his chair and gasping for air. 'Oh... oh... I cannot seem to catch my breath.'

Noel shook his head and put down his tablet. 'Monsieur Bouchard, we are a well-respected establishment. We have five stars. Customers expect a certain level of excellence.'

'I realise,' Ethan told him. 'And we are going to provide them all with excellent traditional French dishes with a layer of a memory from their childhood. Think of it,' he continued. 'All those heart-warming times that their grandmother made them a rich hearty meal and shared stories from long ago.' He smiled at Noel, getting up from the table and elongating his stride across the breadth of the window, making the pigeons lined up on the chimney pots outside suddenly take flight.

'We do not have that style here currently,' Noel reminded. 'Remember the science behind the menu that Miss Durand had created.'

'Delicate and refined,' Ethan stated, remembering the

watchwords that had formed the basis of Ferne's vision for the hotel's food. 'A whisper on the taste buds.'

'The very opposite of *this*,' Noel said, pointing to the tablet he had discarded on the table.

'Yes!' Ethan said, widening his arms. 'The exact opposite is *exactly* right! It is also the exact opposite of most five-star establishments in Paris if my research is correct.' This wasn't about stamping over what Ferne had created. What Ferne had designed for the brand had been right *at the time*. This change was what Ethan thought was needed now. Whether he was proved right or not would be determined by the customers' response to it. But first he had to make it fly with Silvie and, he supposed, Louis.

'This is not the food for a five-star customer,' Noel told him.

'Says who?' Ethan asked. 'And, Noel, tell me, what exactly *is* a five-star customer?'

'A customer who will be able to pay our room rates,' Noel answered.

'Once? Or every day?' Ethan swung back to the table, placing flat palms against the wood.

'What?' Noel asked, not seeming to understand.

'Noel, I ask you, who are we to judge our clientele by the amount of money they may or may not have in the bank… or by what car they drive, or the clothes they wear?' He was striding out again now, every step reinforcing his belief that this was the road he wanted the Perfect Paris hotels to go down. 'Our customers come to us from all walks of life. Some come here, they stay a few nights and hand over their platinum credit cards. Others they pay with a voucher they have received for a gift.' He stopped striding and looked directly at Noel again. 'But all of them. They have one thing in common.'

'They all like a high thread count for their sheets?' Noel asked in a tongue-in-cheek manner that Ethan would have thought was bordering on insolent if he hadn't known the man was responding with the hotel's continued future uppermost in his thoughts.

'They all seek *comfort* before opulence,' Ethan said with authority.

'I am not sure—'

Ethan cut him off. 'I have checked the customer feedback for the last twelve months. Every positive comment was about how the hotel made people feel. "The mattress gave me a sleep like no other", or "the views from the room were incredible". Another one was "Noel understood exactly what type of restaurant I was looking for and gave us the family meal of our holiday",' Ethan informed. 'No one mentioned the food in our restaurants being a whisper on their taste buds. I do not know why we have not looked deeper into this before.'

'With respect, Monsieur Bouchard, for the past twelve months I do not think you have been in a place to look deeper into anything.'

Ethan mused on his point only briefly. His assistant was right, of course, but he was ready *now* and it was going to be his aim to strike while the iron was hot, while Louis was still mourning the loss of his chance to immediately sell the hotels out from under him. This *was* about Ferne. He would ensure her foundations survived and that they continued to build and grew even stronger.

'Well, I am in the right place now,' Ethan responded. 'And we are starting with the food of poor people.'

'At Christmas time customers are looking for fine dining,' Noel said, shaking his head and drawing the tablet closer to him again, taking another look at the menu.

'No,' Ethan disagreed, moving around the table to stand next to his assistant. 'At Christmas time customers are looking for full stomachs in a warm and inviting atmosphere.' Ethan sniffed. 'Can we get rid of the ice rink? I do not know what I was thinking. Instead, maybe we can have… Santa or… perhaps… animals!' He held a finger in the air. 'A turkey… and rabbits. Some things that children can stroke.'

'Stroking?' Noel said with a tut. 'As you should be aware, the hotel currently operates a "no touching" policy in all its communal areas with regard to artwork, ornaments and for the seasonal period, all the Christmas decorations.'

'I realise there was a real need for this earlier in the year but… I want it lifted,' Ethan said with a deliberate nod. 'The time for feeling things from a distance in Perfect Paris is over.' He made sure Noel was in no doubt that he was serious about this decision. 'And the menu… I would like it rolled out as soon as Chef has given the go ahead.'

It now looked like Noel was going to faint.

Forty-Two

Le Marche aux Puces, Saint Ouen, Paris

'What do we have to bring tonight?' Rach asked, leading the way through the famous flea market, her arms already full of shopping bags from the many boutiques they had stopped at on the way. This market was another location on Ethan's map. It was a labyrinth of hodgepodge stalls selling everything from vintage furniture – antique mirrors all highlighted with festive fayre – to books, shoes and vinyl records some in better condition than others. To Keeley it felt like it was a treasure trove and she was definitely going to be looking for Christmas gifts for her parents here. It seemed like the perfect place to discover something truly unique.

'Silvie said not to bring anything,' Keeley answered, pausing by a stall that sold jewellery. There were thick silver rings alongside the most delicate bands of gold with stones running around the circumference of them, then brooches encrusted with rubies and topaz. Something like that would be ideal for her mum. Something to wear and show off at book club or to use as a weapon in Krav Maga. 'But I thought we would take some wine and maybe some flowers. What do you think?'

'I think perhaps I should have answered Louis's last text message about dinner.'

'He texted you again?' Keeley asked, looking away from the jewels to her friend.

'It was the one text. I didn't reply. But he didn't follow it up with a second one. And he could have called,' Rach said. She picked up a silver ring and blew some dust from it.

'Did you want him to call?' Keeley asked. 'You did say you thought he was cute.'

'But I obviously didn't think he was cute enough to answer his text.' She put the ring back down. 'I don't know. I think maybe I should start waiting.'

'Waiting?' Keeley wasn't quite sure what Rach meant. Rach never really waited for anything in her life. She was a go-at-life-at-two-hundred-miles-an-hour kind of person. She hated even waiting for the time it took the kettle to boil for her coffee.

'For the person who looks me in the eye and doesn't care I'm wearing pyjamas,' Rach elaborated.

'Rach,' Keeley said. 'Are you really *really* worried about that?'

'Not worried about it,' Rach said quickly. 'Just, you know, thinking maybe I might have sometimes... underrated myself in the dating arena and, you know, possibly made poor choices in case, maybe, the choices dried up completely.'

'Oh, Rach,' Keeley said, gathering her friend in her arms and hugging her close.

'Don't make me emotional,' Rach ordered. 'I put *special* mascara on today.'

Keeley let her go but kept her eyes direct and focused. 'Your man choices are not going to dry up if you say no once in a while. Saying yes should be about how *you* feel, not anyone else. And it shouldn't be because you're worrying that the next invitation might be a little while coming.' She took Rach's hand and squeezed. 'You're talking to Kidney Girl, remember, the woman who can't usually say anything to a member of the opposite sex without adding in her transplant life story.'

'Or a terrible joke,' Rach said, a smile appearing. 'Do you remember that time at the curry house with the cute waiter? You said to him "how do you ask a kidney doctor if they are there?"'

Keeley cringed as she remembered the punchline. 'Are u-rine?'

'He didn't know where to put his face let alone his poppadoms.'

'See,' Keeley said. 'Nothing for you to worry about not responding to a text if you don't want a date.'

'Except Louis will be there tonight. At Silvie's house. *His* home.'

'And it will be fine,' Keeley reassured. 'I promise.' She gave Rach's hand another squeeze. Except Keeley herself was already nervous about tonight. The closer the evening got, the more the anxiety started to take hold and she was left second-guessing every one of her emotions. Yes, Silvie was nice, in fact she was more than nice, and Keeley had very much enjoyed their lunch, feeling that she had got to know Ferne a little bit better. But the café near the

Louvre was very different to going to Silvie's home. The house that had once been Ferne's home. It was bound to be chock full of memories, a little like her home in Kensington that still held little touches of Bea in every corner. The white ring on the coffee table from Bea's hot chocolate without a coaster when she was fourteen. A hairband down the side of the sofa. A charcoal drawing of the Bristol suspension bridge that was the cornerstone to Bea's GCSE art coursework…

'We could take prosecco,' Keeley began. 'You can't go wrong with prosecco, can you?'

'Are you mad?' Rach exclaimed. 'Of course you can go wrong with prosecco… by it simply not being champagne!'

'OK, change of topic. Tell me about the squirrels,' Keeley said as they moved to another section of the absolutely huge market. Here there were maritime items, ships wheels and maps, anchors – yes, really – and old telescopes. Her dad would have got himself lost in here for days.

'Tell *me* what time you got back last night, because you avoided saying anything at breakfast except that you thought the bacon was a lot thicker than it was the day before and you probably shouldn't have had three slices,' Rach countered.

'Squirrels,' Keeley said, halting by a canister of umbrellas.

'Ethan,' Rach replied.

Keeley blushed fiercely despite doing everything she could to try and stop it happening. 'Oh God, Rach.'

'What?' Rach exclaimed. 'What happened?'

Keeley's insides were squirming now as the bubbling passionate fusion threatened to come pouring out. She had to calm.

'We kissed,' Keeley breathed, not doing the best job at containing her emotion at all. 'We kissed and it was... well...it was the best kiss I've ever experienced.' And it really had felt like an 'experience'. A moment to be thought about continually until it hopefully happened again and led to more. Was that what she wanted? More from this man she barely knew?

'Oh my God,' Rach exclaimed, reaching out and seeming to steady herself on one of the umbrellas, the one with a handle carved like a crocodile. 'You've... never looked like that before. Not with anyone.'

How *did* she look? Keeley turned sideways and caught a view of her reflection in an Art-Deco mirror. Her hair colour had finally settled and was no longer leaking onto everything and the tint in it really suited her skin tone. But it was her eyes where the real difference lay. Even she could see it herself. *Hope. Excitement. Life.* It was all there now. All the givens she had basically given up on.

'Jesus,' Rach whispered. 'You're in *love*.'

'No,' Keeley answered quickly, turning away from the mirror and taking hold of her friend's arm to move them both forward, Rach's bags brushing against her shins. 'It can't be that. Because I've known him five minutes. And I've kissed him once.'

'And you know that's exactly what happens in the movies.'

'But we're not in a movie, are we? And he lives in France and I live in England.'

'Details.'

'Pretty significant details.'

'We got here in a couple of hours.' Rach gasped. 'Or you

could go completely retro and be pen pals like in the olden days. My mum used to get French letters.'

'I'm not in love with him.' But even as she said the words, Keeley knew, whether it was love or not, it was definitely something more than a passing infatuation. It was the way they seemed so in tune with each other's thinking. How things always flowed so easily since their very first meeting. It was how she felt when he held her hand… 'Squirrels,' she blurted out. 'Tell me about the squirrels now.'

'You have to promise not to be mad.'

Keeley dodged around the huge wheel of a Pennyfarthing bicycle and led the way towards a stall selling a selection of artwork, dust still on the frames. 'Why would I be mad about squirrels?' And then realisation seemed to sink in. This story could only be about Mr Peterson's property.

'Oh, God. What's the demented taxidermist done now?' Keeley asked.

'Promise you won't be mad,' Rach said for the second time. Now Keeley was a little bit concerned.

'Tell me, Rach.' Her best friend made big eyes that seemed to say she wasn't going to crack unless the declaration was made. 'I promise I won't get mad.'

'OK,' Rach breathed. 'Your mum has been working on the Peterson place since we left. That's why Roland signed our holiday forms without too much of a grumble. I was sworn to secrecy and… please don't hate me.'

Keeley watched Rach close up her eyes and grimace as if in real fear of her reaction to this news. This was typical Lizzie. Even when Keeley wasn't in London, wasn't there doing her job at House 2 Home, her mum was in the background, managing life for her.

'You should have told me,' Keeley said, sighing.

'I know,' Rach said, opening her eyes. 'But I knew it would unsettle you and you were already dealing with coming here and everything so…'

'So, what has that got to do with squirrels?'

Rach sighed, repositioning her fingers around the handles of her bags of goodies. 'A trio of them burst out of Mr Peterson's airing cupboard, got caught in Lizzie's hair and one of them bit her. She had to go to the hospital for a tetanus shot and some Steri-Strips.'

Keeley was already reaching into her bag for her phone. No matter how irritating her mum was with her need to protect her, she didn't want to see her in harm's way.

'She ordered me not to tell you,' Rach said quickly. 'She said, if I did, she'd tell her book club friends not to buy from Price Squash.' She blinked. 'Adie has six children, Keeley. And they all eat like Eddie Hall doing a food challenge.'

'Go and find us some coffees,' Keeley ordered. 'I'm phoning her right now.'

Forty-Three

'What are we here for? Bo-Bo is bored.'

Jeanne said the sentence through a mouthful of the biggest brioche Ethan had ever seen. A man had been selling them near the *Porte de Clignacourt* metro station. They had alighted there and Jeanne's lips had started to quiver at the sight of them. Her small but strong hands had tugged at his sleeve like he had been completely oblivious to the stand and then she had given him those dewy, slightly piteous eyes she was obviously well practised at pulling out when necessary.

'We are here to find inspiration.' Ethan breathed in, drawing the cold air into his lungs like he was determined to also suck inside every nuance of the ambience of the enormous, sprawling flea market. It did always feel to him that it was a living, breathing beast, each stall owning its own pulsing heart of speciality.

'You are in charge of props for a period drama series on TF1?' Jeanne asked, pulling Bo-Bo away from a toy crib where he was sniffing around a quite disturbing-looking old-fashioned doll with half her porcelain face missing.

'It is for the hotel,' Ethan said, stepping towards a large dresser housing many oddly shaped lamps.

'Which one?' Jeanne asked, chocolate now smeared over her top lip. 'Because I now know there are five hotels.'

'All of them,' Ethan told her. 'But I will start with Tour Eiffel.'

'But,' Jeanne began, still munching, 'according to your website, that is not your "flagship" hotel.'

The kid was smart. Always smarter than he gave her credit for. And she had most obviously been making full use of his Wi-Fi today.

'Is it because Keeley is staying at that one?' Jeanne asked. 'And you want to impress her? Even though she does not know that you own it?' She screwed her petite features up, wrinkling her nose. 'I think there is a flaw in your plan to excite her.'

Ethan looked at the girl then, expertly tightening the lead on her dog while pushing the giant brioche into her mouth. 'You think everyone is impressed by money?'

She shrugged, the neck of her too big T-shirt almost swallowing her head. 'Are they not?'

'Does money impress *you*, Jeanne?' Ethan asked. He wanted to know the answer, because whatever she said would give him an even deeper insight into her mind. This child from the street with all her brashness was, in his opinion, as vulnerable as she was intelligent. Jeanne seemed to quieten a little then, chewing but also looking like she was wholeheartedly considering her reply.

'Money buys you opportunity,' Jeanne said finally.

'How so?' Ethan asked her. 'Because I believe most people would say that perseverance and determination really make for opportunity.'

'I show up in the reception of one of your fancy hotels and

the first thing the evil man behind the counter wants to do is call me a thief. Just because of the clothes I am wearing.'

Ethan couldn't deny that was the case. He had spoken to Antoine about being judgemental on a few other occasions. 'Antoine likes neat and tidy. He has very high, possibly unreachable standards. He is too quick to react to those.'

'How different would his reaction have been if I had say... styled my hair pretty, put on some make-up, a new dress perhaps, cleaned underneath my fingernails, worn shoes with a heel and... arrived to apply for the job of a chambermaid?' She nodded with satisfaction at her answer. 'I would need at least *some* money for the dress and the shoes and the make-up, for me just to be taken seriously and be given the opportunity.' She nodded. 'Money equals opportunity.'

'You do not think you can be yourself and find success in life?' Ethan asked.

'I do not think it,' Jeanne carried on. 'I know it.'

'I cannot believe that is true.'

'Hello! I live on the street and have to beg for food to survive. No one wants me to be myself. Nobody wants me to exist at all.' She gave a piece of brioche to Bo-Bo. 'People turn away from people like me. They think if they cannot see me then I do not exist. Not all of them are bad people. They just do not want people like me on their conscience.'

Her words rained down on him. He had thought the same thing over and over so many times before. His heart ached for her but it also ached for himself too. He had been so lucky. He'd had Ferne back then. Her kindness, their friendship, the bond they shared that never seem to acknowledge their difference in class. It had been everything.

'Listen to me, Jeanne,' Ethan said, putting his hands on her shoulders. 'Never apologise for being here, understand?'

'Did you?' Jeanne asked him, swallowing her mouthful of food.

'Did I what?' Ethan breathed.

'Ever apologise for being here.'

Sucked back into a reverie he would rather forget, Ethan recalled the mantra he and the other children had been made to chant at the orphanage. *Be seen not heard. Speak only when spoken to. Respect elders. Think not of yourself.* It had been drummed into every child until it was the very first thing Ethan thought about on waking and the last thing that drifted through his mind as he prepared to go to sleep. It had broken him. Eventually, he had decided to leave the roof over his head for a life on the street where nothing was guaranteed, not even his next meal… It had scarred him, there was no doubt about that. But he had moved beyond it. With help from Ferne. One person's belief in him had made all the difference.

'I know you are like me,' Jeanne continued as Bo-Bo began to sniff around a stall offering crafts made from old off-cuts of wood. 'Or you were like me, in some way.' She bit into more brioche. 'People like us know each other. You watched me in the hotel, trying to get the chocolates from the Christmas tree. Perhaps I was not subtle enough, but really I think you noticed me because you had been in the same situation yourself once.'

He put an arm around Jeanne's shoulder, steering her out of the path of a man on a bicycle. Bo-Bo popped his snout out from under the stall. 'I was like you,' Ethan admitted as they continued to walk. 'I never knew who my parents were. I was left outside an orphanage when I was a baby.' He sucked in a breath. 'I was there for ten years until I could not stand it anymore.'

'Where did you go?' Jeanne asked.

'Well,' Ethan began, moving towards a glazed 'shopfront' with armchairs, dining chairs and all manner of seating outside it. Some of the chairs would not have looked out of place in a banquet hall, others seemed like they once belonged in a school. 'When I was eight, I snuck out of the orphanage one day and I met a girl...'

'Oh, please,' Jeanne stated. 'Not a romantic story. I cannot stand it. It is enough with the making love hearts with your eyes at Keeley.'

'No,' Ethan said. 'It is not a romantic tale. It is a tale of friendship and... family.' He thought about Ferne, but also he thought about Silvie and Pierre and... Louis. They had been the only family he had known and despite still feeling he was a little bit of a cuckoo, they had been there for him. 'I had two years of visiting a very nice home in the suburbs and being taken on outings you could only dream of.' He smiled at Jeanne. 'With food you definitely dream of.' He plumped down into one of the armchairs and spread his fingers over the fabric on the arms. It was rich, sumptuous green velvet but with small threadbare patches that seemed only to enhance its appeal. 'But after each visit, I would go back to that freezing, soulless place where the people who were supposed to care and look after made it clear I was no better than something that was stuck to the sole of their shoe, and I would long to be anywhere but there.'

'You lived on the street?' Jeanne asked, sitting down in the chair opposite, Bo-Bo deftly leaping up onto her lap.

'I lived on the street,' Ethan answered with a nod. 'I spent weekends with the family that took me out for visits, but I never moved in under their roof.' Perhaps by refusing that offer – because it *had* been offered – he had made *himself* the cuckoo. That self-appointed status he was always using as a default position. 'Perhaps I should have.'

He hadn't realised he had said those last words out loud until Bo-Bo let out a bark and brought him back to the now. Jeanne hadn't said anything and he wanted to get across to her the point he was trying to make in all this. 'I see your independent nature, Jeanne. I know you think you are tough and you can take on the world, but do not be afraid to take *help* from the world too.' He swallowed, watching her features soften and her fingers squash the food in her hands. 'I cannot be anything formal to you. My life, it is still as up in the air as it has always been. I do not have myself together.'

'You own five hotels,' Jeanne stated.

'I *part*-own five hotels and, believe me, that job gets more difficult by the day.'

'You said I could stay… for a bit,' Jeanne reminded him, her tone cutting him to the quick. 'You said we could go to the circus.'

'I did,' he answered. 'You can, and we are, tomorrow evening.'

'Then what is this "I cannot be anything formal to you" speech about if it is not to get rid of me already?'

Ethan sighed, his body resting so comfortably in the old part-worn chair. It was like it was a piece of his own furniture, its cushions moulding to the shape of his body. 'I would like to help you, Jeanne. Like someone once helped me. But we do not have to become a deep part of each other's lives.' He was not ready to be someone's role model or moral guidance. 'I will be your... benefactor. You can stay at my apartment whenever you like, there will be food in the fridge, but we will not always sit around the table together sharing anecdotes of our days.'

'That would be the worst,' Jeanne agreed with a nod.

'And you should go to school,' Ethan told her.

'What?!'

'That is my condition of you sharing my space.'

'But what about Bo-Bo. There will be no one to look after him all day,' Jeanne started to protest, wriggling with the dog still on her lap. 'And the school will want many forms filled in with who I am and where I come from and who is my guardian and—'

'Jeanne, do you think this will be my first time making up a story to suit my purposes?'

'What will I learn at school that I will not learn from the streets... or working at a hotel? There are five of them for you to choose from. I do not mind starting from the very bottom. I can clean.'

Ethan studied her, chocolate somehow now all over her face. She was so young. He had no idea how young and he wasn't sure the girl really knew herself...

'We will do a trial,' Ethan told her. 'You will share my apartment between now and the end of the Christmas holidays and, if the arrangement is acceptable, you will commit to school.'

He watched her mulling over the suggestion. He could almost see her brain working things over. The pluses, the minuses, if this attachment to his offer was really going to be what she wanted. Of course she could flee into the night at any time, or she could stay for the duration of the festive break and then flee into the night and renege on the whole idea. But, for now, he was guessing Jeanne had nothing to lose and he would at least know she was safe for a while. One less kid on the pavements of Paris with no one looking out for them…

'Bo-Bo sleeps with me,' Jeanne said suddenly. '*In the bed*. Not on the floor or on a fancy dog bed he will hate. With me.'

Ethan shrugged. 'He was meant to sleep with you last night, but he ended up in my bed. And he snores.'

'You have terrible taste in jam,' Jeanne countered. 'Strawberry is the best. Not this horrible bitter orange in the cupboard.'

Ethan smiled. He didn't even know he had orange jam. 'So, we are agreed? A mutually beneficial arrangement for a few weeks?'

'Mutually beneficial?' Jeanne asked, her eyebrows rising up into her hat. 'How does this benefit you? Is there a clause I have missed? If it is eating the jam I would rather eat Bo-Bo's—'

'You can work at the hotels. At the weekends. Until you are allowed to be officially employed, you will be my second assistant. That will involve anything I ask you to do.'

'Like what?'

'Like… making coffee or organising the new ornamental features we are looking at today.' He relaxed into the seat a little further. 'What do you think to these chairs?'

'I think,' Jeanne said, sitting further back in hers, her feet coming off the floor completely, 'they have lived a life already.'

'Yes,' Ethan answered, a smile on his face. 'Exactly that.'

Forty-Four

'Squirrels' teeth never stop growing. Did you know that, Keeley?'

'No, Dad, I didn't know that. So, is Mum really OK?'

Keeley watched Rach, a stall to her left, ferreting through a selection of garments laid out jumble-sale style. Rach was far more high-street fashion than she was vintage. Perhaps she was looking for a gift.

'You spoke to her, love,' Duncan reminded.

'I spoke to her for two minutes before she palmed me off with talk about baking for the knitting group.'

'It's the crochet group tonight,' Duncan said. 'Knitting's on Friday week and cooking for the choir's this Saturday. A Christmas bazaar with songs by Cole Porter.'

'She shouldn't have even been at Mr Peterson's place,' Keeley said, frustrated. 'She shouldn't be standing in for me like that.'

'She wanted to help and she wanted you to be able to go to Paris.'

Keeley closed her eyes and let out a sigh. Despite all her early protests and desperate reservations, it seemed Lizzie had done everything in her power to ensure this trip *had* gone ahead. Stepping into the breach to help Roland at the estate agency so no one was inconvenienced by the late notice for the trip, ensuring she had a job to go back to. Albeit a job she desperately wanted to move onwards and upwards from. One step at a time…

'So, how's it going there?' Duncan cleared his throat then whispered. 'Managed to eat some cheese?'

Keeley smiled at her dad's air of naughty schoolboy. 'I've had a little bit.'

'Good girl. A little bit never did anyone any harm.' He paused. 'But don't tell your mother I said that.' He seemed to wait a beat before continuing. 'And… Silvie, she's alright, is she?'

'Silvie's very nice,' Keeley answered. 'She's a little older than you and mum, smartly dressed, she speaks excellent English which is good because I don't speak much French. She met Rach and me at this lovely café near the Louvre and we're going to her house tonight for dinner.'

'And did you talk?' Duncan asked. 'You know… about her daughter?'

'Yes,' Keeley said. 'Silvie showed me a photograph and told me about the kind of person Ferne was. She was beautiful, Dad, and she sounded like someone I… might have liked to have been friends with.' She hadn't thought about that until the sentence had passed her lips. It was true though. From what she had already heard about her donor, Ferne was kind and fierce and very much loved. Who wouldn't want to have someone like that as a friend? 'And… I told Silvie about Bea. She didn't know, you know, that Bea had… passed away.' She still found it so hard to say the word 'died'. In her mind, Bea was still out there somewhere, perhaps building bridges out of clouds…

'I suppose she wouldn't,' Duncan answered, his voice catching a little. 'So, it's all alright then. You're not unsettled by anything or… worried about anything.'

'Dad,' Keeley said, watching Rach unearth what looked like something Gucci from the pile of clothing. 'Mum's standing right with you now, isn't she?'

Duncan let out a sigh and Keeley heard a whispered, 'I told you she would know,' before a sound seemed to indicate something on the call had changed.

'I've put you on speakerphone,' Duncan answered.

'Mum—'

'Don't be cross with me, Keeley. I can sense you're going to be cross with me,' Lizzie started.

'I'm cross that squirrels attacked you when you were somewhere you shouldn't have been.'

'I'm cross that someone keeps three squirrels untethered in an airing cupboard, ready to attack any unsuspecting individual who happens to consider tidying the towels. Buyers look in cupboards. We looked in cupboards before we bought this house, didn't we, Duncan?'

'We did,' Keeley's dad concurred.

'You do know Mr Peterson is a taxidermist,' Keeley remarked.

'Of course I know that! What I didn't realise was he kept *live* animals in unusual places.'

'The man does have a certain reputation for things like that.'

'They were supposed to be dead,' Lizzie continued. '"Drying" was actually the word he used. Who leaves living animals to "dry"? It's as bad as leaving a poor dog in a car on a hot summer's day with no window open.'

'But you're OK, Mum,' Keeley asked for what felt like the millionth time.

'I'm fine. And the lovely doctor said there's not going to be any scarring.'

'Scarring! Mum! How bad was it?'

'Their teeth never stop growing apparently,' Duncan chipped in.

'Mum!'

'Keeley, I'm fine. Honestly. There's no need to worry about me. You just carry on having a lovely time with the smartly dressed new mother figure who has an excellent command of a second language,' Lizzie said with a sniff.

'Mum,' Keeley said with a sigh.

'I mean it. Have a lovely time but…' Lizzie paused.

'But what?'

'Come back, won't you?'

'Of course I'll come back… Mum, Dad, I've got to go now, Rach is about to disappear into a pile of dresses.'

There were shouts of 'goodbye' and one final 'don't forget me' from Lizzie before Keeley ended the call. By the time she got over to the clothing stall, Rach had put her purchases on the ground around her feet and was scrabbling around, elbow deep in material and drawing the attention of the stall owner.

'Rach,' Keeley said. 'What are you doing?'

'There's Gucci under here,' Rach gasped. 'And I don't think it's knock off. These ones are all a decent length, so if I get them I won't have to borrow anything of yours to wear tonight.' There was a growing pile of garments on the stall next to her she seemed to be half-guarding with her body.

'Rach, slow down. You're in danger of knocking off some

of these beautiful vintage items on the floor.' Keeley had caught the stallholder's eye and said the words 'beautiful' and 'vintage' like she might have said 'one and only much longed for baby'.

'Did you hear what I said?' Rach asked. 'Gucci.'

'I did hear but...' Keeley stopped talking when something caught her eye. Was that... Bo-Bo? She shook her head and closed her eyes, then quickly opened them again. Looking over to stalls selling artwork and chandeliers she watched the dog spinning around, no lead on the end of a collar. But why would Bo-Bo be here? It was a bit of a Metro journey for Jeanne to take but, then again, she was a girl who seemed to be able to defy all the usual prerequisites for a person of her age. It could be any scruffy brown dog really though. Couldn't it?

'Fuck! There's a handbag here I saw on eBay!' Rach exclaimed, still rifling through the wares at a rate of knots.

The dog barked and then bumped into a hostess trolley filled with glassware. The glasses started to rock and reel and that's when Keeley made a decision. Rach was going to have to deal with the anger of the stallholder on her own if those frocks ended up in an inch of snow on the ground. Whether the dog was Bo-Bo or not, she was going to have to do something!

Forty-Five

Animals were going to be the death of Ethan. Not a minute after his talk with Jeanne about 'sharing space', Bo-Bo had somehow slipped his leash and gone bounding off into the thick of the market. Before he took off, Ethan had ordered Jeanne to stay exactly where she was. He didn't want to lose child and canine, but he suspected, as soon as his back was turned, Jeanne was going to be in pursuit too. Bo-Bo was fast and he had lost sight of him completely a couple of times. Until now. The dog was just up ahead, turning around in circles, until suddenly he banged against a trolley full of delicate-looking glasses.

'*Merde*!'

Ethan sprinted forward, rushing to connect with dog or trolley. Instead what happened was he connected with a person. And before he knew it he was tumbling onto the ground.

'Oh, gosh! Oh, *monsieur*, I am so, so sorry!'

The voice was familiar. Seeing stars in his peripheral Ethan looked up, wondering if he had banged his head. There was barking, smashing glass, something wet against his face… and he felt sure he could hear… Keeley?

'Ethan!'

That was most definitely Keeley's voice. And the wet sensation was still there. He then realised it was Bo-Bo's rough tongue, licking at his face. 'He… has no lead.'

'I have the lead!'

That was Jeanne's voice. So, she had not done what she was told and stayed where he could find her. But she was thankfully here and not missing. Ethan shook his head and attempted to stand.

'Are you OK?' Keeley asked.

He felt her hands then, holding onto his arms and helping him up off the ground. He urged his body to comply. The last thing he needed right now was bumps, bruises or a face as red and lumpy as Louis's.

'I am OK,' he answered, finally standing and trying to make sense of the scene. There were a few broken glasses on the floor and the stallholder was already out sweeping away the destruction. 'Monsieur, I am very sorry for the damage. Let me pay for it. It is my dog that has caused this.' He reached into his pocket for his wallet.

'He's *my* dog,' Jeanne said, Bo-Bo now back on his lead and dancing around a little bit less.

The owner of the stall accepted more than half of the Euro notes in his wallet. Those glasses had to be from at least the Victorian era or maybe he had just been taken for a ride. At this moment Ethan didn't care. He faced Jeanne. 'You must control him better.'

'I was,' she exclaimed. 'It is the new lead the man who doesn't like anything touched put on him. I have not got used to it yet.' She smiled. 'Can I get another brioche?'

'Jeanne! Another one?' Ethan exclaimed.

'Please!' She put her hands together in a begging stance and almost dropped Bo-Bo's lead for a second time.

Ethan pulled another note from his wallet and gave it to her. 'One brioche and two coffees. Ask them to wrap the brioche so you can put it into your pocket while you carry the coffees.' He took the lead out of Jeanne's hands. 'And I will look after Bo-Bo.' He ensured a good grip on the lead. 'You remember where the stall is.'

'I've got it,' Jeanne answered with a nod. 'Two coffees and two brioches.'

Before Ethan could protest about the doubling of the brioche order, Jeanne was off into the hubbub again. Ethan tried to elongate his spine, the tumble definitely having strained something. Finally he smiled at Keeley and gave a small bow. 'Good afternoon.'

Keeley laughed. 'Good afternoon.' She gave a curtsey, holding the edge of her bright red coat and doing a quick bob.

Ethan sighed, giving himself a little time to be mindful. His body was already starting to loosen, simply from enjoying her smile. 'We must try to stop meeting like this,' he said. 'Or one of us might get really injured.'

'I agree,' Keeley said, nodding. 'My bruises from my brush with you and the penguin are still stuck between blue and purple.'

'It is the animals!' Ethan declared, putting his arms to the heavens. 'They are to blame for everything.' He put his arms back down and smiled at her. 'What brings you to *Les Puces*?'

'Well, it's getting closer to Christmas and I need to get

some gifts organised. Plus Rach is a huge fan of shopping and... well...' She looked a little bashful then. 'It was on your map.'

He had put the market with over three thousands stalls on the map he had made for her because it had been one of his regular places to visit. In the darkest times of his youth he had escaped here with half a dozen other orphans to take part in picking the pockets of anyone they had marked as having money. He had also come here with Ferne, trying to find a chink of treasure, a hidden or long-forgotten work from Picasso or Matisse, antique furniture as a gift for Silvie. Two very different sides of his time spent here. Two eras of his life as far removed from each other as could be.

'It is a unique place,' Ethan remarked. 'Shall we walk?' He offered her the arm that was not bearing the weight of a feisty Bo-Bo.

He watched Keeley turn, her eyes on a table a little way away.

'Rach is over there, but she looks to be in a deep bartering session.'

'Not far,' Ethan assured. 'Jeanne will need to find us.'

Keeley took his arm and her touch sent his head spinning for the second time today. Their connection just somehow felt *right*.

'Today people come here expecting to spend a lot of money. There are antiques everywhere,' Ethan told her. 'Some stalls are a subsidiary of an established business elsewhere in Paris. They move some of their pieces here into the hub where rich collectors and interior designers, like yourself, come to find extravagant pieces to fill an investment request or style a home.'

'There are so many stalls and shopfronts here,' Keeley answered as they strolled, Bo-Bo still pulling enthusiastically. 'I've really never seen anything like it.'

'You will need an entire week to walk around it fully,' Ethan said. 'It is seven hectares.'

'Oh my God! My legs ache just thinking about it.'

'Mine too,' he admitted with a laugh. 'But I believe Bo-Bo would consider it.' The dog was sniffing his way across the concrete.

'So, are *you* looking for Christmas gifts?' she asked. 'Is that why you're here?'

'*Non*,' he replied. 'I am looking for items for my hotel.'

'Hotels,' Keeley said.

Everything froze for a moment. Did she know he was the part-owner of the hotel she was staying in? How did she know? Had Jeanne somehow gone back on her word and communicated it? Why *hadn't* he wanted her to know he was connected to Perfect Paris? Because negotiations were still continuing with regard to the brand's future? Or because talking about the hotel chain would mean talking about Ferne?

'You said "hotels" last night when we were talking,' Keeley said. 'Unless I misheard. Do you have more than one?'

He wasn't going to outright lie to her. He nodded. 'I actually have five.'

'Wow!' Keeley exclaimed. 'I mean… socks are what most people usually own five of. Or books. Or mugs. Or—'

'I do not want you to get the wrong idea of me,' Ethan said quickly. He was now acting like he was almost ashamed of his status of hotel chain owner.

'The wrong idea?'

He nodded, feeling a little like he was going to be fighting with these next words. 'I am not Mr Hotel. I... merely helped a friend to build her dream and then I was left to carry it on.' He swallowed. This was much harder than he had envisaged. 'It is not my vocation. Or rather, it was not. But I feel now as if it maybe could be. *You* have actually made me feel like it could be.'

Ethan had stopped walking now and Keeley halted too, their arms still linked together. His words peppered her heart, marking it with slow, soft indentations.

'I am not here with the mind of an antique dealer. I am not even here with the vision of an interior designer. I am here to do what you suggested.'

'Oh,' Keeley said, not sure she understood.

'I am here looking for things that matter,' Ethan continued, stepping in under a canopy. 'Or rather, things that *have* mattered.' He wandered under the ceiling wound with vines and ivy then picked up a mirror that was lying on top of an oriental-style chest of drawers. The wood was old and cracked in places and the glass was smeared and dotted with blemishes. 'I want to redesign my hotels and make them all about the comfort and all about the story.' He held the mirror up to their faces so they could see their reflection. 'Touch. Taste. Feel.' He carried on. 'I want the hotels to evoke memories and create new stories, inspired by old stories.'

Keeley could feel her insides reacting to what he was saying. His words were everything she felt about how she wanted her own interior design business to go. She wanted to get to know her clients, understand exactly what their vision was and then dig a little deeper. She carried on looking into the mirror with Ethan.

'You have brought everything into focus,' he whispered.

Their framed reflections in this old mirror was like looking at an old photograph, its edges blurred, slightly rumpled, but the two people were knitting together so easily, so perfectly.

'Can I help you? Look for things?' Keeley asked as her heart thumped in acknowledgement of how she was feeling here with him.

'You do not know how much I was hoping you would say that,' Ethan replied.

His phone bleeped from the pocket of his coat and he put down the mirror. 'Excuse me,' he said to Keeley. 'Things with the hotels are busy at this time of year. It might be—'

'It's fine,' Keeley answered. 'I'll make a start.'

He watched her walk further into the depths of the makeshift shop all corrugated sheeting and wood that looked like it might fall down at any second. Smiling, he took his phone from his pocket and saw it was a message from Silvie.

Please come to dinner tonight. No talk about Perfect Paris and Louis will be on his best behaviour. I would really like you to meet the girl Ferne was able to help. X

Ethan shuddered. *The girl Ferne was able to help*. So the person who had his best friend's kidney was a girl. He thought about Jeanne, just for a few seconds, and then he put his phone back in his pocket. There was no way he was going to go.

Forty-Six

The Durand House, Neuilly-sur-Seine, Paris

'This looks like something from a film set,' Rach remarked later that evening as the car that Silvie had sent for them pulled up outside a substantial property with a large paved driveway. 'It's almost as big as the town hall and the chateau we went past.'

There were four columns lined up along the front almost like sentries waiting to confirm their invitation to the house. It was a little imposing in its grandeur and Keeley wasn't sure what was going to come from the inside. The very large Christmas tree was slightly more welcoming in its appearance. It was as broad as it was tall, and it was covered in perfectly organised lights, baubles and tinsel. Keeley opened the door before the driver could get there to do it for her and she almost expected a choir to appear to regale them with carols. Boots crunching down onto another layer of snow she took a deep breath, stilling herself and acknowledging the surroundings. Snow was wispy in the air now, nothing to cause a concern of getting stranded later, but, with the plummeting temperatures, it meant the ground was still crisp and white.

'Keeley! Rach! Come in! Come in!'

Expecting a servant, Keeley was surprised to see Silvie standing at the entrance, beckoning them towards the house, wearing no coat. Keeley stepped up her pace, wanting the woman to get back inside and out of the wind.

'Are you glad we bought the expensive red wine now?' Rach whispered in Keeley's ear as they both made steps towards the house.

'I wish we had bought the larger round of brie and those vintage plates with the birds on them,' Keeley said with a gulp. Was this really the house her kidney donor had grown up in?

'Don't mention birds,' Rach begged. 'It always gives me a nasty Mr Peterson flashback when one time he was mounting a crow.'

Keeley smiled as they reached Silvie's front door and she offered out the wine and cheese. 'Hello, I know you said not to bring anything but... we did.'

'Oh,' Silvie said. 'There was no need... but thank you so much.' She took the gifts and looked appreciatively at them both. 'I do love a good *vin rouge*.'

Rach was already nudging Keeley that her choice was spot on and Keeley gave her an elbow back.

'Come in, please, it is so cold tonight even the Christmas tree wants to come inside.' Silvie smiled and led the way into the home.

There was another tree over the threshold, this one slightly smaller, but just as tastefully decorated, if your taste was regimented and covered in gold. It was a world away from anything Keeley had looked at with Ethan that afternoon. As a maid took Keeley's coat, then offered the same service to Rach, Keeley thought about her time at the *marché* with Ethan. They had rummaged! At one point, they had each been holding one of Jeanne's legs while she climbed into a mammoth Arabian-style basket to retrieve a wooden trug that had caught Ethan's eye. And they had laughed so much. Sleeves rolled up, hands on items while they closed their eyes and tried to feel an aura the certain object might be offering up. Although Keeley had talked about the memories décor could evoke, she had never actually held something to see if it projected a certain vibe. But, in some cases this afternoon it had. And Ethan said he could feel it too. Sometimes there had been a warmth, sometimes not, but being mindful while you were cradling a coat hook or a collection of hand-painted wooden nutcrackers definitely helped the purchasing process. And Ethan had purchased a great deal that was, this evening, being collected.

'You have a lovely home,' Rach remarked, eyes on stalks at the chandeliers hanging from the ceiling and the stair banisters through which wound gold and red ribbons with fir cones and bells dangling from them.

'Thank you,' Silvie answered. Keeley thought their host sounded suddenly a little subdued. Perhaps it was the word 'home'. She knew herself that home didn't really feel quite the same without Bea there. She suspected Silvie felt exactly the same without Ferne.

'Good evening.'

It was Louis, appearing in the entrance hall. He was wearing smart trousers, a white shirt with a pale lemon-coloured jumper over it. He smiled at them both and Keeley watched Rach look a little nervous, her fingers going to the hem of the dress she was wearing that she bought from the market.

'Hello,' Rach replied.

'Come through,' Silvie insisted. 'There is much more to my house than the hallway.'

There *was* a great deal more to the Durand's home than the elaborate hallway. The house flowed under archways and into a reception room where chaise longues hung out with large urns full of festive flowers and bright red berries, fir cones drizzled with silver. Then it was a lavish sitting room with elaborate floral-patterned sofas straight out of the pages of a magazine and fur rugs that hopefully weren't as real as they looked. They'd had canapes in this room, just the four of them, plus two very attentive staff filling up their glasses with a rather crisp, clean white sparkling wine. Then they have moved into a dining room fit for royalty. The table was huge for four. It would have been huge for ten. And it was beautifully laid out, a dramatic miniature fir tree in the centre spot, around which was a ring of candles creating a warm glow.

Keeley had a warm glow on her cheeks now and it was most definitely the wine. A dry, rich, white that was meant to complement the goose they were eating. It was actually a Christmas Day spread from the giant bird to the roasted potatoes and mix of *legumes*.

'Tell me,' Silvie said, pausing in her eating for a moment. 'What did you do today?'

'Well,' Rach began, enthusiastic after more glasses of wine

than Keeley had indulged in, 'I did my very best to wear Keeley out taking her on a tour of all the best boutiques and then she wanted to go to a flea market. I thought that sounded pretty un-chic until we got there and I saw how ginormous it was and… I found some designer bargains amid the old stuff.'

'We went to *Les Puces*,' Keeley elaborated. 'In *Saint-Ouen*.'

Louis and Silvie shared a look, both smiling a little as if Keeley had said something in secret code.

'Ferne liked to go there,' Silvie remarked, smiling as one of her staff came and topped up her wineglass.

'Really?' Keeley remarked. Despite the things she had learned about her donor, she had envisaged Ferne being more on the Rach side of shopping, except maybe with more Parisian flair than bootleg bargains.

'Ferne always thought she could detect an heirloom from a million miles away. Something that had been discarded as rubbish,' Louis told the table. 'I remember one time she arrived home with the most hideous clown. It was a wooden puppet, almost life-size, with the most crude artwork.' Louis shook his head. 'What did she call it, Mother?'

'Augusto,' Silvie jumped in. 'And she said it with such an Italian accent.'

'Augusto!' Louis proclaimed, his hand gesturing out in front of him as he sat, like he was introducing the dessert as a dinner guest. It was funny but Rach laughed a little louder and harder than anyone else, eventually having to cover her mouth with a napkin.

'Even at eleven years old, Ferne was determined that this puppet was the first work from a great modern-day sculptor…' Silvie began.

'Or, at the very least, one of his toys,' Louis added.

'Did you have it valued?' Keeley asked, finding herself sitting forward on her chair.

Silvie laughed. 'No! Of course not! You only had to look at it to see the stallholder must have thought all his Christmases had arrived when someone actually wanted to take it from his hands.'

Keeley felt aggrieved on Ferne's behalf. However, she supposed, if it was found to be worthless in monetary terms that might have broken a little girl's heart more than the never knowing. But, still, perhaps the puppet might have been a treasure of some kind. It obviously already had been to Ferne.

'If you saw the horror you would know what we are talking about,' Louis said.

'I still have it,' Silvie announced, sipping her wine.

'You do not!' Louis said.

'I do,' she insisted. 'It is in Ferne's bedroom. Hidden in the cupboard so it does not scare the staff.' She smiled a little then. 'Ferne and her strays.' She shook her head. 'And now the animal charity having a say in how we run the hotels.'

'You run hotels?' Rach asked, eyes out on stalks. 'A *chain* of hotels?'

Already Keeley could see that Louis was about to go a few rungs up the ladder as far as romantic suitability was concerned.

'Oh!' Silvie gasped. 'Did I not say? Not over lunch?' She pressed her napkin to her lips.

'You told me that Ferne was in hospitality but…' Keeley began.

'We are... Perfect Paris!' Louis announced. Keeley half expected him to do jazz hands to highlight the point. So, the hotel they were staying in was *owned* by Silvie and Louis?

'Are you for real?' Rach asked. 'That's amazing. I mean it's... spectacular! The gourmet food and the... animatronic festive things... I might have thought *Sleeping Beauty* on ice was a bit out there on a rink the size of a postage stamp but... it's artsy, isn't it? People love artsy, especially at Christmas time.'

'Keeley,' Silvie said softly. 'Is everything OK?'

Keeley knew she had gone a little quiet but she was processing. Somehow it felt a little odd that they had been staying in the hotel where Ferne had worked. *Had* Ferne actually worked there?

'I'm... fine.' Keeley took a sip of her wine from her glass. 'Did Ferne work at the hotel? The one we are staying in?'

'Sometimes,' Silvie replied. 'Although her office was at the flagship hotel in the Opera district. Perfect Paris was her dream after she stopped buying puppets. She wanted to create a haven of luxury in the middle of the city.'

'And it *is* luxurious,' Rach agreed, smiling at Louis.

'But times are changing,' Louis said. 'One of the reasons I am here was to arrange the sale of the hotels. We had a number of larger brands interested in buying the chain but, there is now an obstacle to overcome and—'

'And we do not need to talk about such boring matters as business at the dinner table,' Silvie interrupted.

'What was the other reason for you being here?' Rach wanted to know.

'To meet Keeley, of course,' Silvie said softly. 'Tell me, how was the ballet the other night?'

Keeley's heart arrested. Had Louis not told Silvie that Rach had met him at the ballet instead of her? Now she didn't know quite what to say and she hurriedly filled her mouth with food so someone else had to answer on her behalf. The goose wasn't slipping down quite so easily now.

'Ah,' Louis spoke up. 'Unfortunately Keeley was...'

'Not feeling well,' Rach chipped in. 'A temperature and a sore throat. Only a slight one. Nothing major.'

'You are sick?' Silvie questioned, putting all her focus on Keeley. Her concerned look forced Keeley to munch until she had to swallow.

'No, she's fine,' Rach said. 'She's fine *now*. But she was a little, tiny bit, under the weather for the ballet. So, I met Louis in her place.'

Silvie's expression was suddenly a mix of disappointment and upset and the woman reached for the wine bottle before any of her staff could get there to do it for her. Topping up her glass she looked to Louis. 'You did not tell me.'

'I...' Louis started, sounding flummoxed. 'I told you the ballet was wonderful and that we had a very nice time.'

'Yes,' Silvie hissed. 'But I presumed you had gone to the ballet with Keeley!'

'I thought the ballet was wonderful too,' Rach jumped in. 'I even cried. And I don't really cry at stuff like that. You know, I'm more of a "got my finger caught in the coffee machine" kind of crier than the emotional kind.'

Keeley reached out and put a hand on Silvie's arm. 'I'm so sorry I didn't go to the ballet. I was going to. I thought about it, maybe even a little too much and then, I don't know, it all suddenly felt... a bit too much. And I know that sounds incredibly selfish when you've invited me here and everything but… I thought you would understand.' She took a breath. 'I hoped you would understand.'

Keeley waited then, watching for Silvie's reaction. She hoped she hadn't upset her host and irrevocably changed the dynamic between them. Silvie *had* said there was no pressure. But perhaps she hadn't meant that quite as sincerely as she said she had.

'*Mother*—' Louis began.

'It is alright,' Silvie breathed, offering Keeley a small smile. 'When we have finished the goose, shall we go to see Ferne's room?'

Keeley nodded. 'Yes. I would really like that.'

Forty-Seven

'*Voila*,' Silvie said later, opening the door of one of the rooms upstairs.

They had finished the main course and were waiting for the chef – yes, Silvie had a chef – to arrive with the dessert. While Rach seemed slightly wine-besotted with Louis, Keeley was now eager to see inside Ferne's space.

The door swung back and revealed the kind of sized room most people would kill for their central living space, let alone a bedroom. It was so vast it could easily have been sectioned off into a sleeping area, a sitting area with even room for a full bathroom if required. It was like a whole apartment, something Keeley envisaged *sharing* with Rach when they began their accommodation search. Keeley hesitated on the threshold for a moment, until Silvie urged her forward. 'Please, go inside.'

Keeley stepped inside the cavernous area, eyes roving, picking out this and that and trying to capture everything there was to learn about her donor. This bedroom seemed pristine, like maybe time had stopped. For some reason she could envisage drawers being open, clothes with sleeves draping down from the units, open make-up pallets with stray brushes, music in the air…

'It's beautiful,' Keeley breathed. Maybe it wasn't to her own taste, but it was divine in design. With its flocked wallpaper – a pink and silver embellishment that seemed to speak of the liking for both finery and girlie – the bed a king-size with a mattress so thick you might need a step to launch yourself onto it and cushions – silk, fur, feather, sequins – it was, without a doubt, a perfect boudoir.

'Ferne was a little spoiled,' Silvie admitted. 'She was my only daughter. *And* she was really… how do you say in English? A daddy's girl.'

Keeley smiled. 'My mum would say the same about me.'

'Would she be right?' Silvie asked.

'No,' Keeley admitted freely. 'But my mum has always been the one to hand out the tough love. While my dad is the one Bea and I could sweet talk into anything.'

Silvie smiled then as they edged further into the room. 'Pierre was always sweet-talked by Ferne. If it had been up to him, our house would have been filled with dogs and candy floss, with members of Ferne's latest boy band obsessions coming on weekends.' She sighed. 'He was always a little harder with Louis.'

Keeley stepped on into the room, her feet sinking into the soft pile of the carpet. This was the suite of a princess. At first glance it could be the sleeping palace of a child, but there were touches of Ferne the young woman too. A pin-board of photographs on one wall, a map of the world with pins in it – destinations she had been or ones she would now never get to? – a computer station with an Apple Mac lying dormant, a coffee mug full of pens, unopened letters, a cactus plant…

'When Pierre died I went through everything and

only kept what we really needed to save. But with Ferne, somehow, I… could not bear to let anything go,' Silvie admitted, her voice tight. 'She had her own apartment but she almost always stayed at home.'

'I understand,' Keeley breathed. 'Bea's room at home… well, before… we lost her… she was always talking about changing her décor. She wanted me to help her and we had looked at hundreds of magazines and style brochures I'd ordered and she never could make up her mind on furnishings. Bea liked to be surrounded by practical and calm. The only thing she *had* settled on was knowing she wanted it painted a light, soft shade of aqua.' Keeley shook her head. 'I remember my dad arriving at the door of her room in the summer, a huge tin of aqua paint in his hand, telling my mum he was going to paint it the colour Bea had always wanted it.' Tears were gathering in her eyes now. 'My mum went mad. It was change. It might have been what Bea had talked about and planned out, but it wasn't the same now she wasn't around. My dad thought it would help us move on, remember Bea by turning her room into how she wanted it but… my mum… and I… wanted to hold on to everything of Bea that was left. Just the way she left it. Her finger marks on the door frame, the sheen of hairspray across the mirror, the last pillowcase she lay her head on that my mum presses her nose against even now.'

A tear began to slide down Keeley's face, and she looked to Silvie, finding the woman was getting emotional also.

'I can relate to those feelings.' Silvie sniffed. 'That is why I keep the room exactly how it is. The maid is not even allowed in here. To clean it would be to disturb the last traces of my daughter.'

Keeley swallowed, wondering if she should reach out to her. They did have so much in common when it came to loss. Keeley put a hand on Silvie's shoulder and gently squeezed. 'Thank you for showing me Ferne's room.'

Silvie sniffed again, recomposing herself. 'You think we are finished?'

'Well, I… didn't want to pry.'

'Nonsense,' Silvie said quickly. 'Come, help me up onto the bed.'

Keeley smiled as the woman headed towards the extremely high mattress and attempted to get on. Giggling, Silvie beached a little on the edge and Keeley had to hurry to her side and aid her in getting on top of it.

'Honestly,' Silvie exclaimed, straightening her form. 'I never could understand why Ferne wanted a bed so high.' She smiled. 'Come up here with me.' Silvie patted the space next to her.

'Are you sure?' Keeley asked.

'But of course!' Silvie patted the bed again. 'Come!'

With quite substantial effort and a little help with balance from Silvie, Keeley managed to finally get on top of the bed. She stuck her legs out in mid-air and wiggled her feet. 'Maybe that's why the bed is high,' Keeley mused. 'It feels a little bit like you're flying up here.'

'Ferne never stayed still,' Silvie mused. 'Staying still for a moment bored her.' She sighed. 'My daughter was always about the "doing". I do not remember the times when she stood still. Perhaps only in the shower.'

Keeley took a deep breath. There was something, one question, she had been wanting to ask Silvie from the moment they had met. 'Silvie, do you think, if Ferne had been given the choice, she would have donated her kidney to someone like me?'

'Someone like you?' Silvie asked, her brow furrowed.

'Someone ordinary,' Keeley answered. She felt immediately scrutinised and realised she should probably elaborate a bit more. 'Being here in Ferne's space, I can start to see what a full life she led and I don't know if I can... do her justice.'

'Oh, my dear,' Silvie said so gently. 'Ferne and I discussed donation when our country changed its law. Neither of us could see any reason why we would opt out of giving someone the gift of life if ours was not going to go on.'

Keeley nodded. 'Thank you.'

'And as for being ordinary... *bof*! You, Keeley, are exactly the kind of person Ferne would want to carry on living for her. From what I know, and I do wish to know a lot more before it is time for you to leave, you are warm... and kind... and generous with your time for others. You have a soft heart and a keen mind. I think you and Ferne would have been great friends.' Silvie put her hand over Keeley's. 'I think you could be great friends with Louis too.' She looked a little forlorn again. 'I do worry about him. Alone in America, working all the time. I worry that perhaps he made choices he thought his father would have wanted him to make.'

'I really am sorry about the ballet. I...'

'It is no matter,' Silvie said, shifting her weight across the mattress a little. 'But I do hope there will be a little time for you to get to know Louis better while you are here in Paris.'

Suddenly a loud clanging filled the entire room and Keeley clutched at her chest.

Silvie fell about laughing. 'The way we announce the next

course here in the House of Durand is surprising, yes?' She shifted forward a little, teetering on the edge of the mattress again. 'That is a reminder of my Pierre. He always liked the ceremony.' With a bit of a bounce, Silvie sprung down off the bed and Keeley panicked as the woman listed a little to the left, heading towards a collision with the nightstand.

'Oh!' Silvie cried out.

Keeley managed to take hold of the woman's arm and steady her landing a little while trying to manoeuvre herself off the giant mattress. A few things fell from the bedside cabinet then – a photo frame, a couple of books, thankfully not the lamp…

'Are you alright?' Keeley asked, her feet finally finding the carpet as Silvie straightened up.

'Yes, yes,' Silvie said quickly, her voice light. In fact, she sounded very much like she was laughing. 'How did my daughter get in and out of this bed every day?'

Keeley smiled. 'I don't know… but it was probably a lot of fun.'

'I have made a mess,' Silvie said, bending a little stiffly to gather the items that were on the floor.

'Let me help,' Keeley said, picking up the photo frame. Inside was a picture of Ferne, her blonde hair poker-straight, her face made up like she might be about to attend a party. 'This is a lovely photo.' Keeley put it back on the nightstand.

'That was taken at a Christmas party. Our party nights at the hotels at Christmas time are very popular.' Silvie sighed, looking at Ferne's image. 'Ferne loved those parties. She was in her element, working the room, making sure everyone was having the best of times.'

The gong sounded again, this time somehow, even louder and they both laughed together.

'I think they are getting restless and want our presence,' Silvie said. 'I believe the dessert is something with chocolate tonight.'

Another food sin that Keeley should probably not be so fond of. She gathered up the last books from the floor and went to put them on the bedside table. But, as she did so, something fluttered out from between one of the pages and sank to the carpet. While Silvie headed for the door out, Keeley picked up the piece of paper and couldn't help but look at it. It was a photograph. A Polaroid. A little faded, obviously well-worn through time and touch. But the image looking back at Keeley stole her breath. *Those grey eyes*. No, it couldn't be. She shook her head. She was being ridiculous now, seeing him everywhere.

'Keeley,' Silvie called from the threshold to the room.

She swallowed, feeling somehow guilty. And then she put the photograph back between the pages of the notebook. 'Coming.'

Forty-Eight

L'Hotel Paris Parfait, Opera District, Paris

'This is one of your other *little* hotels, is it?' Jeanne asked, swinging her legs so they continually knocked against the leg of the dining table they were seated at. Ethan had managed to get Bo-Bo – with Jeanne's disgruntled approval – to accept being stationed in the garage while they dined in the hotel's restaurant. Silvie had sent him a second text reiterating her invitation to dinner earlier. She had sounded like she might really want him to come, like it really might not have been another kind of business ambush. Except that person would be there. The girl. What was he going to say to her? How could he even look at her knowing that she was there because Ferne was not? He considered ignoring the second text just like he had ignored the first but, in the end, he had sent a polite decline with no emotion attached to it. If he gave no energy to it, it would go away. *She* would go away. He was busy. He was focused. He didn't have time for his thoughts to stray beyond improving the hotels. He already had a child and a dog he hadn't planned for…

'Why do I sense that you do not like it?' Ethan asked her.

'It looks like a courtroom,' Jeanne said with a sniff. She wiped her nose with the back of her hand. 'A courtroom with too much blue and silver glitter. It looks like a troupe of can-can dancers high-kicked through here on their way to jail.'

A courtroom. Ethan studied the dark wood he had always thought looked regal and majestic. Perhaps Jeanne was on to something. Except the changes he had in mind for the hotels didn't incorporate a full re-fit – that might go some way to bankrupting them. He would have to do the best he could to soften hard edges and introduce warmth in other ways. He would begin with some of the items he had purchased from *Les Puces*.

'If you were not my boss I would hate you,' Noel greeted, his hands holding a tray.

'I am sure hating your boss is a prerequisite in most businesses,' Ethan answered, deftly spreading his napkin over his lap. 'I can deal with a little hate today, as long as I am going to love the food.' Ethan leaned forward in his seat and sniffed the air. The most fragrant scent was rising with the steam from two rustic bowls on the tray Noel was balancing. The bowls belonged to a large set he had found hidden away in a suitcase under a table in the large market. They looked like something Jesus and his disciples might have used during The Last Supper. Thick, unrefined and slightly uneven rims in sturdy pottery with a deep bowl. They were exactly the right style to serve the spin on paupers' food he hoped his chef had perfected in double quick time. He was going to see where he could source similar tableware for *all* the hotels if this new avenue proved as popular as he hoped it would.

Ethan breathed in the aroma of chicken, sausage, thyme, red wine and garlic and, if his stomach had hands, it would be applauding. He looked at Jeanne then and watched as she took the bowl from the tray before Noel had a chance to set it down. Grabbing a spoon, the girl attacked the food like she attacked *any* food put in front of her. But then, as the first mouthful must have hit her taste buds, she paused, closing her eyes and loudly snorting air through her nose in a show of nothing short of exaltation.

'This is... so good,' Jeanne announced, a cannellini bean falling from her lips.

Noel placed a bowl in front of Ethan and shook his head. 'I have seen better bowls put in front of dogs.'

'But feel it,' Ethan said, his hand wrapping around the pottery, the warmth from the meal seeping through it, its solidity somehow strong and comforting. 'This is... hunkering down during a snowstorm... or having a flu and being given that first taste of food you have not been able to smell or stomach for a week or—'

'Knowing this might be the only meal you get for a week and it makes you remember someone you lost.'

This last thought came from Jeanne, but the girl wasn't truly engaging with him and Noel. Ethan wasn't sure she even knew that she had spoken at all. She was eating more slowly, carefully scooping up the *cassoulet* with her fork and looking like she was being completely present in her own moment with every portion she took. It was as if she was finally giving something, including herself, space and time to breathe.

'Has anyone else ordered this dish tonight?' Ethan wanted to know.

This was the most mini of trials, but he needed to get some feedback if he wanted to go all out for Christmas. He was hoping that reviews would be positive. He wasn't sure what he would do if they weren't positive.

'Eighty per cent of diners have ordered it so far,' Noel said with a sigh of disapproval. 'Chef tells me he has not made this since he lived with his grandmother. Before cooking school. When he was around twelve.'

Ethan couldn't halt his smile. He *had* been right to go with back to basics. He had felt it. And Keeley, she had *made* him feel it.

'One moment and I will bring you some more water,' Noel said, picking up the jug from the table.

As his assistant departed, Ethan lifted his fork, preparing to eat. And then he stopped.

'Are you not going to eat it?' Jeanne asked.

'Food can talk to us, can it not?' Ethan asked her.

'You are mad.'

'I see it talking to you.'

'You do not *see* talking. You hear it.' Jeanne wiped sauce from her mouth with her sleeve.

'How does the food make you feel, Jeanne?'

'A lot less hungry than I was before I ate it.'

'Well, I feel rich,' Ethan proclaimed, the idea really hitting him in the soul. 'I am sitting here with this *cassoulet* and I feel like the richest man on Earth.'

'You *are* rich,' Jeanne reminded. 'You own five hotels.'

'It has nothing to do with the hotels. It has to do with... food on the table and... a fire in the grate and... the Christmas music in the air.'

'And your heart filled with love? Blah blah blah.'

Ethan still hadn't eaten a mouthful, although the aroma was continuing to wind its way through him, as were Jeanne's words. *Was* his heart filled with love? He was too scared to think to those depths, but what he did know was that his heart was here, beating, awake and more alive than it had been in the past year. And his mind, well his mind was full of Keeley plus this strange little girl he seemed to have given a home to…

'Do you make Christmas dinner at your hotels?' Jeanne asked suddenly.

'Of course!'

'On Christmas Day?'

'Yes, of course. We have many guests who stay here all over the festive period.'

'But can *anyone* come here, on Christmas Day, and eat the food?'

'Yes, of course,' Ethan started. 'But ordinarily we are fully booked a long time in advance.'

'Oh,' Jeanne said, shoulders sagging a little. 'Not everyone then.'

Not everyone. Those two words hung in the air, somehow contrasting firmly with the delicious fragrant food, the air of joy to the world coming from the light conversation around them and the festive music being played by the pianist near the bar. *Not everyone*. How many times had Ethan been excluded in his lifetime? You never forgot how that felt.

'I can change that,' Ethan whispered.

'What?' Jeanne almost missed her mouth with the fork.

'This year,' Ethan continued. 'We can make Christmas for everyone.'

He didn't wait any longer. Digging his fork into the meal,

he heaped up chicken, sausage and all the other flavours and brought it to his mouth. Closing his eyes, as well as his lips, he experienced all the textures and tastes, the nuances of herbs on his tongue, mixing so perfectly with the thick yet tender chunks of meat. It might have been based on a poor man's meal, but it really did taste like it was fit for a king.

This was going to work. He was going to *make* it work.

Forty-Nine

L'Hotel Paris Parfait, Tour Eiffel, Paris

'The bread's got better. Have you noticed? All the time we've been here it's been fine, you know, white thin sliced and a few rustic baguettes, but now it's like they went out and bought a bakery,' Rach remarked the next morning as they sat eating breakfast.

'Mmm,' Keeley answered. She had been saying 'mmm' quite a lot in response to Rach's questions since last night. Last night, when she had returned to the dining room at the Durands and a chocolate bombe, she just kept seeing that photo in her mind's eye. *Those grey soulful eyes*. Did someone else have that same intense look? Or was it... could it really be... Ethan? And then Keeley's mind started galloping away with that idea. If it was Ethan, why would Ferne have a photo of him? Inside a book. At the side of her bed. The obvious explanation was that they had been together. Ethan and Ferne. Ferne her kidney donor. Together. A couple. Ferne in a relationship with the only man ever to bring her out in goose bumps just from thinking about him... but that was crazy! Until, that was, you started thinking about the 'hotel' connection. Ethan said he part-owned hotels. The Durands owned the Perfect Paris chain. What if the two things were connected? That would make the photo fall into perfect place. And why, oh why, hadn't Keeley asked Silvie any of this last night? One question, one answer, would have provided her with clarity. She could have thought about the 'what then?' afterwards.

'Do you think Antonie looks hot today?'

'Mmm.'

'That's it. You really *aren't* listening, are you?' Rach exclaimed, pouring herself a glass of orange juice.

'Mmm.'

'Keeley!' Rach shouted.

The bellow had Keeley jumping in her chair and connecting her elbow with her bowl of healthy fruit she had known she wasn't going to eat from the moment she ladeled it in there. 'What?' She took a breath. 'Sorry. What did you say?'

'I said Antonie looked hot and you said "mmm" which means you weren't listening to me.' Rach explained. 'You haven't been listening to me since last night. What happened upstairs with Silvie? Did it get a bit creepy being in Ferne's bedroom?' Rach gasped. 'She didn't get out that puppet, did she?'

Keeley shook her head. 'No.'

Should she ask Rach's opinion? Tell her about the photograph? How sure was she that it could have been a picture of Ethan?

'Louis asked me out again last night,' Rach announced, sipping at her juice.

'Oh,' Keeley answered. 'And what did you say?'

Rach took a breath. 'I said no.'

'You did?'

Rach nodded firmly with a big smile on her face. 'Well, it would have been easy to say yes, wouldn't it? He's cute now the allergy's worn off a bit. I'm hot. But... he would have been another "for now" not a "forever".' Rach sighed. 'And, you know, I might not exactly be looking for my "forever" yet, but I am, I think, looking for my "for more than a fortnight".'

Was that what Keeley was looking for too? Or was this connection with Ethan only going to last as long as their stay in the French capital? Did it matter? She hadn't exactly been rife with romance this past year, unlike Rach.

'Please tell me I didn't just say no to something I should have said yes to!' Rach begged. 'I mean he's good-looking and he's rich and he's into me and he has that slight vulnerable edge of sadness filtering through his preppy jumpers and—'

'Does he?' Keeley asked.

'You can tell he loved his sister,' Rach carried on. 'Just in the way his expression changes when he talks about her. He sounded so proud of the work she did at the hotels and he showed me some photos of them when they were kids. Both of them really glowed up!'

'Ferne had a massive bed,' Keeley said with a smile. 'And the mattress was so comfortable.'

'Better than Premier Inn?'

'I'm not sure—'

'Apparently a family friend was meant to be at dinner last night. Someone Louis doesn't get along with. Whoever that is, they're apparently a thorn in his side at the moment. Might have made for a bit of excitement if they'd turned up.'

'Silvie didn't mention anything to me,' Keeley answered.

'I think Silvie was focused on trying to matchmake you and Louis. If only you hadn't met a man with a penguin and a dog on its last legs.'

'You saw for yourself that Bo-Bo's fine now.' She sighed, her mind still delivering her that grainy Polaroid image.

'And are you fine?' Rach asked a little softer now.

Keeley nodded. 'Yes. Of course. Dinner last night was nice. I feel I know Silvie and Ferne even better now.'

And, all she had to do, if she really wanted to know if there was a possibility that Ferne might have a photo of Ethan in a book beside her bed was ask. Or she could completely forget she had ever set eyes on it and whoever it might be in the picture.

Keeley offered up her coffee cup. 'OK, let's have a toast.' She took a breath. 'Here's to having a little French fun today. Let's see some more sights, do a little Christmas shopping, not worry about anything. What do you say?'

'I say *oui*,' Rach replied with a grin. '*Magnifique*.'

Fifty

Cirque Pinder, Paris

'She has been excited all day,' Ethan said that night, his eyes on Jeanne who was galloping ahead towards the grand entrance. A yellow and red striped big top, French flags flying from the uppermost struts was standing ahead of them, the sound of a fairground organ filling the night. 'All day long it has been "what time is it?" and "how many hours to go?".'

Keeley smiled. Her stomach was full of butterflies despite the date pep talk Rach had given her before she'd left their suite for the car waiting outside. She needed to chill. She needed to take things at face value and forget the 'what might be's'. *Mindfulness. Calm.* And if she really *couldn't* do any of that she just needed to ask Ethan if he knew Ferne Durand and see what happened next. Except what did she say if Ethan *was* somehow connected to Ferne? Was she just going to blurt out 'by the way I had a kidney transplant a year ago that I haven't mentioned and I'm the proud owner of one of Ferne's kidneys?' She shivered at that thought. It was much better to still hope that there was no association at all. If there was no association then nothing had to change. She could still enjoy exploring the connection they had made together. And it was the thought of that opportunity being taken from her that was concerning her the most.

'You are quiet,' Ethan said, nudging her arm a little as they walked towards the archway bearing the name 'Pinder' in lights.

'I'm taking it all in,' Keeley answered. 'I've never been to a circus at Christmas time before.'

'For me, I feel it is the perfect time to go,' Ethan said. 'The snow on the ground, the carol singers outside, the electric atmosphere inside the tent.' He pointed ahead to Jeanne. 'The very excited child.'

Jeanne was looking back to them now, a scowl on her face that was visible even from this distance and likely in response to the pace of their stroll.

'I know it is unorthodox,' Ethan began. 'To bring a child along on a date. But, from what I remember of this circus, she is going to be transfixed from the very beginning.' He edged a little closer. 'So transfixed that she will not notice if we... sit a little close to each other and maybe...'

A date. It was definitely a date. Now Keeley's heart was *definitely* telling her to forget everything else. She could close off all the dialogue in her head, concentrate only on how this man was making her feel. Before she knew it, her fingers were finding his and she curled them around his hand, loving the way they felt when they were fitted together. He didn't need to finish the sentence. She knew completely what he meant.

*

The scent of the sawdust, plus the slight smell of heat from all the spotlights stirred Ethan's memories as they entered the big top to a rapidly growing audience. Everything here was a harkening back to when he was Jeanne's age, seeing exotic animals and crazy characters for the very first time.

'Are we close?' Jeanne asked, tugging on his sleeve. 'Will I be able to see everything?'

'Are we close? I do not know,' Ethan answered, drawing the tickets from the pocket of his coat. 'I did not think to—'

Jeanne snatched the tickets from his hands and then her face lit up like Christmas might have arrived already. 'The front row! The very front row!'

He smiled at her pure joy, so richly transparent. He instinctively knew she would like to sit in the very first row and he had been almost as excited as he knew she would be when he had found there were still seats in that area available. What he hadn't been expecting though was what quickly came next. Jeanne threw herself at him, stick-thin – yet surprisingly strong – arms going around him in a bear hug of mammoth proportions. It caught him off guard. He wasn't quite sure what to do. For a brief second he didn't do anything and then he caught sight of Keeley and she put her arms out, mimicking a hug. Yes! He should hug Jeanne back. That was exactly what he should do. Except affection like this, it did not come naturally. Finally, he grouped his arms around her and gathered her a little closer, patting her on the back. Why was he so bad at this? And why was he so bad at this in front of Keeley? What must she think of him?

'Can we get popcorn?' Jeanne asked, stepping back, cheeks flushed, eyes showing signs of unshed tears.

'Maybe in a while,' Ethan offered.

Jeanne waved the tickets in the air and was off again, gamboling down the aisle and making for the front rows of seating right next to the ring.

'She is so excited,' Keeley said. 'More excited than Rach was to discover designer fashion brands at a flea market.'

'I suspect this will be the first time she has been anywhere close to anything like this,' Ethan replied. He was still watching Jeanne, finding himself a little concerned when she was too far away. What was the impetuous child doing to him? She was making him care, opening him up in ways he never thought could be possible in his life.

'Is she staying with you?' Keeley asked. 'At your apartment above a bakery?'

He turned to Keeley then and smiled, nodding. 'It really is small,' he answered. 'When Bo-Bo comes into the living area it is like sharing the space with a large horse.' He sighed. 'But, what else could I do? She has nowhere safe to live. The alternative would be…' He didn't finish the sentence.

'There must be someone you could call for help,' Keeley suggested.

'Help' *would* come if he called it. 'Help', he knew from experience, would end up being worse than all anyone's nightmares rolled into one. He didn't want to think about that option. And that was why he was letting Jeanne stay. 'I have said she can stay for a while. After Christmas, we will see.'

There would be no 'seeing'. He had made Jeanne a promise and he had meant it. He would get her into school if she stayed. He did not have the first idea what he was doing attempting some kind of parenting, but he could not let her go back to how he knew she would be living. Cold. Desperate. Having to make friends with unsuitable people simply to get warm standing around a fire.

'That's very kind of you,' Keeley said.

'She will run the rings around me,' Ethan answered. 'Exactly like the horses we are going to see in a few moments.'

'I like that you care about people,' Keeley told him as they arrived at the very front row of seats. 'I think you find it difficult to know what to do when you *do* care about people but… caring in the first instance that's the most important thing.'

'Oh,' Ethan whispered, dropping his face a little nearer to hers. 'Believe me, I know what to do when I care about people. I am just… a little out of practice.'

And then he kissed her. Firm and intentional, leaving no doubt about the depth of his feelings. Right away her lips responded and the glow that reappeared around his heart whenever their mouths met in a kiss, brightened to a new level.

Jeanne cleared her throat like perhaps she had caught the annoyance of hairballs from Bo-Bo and Keeley backed away from him, her cheeks a little flushed.

'I believe it is a family show,' Jeanne said, sitting high and proud in her chair, hat as far pulled back from her face as it had ever been.

Family. Settling down in his seat next to Keeley, Ethan thought about the fact that family had always seemed such an unlikely scenario in his life, until Ferne. And now, with

Ferne gone, with Louis uncomfortable with Ferne's last wishes regarding the hotels, he had thought it unlikely the universe was going to reach out to him for a second time. But as the lights around them dimmed and the spotlight focused on the circle of sawdust, the ringmaster approaching, Ethan took Keeley's hand in his. Maybe the world could be on hold for a time and, perhaps, the reaching out did not, after all, have to be commenced by fate.

'Horses!' Jeanne breathed louder than Ethan suspected she had expected. 'And… acrobats!'

Keeley turned to look at him and as their eyes met there it was again, loud and clear, a cluster bomb of internal reactions Ethan wasn't at all familiar with. It was demanding loud, screaming, this was right! And then Keeley whispered to him, 'I'm almost as excited as Jeanne.'

He smiled, squeezing her hand. '*Moi aussi*.' He let out a breath of content. 'Me too.'

Fifty-One

'The bikes were the best... no, the clowns... no, the acrobats on the horses... no, wait, *ses furets*! *Oui, ses furets*!'

Yes, there had been performing ferrets that had brought back all the Mr Peterson vibes and had Keeley wondering exactly how big the squirrels that had attacked her mum had been. The performing ferrets were certainly bigger than any stoat-like creature she had come across before, on a nature documentary or once in the closet of a particularly wealthy estate agent customer.

'You have named almost every act that performed,' Ethan said laughing.

'Apart from the ringmaster,' Keeley told Jeanne. 'And he was very good too.'

Jeanne was chomping on a hot dog now as they walked away from the big top over the grass and towards the area where the car was going to collect them from. It was freezing, the snow cracking with every foot laid upon it, breath visible as they chattered. The circus *had* been amazing and, as it was near to Christmas there had been some lovely festive touches to add to all the hair-raising feats and slapstick from the clowns. Ethan had laughed hard at the clowns, their stupidity off the scale, with most of the endings to their sketches predictable but hilarious all the same. And his laughter had warmed Keeley right the way through. To her it was the sweetest sound, because it felt somehow like that slight tenseness he tended to carry was relieved in that moment. Ethan laughed openly and genuinely, always with a whoosh of stress expelled along with that laughter.

'Bo-Bo would have liked it,' Jeanne carried on.

'Bo-Bo would have tried to eat the ferrets,' Ethan said.

'He's a good dog!' Jeanne exclaimed.

'I can vouch he knows how to play dead very well,' Keeley answered.

'He will be pleased to see you,' Jeanne said, a smudge of tomato ketchup on her cheek.

'Where is he?' Keeley asked, 'Is someone watching him?'

'He is at my apartment,' Ethan said. 'He has the entire, yet small, lounge to himself, together with water, too much food and I hope no unexpected accidents on the floorboards. I was also instructed to leave on the TV because he may get lonely.' He paused then and looked to Keeley, his expression giving the impression he thought he had said something wrong. 'That is... you do not have to come... to my apartment... I was not saying that was a firm plan. We can always... go somewhere else or... nowhere at all.'

'*Mon Dieu*,' Jeanne said shaking her head as she stopped walking and stared at Ethan. 'You always do far too much talking!' She chewed up her mouthful and then started talking again. 'You have hot chocolate. You have red wine. Offer one of those and Keeley will come.' She looked to Keeley then. 'Won't you?'

Keeley nodded. 'I would really like to see where you live. Where you *both* are living at the moment.'

'The three of us. Do not forget Bo-Bo,' Jeanne warned. She stepped closer to Keeley then and stage-whispered very poorly. 'He has cheese in the refrigerator but not very much else. He needs to get groceries.'

'Dog food, red wine and cheese,' Ethan added with a shake of the head. 'My priorities now.'

'And he doesn't have a Christmas tree yet. You will get a Christmas tree soon, won't you?'

'There is not space for your dog *and* a Christmas tree in my living room.'

'*Connerie*!'

'Jeanne!' Ethan shouted.

'*Quoi*?'

'Do I want to know what you two are saying?' Keeley asked.

'*Non*,' Ethan and Jeanne answered together.

'Fine,' Keeley answered with a smile. 'I look forward to my conversation with Bo-Bo.'

Fifty-Two

Ethan's apartment, Opera District, Paris

The car pulled to the kerb on the narrowest of streets that seemed only really large enough for two bicycles to pass. Townhouses rose upwards from the pavement, iron Juliet balconies aglow with festive fairy lights, the sound of jazz a whisper in the night air. Milo, the driver, had opened her door and Keeley stood in the street regarding the place Ethan lived. It suited him. It was everything she thought it would be. Individual and soulful, just like him. She hurriedly fastened up her coat then, before ducking her head back into the rear of the vehicle.

'Do you need any help?' she whispered.

'No,' Ethan replied. 'It is OK.'

Milo opened the door on Ethan's side of the vehicle and Ethan stepped out onto the road, before diving back in and gently pulling a sleeping Jeanne into his arms. 'Thank you, Milo. I will call you when Keeley wishes to go back to her hotel.'

'*D'accord.*' Milo touched his hat and got back into the car.

'She's fast asleep,' Keeley said, walking next to Ethan has he headed towards an archway built into crumbling brickwork. Just to the right was that bakery on the corner he had told her about, a dim light coming from inside that suggested someone was already at work to make the next morning's baguettes. It was so charming. It wasn't anything like the hustle and bustle around the Eiffel Tower. It was traditional yet also a little quirky, with brightly painted front doors, some with tiny hedge-edged front gardens creeping onto the pavement with room only for one small table and a chair. Keeley followed Ethan under the archway and into an inner courtyard not visible from the street. There were old-fashioned streetlamps, an area fenced off in the centre with wrought iron benches and more lights hanging from trees growing among the slimline homes. It looked like a walled garden solely for its residents.

'Keeley,' Ethan whispered. 'Could you... help me? The key to my apartment is... in my pocket.'

'Oh, sorry, yes,' Keeley said. 'Where? Should I...'

'The left side,' Ethan said, turning a little to aid her search. 'Or maybe the right. I do not remember.' He flushed a little and it was cute. '*Je suis désolé*. Sorry.'

Keeley slipped her hand inside the pocket of his coat, needing to stand close to get her fingers in to the very bottom. She was conscious of his proximity and could only imagine what he smelled of. She tried to inhale and inject some vigour to her dulled senses like she had when they had overlooked the Seine. *Masculinity. Mystery. Adventure.* Although she wasn't sure it was possible to actually smell any of those words her brain had dealt up. She swallowed and made herself focus on the task in hand. There was nothing in his left-hand pocket.

'Sorry,' she breathed. 'There's nothing there.' She moved around the still sleeping Jeanne, and dug into his other pocket. This time she produced a set of keys. 'Which one?' she asked. 'I'll open the door.'

'The brass one,' he whispered.

It was a nice front door, the paint a faded green and peeling off in places, but in complete keeping with the rest of the courtyard of doors and the old, scuffed brickwork. She slotted the key into the lock and turned, stepping back as the door opened and she let Ethan with Jeanne in first. Keeley followed, moving in behind Ethan, taking in the bare brick walls and aged wooden boards beneath her boots. A black iron spiral staircase led upwards and Ethan seemed to have to rearrange Jeanne slightly to avoid knocking any parts of her against the curve of the stairs.

There were photos on the bare bricks – black and white prints of city scenes and people. Some places Keeley recognised – the Eiffel Tower, Notre Dame – and others she didn't – street cafés, a man playing an accordion. It was minimalist, but it was a small area down here. A front door, a hallway and this staircase that wobbled quite a bit with every step she took.

She reached the top and Ethan turned to look at her.

'I will put her into bed,' he whispered. 'The lounge is through there.' He indicated a closed door just in front of her.

'Are you sure you don't need any help?' she asked him.

'No,' he said. 'I won't be long. Please, sit down, relax.' He turned then, manoeuvring into another room on what was a pretty tiny landing area.

Keeley put her hand on the door handle and opened. With the very first crack of opening, Bo-Bo came barrelling through, barking and whining and nearly knocking Keeley sideways in his attempt to get out. The dog made for the room Ethan and Jeanne had gone into and Keeley stepped on into the living area.

It was small but perfectly formed. Wooden floorboards again, a floor-to-ceiling bookshelf against one wall containing all manner of items. There were many books, then piles of magazines, toy cars, board games, Rubik's cube style puzzles, empty wine bottles with burned down candles poking out of them, others that looked like they contained copper strings of lights. Some people might describe it as cluttered, but to Keeley it looked like all of the places she had been with Ethan during their time together. It was acutely him.

She moved to the window – only a few steps and she was there – and looked out over the street below. Even with the window closed against the cold she could still hear the subtle jazz and see those lights on the balconies.

'Jeanne's bedroom has a view of the courtyard garden,' Ethan said.

Keeley hadn't heard him enter the room and she swung round, knocking something on the floor with her boot. 'Oh, sorry, I think I...'

'It is OK,' Ethan said, crossing the room in two paces and bending over. 'It is Bo-Bo's water and food bowl. I will move them.' He picked up the bowls she hadn't seen and strode another two paces and through a small arch in the wall into what Keeley could see was the tiniest of kitchens.

He came out again, standing under the arch, looking a little unsure of himself. 'You would like hot chocolate?'

'If it isn't any trouble,' Keeley answered. 'The person who invited me has fallen asleep and the dog who was supposed to be pleased to see me couldn't wait to shoot past me.' She smiled.

'The dog is trying to wake Jeanne up,' Ethan replied. 'Licking her face like she is an ice cream.'

Keeley stepped towards him. 'Let me help.'

'It is OK,' Ethan said. 'The kitchen… it is… *petite*.'

'I don't mind,' Keeley said. 'I would like to see it.'

Ethan smiled. 'There is only about a metre to regard.'

'Aren't the very best things supposed to come in small packages?' The second the sentence left her lips she blushed.

His smile widened then, a look of pure sexy mischief dancing in his eyes. 'Ah, Keeley,' he breathed. 'But, sometimes, also what you see is not always what you get.'

Now her blush was turning bonfire hot and she wondered whether she could stand next to him in a confined kitchen space without wondering exactly what the true dimensions of his package was…

Ethan laughed then. 'Come.' He beckoned. 'I will show you what the French stockpile in their cupboards.'

Fifty-Three

Ethan wanted to impress her. It was stupid, wasn't it? To want to impress someone he had learned put more weight on feelings and comfort than she did on the size of someone's living space or whether they had top-of-the-range kitchen appliances. Yet still he wanted her to like the place he lived the way *he* liked it. There was a reason it was small. There was a reason he hadn't moved to a different part of Paris, somewhere considered more affluent. This was who he was. This was all he needed.

He had made hot chocolate and then he had lit the wood burner. It was the tiniest of fires against one bare brick wall, so close to the sofa that if you stuck your feet out too far you might catch your toes on the front of it. But it didn't need to be of a size to adequately heat the living room. And it *was* warm now, perhaps a little too warm considering he and Keeley were sat close together on the only two-seater sofa he had found to fit in the room.

'How is your hot chocolate?' Ethan asked, plucking his mug from the coffee table and taking a sip.

'It's very good,' Keeley admitted.

'If I wanted to impress you I would tell you it is my mother's recipe,' Ethan said.

'It's not?'

'It is out of a jar, with a touch of milk, blended together to form a paste, before you add the hot water.'

'And now I have your secret to making it so well,' Keeley said.

He smiled. There was a question he had been wanting to ask her almost since they had met, but he had battered it away as unimportant. If he asked it now he knew it would change things from living in the moment to making plans for something else. But his need to know the answer was now creeping up as December started to accelerate in numbers...

'Keeley,' Ethan began.

'Yes.'

'How long are you staying in Paris?' It was out there now, but it felt altogether too blunt. He followed it up. 'I do not know if you are... here on holiday or... with your work or... something else.'

'A holiday,' Keeley answered. She cleared her throat and leaned forward to put her mug of hot chocolate down on the coffee table. 'Rach and I... well, we had some time off that needed to be used up before the end of the year and... we had never been to Paris before so...'

'And you are returning when?' He swallowed. He was now feeling anxious about her answer. What if she said she was leaving soon? Before Christmas. Sooner...

'We haven't actually fixed a date yet,' Keeley said. 'But my parents are expecting me back for Christmas Day. And if I don't get back for Christmas Day it's likely my mum will phone the British Embassy.'

Ethan smiled. 'OK.' *Soon*. But not so soon they couldn't

spend more time together. This was good. Or at least, better than bad.

'What about your mother?' Keeley asked then, sitting a little sideways so she was facing him. 'Would she phone the *gendarmes* if you were overseas and didn't come back when you said you would?'

'Ah,' Ethan said with a sigh. *His mother. His parentage.* The thing he never talked about. Immediately he got ready to change the subject or trot out the usual tired lines he gave to girls in bars who wanted more than a physical connection during a one-night encounter. But the words weren't coming as easily as usual and one look at Keeley's expression – soft, inquisitive, ready to be fully invested in his answer – told him this was not the time for brushing this off. 'I... do not know my mother.'

He turned a little side-on too and watched the confusion appear on her face. 'I... do not know my father either.' He shrugged, as if this was the most normal thing in the world.

'You don't know them very well?' Keeley asked. 'Or you...' She stopped, as if trying to get her mind to catch up. He filled in the gaps for her.

'I do not know them at all. I have... never known them,' he stated. 'The story is that I was left at the orphanage as a baby. No note. No information at all. Just me.' Saying the words was still uncomfortable even though time had marched on. He didn't give himself permission to dwell very often because what was the point? It achieved nothing. 'I am... very much... like Jeanne.' He shrugged again. 'Perhaps that is why she is here with her very annoying dog.' He smiled, cradling his mug in his hands.

'I can't imagine not knowing who I came from,' Keeley said. 'Sorry… that was really unfeeling. I didn't mean—'

'It is OK,' Ethan told her. 'But I have never known any different.' He placed his mug back on the table. 'Everyone around me at the orphanage was in the same position. Later, everyone I came into contact with on the street was either in the same position or hiding from the family they *did* have.'

'So how did you build up a business? Where did you begin? What about school?'

'So many questions,' Ethan breathed, a hint of a smile on his lips.

'Sorry,' Keeley said. 'Am I asking too much? Is it—'

'*Non*,' Ethan said. 'It is OK.'

It was OK, wasn't it? To share the truth of his past with Keeley? Usually there was hesitation and a small voice telling him not to tell his story, but this time the little whisper from his subconscious seemed to be cheering him on. 'The reason I am here and not still living on the street. The reason I have a reason to get up in the mornings is because… I met a girl.'

Keeley felt her heart plummet and she was back in that bedroom picking up a photograph from the carpet. Was this the moment she was going to find out what she was undoubtedly the most terrified of? She tried to calm her inner turmoil and not let it show on the outside. How did you do that when everything itched and pulsed?

'That girl, she made me realise that the world is a complicated place, but that at the heart of everything is the simple knowledge that no matter what our background, or our beliefs, or our status… we *are* all the same,' Ethan said with true conviction. 'We are all in this world together and she showed me that I counted exactly as much as the next person. And she taught me never to apologise for being who I am.'

'She sounds like a wonderful person.' Keeley knew her lips were trembling. She should ask the question now. She should ask Ethan the name of the girl, and pray she was wrong. But the raging fear that she wasn't wrong, that she already knew the answer, was overpowering everything. She wanted so much to be wrong. She didn't want confirmation. Because if she had confirmation it would open up a whole different avenue of discussion that once travelled down could not be retraced.

'She is,' he answered softly.

'Were you in love?' Keeley asked. *Say no. Please say no. Say the grey eyes in that photo weren't yours.* She was holding her fingertips together, crushing the pads against each other.

'No,' Ethan breathed, his lips forming a smile. 'No, never in love. Not like that. The best of friends. She... has a piece of my heart, and everything she has given to me is something I can never repay.'

He looked so sad now, so lost. All Keeley ached to do was reach out to him, to let him know how special *she* thought he was. But if she did that, if she made that deepest of statements now, here by the cosiest of fires in the most comfortable of places, full of Ethan's eclectic personality and sizzling masculinity, there might be no going back.

'I do not think I have ever been in love the way it is described in books or in TV shows,' Ethan admitted. 'Have you... ever been in love?'

Keeley was finding it increasingly difficult not to show everything she was feeling in her body language now. She knew she had never felt with anyone else the way she felt here next to him. Could she admit that out loud? Erica invaded her thoughts then and the promise she had made her friend. *All in. Every time.*

And then there was Bea. Forthright and pragmatic even in love. You liked someone, you told them. You got on with it. Bea had never been afraid to live her truth. It felt like Bea and Erica were both staring hard at her now, pleading with her to say what she felt.

'I think love might be what's happening to me now,' Keeley breathed. She looked into Ethan's eyes, breath catching in her throat. 'I think it's frightening… and uncontrollable and it… doesn't discriminate between people who are ready for it and people who had no idea it was going to happen.' She took a harried breath. 'I think it might be meeting someone unexpectedly and… chasing a penguin… and finding hidden Paris and raising a dog from the dead…or maybe even… riding extinct animals on a carousel…'

'Could it be… showing someone your very favourite café without worrying they will not see it the same way as you do?' Ethan asked. 'Or, maybe, feeling more in tune with someone than you have ever felt your whole life as you look through trunks and shelves and baskets at a flea market.'

He had edged closer to her. Keeley could feel his knees pressing so lightly against hers, the sofa no bigger than a not-very-generous loveseat. 'Is it thinking about making postcards?' she asked him. 'Of places that don't usually have postcards?'

'I think perhaps it could be all of those things,' Ethan whispered. 'And maybe so much more.'

Nothing else mattered, did it? Nothing except the delicious sugar-coated sensations that were caramelising her heart. Keeley reached for him, wanting to feel if the beat of his heart was echoing hers. With a trembling hand she touched his chest and, as her fingertips connected with the fabric of his shirt, he tipped forward, placing his hand on top of hers. Now she was breathless, motionless, simply still and able to recognise the thrum of his core exactly as urgent as her own.

Keeley gazed at him. It was like somehow she had known him her whole life. She took in the way his slightly wild crop of hair never quite looked the same, the tiny crinkles at the corner of his beautiful eyes that increased when he laughed or concentrated hard, his firm jaw and those oh-so-smooth lips. Looking at him, being with him was like coming home to a familiarity no one had let her know existed out there, ready only for her.

'Keeley,' Ethan said, a hitch in his voice.

She didn't want to speak anymore. She wanted to be a little selfish. She wanted to believe this was somehow meant to be.

She leaned into him, in no doubt of what she wanted, connecting their lips in a kiss that sent crackles of heat right the way through her. And Ethan's response only sent her temperature soaring higher. He returned the kiss she had started and it was like before on the street – strong, sensual, passionate – yet this time the intensity seemed to have increased ten-fold. This wasn't a kiss you broke away from. This was a kiss you leaned in to and made last.

It was Keeley's fingers that moved to buttons first and hastily, keeping their mouths together, she began to unfasten Ethan's shirt. Her heart might have been jumping a jive, but her mind was clear. There was nothing she wanted more than to move this on a level. Except she still didn't know. And maybe she *did* need to know before this went further. She drew her mouth away from his, breathless, knowing her pupils had to be as large as giant chocolate buttons as she regarded him, shirt half on-half off, his hair even wilder now her fingers had raked their way through it. 'Ethan,' she said.

'*Oui*.'

She could see the deep concern in his face, almost as if he felt he had done something wrong. Perhaps this was the kind of complex that someone who had obviously brought himself up had hanging over him all the time. But this vulnerability and exposure of his inner self to her only fuelled her feelings for him.

Keeley reached for his hand, interlinking it with hers. 'What was the name of the girl? The one who has a piece of your heart?'

He squeezed her hand and kept his eyes on hers. '*Crevette*,' he answered. '*Ma crevette*.'

Not Ferne. Definitely not Ferne. The absolute relief quickly mixed together with total joy at his reply and Keeley kissed him again, hurrying to relieve him of his clothes. She discarded his shirt and looked in appreciation at his trim torso before resting her lips on his shoulder blade, then kissing a pathway down his chest.

'Keeley,' he said, raising her head with one hand and looking deep into her eyes. 'You are sure?'

It was a gentleman's question and Ethan was every inch the gentleman even if he did not realise it. She smiled and kissed his mouth again. 'Yes,' she replied. 'Yes, I'm sure.' She palmed his face again. 'Show me your bedroom.'

Needing no further reassurance, Ethan scooped her up in his arms, holding her tight as she kissed him again, and he carried her out of the room.

Fifty-Four

Place de la Bastille, Paris

'Today, nothing remains of the prison,' Noel began the next morning. 'In my opinion this is a good thing. I feel if the ruins did remain, then Paris would be inundated with tourists wanting there to also be cardboard cut outs of Russell Crowe or Ann Hathaway for them to have selfie photographs with.'

Rach drew in a breath, looking like she was also inhaling snowflakes that were dropping at pace from heavy grey clouds above them. 'Why did we agree to this particular sightseeing expedition at stupid o'clock?'

Keeley stifled another yawn. 'Because Silvie arranged it for us and she's meeting us for lunch. And she paid for our whole trip here and—'

'Alright! Alright! I get it,' Rach said with a sigh. 'Although I'd be slightly more grateful if I had a large strong coffee in my hands right about now.'

Noel cleared his throat in a manner that gave off irritation. 'Are you interested in the history?' he asked. 'Or would you rather we skip to the boutiques again? There are at least a hundred other places I could be, although I am too polite and too in need of my job to tell Madame Durand that.'

'I'd like some of the history please,' Keeley told him. Despite being London-Marathon-in-a-heatwave-wearing-a-bear-costume-kind-of-exhausted she was also feeling energised. Perhaps it was the soul-searing sex with Ethan or maybe the early-morning wake-up when Bo-Bo decided to leave the comfort of Jeanne's bed for the master bedroom. Or maybe it was the knowledge that something had changed in her. Keeley Andrews, penned into a pre-ordained life model where everything is triple-checked and planned with the fine detail of crisis management, was breaking out of her fragile mould.

'Keels!' Rach moaned.

'Come on,' Keeley said, putting her arm around her friend and walking closer to the July Column that was ahead of them. 'It's good to learn about what happened in the past. It makes you appreciate what we have now.'

'Did you actually have sex last night or did you just spend the small hours reading books?'

Noel cleared his throat again. 'The prison that was here was stormed in 1789 at the very beginning of the French revolution. Now the only thing that remains of it is the outline traced in stones that differs from the rest of the pavement. I will show you.' He strode on.

'You haven't told me all the details of it yet,' Rach reminded, taking Keeley's arm. 'And if we are going to be best friends as well as apartment sharers when we get back home then I am expecting all the details of everything, even more so than I normally do.'

Sex with Ethan. Keeley's whole body was still humming from it. It was like her skin had been lightly glossed in a golden syrup and was still softly simmering from the heat they'd made together. She couldn't stop herself from smiling. Even the snowflakes that seemed to be settling – and sticking – on her eyelashes more than anywhere else weren't as annoying as they might have been.

'It was,' Keeley began, 'incredible.'

'Give me it in a food analogy,' Rach ordered, expression eager.

'It was like... devouring the best Chinese takeaway you've ever had, really *really* slowly, and feeling completely warm and full and... the end result is not putting any weight on and ending up with the figure of Emma Willis.'

'Jesus!' Rach exclaimed. '*That* good.'

'*That* good.'

'Did he—' Rach started.

'*Regarde*!' Noel all but shouted. '*Opera Bastille*.'

Keeley looked up at the silver façade just ahead of them. It was all chrome and glass and granite. Nothing like the tiny alleyways and courtyards she had been hoping to see on this morning's tour.

'It was built in 1989 by a Canadian architect and you can take part in a tour inside if you so wish,' Noel informed them. 'It is approximately ninety minutes long.'

Keeley looked at Rach and Rach looked back at her. If Keeley was honest she was enjoying the snow, the Christmas trees sparkling from business premises along their route, the sound of carols in the air, even the city traffic was oddly pleasurable today. 'Could we carry on walking? Is there somewhere nice we can stop for coffee?'

'Now you're talking my language,' Rach said happily.

'As you wish,' Noel replied.

Noel had led them underneath a large red canopy where patio heaters were warming the patrons sitting underneath it. He had then instructed a waiter to take their order while he disappeared somewhere else citing he would be back in an hour's time. Keeley thought their guide seemed slightly more harassed than usual today, his mind definitely elsewhere. Their coffees having arrived, it was pleasant sitting here, the chill taken out of the air by the heaters and still very much able to people-watch, Parisian life going on around them.

'So,' Rach said, sipping at her coffee. 'Tell me, are you still not Kidney Girl or did you tell Ethan last night while he was all over you like chow mein?'

'Still not Kidney Girl,' Keeley admitted.

'Whoa! It must be a record.'

Keeley smiled. 'We might need to phone Guinness.'

She couldn't deny, despite feeling like a bubbling ball of mercury waiting to rise up the thermometer, it had been on her mind the whole time Ethan had been stripping her of her clothes in his bedroom. She was going to be naked, fully exposed, for the first time since the accident. Would he find her scars off-putting – the four almost dent-like marks at her centre and the other longer curved scars at one side of her body. Would he ask about them? And if he did ask, what would she say? In the end, this morning, while she was dressing again and wanting to leave before Jeanne awoke, Ethan had finally asked her about them and she had given him the only answer she was ready to at the moment.

'He kissed my scars,' Keeley told Rach, the memory of Ethan's hot mouth tracing every line making her shiver all over again. 'And this morning he asked me what had happened.'

Rach shifted forward on her seat. 'What did you say?'

Keeley smiled. 'I told him if he thought my scars were bad he should have seen the shark.'

Rach laughed.

Keeley knew she had to tell Ethan the truth. She also knew she *wanted* to tell him the truth. But telling him would mean talking about her weakened immunity, her probable need for further transplants and her shorter-than-average life expectancy. She just wanted to complete one perfect Paris night without any of those complications. That wasn't a lot of ask for, was it?

'What did he say to that?' Rach asked her.

'He said he was never going to go swimming with me,' Keeley answered.

Fifty-Five

L'Hotel Paris Parfait, Opera District, Paris

Ethan had never felt so energised. Suddenly he felt he had become superhuman. Today he was the personification of organised and capable, the leader of the hotel he should have been when they went through the despair of losing Ferne. He placed a deep green velvet chair in the corner of the dining room, next to the fireplace he had got Jeanne to decorate with whimsical ornaments that looked like they might have come from the circus. Bright turquoise fir cones mingled with nickel bells and dancing fairies on strings, aged Santas on sleighs and red apples with silver centres reflected the flames flickering in the grate. An old-fashioned radio with big chunky buttons on the mantle was playing a festive soundtrack as Ethan worked, making tweaks, re-arranging, bringing in more pieces from the hotel's garage.

'What the hell is going on?'

It was Louis's voice, audible from the dining area, even above the music, but definitely coming from reception.

Ethan straightened the collar of his shirt as well as his demeanour and headed out of the room.

'Antoine, why are there *rabbits* in the reception area?' Louis boomed. 'And why are guests *touching* them?'

Before his concierge could reply Ethan stepped up and stepped in. 'Christmas, Louis, it is all about "birth" and "new life". And it is also about children. The festive petting area is somewhere the kids staying here can share a hands-on experience with their family.' Ethan smiled. 'Happy family, Happy Christmas.'

'This,' Louis began, his cheeks turning so red Ethan wondered if the man might have an allergy to rabbits as well as penguins, 'is a health and safety disaster waiting to happen! Animals! In a five-star hotel!' Louis scoffed. 'Is this a joke? Some sort of twisted payback about the animal shelter inheriting a share of the hotels?'

'What?' Antoine gasped. Ethan noticed his concierge was now wearing latex gloves.

It was Ethan's turn to be angry now. He put a hand on Louis's shoulder and moved him towards the small rabbit enclosure, but away from Antoine. 'You cannot speak of private business matters in front of the staff. It is confidential and it unsettles them.'

Louis snorted. 'So, now you are all about the business? Now, at the final hour, when you have been basically neglecting everything my sister built up and running the hotels into the ground for the past twelve months.'

'That is not fair, Louis,' Ethan said, narrowing his eyes. 'You know how tough things have been for the whole tourist and travel industry.'

'And I also know you have been spending your time

frittering away my sister's money while my mother has been trying to work out an exit plan from her involvement with the hotels without ruffling your feathers,' Louis continued, pointing a finger in Ethan's face. '*I* do not care for your feathers!'

Ethan bent over the small wooden fenced enclosure and plucked up a baby rabbit, holding it in his hands and smoothing his fingers over its fur. 'You do not care for anything other than money,' Ethan said, rubbing the space behind the rabbit's ears. 'That has always been your way. That is why you are nothing like your sister. You lack all of her *joie de vivre* and passion. You left France, you left your family, to chase the cash in the US and you never once looked back. Ferne's drive was for life. Yours, it is still for dollar signs.'

'Speaks the man who is holding a rabbit in the middle of a reception area! You, Ethan, are ludicrous! And you always have been!'

'And you,' Ethan said pushing the rabbit towards Louis, 'are terrified of anything you cannot make into a spreadsheet! Numbers! Averages! Be careful not to actually get emotional about anything!'

'You won't win,' Louis told him.

'And still you are so stupid! This is not about winning!' Ethan retorted. 'It is about taking the hotels in a different direction. A direction I know Ferne would be so proud of.' He cuddled the rabbit to his chest. 'Fluidity. That was what Ferne was all about. Smooth. Elegant. Adaptable. She would think always outside of the box.'

'And look how that ended for her,' Louis bit back.

If Ethan hadn't been holding the bunny, if a family of

four with two excited children hadn't bounded over to the pen of animals as soon as they arrived inside the hotel, he would have struck out at Louis's careless comment and given the guy another red mark on his face.

'Did you even know your sister at all?' Ethan spat.

'I knew her as well as I was able to know her, with someone else always there. Someone who always seemed to be right there in what should have been my place!'

Louis's comment rocked Ethan for a moment and he began to see a different look in the man's eyes. What was hiding there? Regret? Sadness? Envy? No, it was not possible that Louis might be jealous of him. Unless this really was not about possessions and wealth... but family.

'Louis, I—'

'Where is your plan?' Louis interrupted, the shutters up again.

'Well, there are going to be many changes,' Ethan told him. 'And I am going to showcase them all at Christmas. Then I will present Silvie and the representative from the animal shelter my plan for the development of the chain over the next three years.'

'You have made a three-year plan?' Louis immediately scoffed.

'It is not finalised yet but—'

'As I thought! The way you always are! All of the dramatic presentation and nothing to back it up!'

'You will see,' Ethan said. 'I am going to make the hotels even more of a success and I am going to do it on my terms and... in Ferne's honour.'

Ethan hadn't expected the raw emotion to come rolling up over him but there it was, wrapping itself around him, seeping through his skin, finding its way into every cell until it found his heart. The tiny rabbit was quivering in his hands, and then Louis broke the silence.

'My mother wants you to come to lunch,' Louis said, still sounding a little stiff. 'That is really why I am here.'

'Today? Now?' Ethan asked, checking his watch as he still balanced the bunny in his palms.

'You could not make dinner at the house to meet—'

He didn't need to hear any more. 'And I cannot make lunch today. I have too much to do here. Plus, a three-year plan to finish.'

'Ethan,' Louis said a little softer. 'We cannot keep running away from the fact that Ferne has gone.'

'That is where you are wrong,' Ethan answered, pressing the rabbit to Louis's chest and giving the man no choice but to take it. 'I am not running away. For the very first time I am creating a future to run towards.' He smiled then, enjoying Louis's disgust at having to handle the animal. 'Do not forget to wash your hands,' he said. 'There is also an antibacterial hand gel station by the door to the bar. Bye.'

Fifty-Six

I ned to see a pic. I want to no what he looks lik. Dying girl shud get wot she wants.

The spelling was all off and that wasn't Erica at all. There was also an emoji of a skull and crossbones that might have been funny if it didn't have such tragic connotations. Keeley ran her fingers over the text and imagined the effort it would have taken for Erica to press the icons considering how weak she was.

'Is everything OK?' Ethan asked, pressing a kiss to her temple as they walked alongside each other. They had got off the Metro only five minutes earlier, with their final location apparently a surprise for her. A new crisp layer of snow on the ground, Paris was becoming more and more festive as every day passed. It was getting to that stage where Keeley was becoming accustomed to being here, getting used to speaking a few words of French, craving the chance to have cheese without a disapproving Lizzie look and strolling along the cobbled streets discovering the tourist trail of the city as well as its hidden parts. Including the parts of Ethan she had discovered last night...

Keeley smiled at him. 'You'll think it's silly if I tell you.'

'I would never think that,' he assured her.

'Well… my friend at the hospice I told you about… Erica. She… wants to see a photo of you.' She was blushing straightaway. She might have slept with this gorgeous guy, but were they at the taking photos stage? Which one usually came first in this whole holiday romance scenario? Probably, weirdly, not the taking photos part.

'What is silly about that?' he asked. 'Unless…'

Then he pouted as if suddenly struck by something. How was it fair that a man had lips to-die-for like that?

'Unless?' Keeley asked.

'Unless you would rather send her a photograph of… Alec Benjamin?'

Keeley laughed. 'Do you even know who Alec Benjamin is?'

'I have had a crash course this afternoon. Jeanne hacked into my Spotify. I could probably sing you all the songs.'

She smiled. This was a man she definitely felt so comfortable with. 'Would you mind?' She quickly continued. 'The photo… not the singing. Unless you want to.'

'Of course,' Ethan said. 'A selfie. Come on,' he encouraged. 'Here, with the *Palais Garnier* in the background.'

The *Palais Garnier* was a magnificent sight. Golden-coloured effigies stood proudly at the forefront of the roof, with smaller busts in-between and a large green figure at its centre. Keeley was sure Noel would have been able to tell her the history behind it all, but this time she would have to refer back to her guidebook when she returned to the hotel. Sometimes thumbing the pages of a reference in the moment killed the magic. She took her phone from her bag and turned the screen around to capture them both, lining their faces up and eager to get some of the best bits of the statuesque building behind. She felt Ethan slip his arm around her shoulders and draw her closer, that gorgeous, wide smile, appearing on those lips…

'For your friend,' Ethan said, still smiling for the pose.

'Erica,' Keeley breathed, widening her smile too. She pressed the button and committed the picture to her camera roll.

Ethan let a breath go then, cupping his hands together and blowing into them.

'Is everything OK?' Keeley asked him. 'You haven't told me where we're going.'

He grinned. 'You are right. I have not.'

'You seem nervous,' Keeley said. He did seem nervous, or perhaps it was more a case of nervous energy.

'Maybe a little,' he admitted.

'Why? What's all the secrecy?'

'Come, I have something to show you. But first, we are going to play a game.' He took her hand in his, squeezing it a little. It was both comforting and somehow super-sexy. A game? She hoped it wasn't the kind found beneath the pages of an erotic novel. She might have felt liberated by the complete abandonment of her apologise-for-everything Britishness in their love-making last night but she wasn't sure bedroom games were quite her bag this soon…

'Now you look a little scared,' Ethan remarked. 'It is nothing difficult, I promise.'

Keeley was trying not to think of all the 'easy' half-hours she had spent with items labelled 'body contouring'. Perhaps she should have asked more questions of Rach prior to this.

She had left her friend in the hotel suite, zinging between emails to a salubrious House 2 Home client she apparently had to give attention to even though she was on holiday and ringing down to reception deliberately asking for things not on the room service menu and intentionally calling Antoine Antonie.

'OK,' Keeley answered a little stiffly.

'Hey,' Ethan said, putting his arm around her and pulling her gently against him. 'If you are not one for surprises, I can tell you. I do not want you to feel… less than "comfortable" about tonight.'

He had purred the word 'comfortable' and the happy sparks were back.

'I trust you that it's going to be a surprise I'm going to like,' she answered him.

'*Je promets*,' he whispered, his mouth close to her ear. 'I promise.'

Ethan's heart was somewhere between his throat and his ears as he pushed open the ornate iron gates that led into the rear entrance of Perfect Paris Opera. This was one of the reasons this hotel was so popular. Its fabric seamlessly blended between being a large building fit for hundreds of guests, but also with the quaint, appealing throwback features hinting at the villages of France and the countryside. And Ethan was going to make it his mission to do the same for the internal décor going forward. Tonight he had made this garden courtyard just for them, with himself and Jeanne working hard all afternoon to get it perfect. He looked to the windows of the hotel then, imagining the girl and Bo-Bo peering out at them. There was no evidence of this yet.

'Oh, Ethan!' Keeley breathed. 'This is… beautiful.'

Her tone was exactly what he had hoped for. He watched her walk into the middle of the walled courtyard, the trailing ivy still present on the rough, old brick walls at this time of year, strings of tiny golden lights interwoven amid their vines. There were candles everywhere. Plain Mason jars holding tealights sat all along the path to the main building some also perfectly positioned on the small bistro table set for two – a bottle of red wine breathing in its centre – and finally there were half a dozen more marking out the perimeter of the *petanque* court. Lights on the wall focused their attention on the strip of sand and shining silver balls.

'What is this place?' Keeley asked. 'Is it another part of hidden Paris no one knows about?'

'*Non*,' Ethan answered. 'This is… one of my hotels.'

Keeley turned around then, her gaze moving from the twinkling romantic garden he had made, to him. 'Is it really?'

He nodded, at last feeling nothing but the deepest pride in what he and Ferne had achieved over the time they'd had together. 'It is.' He swallowed. 'Is it… what you imagined?'

'Gosh,' Keeley said. 'I don't know what I imagined. I suppose I thought it might be a little like the hotel I'm staying in. Although things there have changed a little bit over the past few days.'

'They have?' He held his breath, wanting her to say the changes were all for the better.

'Yes,' she answered. 'The bread is much *much* nicer and

the too big Christmas tree in the lobby has gone. Now it's one a little less dramatic.'

She *did* approve. But he didn't want to say anything yet. He wanted the interior of *this* hotel – the one he had put his heart and soul into today – to be another complete surprise to her... together with his proposal.

'So,' he said, spreading his arms wide, 'a good surprise? A garden in the city, a little red wine and a game of *petanque*.'

She was smiling. 'I've never played before. You are going to have to teach me.'

Her words thrilled him. He wanted to teach her many things. She had taught him a few things last night. She had taught him that sex could be so far removed from anything he had experienced before that it was almost another act entirely. There had been moments during the day when he had recalled a snapshot from their night together and his own lack of self-preservation, the freedom of his heart, had astounded him all over again. He had loved longer, harder and deeper last night than he had ever thought possible. And their lovemaking had most definitely been as much about the togetherness of their minds, hearts and souls as it had been about their bodies. Maybe even more so...

'But of course,' Ethan told her, stepping towards the sand. 'Come.'

Fifty-Seven

'Yes! Yes! I win! I win!'

Keeley laughed as Ethan threw his hands into the night air and began to dance around the boules arena like he had just scored the winning goal in the World Cup. This was the third time he had won. Despite his expert tuition – that had involved much close contact she had absolutely enjoyed more than the game itself – Keeley just wasn't skilled at the art of 'chucking'. In fact, she was almost worse at *petanque* than she was at darts.

'You are not celebrating with me,' Ethan said, finally putting his arms down and stilling his moves. 'You are a bad loser.'

'Oh, no, hang on a minute,' Keeley protested, all smiles. 'That is very unfair.'

'You are not congratulating me on my victory,' Ethan continued.

'You haven't actually given me much of a chance,' Keeley said, still laughing at him. 'Anyway, it's not the British thing to go around congratulating others who have beaten us by waving our arms in the air like we've won ourselves.'

'*Non*?'

'No,' Keeley admitted, taking steps towards him. 'We

might get a little sour at having lost primarily, but then we always give a firm "well done" handshake even if we're still not quite satisfied with the result.' She held her hand out to him.

'You are sour?' he asked her, one eyebrow raising.

'No one likes losing,' Keeley said. 'Particularly if you're someone who hasn't ever felt you're very good at anything.'

She watched his face morph into a deep-set frown then. 'You do not think you are very good at anything?'

Keeley shrugged then, realising perhaps this conversation about winning and losing had suddenly got a little deep. 'Well, you know, some people are naturally good at things and some people just aren't. And those people, they have to work a little harder to achieve good things.'

'Oh, Keeley,' Ethan breathed.

She almost felt his exhalation inside herself and it was as heartening as it was confrontational. She shivered as he took her hand.

'What I am about to show you,' he said so gently. 'It is all your doing.'

She swallowed, trying to read the emotion in his eyes. What was he going to show her?

'Come,' he said, gently tugging her hand and heading for the glass-paned door to the inside.

Once inside the porch area, Ethan drew them to a halt and Keeley tried to look over his shoulder to the interior of this hotel. He barricaded her view, smiling at first and making a joke of shifting a little this way and that. Then he stilled and that seriousness was back on his face again.

'Before we go inside,' Ethan began. 'I want you to know that… it is not perfect yet.' He sighed. 'That is, not in the way I want it to be perfect.' He took what sounded like a nervous breath, his free hand going to his hair and briefly edging it backwards. 'But with the small amount of time I had… it is better than I could have imagined.'

'What is it?' Keeley asked him.

He smiled like he was wearing his whole heart in his expression. 'I only hope that you like it.'

Pressing his back to the door, he leaned into it, opening it, and, still holding her hand, he steered her inside.

Keeley's feet met carpet and then the most sumptuous rug that her boots sunk down into in the best of ways. Tiny glowing droplets like strings of sparkling rain hung from wooden beams and along every wooden surface. And there, right in front of her, was an open fire, in a snug sitting area, logs crackling, woollen stockings hanging from nails on a broad chunk of mantle on which rested berry-red baubles, pinecones and silver stars. A Christmas tree covered in a mish-mash of ornaments was in one corner, wrapped presents under its branches. Immediately Keeley recognised the chairs ahead. She stepped forward, into this large yet cosy room, festive tunes playing from an old radio and stepped up to the mismatched chairs. One was a russet-red, the other a moss-green, both their backs covered by plaid rugs that brought every nuance of shade in the room together.

'You bought these at the flea market,' Keeley said, running her hand over the velveteen fabric.

'I did,' Ethan replied. 'And the radio… and some of the decorations and… quite a lot of other things in many other parts of the hotel I will show you.'

'*You* did all this?' Keeley asked, stopping in front of the fire and turning to face him.

'*Non*,' Ethan answered. '*You* did this.'

Ethan could see that somehow she still didn't fully understand. He had to tell her. He wanted to make it absolutely clear.

'What you said to me...' He paused, wanting to get the words absolutely right. 'What you have been saying to me from the moment we first met. About "moments" and "feelings" and "memories".' He swallowed. 'I listened. And finally, I understood what I had to do for the hotels.'

'I... don't understand,' Keeley said.

Ethan took her hands in his. 'I have been hiding for the past year, Keeley. I have been... swimming through honey, er, walking the wrong way up an escalator... not knowing how to carry on, not even knowing if I *should* carry on... until I met you.' He laced his fingers through hers, loving how her skin felt next to his. 'You showed me the way,' he breathed. 'You reminded me of all the things that make life important. You taught me again that being special is not about having the cleanest contemporary lines or the most expensive champagne on the menu, it is about the individual. People. People are what matter.'

'Ethan... I don't know what to say. I—'

'Say you will help me,' he asked her. 'Because *this*... this is what you are naturally good at. *Amazingly* good at.'

He watched Keeley's eyes move from his and his gaze moved too, looking around at the room he had entirely made over today in a style she had brought him to. A style that said 'home'. A style that he hoped had 'comfortable' written all the way through it.

'This is beautiful,' Keeley breathed. 'It really is.'

Ethan could see the sheer wonder in her eyes now and it was bringing out every internal reaction he owned. He wanted to please her. He wanted to make her smile so he could indulge in looking at the cutest of dimples that appeared on her face when she did.

'But it could be better,' he said quickly, wanting still to elaborate. 'With your help it could be so much more, I know it.' He put a hand to his chest then. 'I feel it.'

'You want me to help you re-model this hotel?' Keeley asked him as if only now realising what he had meant.

'Not just this hotel,' Ethan said. 'All of them.' He tried to temper his enthusiasm just a little. It was a big ask, he knew. But he had never wanted anyone's answer to be yes so much.

'I—' Keeley began.

'Don't say no,' Ethan said, his words jumping in. 'Please, take your time before you give me an answer but please, do not say no. Not yet.'

'Ethan, I don't know what to say.'

'Do not say anything,' he pleaded. He knew she was not here for very long, but he also knew he wanted that to change. He hadn't completely thought through the logistics of it, but there was only a tunnel separating them and hopefully no tight border restrictions in their future. It could be done, couldn't it? 'Maybe only tell me now... that you like the beginnings of what I have done. Tell me that you do not think my new vision is completely off the mark.'

'Ethan, it's completely perfect, it really *really* is. And, no one has ever... listened to me and... done something like this. I mean, in my job I would provide detailed ideas and swatches of fabrics and mood boards but…'

'Your words gave me a mood board all on their own,' Ethan told her.

'It reminds me of Christmas at my Grandma Joan's but with… much better decorations and none of the awful liqueur chocolates,' Keeley said. 'Or one of those beautiful log cabin hideaways you could be tucked away in when it's snowing outside on the mountain.'

She sounded so enthralled and her expression was telling him everything else he needed to know. Except he didn't really need Keeley to tell him he had got this right. He'd known he had succeeded because when he had stood back and admired for himself before they had met up tonight, he had *felt* it was right. And that feeling, that utter joyous, riotous feeling was still very much running through him now.

He held her hands again, joining them together as the fire crackled and popped and the festive music sang of cold winter nights and starlit skies. She was the most beautiful woman he had ever set eyes on. But what attracted him even more was the fact she was just as stunning on the inside.

'Keeley,' he breathed, his face moving towards hers.

'Ethan,' she answered, her lips dwelling a little on his name.

He was going to kiss her now and he wanted to carry on kissing her for the longest time…

'Woof!'

Before Ethan could connect their lips, a brown wiry four-legged creature bounded into the snug and began leaping up at Keeley.

'Oh! Bo-Bo!' Keeley exclaimed, trying to pet the dog but also looking like she was trying to stop his claws grazing her legs.

'Down Bo-Bo!' Ethan ordered. He looked to the door, a little unhappy that their moment had been interrupted. But then he saw Jeanne. He swallowed and instantly his mood lightened. She was finally wearing one of the tops he had bought her and some jeans that actually fitted her frame. Completing the picture of alteration was the fact that her long dark hair was down and brushed and it was not covered by a hat.

'Jeanne,' Keeley breathed. 'I... didn't realise you were here.' Bo-Bo started turning happy circles, his loud barking ceasing and a joyful yelping taking its place.

Ethan knew Keeley had wanted to say something else, something about Jeanne's change in appearance but she had stopped herself. Keeley knew, like him, that any attention brought to the matter would only turn the girl angsty all over again.

'Of course I am here,' Jeanne answered, taking hold of Bo-Bo's collar. 'I wanted to see what you thought of the new place. I helped to decorate the tree and I helped Noel tell the guests that this area was off limits for tonight.'

'Oh,' Keeley said. 'You stopped your guests coming in here for me? Now I feel incredibly guilty. It's so lovely, everyone should be able to enjoy it.'

'And they will,' Ethan assured her.

'Monsieur Bouchard!'

It was Noel calling him from the corridor, beckoning like there might be a problem. Ethan felt the tension in his shoulders. 'Excuse me for a moment.' He turned away. 'Yes, Noel.'

Keeley watched Ethan leave, walking swiftly out of the room towards someone who looked a little familiar. *Noel*. Could it be? Their tour guide? The person Silvie had organised to show them around the sights of Paris. She swallowed. Noel worked here. At Ethan's hotel... Warning signposts were starting to pop up like unwanted pimples before a party. It had to be coincidence. Maybe it wasn't *that* Noel. She had only caught a glimpse of this man. It could have been someone who looked a little like him. OK, *a lot* like him... Keeley glanced down the corridor again to where the two men were conversing. She could only see Noel's back. Perhaps it *was* him. Perhaps he worked at numerous hotels. That had to be it. He was a tour guide unconnected to any one place. It was natural he would spread his expertise across many establishments. She felt a little better, better enough not to feel cross when Bo-Bo started to lick her leg.

'I knew you would like it,' Jeanne said with confidence. 'I *love* it. It is like the complete opposite to anywhere I have ever spent time. Apart from my auntie's house.' She sniffed. 'If she even was my real auntie. Who knows?'

Jeanne was touching the decorations on the tree now. Keeley joined her and watched the girl caressing the wings of a rather sparkly angel, albeit with a bit of a tarnished face.

'I love it too,' Keeley told her. 'It's everything a great hotel should be and more.'

'Ethan's going to change the name too, you know,' Jeanne said. 'That was his idea. Not mine. And only if his co-owners agree. I cannot see that the animal shelter will disagree. Not now there might be the chance to have an "adopt a dog" area for them here after Christmas. *That* was my idea. Dogs are so much better than rabbits, do you not think?'

Keeley frowned, not really understanding much of what Jeanne had just spat out very quickly. 'Change the name?'

'The name of the hotel chain,' Jeanne said, eye-rolling quite clearly at Keeley's inability to keep up with the conversation. 'It's going to be hello to "Welcome Paris – your home from home" and goodbye to that awful "Perfect Paris – always excellence".' Jeanne blew a raspberry. 'Aimed at rich people. So pretentious.'

Keeley's heart felt like someone had just stabbed it with a poker-hot log from the fire in front of her. It was such a stun she held onto her chest in case it decided to burst out and fall into the embers. 'What... did you say?'

All the while she waited for Jeanne to say something else her mind was coming up with questions. Why? How? Those grey eyes in the photo *had* belonged to a young Ethan. She was so stupid. She should have owned that knowledge and not tried to push it out of her mind. But she had asked if Ethan had been in love and he had talked about someone called Crevette. *Not* Ferne. This couldn't be happening. It simply couldn't. She took hold of Jeanne's arms in a bid to make the girl hurry up and answer, as well as to steady her quaking body.

'Ow!' Jeanne exclaimed. 'You're pinching!'

'Sorry,' Keeley said, letting go. 'I'm sorry.' Her eyes looked around the room for evidence of the name of the hotel they were standing in. There had been nothing outside. No name on a sign. Zilch. Except the rational side of her mind was telling her quite clearly that the entrance to the garden and the *petanque* court was not the front and centre of this place. She needed to be calm though. She needed to breathe. Except the heat from the fire was making it almost impossible. Cosy was quickly turning into stifling.

'Are you OK?' Jeanne asked, curiosity coating her features. 'You look a bit weird.'

'Jeanne,' Keeley said, moving away from the fire and backing towards the glass-paned door. 'What's the name of this hotel? The name of Ethan's hotel?'

'Opera,' Jeanne said, both eyebrows meeting in the middle of her forehead. 'Are you having a stroke?'

'Opera?' Now Keeley didn't understand at all. Her heart was still racing into blind panic and she really did have to get out of the warm room.

'Yes,' Jeanne continued. 'This one is called Opera because it is in the Opera District. And he has four others. All the hotels are named after the districts they are in, plus the brand... Perfect Paris.'

And there it was in all its finality. The answer Keeley was looking for. The answer she never wanted. It was like her whole body had seized up, except her heart and her brain both now in a battle with each other to see who was going to break first.

'I... have to go,' Keeley said, the lump in her throat making it difficult to commit the words to air.

'Go?' Jeanne asked, putting her hands on her hips. 'Are you not staying for dinner? I thought Ethan was going to treat you to the new menu. The chef has made a *cassoulet* with sausage. We liked it, didn't we, Bo-Bo?'

Keeley's vision was starting to swim and she needed that fresh snow-ridden air more than anything else. Her eyes went up the corridor to where Ethan was still talking to Noel. *Ethan*. Gorgeous, enigmatic Ethan she had connected so perfectly with in every single way. She couldn't see him now. She couldn't talk to him now. She had to leave. She had to just get out of there.

'Jeanne,' she said, leaning heavily against the door, her body weight causing it to open a little, bringing the cold air in. 'Please could you tell Ethan that I'm not feeling well.'

'You are not feeling well?' Jeanne asked, one eyebrow elevating. 'Or you wish me to tell Ethan you are not well.'

'I have to go,' Keeley said. 'I just have to.' She attempted a smile at the girl but all the while she was backing away. The very last thing she saw before her feet hit the ground of outside was Bo-Bo dropping into a sit with a whine of displeasure.

Fifty-Eight

L'Hotel Paris Parfait, Tour Eiffel, Paris

'I am going to get a key card from Antoine and I am going to go into her room.'

Ethan was out of breath. He had broken into a run the second the car had stopped at the traffic lights still a few yards away from the hotel. He hadn't wanted Jeanne and Bo-Bo to accompany him, but Jeanne was never very good at taking no for an answer and he just wanted to get going. As soon as Keeley had ignored his twelfth call and the tenth text message he could sit around no longer. He had to know why she had left. What he had done? Or, maybe, what he *hadn't* done?

The snow had started to fall again and it was rushing across his vision as he barrelled past tourists on the street, all of them wanting that night view of the Eiffel Tower lit up in all its glory.

'If you get a key card and burst into her room she will think you are crazy,' Jeanne said, catching him up. '*I* think you are crazy.'

'I think there must be something you are not telling me,' Ethan said, snow landing on his lips with every word that met the air. 'What did she say to you again? Did she not like how the room looked? Was she really upset she did not win *petanque*?' Ethan asked.

'I told you,' Jeanne said. 'She told me she was not feeling well.'

Ethan blew out a breath. 'But you and I both know that was an excuse.'

'I never said that,' Jeanne said straightaway.

'You did not need to say it,' Ethan answered. 'Everything you feel is always written all over your face, Jeanne.'

'That is not true.'

'Why would she not answer my calls or my messages?' He wanted to run faster, be there sooner, but even Bo-Bo was heavy breathing from the exertion and, whether it was official or not, he had made himself responsible for Jeanne's welfare.

'Perhaps she is in bed asleep. Or being ill in the bathroom. Or a combination of the two,' Jeanne offered.

'I do not believe that,' Ethan said. 'Something is wrong. I know her,' he continued to protest. 'I really *know* her and I know that she would not have left unless something was really wrong.'

'OK,' Jeanne said. 'OK, I get it. Maybe something *is* wrong but... stop!' She grabbed hold of his jacket sleeve and used all her might to pull him to a halt. 'Please, just stop!'

The last word was a literal scream and Ethan cooled his heels and stopped his forward momentum. Instead he changed tack, beginning to pace up and down over a few yards while he waited for the girl to tell him whatever she was going to tell him. He felt that every minute that was passing was taking him somehow further and further away from Keeley.

'You need to keep cool,' Jeanne said to him with what sounded like a good deal of authority.

Ethan put his hands through his hair. He felt completely not cool. He felt absolutely out of control. He hadn't felt this out of control since a year ago. He didn't like it. Not one bit.

'Not your appearance!' Jeanne exclaimed.

'I wasn't "doing" my hair!' Ethan blasted. 'I was getting the snow out of it and waiting for you to tell me why we have stopped when we should still be going.'

'Because you are not in the right place of mind to talk,' Jeanne told him.

'I am… exactly in the right place of mind to talk,' Ethan insisted. Except his words had come out in a hurry and he could feel the irritation and downright fear bubbling under his skin. This felt like… being in Paris when his best friend was lying in a hospital bed in London. This was like getting to the *Gare Du Nord* determined to reach Ferne when Silvie made that phone call. He did not want this to turn into him collapsing on the riverbank wanting the water to swallow him up…

'No, you are all… scrambled,' Jeanne remarked, beginning to walk around him in a circle, Bo-Bo copying her exact moves. 'Your brain is not thinking with logic, it is thinking with panic. And it will react with anger if you do not receive the answers that you want.'

He shook his head. 'That is nonsense.' He swallowed, not believing his own answer.

'What are you hoping to achieve by bursting into Keeley's room and demanding an explanation?' Jeanne asked.

Ethan shrugged. 'Isn't it obvious? An explanation!'

'Do you not think, that if she wanted to give you an explanation of how she is currently feeling then she would have stayed instead of leaving?'

'I do not know,' Ethan said. 'How am I supposed to know?'

'*I* know,' Jeanne assured him. 'I know that if someone runs away like that it is because they do not want to talk.'

'Well... what about... if they only *think* they do not want to talk? Have you thought about that?' Ethan asked, watching Jeanne. She was still circling him like she was a bird of prey ready to drop down and then feast. She somehow looked doubly threatening with that thick dark hair framing her ivory skin.

'I think that is not your decision to make,' Jeanne said. 'I think this is up to Keeley.'

'She won't answer me! I have called. I have sent messages. What else can I do?' Ethan threw his arms in the air and a pigeon took flight from the pavement, soaring through the driving snow and up into the sky.

'Give her some space?' Jeanne suggested. 'At least do not behave like a mad clown.'

'I am not a mad clown,' Ethan insisted, in a way only a mad clown would.

'Then stop acting like it,' Jeanne said, ending her sentence with a finger point.

'I am... confused and... concerned and...' He didn't quite know what to say next so he stopped talking altogether.

'You are in love with her.'

'No!' Ethan said all too forcefully. 'No, of course not.' He felt like he was betraying his own soul by the vehemence he was showing now, but what was the alternative? Admit the opposite. That he *was* in some sort of… love? He was shaking his head at himself now.

'You are in love with her,' Jeanne repeated.

Ethan growled in frustration, clenching his fists together as Jeanne finally stopped circling around him. Maybe he had said too much too soon. He had asked her to help him make his hotels into the kind of 'comfortable' she had talked so passionately about. After their night together he had thought they had shared themselves completely. Except there was that large scar on her belly she had laughed off when he had asked her about it… Fear *was* in complete control of his reactions now. What if there was something wrong with her? What if she was sick?

'I have to see her,' Ethan said, powerwalking towards the hotel. 'Not crazy or angry, perhaps not cool either but… I have to see her.'

'Wait!' Jeanne called. 'Do not ask anyone for a key card! Ethan!'

Fifty-Nine

The Durand House, Neuilly-sur-Seine, Paris

Keeley was still shaking like the branch of a Christmas tree being attacked by a cat as she sat on a two-seater chaise longue by the fire in Silvie's living room. She was nursing an elegant cup and saucer that was mainly filled with coffee, but had also been liberally splashed with brandy that came from a decanter that looked like it could star alongside Fiona Bruce.

'Keeley,' Silvie said, padding closer to her, another blanket in her arms. 'You are still cold?'

Keeley shook her head. She wasn't cold, she was grieving. She was mourning the loss of the first relationship with a man she'd had that had any real value to it. Something so unexpected. Something that had happened so quickly yet snowballed and snowballed until it had meant the world. Tears slipped from her eyes, one of them dropping into the dark coffee.

'Keeley, tell me,' Silvie begged. 'Tell me what has happened to make you this way.'

Keeley sniffed, turning her head a little to face the French woman. An employee had opened the door to Keeley's ringing on the doorbell as the taxi drove out of the Durands' gate. Her face red from tears and her hair covered in snow, she had stood by the giant Christmas tree, the weather dripping off her boots and pooling on the tiles. Silvie had appeared on the stairs dressed in a full-length light pink silk dressing gown, kitten-heeled slippers on her feet, two large plastic curlers in her hair that she was taking out as she regarded her. And Keeley hadn't said anything. She had just kept on silently crying, shoulders quivering, emotion seeping out of her until Silvie had ushered her inside, stripping her of her coat.

'Keeley,' Silvie breathed. 'Please. I am worried for you. Have you been… attacked? Are you hurt? Where is Rach?'

'No,' Keeley breathed. She looked at the coffee cup, wondering whether to drink some of the liquid or to put it on the antique-looking table next to her. 'And Rach… is OK.'

Keeley hadn't gone back to their hotel. She had hailed a taxi and come straight here looking for answers she hadn't had the strength to ask anyone the questions for yet. She needed to try and distance herself from her feelings for Ethan for a moment and quieten the roar of her heart to get to the truth.

'Then what can I do?' Silvie asked her, eyes full of deep concern. 'Please, Keeley, tell me what I can do.'

Keeley reached for her hand then, drawing the woman closer until Silvie dropped down into the seat next to her. The blanket fell out of the woman's arms and hit the floor.

Keeley took one of the biggest breaths she had ever taken,

feeling the air fill her entire body, and her eyes drifted then to a photograph on the mantle. *Ferne*. She let out a sigh, really concentrating, trying to look into the heart of the woman who had given her the ultimate gift. Had Ferne loved Ethan too? Was that what she was going to hear from Silvie when she dared to ask? How could that happen? How could fate *allow* that to happen?

'Keeley, you are worrying me,' Silvie spoke then. 'Are you ill? Do you need me to call a doctor?'

'No,' Keeley said straightaway. 'It's... not like that.' She gave Silvie's hand a squeeze. 'I'm sorry,' she breathed. 'For turning up here and, well, for... turning up here.'

'Keeley, you can come here any time. It is my wish to spend as much time with you as you are willing to give me. I have not pushed things because, well, we both know it is a difficult situation and I really would not wish for you to feel uncomfortable.'

'I don't,' Keeley reassured, nodding. 'I really don't.' She swallowed. 'At first, perhaps, because I was nervous, I felt a little overwhelmed. But, getting to know you, it has been so nice and *you* are so nice. And I feel like I know Ferne so much better now.'

She felt Silvie squeeze her hand back and it only made her want to start crying again. Except, if she wanted answers she needed to hold it together. 'But what I need for you to tell me about now is... someone else.'

'Someone else?' Silvie asked, frown lines arriving on her forehead.

Keeley nodded. 'I... want you to tell me about...' This was so hard. Because as much as she wanted to know, there was still a big part of her that didn't want this to be the case. She swallowed. 'I want you to tell me about... Ethan Bouchard.'

'Ethan?' Silvie asked, now looking even more confused.

Keeley nodded. 'You know him, don't you?'

'Yes,' Silvie began. 'Of course. I was hoping so much to introduce you to each other. I invited him to dinner here and to our lunch today, but he said he was busy with something for the hotels.' She sighed. 'And losing Ferne was as hard for Ethan as it was for the rest of the family. And, to be honest, I think that he was a little overwhelmed about the prospect of meeting someone with that kind of... tie to Ferne.'

Keeley squeezed her lips together and closed her eyes for a second, all her worst fears being rapidly realised. She hadn't got this wrong. Ethan *was* connected to Ferne. His hotels and the Perfect Paris hotels were one and the same. She should have seen it before. The moment they had first met chasing Pepe – it was right outside her hotel – Perfect Paris Eiffel Tower. Why hadn't she asked the right questions from the outset? Why had it taken until now to know?

'Does he know who I am?' Keeley asked. 'Does he know my name?' He couldn't know, could he? He couldn't have, all this time, been playing some kind of game with her feelings?

'I... do not know,' Silvie said, looking confused. 'When I first mentioned it, he shut me down so fast. I...'

Silvie pulled her chair a little closer, recapturing Keeley's hand. 'Have the two of you met already?' she asked. 'Ethan spends much of his time at our flagship hotel in the Opera District, but I know he has been determined to do something special this Christmas at all the hotels. We have had... certain difficulties of late, but we will... work through them... as a family.'

As a family. Keeley couldn't stop her body reacting to that sentence. What did that mean? Tears were seeping from the corners of her eyes again.

'Who is he?' Keeley asked. 'To you… and to Ferne?'

Silvie sighed, sitting back a little and raising her slipper-covered feet towards the fire. 'That is a question the Durands have been asking themselves for around twenty years.' She smiled. 'Ethan, he is like an… adopted son you could say… just without the paperwork. Ferne, she started bringing Ethan to this house when he was perhaps eight or nine. And, when we found out where he was living, we arranged official visits and trips out, weekends here. Then, eventually, as the years went by, he was more here than anywhere else.' She smiled again. 'So you *have* met him. I am glad. He was a very big part of Ferne's life. He knew her the best out of everybody.'

Keeley nodded, her body beginning to shake again. 'They were in love, weren't they?'

'Oh! No!' Silvie said immediately, her head shaking. 'Goodness, no. Ferne, she was never interested in boys in that way.' Silvie looked directly at Keeley then. 'I never had any doubt about that.' She patted Keeley's hand. 'Before Ferne left for London… before the accident… she told me that she had just started to date someone new.' Silvie smiled. 'She said that if it was still going well after Christmas then she very much wanted me to meet her.' Silvie sighed. 'Ferne had many dates, but she had never suggested I meet anyone before. I did not think that the place I would be first meeting Nicole would be Ferne's funeral.' She sighed again. 'But… I was very glad to meet her. I could tell that she cared for Ferne very much and it was nice to know that my daughter was at her happiest romantically before she passed away.'

Despite Silvie's sad story, a flicker of hope burned brightly in Keeley's heart. Ferne and Ethan had never been together, never been in love. But he hadn't wanted to meet her. Hadn't wanted to share dinner with the person who had the kidney of someone he was close to. What did that mean for them now?

'Keeley,' Silvie said softly. 'Ethan and Ferne, they were the very best of friends. At times, inseparable. And, at the beginning, I did have my concerns about the relationship. Ethan, he was always an unknown entity. I think he will forever be a little like that. But what I have discovered, from getting to know him, is that the core of a person does not come from the people that made them, it comes very much from the nurturing.' She took a breath. 'Has he told you the kind of life he was leading when he was young?'

Keeley nodded. 'A little. But I... didn't push.'

'Well, you should know that someone who has had the kind of treatment I imagine Ethan has had goes one of two ways. There is the tragic way, where they can never find the exit from the vicious circle they have grown up with, or there is the way where they take everything that has been dealt to them and they turn it on its head and rise above it.' Silvie adjusted herself in her seat. 'It takes the strongest of characters to do that. Can you think how it might be? To not let the scars of your past taint your future? I am not saying that his upbringing has not affected who Ethan is today, only that he has somehow successfully used it as a weapon to drive him to better things. Yet still, all the time, Ethan believes he is not good enough, when the truth is, actually he is better than all of us.'

Keeley took in everything Silvie had said. It was a brief

story of the man she already knew had a good heart. And she knew that because he had shown it to her. But that was before. How were things going to change if he found out who she was? How did *she* feel now she knew he had been like a brother to her donor?

'Tell me,' Silvie said gently. 'What is it you *really* want to know about Ethan?'

What did she say now? The absolute truth? That he had captured her heart like no other, but now there was this undeniable bond between him and the woman who had saved her life it felt unsurmountable, almost incestuous.

She shook her head, tears escaping again. 'I met Ethan... when I first arrived in Paris. He was carrying a penguin. And somehow, through every twist and turn of my visit here, he's been there.' She took a breath. 'And, after the shortest time, I found myself *wanting* him to be there.' She swallowed before starting again. 'And then it was as if we were meant to find each other. And I don't understand that at all but... somehow it happened.'

'Oh, Keeley,' Silvie gasped.

'I had no idea who he was. I had no idea he knew Ferne. He told me about his hotels eventually, but still I never connected the two things until...'

'Until?' Silvie asked, still holding Keeley's hand.

'Until when I was here for dinner,' she admitted. 'And we were in Ferne's room and a book fell on the floor.' She closed her eyes, remembering. 'A photo fell out and... I don't know... I wish I hadn't looked. I wished I'd left it on the floor.' She sighed in frustration and gazed at the flames. 'I told myself it wasn't Ethan. As if anyone else could have those eyes?! And then... tonight... he took me to one of his hotels and… it was one of *your* hotels.' She paused. 'Perfect Paris Opera.'

'Keeley, what has actually happened to make you so sad? Has Ethan done something? Said something?'

She shook her head, trying not to fall apart again. 'No,' she said. 'No, he hasn't done anything. Except… get to know me like no one's ever done before.' She wiped tears from her face with the back of her hand. 'And now… it's ruined.'

'What is ruined?' Silvie asked gently.

'Everything,' Keeley sobbed. 'Because I wasn't being Kidney Girl. I promised Rach. And it was really refreshing to just be the person I was before I had the accident and before I lost Bea. I hadn't been that person for so long I had forgotten who she was. And I was starting to get to know her properly again and I *like* her. And now…'

'Now?' Silvie asked.

'Now, not only am I going to have to tell Ethan about my transplant, I'm also going to have to tell him that I have Ferne's kidney.'

Silvie didn't immediately reply and when Keeley looked up it was to see tears were in the woman's eyes too. She suddenly felt very selfish for coming here at all.

'I'm sorry,' Keeley said, standing up. 'I sound so ungrateful. I shouldn't have come. I don't know what I was thinking. I probably wasn't thinking at all. I've insulted you and I've insulted Ferne's memory and—'

'Keeley,' Silvie said. 'Please, sit down. Please.'

The woman said it in such a manner that Keeley didn't refuse. Dropping down to the sofa again she held her hands together, now feeling utterly exhausted.

'You are an intelligent girl,' Silvie began. 'No, not a girl. You are a woman.' She drew the cord of her gown more tightly around her. 'A woman who is living.'

'I know,' Keeley said. 'And I know right now I sound so selfish and completely ungracious but...'

'Do you know what I think? I think you worry too much about everyone else,' Silvie said firmly. 'I think you worry and think about everything so much that you forget the most important person.' Silvie took hold of Keeley's hands again, holding them tight. 'Like you said. *You*.' Silvie smiled. 'It is time to think of *you*.'

Keeley shook her head.

'What are you most afraid of?'

'Telling Ethan.'

'Telling Ethan what?'

'That...' Her brain was firing now, taking in everything Silvie had told her. What part of this whole scenario was the worst? Her admitting she lived a life watching her health with the possibility of more operations in the future and a shorter shelf life than most? Or that Ethan's deceased best friend had gifted a piece of herself and it was her death that had brought them together. Or... that she had fallen in love with him.

Silvie held Keeley's hands in hers again and sighed. 'Do you know, when I invited you here to Paris, in the back of my mind, I had this very *very* silly idea... that perhaps you would meet Louis and you and he would...' Suddenly all Lizzie's warnings about being held hostage tap-danced into Keeley's conscience.

Silvie shook her head. 'So silly. What was I thinking?' She took a breath. 'Keeley, I want you to know and believe that

that was never my principal thought when I reached out. It was always about getting to know you and finding out how you were. I had thought about approaching the hospital before, but I was not ready before. And then, as time went on, and the thought came again and would not let go, I began to pray that I had not missed my chance to connect. And the more I hoped, the more I realised I *had* to take the chance. What harm was there to call them? To ask if you had left your details accessible if I did ever decide to write. And when they passed on the email address I was delighted. I think I drafted that short email about a hundred times and I still was not sure it was right. Would you reply? Or would you decide that to know me would perhaps set back your recovery and your healing. And I had no idea about your poor, poor sister.' She paused for a beat. 'But then I met you and I really began to get to know what an incredibly kind and beautiful person you are. You are exactly the kind of person Ferne would be cheering on if she were still here. Someone strong and independent, a caring friend with a gentle and beautiful spirit. Someone who thought nothing of jumping on a train to meet a very stupid, sentimental old woman.'

'Silvie,' Keeley said.

'Yes, my darling girl.'

'I think,' Keeley began. 'I think… I am in love with Ethan.'

Silvie nodded, long and slow, her hands still cupping Keeley's so tenderly. Like a mother. 'Then, you must tell him.' She smiled. 'Tell him everything.'

Sixty

L'Hotel Paris Parfait, Tour Eiffel, Paris

'Wake up! Wake up!'

It was Jeanne's voice very close to his ear and for a moment, Ethan didn't know where he was. Then it all came back to him. The previous night, everything being so perfect and then suddenly not. He could sense, more than see, it was morning, but a quick look to the curtains showed there was light behind them and he was lying in the middle of a king-sized bed in one of the rooms at the hotel with a dog between his knees. Bo-Bo let out a yelp as Ethan tried to sit himself up.

'What time is it?' he asked Jeanne, moving his arm to check his watch.

'It's time you got up,' Jeanne ordered, bouncing up and down at the end of the bed and rocking his hangover. Just how many bottles from the minibar had he consumed? And why was there an animatronic snowman in the corner? It was stood, by the desk, next to the window, moving very slowly from left to right, glowing on and off and bringing a stick-like arm to its head and eventually managing to tip his hat.

'What is a snowman doing here?' he asked, muzzing his hair with his hands then rubbing at his eyes.

'Ah, well,' Jeanne began. 'You brought that upstairs last night. After the fourth glass of Pernod. You said that it was not going to go with the new décor and it was scaring the rabbits.' She smiled then. 'I love the rabbits by the way. Can we get one for home?'

So much of that sentence pitter-pattered over his brain. *Pernod. Rabbits.* But it was the use of the word 'home' in relation to his apartment that impacted the most. Suddenly Jeanne's cheeks reddened and she stopped bouncing, as if realising what she had said.

'The apartment I mean,' she corrected herself. 'Your apartment.'

He smiled at her. 'You think Bo-Bo would be able not to eat it?'

Jeanne looked at Bo-Bo as if giving the question the deepest of consideration. She patted his head. 'No,' she concluded. 'He would definitely try to eat it.'

Ethan grabbed for his phone on the nightstand then. *Keeley*. He had to speak to Keeley. Before he could reach it, Jeanne snatched it up and held it to her chest.

'Jeanne! Come on!' Ethan ordered, holding out his hand.

'Calm,' Jeanne reminded him. 'Remember what we talked about before the third Pernod?'

Ethan didn't actually remember drinking any Pernod although his sore throat and taste buds definitely told him otherwise. 'Jeanne, please give me the phone.'

'She has replied to your messages,' Jeanne announced.

Ethan made a grab then, lunging over the mattress and missing the object by mere millimetres as Jeanne leapt off and away from him, Bo-Bo flying off too.

'Jeanne!'

'No!' Jeanne said, shielding the phone as Ethan got off the bed and strode towards her. 'Calm.'

Ethan shook his head and groaned. 'You were never talking about "calm" when I met you. You were quite happy for the shouting and rudeness then. Now you sound like an inspirational app.'

Jeanne held the phone up in the air as if that was going to stop Ethan from getting it. She was a little over five feet tall and although she still had long, skinny arms, he was quite able to reach the phone if he so desired. But he held off and instead folded his arms across his chest and waited for her to carry on. Bo-Bo looked very much like he would start nibbling at Ethan's ankles if he took another step towards his mistress.

'She has sent you one message,' Jeanne informed. 'It is very short.'

'Let me see it!'

'In a moment,' Jeanne said. 'When you are calm.'

Ethan knew she was right, despite all the dramatics. He took a long slow breath inwards and tried to stop looking at the snowman. He was going to destroy the snowman. And make sure Noel was never in charge of decorating the hotels for Christmas ever again.

'Better?' Jeanne wanted to know.

'Better,' he answered. He wasn't better. He wasn't even sure what better looked like at the moment. The only thing he *did* know was Jeanne had talked him out of making contact with Keeley last night, even confiscating the key card he had demanded from Antoine so he couldn't take the elevator up to her room. That perhaps had been the right course of action. Everyone knew a new day brought new perspective and there was absolutely nothing he couldn't put right as soon as he found out what had gone so wrong.

Jeanne handed out his phone and he took it, eager to see what Keeley had said in response to his pleas from last night. It was actually those pleas he saw first. A whole stream of them going down his phone in blue.

Are you OK?

What is wrong?

I am worried about you x

Did I do something wrong? Say something wrong? Please call me x

He sounded deranged. He didn't sound like a person who even deserved the attentions of a woman like Keeley. He swallowed and focused his attention on the short text at the bottom of the messages. Keeley's reply in grey.

I am OK. But we need to talk. Meet me at 11 a.m. outside La Valentin, Passage Jouffroy.

Passage Jouffroy. He shook his head as a memory arrived. That was it. A location and time. The need to talk. No sentiment added on the end. His heart was sinking faster than dog food in Bo-Bo's bowl. He didn't know what to do. He checked his watch again. It was a little after nine. He had time to go to Keeley's room now. Speak to her now. But he knew in his heart that was not the right thing to do. He let out a sigh, eyes still on the words as if looking for a hidden meaning.

'What do you think she means?' he finally asked Jeanne, slumping down to a sitting position on the bed.

'I think she wants to talk to you,' Jeanne answered, plumping down next to him, Bo-Bo jumping up too and nuzzling any body part he could get access to.

'But what does that mean?' he asked. 'You are a w…' He had been about to say the word 'woman'. She couldn't be more than… ten? Eleven? 'How old are you, Jeanne?'

'Old enough to know that you should not be thinking about storming her room now, when you did so well – with my help – not doing exactly that last night.'

'How old are you, Jeanne?' Ethan asked again.

Jeanne shrugged her shoulders. 'Somewhere between puberty and *5eme* at a guess.'

Ethan looked at her, taking her in anew. How had this happened? Going from being single, slightly wobbling on the rails of life, to being a guardian of a maybe-eleven-maybe-twelve-year-old and a wiry long-limbed hound, his heart aching for someone he had fallen in love with… He had fallen in love with Keeley. He was sure. If Jeanne asked him again now he would not deny it. But the right thing to do would be to wait. He would respect Keeley's request and he would badger her no further. He didn't want to make things worse if there was a chance he could make things better.

'Should I reply?' Ethan asked Jeanne.

'Yes,' Jeanne answered, nudging closer to him, her eyes on the screen. 'But do not say anything ridiculous.'

His thumbs wanted to take over all the keys, telling her he was sorry, even though he didn't know what he was sorry for. He stilled them and waited.

'Just say,' Jeanne started, 'that you are glad she is OK and that you will see her there.'

'That is it?' Ethan asked, unsatisfied.

'That is it. Any more will sound like you are trying to take control of the situation and you do not want her to feel like that.' Jeanne hit him with one of her soul-searing looks again. 'Do you remember, from the streets, how it feels when someone else tries to control your situation?'

A tiny internal part of him pulsed in recognition and he nodded at Jeanne. 'OK,' he said, beginning to type. 'I am glad… you are OK,' he spoke the text aloud. 'I will see you there.' He looked to Jeanne again. 'Do I add something? A… x.' He'd said the letter 'x' instead of the word 'kiss' and was immediately embarrassed he was taking a relationship texting tutorial from a minor. Bo-Bo barked. And a dog…

'Nothing else,' Jeanne said firmly. 'Now press send and put your phone away. We need breakfast.'

'OK,' Ethan said, getting to his feet, mildly enthused that at least he was going to get to see Keeley today. 'OK, you are right. We will go down to the restaurant for breakfast. Come, Bo-Bo,' he beckoned.

'No!' Jeanne exclaimed. 'We cannot eat in the restaurant. That will be where Keeley and Rach will be having breakfast. Space, remember?'

'OK,' Ethan said, nodding. 'We will go home for

breakfast.' He recognised that he had said the word 'home' just like Jeanne had.

'We could get a hot dog on the *way* home,' Jeanne suggested, standing up and clipping Bo-Bo to his lead.

'You need to learn to eat more healthily,' Ethan told her.

'I think if you are going to be my guardian that's kind of *your* job.'

'Fine,' Ethan replied. 'Nothing to eat until we get home where we will have cereal.'

'Ohhhhh!' Jeanne moaned. 'A compromise?' she suggested. 'How about cake?'

'How is cake a compromise?' Ethan asked her.

'It is not a hot dog.'

Cake. Suddenly the relevance of Keeley wanting to meet at Passage Jouffroy hit him. On the map he had given her, it was the very last place he had marked.

Sixty-One

Notre Dame Marche de Noel, Paris

There was still repair work going on to the famous cathedral following the devastating fire, but the Christmas market set outside it was a picture of festiveness. Around thirty white tents with pointed roofs housed all kinds of gift ideas and were positioned around a central circle where, amid a ring of small decorated and snow-flecked firs, a band was playing Christmas tunes. It would have been idyllic, true December goals, if Keeley's mind wasn't tracking through everything she was going to have to say to Ethan in just an hour's time.

'You OK?' Rach asked for somewhere near the twentieth time since their conversation on the balcony early that morning.

Bundled up in coats and the duvets from their beds, the women had shared coffee and tears as Keeley had told her best friend everything that had happened at the Opera hotel and later with Silvie. Rach had held her close and told her everything was going to be alright but Keeley knew in her heart that everything had changed now and there were no 'alright' guarantees. She had made the decision to tell Ethan the truth and she had decided on eleven a.m. Except now, even as the clock ticked just after ten, it still felt like an age away. Which was why, shortly after nine, they had decided to travel here. Christmas was still coming. Gifts still needed to be purchased. And Rach loved shopping. It was the ultimate distraction.

Keeley nodded, tightening the belt on her coat.

'Stupid question. I just… don't know what else to say,' Rach admitted as they walked to the next tent selling hand-carved wooden ornaments.

'It's OK,' Keeley answered, scuffing the snow with her boot.

'It's not though, is it? And some of it is my fault.'

'Oh, Rach, it's really not.'

'It is!' Rach carried on. 'Because if I hadn't made such a fuss about you not being Kidney Girl on this trip you might have just – I don't know – met Ethan and told him straightaway about the transplant and Silvie and Ferne and then…'

'And then I might not have had the most amazing time of my life getting close to him.' Keeley sighed. Because that's what she imagined would have happened if Ethan had known from the beginning. He would never have looked at her the same way. Would never have got to know the her she had managed to be since she arrived in France.

'Well,' Rach said, 'like I said after the fourth cup of coffee before we ran out of sachets in the room, if Ethan cares about you like he says he does, then nothing you tell him this morning is going to change that.'

Keeley nodded at her friend, but she didn't really believe that. Silvie had said Ethan had never wanted to meet the recipient of Ferne's kidney. She pointed towards a hut a little further ahead of them. 'Handbags.'

'You're changing the subject.'

'I need to, Rach, seriously,' Keeley said, taking the deepest of breaths. 'Tell me something that's going to take my mind off *this*.' She clamped her hands to her body where her scars were. She turned to Rach then, remembering she hadn't asked her a thing about her evening. 'How did it go with the VIP client?'

'OK,' Rach said, beaming a lot more than the word 'OK' really warranted.

'I'm sensing there's more to this.'

'It's the Bradburys!' Rach announced. 'Confidentially of course!'

The Bradbury family were a big deal in the area. Kind of like a legitimate version of the Wallaces in *Gangs of London*.

'The Bradburys only want to deal with me. Not Jamie. Not even Roland. Me. And they said, they might even have a few contacts they could recommend my excellent house searching expertise to!'

'Rach, that's brilliant!'

'I know! And I'm thinking, I definitely need to ask for a pay rise if I'm going to start attracting clients of that kind of notoriety or, if Roland starts being a skinflint about it, perhaps I need to start thinking about my own agency. Maybe working from home at first and then, well, I don't know, it's just an idea. But I'm excited!'

'I'm excited too!' Keeley said. 'It's amazing.'

'I know! So I… drank some tiny bottles of alcohol from the minibar and then I needed something else. So, I ordered some fizzy wine on Silvie's account which I totally will pay for and…

'And?

'And after I finished the fizzy wine I phoned reception and I spoke to Antoine again,' Rach said, her voice shaking a little. 'And I kept speaking to Antoine and he was as completely annoying as he always is and still I kept talking and talking and winding him up and…' Rach seemed to have to stop talking to catch her breath as she thumped the handbag back down on the stall.

'Rach, what happened?' Keeley put a hand on her shoulder.

'Antoine came up to the suite,' Rach whispered, her eyes glistening with something Keeley couldn't quite translate.

'With more alcohol?' Keeley was hoping the concierge had sensibly brought coffee instead.

Rach nodded. 'A very nice bottle of Burgundy.'

Keeley gasped then, hands flying to her lips. 'I've just realised… you haven't called him Antonie!'

Rach nodded again. 'I know! And, after a while, he didn't call me Rash.'

'Rach! Tell me!'

'I kissed him,' Rach exclaimed. 'I kissed Antoine.' She gripped Keeley's arm. 'And he kissed me back. And… I was wearing my pyjamas.'

Sixty-Two

Ethan Bouchard's apartment, Paris

'How do I look?' Ethan spread his arms out in the centre of his living area, not so far off from being able to touch the walls with his fingertips. Bo-Bo let out a bark, then preceded to try and leap up, his paws on Ethan's dark jeans. 'Down, Bo-Bo!'

'You look fine,' Jeanne answered. 'Although you smell like maybe you have rolled around for a hundred years in a pine forest.'

Ethan slapped his cheeks. He had shaved. He had put on aftershave, perhaps a little too much. He couldn't help it. His insides seemed to be filled with hundreds of tiny fleas performing like they were members of a circus troupe. Whatever was wrong, whatever concerns Keeley had, he could ease them. He would tell her that he felt what they had together was so special. He could not have imagined the way she had reacted to him ever since they had met, how her body had reacted to him only a few nights ago…

'Relax,' Jeanne ordered him. 'You are making me feel

nervous and I cannot make paper chains if my hands are shaking so much I cannot use the scissors.'

Ethan paid more attention to what she was doing then. Laid out on his coffee table were strips of newspaper, magazines, a cereal box and some tin foil. Jeanne appeared to be cutting into each of them, making hoops and connecting the circles together in a chain. 'What are you doing?'

'Getting a little Christmas in this apartment,' Jeanne said with a sniff. 'You have nothing.'

Ethan looked around the living room as if expecting to see at least one greetings card or something else festive he had overlooked. But it was true, there was nothing. Despite the lack of space, he usually had something in here. He sighed. Ferne had always been the one encouraging him to decorate. But Ferne had liked to decorate everything, even if it wasn't Christmas. 'Let me get you something from the hotel.'

'The snowman that tips his hat?' Jeanne asked, all bright eyes. 'Or the reindeer that shakes its head?'

'I am not sure there is the space for any of those in here.'

Jeanne screwed her nose up. 'Do you not eat Christmas dinner either? Because the turkey and potatoes and gravy will not fit?'

Ethan sank down to the sofa. 'Jeanne, I can find you something more than plain cardboard and tin.'

Jeanne raised her head from what she was doing and Bo-Bo looked up from the cleaning of his bottom. 'You do not think my paper chains will be good enough?'

'No,' Ethan said, quickly. 'Of course I do!'

'I made them with my auntie. If she was my auntie.' She sniffed again, getting back to work with the scissors.

'She put on her record player – songs from the church, a choir and organs – and we sat by the fire, eating *buche de Noel* and making chains to hang around the house from whatever there was.' Jeanne smiled. 'One time we made pompoms with wool.'

Ethan nodded. 'We made pompoms often at the orphanage. In fact, we made pompoms for almost every occasion. Perhaps it was because wool was the only substance we could not attack anyone with.'

'Hmm,' Jeanne mused. 'You obviously never tied up any of the staff.'

Ethan got to his feet again. 'I do not want to hear anything else.' He smiled at Jeanne then. 'But when I come back, perhaps I can help you make some pompoms. I remember how.'

'Do you have wool?' Jeanne asked, voice already wholly excited. 'Or can I unpick that horrible green jumper in your wardrobe?'

'You have been through my wardrobe?' Ethan asked, astounded.

'There was not a lock on the door,' Jeanne answered, shrugging as if her response was the most natural thing in the world.

There was a knock at the door then. It startled him and set Bo-Bo off barking. Ethan checked his watch. There was still plenty of time before eleven. But perhaps Keeley had changed her mind and decided to come here.

'You still smell like a forest,' Jeanne remarked. 'But now you look like a ghost.' She shooed him with a hand. 'Go and open the door.'

Ethan left the room, bolting down the spiral staircase to

the front door, heart in his mouth. He had to remember to be calm when all he really wanted to do was throw his arms around Keeley. He pulled open the door, a smile already working its way over his lips until…

'Louis.'

Ethan frowned, looking at the man who was unusually dressed down in jeans and a jumper, a casual jacket zipped up to his chin. He couldn't remember Louis ever coming to his apartment before. And he didn't really know what to do.

'Ethan,' Louis said. He put gloved hands into his pockets and looked as awkward as Ethan felt. 'May I come in?'

'I… have to leave for a meeting.' Ethan stepped outside, pulling the door to behind him.

'Really?' Louis asked, shaking his head.

'Yes,' Ethan said, a little softer. 'Really, I have to leave for a meeting but, we can talk… if talking is why you are here.'

Louis let out a weighted breath and appeared equally as heavy in demeanour. 'I am worried about my mother.'

'She is not well?' Ethan asked.

Louis shook her head. 'Not in the way you mean.' He sighed again. 'This time of year…' He nodded towards the strings of festive lights around the buildings in the courtyard, the sound of a Christmas tune being played on an accordion rising into the air. 'What has happened with Ferne's will…'

Ethan waited for Louis to elaborate.

'I… am worried she is regressing,' Louis told him. 'She has been spending time in Ferne's bedroom again. She has got out all the old photographs, creating collages, reminiscing…'

'There is nothing wrong with reminiscing,' Ethan said. 'Sometimes it can be… healing.'

'That is just it. She is not healing,' Louis said. 'She is going backwards. Instead of using her memories to help propel her into something new, she is going over old ground, living in the past.'

Ethan nodded. It was quite possible that Silvie was doing now all the things he had done *immediately* after Ferne's death. He knew Silvie had been the one who had to deal with most of the practicalities of Ferne's passing, while he had tried to keep on top of the day-to-day running of the hotels as he trudged through his own devastation. Was Silvie's grief only really coming to the fore now? Christmas always did seem to have a way of increasing the ferocity of feelings.

'And what about you, Louis?' Ethan asked. 'What are your feelings?'

'I am talking about my mother,' Louis answered.

'And I am asking about you.'

'Why?'

'Because… I have not taken the time to ask before. Because, perhaps I have *never* taken the time to ask before,' Ethan said, trying to swallow the lump in his throat. 'I am just thinking that… maybe both of us have spent so many years fighting about our place in this family that we entirely overlooked the whole reason for family.'

'I do not follow.'

'Ironically, going against our professional brand, family is not ever about perfection. Just as it is not about any one person that belongs to it. It is about the whole. And it is about all our family's beautiful imperfections.' He sighed.

'It is about your father getting furious when his shoes were not polished correctly. It is about Silvie going through those months when she tried to cook herself. It is about you dying my hair bright orange in my sleep and blaming it on your awful friend Rolo. It is about Ferne being the biggest of bitches when she did not get her way.' He shook his head. 'We should be helping Silvie together, Louis. What do you say?'

'God, Ethan,' Louis said, sighing. 'All this time you knew I was the one to dye your hair?'

'Exactly like you know it was me with the penguin. But I truly did not know you were allergic.'

Louis smiled at him then playfully punched his arm. 'You are an idiot. Still. Even now.'

'You too,' Ethan answered. 'I am sure that will never change.'

'I miss Ferne,' Louis said then, shuffling his feet a little against the cold. 'And I regret not handling things so well when our father died. I shut her out. I shut you out.' He sniffed. 'I shut out my mother and eventually I ran away. I don't want to do that again.'

'So help me,' Ethan encouraged. 'Work with me.'

Louis let out a noise of discontent then. 'I don't know what is for the best anymore. And I am also not sure my mother inviting the recipient of Ferne's kidney here was the best idea.' He let out a noise of discontent, his hands going to his head. 'I have tried my best to support it, but my mother has been a little fixated with trying to get me to spend time with her.'

'I… could not think about that.' He still didn't want to think about it now.

'You should have come to the dinner and the lunch. You could have helped bring some normality to the proceedings. Not that the girls are not good company. They are nice enough. But it gets a little wearing when the only memories your mother is sharing of your sister are the good bits. There is very little mention of the stubborn, foolhardy person Ferne could be. And you know that side of her like I do.'

'The girls?' Ethan queried. Suddenly what Louis was saying was drip-feeding into him a lot more slowly than he needed it to. And there was something, the smallest of thoughts, morphing and expanding, prickling his subconscious as he took it on board.

'She has a friend. A rather nice friend actually but… I do not need the complications of a relationship right now. Not when I am worried about my mother and the hotels and…'

Ethan's head was suddenly full of Keeley. Keeley's laugh. Keeley's smile. The way her hair moved in the breeze of a snow shower, their passionate, perfect night together… *Her scars*. He swallowed as her words came back to him. *It was a shark. He came off much worse than I did*. Momentarily, it felt like he was paralysed and then, when adrenaline started kicking in, pulsing around his body hard and fast, it was pushing scenarios he didn't want to have to contemplate right at him. It couldn't be. Why would it be. *How* could it be?

'What is her name?' Ethan asked, the words scratching their way up his throat.

'What?' Louis replied.

'The… person,' Ethan began, suddenly sweating despite the fiercely cold temperature of the street. 'This… girl. The one that… received… part of Ferne.' He could not even bear to say the words. But, as Louis opened his lips to make his answer, Ethan already knew what was coming. He braced himself against the brickwork of the apartment, flesh against stone, heart achingly waiting for confirmation he didn't want…

'Keeley,' Louis said. 'Her name is Keeley.'

Sixty-Three

Outside La Valentin, Passage Jouffroy, Paris

For ten minutes Keeley had debated whether she should wait outside or whether she should go into the smart *patisserie*. There were so many different varieties of desserts in the front windows, – puffed up macarons, fluffed out croissants, cakes with cream and cherries on top – a collection of colour and textures. All of them looked equally perfect, yet none of them were desirable to someone whose stomach was in knots. Finally, she had opted for staying outside, where she could busy her feet, stamping them down on the tiled floor of the impressive arcade that was Passage Jouffroy, as well as keeping out the cold. Its impressive high glass ceiling let in the bright light of this December day, then, below it, nestled between the frontages of the independent shops and curling wrought-iron lamps were lots of Christmas touches – thick garlands of red tinsel looped around shiny gold baubles and white fairy lights. She breathed in, re-imagining the scent of freshly ground coffee and letting her mind fill in the gaps of exactly what the bonbons and other sweet treats might smell like. Rach was shopping, not far away, ready to arrive should Keeley need her. She was hoping she *wouldn't* need her. She hoped she could cope with whatever this conversation brought.

Keeley's phone started vibrating and she drew it out of the pocket of her coat expecting it to be Ethan. Was he running late? Was he not coming?

Erica. An audio call.

Keeley's heart lurched and she rushed to answer, pressing the phone to her ear. 'Hello.'

'H…ey.'

Keeley screwed her eyes up tight. It *was* Erica but she sounded so weak. So *so* weak. Now was the time to gather herself and say only positive things. Because amid whatever she was going through there was someone in the UK she needed to be super-strong for. 'Hi, Erica. I was going to send you another video. Do you want the River Seine and some of the boats, or do you want cakes and coffee and Parisian walkways?'

There was a pause and Keeley could hear how laboured her friend's breathing really was. She waited.

'No… more… time for… videos,' Erica whispered.

The tears were in Keeley's eyes before she really, truly acknowledged their presence. Her friend was truly losing her battle now. 'OK,' Keeley answered. 'No more videos. Just tell me what you want me to do.'

She turned towards the window of the café, shielding herself from the passing shoppers who were talking as they strolled, sharing laughs and holiday joy. Part of her wished she could be there with Erica now, holding her hand, wetting her mouth with a moist swab, sheening a little balm on her lips. Be the friend she needed, right by her side.

'You,' Erica began. 'You... owe me... a photo.'

Keeley furrowed her brow. What was she talking about? And then, all at once she remembered. The selfie. The photo of her and Ethan from the night before. Before everything had changed. She had taken the picture, but she had never sent it. 'Oh, Erica, I'm so sorry! I took the photo but... I forgot to send it to you. Give me a minute.' She took the phone away from her ear for a second.

'Not now,' Erica breathed. 'When... I'm done.'

Keeley paid proper attention again, pressing the phone back to the side of her face. 'I'm listening. I'm here.'

The sound of Erica's slow rattling breaths was heart-breaking, but Keeley had to keep it together. She simply had to be here and listen.

'You are... the best friend... I ever... had,' Erica made clear.

'Oh, Erica,' Keeley sobbed. 'You are the strongest, most opinionated, most brilliant person I've ever met.'

'I... know that,' Erica wheezed in approval. 'And... I am counting... on you... to... live for... you... and live... for Bea and... for me and... to wear out that kidney... you got given... with all the fun... the world has.'

Keeley was nodding as the tears tracked down her cheeks, her eyes blurring and the flans in La Valentin's window display beginning to lose their vivid shape. 'I promise you. I will do that.'

'Swear it,' Erica ordered, making the words as clear as she was able. 'Swear it... on Nick Jonas.'

'I swear it,' Keeley told her. 'I swear it on Nick Jonas. I

promise.' She sobbed and tried to catch the sound in her throat so Erica couldn't hear her despair. She had to be brave all over again. Face this farewell to someone she loved for a second time. This was Erica saying her final goodbyes and this was Keeley's chance to say goodbye too. She had never had the opportunity to tell Bea how much she loved her, what an amazing little sister she had been, how life would never be the same without her. But she had a chance to say all the things she wanted to say with Erica now.

'I am never going to forget you, Erica,' Keeley told her, her voice full of admiration and, she hoped, strength she never knew she possessed. 'You are one amazing, fierce friend and I am going to do…' Keeley stopped talking. She had been about to say she was going to do her best, but this was the time for being a whole lot more definite than that. 'I am *going* to savour every moment like it's… turkey crisps and Celebrations and… popcorn.' She took another breath, her thoughts gaining momentum. 'I am going to… dance like poodles and I'm going to be—'

'All in,' Erica interrupted. 'All in… every time.'

Erica's statement hit Keeley hard and she crushed her lips together, fearful all her emotions were going to leak out and down the phone line. 'All in,' Keeley repeated. 'Every time.'

It took Erica a few moments to speak again and it was obvious the conversation was sapping her strength. 'Don't… say goodbye.'

'I won't,' Keeley replied, turning away from the café window and again facing the shoppers flowing through the nineteenth century passageway. 'Because… it's not goodbye.' Her tears were falling faster now. 'I'm in France and I have had you here with me the whole time. So... it's *à bientôt*,' she said. 'Only *à bientôt*.'

'What you said,' Erica rasped out before the call ended.

Keeley held the phone away from her, not quite ready to let go yet. But then she tapped at the screen, eager to do one more thing she knew would make her friend happy. Finding the photo of her and Ethan she took a second to let the image hit all her senses. She ran a finger over Ethan's face, along that jawline, down his aquiline nose to the breadth of his smile. *She* looked so happy, carefree and that was something she hadn't felt in such a long time. Whatever happened next, how could she ever regret meeting Ethan exactly as she had met him? By chance. Absolutely, completely by chance. With a penguin.

Keeley added the photo to Erica's message stream and watched the picture send and be delivered. Those three bubbles immediately appeared and then, eventually, came Erica's reply: a single red heart.

Keeley's own heart swelled and she leaned against the window of the patisserie to try and steady herself. The shopping arcade was starting to spin a little.

'Keels?'

Rach's voice brought Keeley back to. 'Oh, Rach, I—'

'Has he not turned up?' Rach snapped.

'I...' Keeley checked her watch. She hadn't really noticed how fast the minutes were ticking by. 11.30 a.m. For whatever reason, Ethan wasn't coming.

'Come on,' Rach said. Once she had coordinated shopping bags, she put an arm around Keeley's shoulders. 'Let's go in here and have a cake or something.'

'I... can't eat anything,' Keeley said, still feeling a little wobbly on her feet.

'Coffee then and you can watch *me* eat something.'

A familiar bark halted their advance into the café and before Keeley could move, Bo-Bo was there, up on his hind legs and leaping to lick her face.

'Bo-Bo! Down!'

'Bloody dog!' Rach remarked. 'It needs to learn a little social distancing.'

Keeley looked to Jeanne who was wearing a coat a few sizes too big for her with the buttons done up wrong. It was like she might have put it on in a hurry.

'Hi,' Jeanne said, pulling Bo-Bo's lead a little tighter in her fist.

'Hi,' Keeley greeted, her voice almost failing her. 'Is Ethan OK? Is something wrong?'

Jeanne shook her head. 'He is not coming. But, I am positive... given a little time he will...' She didn't finish the sentence.

Keeley didn't understand. Ethan had been so desperate to speak to her last night. And this morning, in reply to her message, he'd said he would be here. Why wasn't he here now when she so desperately needed to tell him her truth?

'Well, where is he?' Rach demanded to know. 'Because standing someone up isn't cool.'

Jeanne pulled Bo-Bo to heel again and the mutt sat down next to her. 'He knows,' the girl said softly. 'About... your connection to... his best friend. To Ferne.'

Keeley crumpled, her fingers finding Rach's bag-filled arm and her body listing. This wasn't what was supposed to happen. *She* wanted to be the one to tell him. How did he know? Who had told him before she could? Surely not Silvie...

'How does he know?' Rach asked the question, gathering Keeley close to her and letting the bags drop to the floor. 'It's OK,' she whispered to Keeley. 'It's going to be OK.'

'Someone called... Louis?' Jeanne said. 'I heard it all... from the top of the staircase and, well...' She sniffed, then wiped at her nose with her sleeve. 'So, I came because I wanted you to know that... I am going to look after him, the way he has looked after me and... when he has had time to think... he will want to see you. I know he will.'

Keeley couldn't concentrate on what Jeanne was saying to her, all she could feel was the bottom falling out of her world again. Erica. Ethan. Everything. She felt her body slide down to the floor.

Sixty-Four

L'Hotel Paris Parfait, Tour Eiffel, Paris

Five days later

'Antoine,' Rach purred. 'Do you have any more of those sugar-coated sweeties that were on your desk?'

'Are they for the general festive decoration? Or are they for your own consumption?' Antoine asked.

Keeley looked up from her clipboard and focused on her best friend leaning across the desk and displaying more than the probably accepted level of cleavage for the cold weather. She shook her head at the conversation, but all the while she was smiling. Rach's budding relationship with their concierge was a bright spot in an otherwise turbulent few days. Having been picked up off the floor inside Passage Jouffroy, Keeley had spent the first twelve hours or so bundled up in bed only sitting up to take the sips of water Rach offered at regular intervals or actually getting out from under the covers to visit the toilet. Then, the following day, the phone call had come, Nurse Walters informing her that

Erica had passed away. It had hurt. So much. Even though she had known it was coming. Through Keeley's fresh tears, the nurse had assured her it had been as peaceful as it could have been and that someone had been with Erica, holding her hand. Even the slightly gruff health care worker who witnessed death on a daily basis had sounded emotional. After that phone call she remembered vividly the promise she had made Erica. All in. Every time. That was a mantra for life and not reliant on anyone else's thoughts and feelings on the subject. It was then she had finally got out of bed. She'd washed and dressed and she'd begun a new day here in Paris with a list of things she wanted to do.

And during the days that followed she had got Silvie's go ahead to get stuck into a transformation of the hotels. Silvie had seen how areas at Opera had altered and what a difference it was making to the overall ambience of the place. Plus, the woman had also eaten some of the new simplified yet flavourful dishes on the menu and agreed they were to be immediately introduced. The jury was still out on the rabbits…

From the moment Keeley had taken that après-meltdown shower and no dye had leaked from her hair she had told herself this trip could still be all she wanted it to be and more. She didn't regret coming to Paris. She didn't regret meeting Silvie, or travelling around the gorgeous city, or learning more about Ferne. Whether she was meant to be here for Silvie, for herself, for Erica, or maybe even for Bea, it had been the right decision to come, despite the broken heart she was nursing. Because although her heart was crushed and possibly would never be fully mended, so much of the rest of her had started to heal.

'Well,' Rach said, her fingers prowling across the desk towards the slimline tie of the beaming concierge, 'my clever friend, Keeley, has sourced some lovely hand-painted wooden Christmas eggs on strings that we can fill with sweets for the tree.'

'As long as the sweets are allergen-free,' Keeley reminded, ticking an earlier completed task off her list.

'These,' Antoine said, producing the bowl from underneath his workstation. 'Are almond nuts.'

'Nuts,' Rach said long and slow.

Keeley shook her head again. 'I'm trying to get a hotel ready for Christmas over here.'

She swallowed, realising what she had just said. What *was* it she was doing exactly? Taking a job that had vaguely been offered her before the person that offered it had realised she had been holding back quite an important piece of her life from him. And neither of them had known quite how intertwined that had all been. Put simply, she was keeping busy. And she hoped she was doing good. Because Ethan had gone to ground. Well, not exactly gone to ground, Jeanne and Noel – who was far more Ethan's assistant than he was tour guide she had discovered – were reporting on the movements they were observing. Apparently, Ethan slept in his bed, but left early in the morning for who-knew-where. All Jeanne knew was that he left food for her but that there was no evidence he was eating anything himself. He made the briefest of appearances at the hotel in the Opera District, but only to delegate to his staff or, if the particular delegation was above their paygrade then he was passing the responsibility to Louis. Jeanne also said there were still no other festive decorations in the apartment except the paper, cardboard and tin foil chains she had made.

Keeley put her hand to one of the drapes she was hanging above the archway that led from reception to restaurant. She had thought about Ethan while she was drawing every brief outline plan for the communal areas of the hotel. He was in every idea and thought as she tried to carry on with what he himself had started. The hotels were going to become a home from home, just like the new slogan suggested. But right now she was working on them being a home from home with the added enhancement of Christmas. She was thinking not along the lines of Santa's grotto, but more that cosy log cabin vibe she had got the night Ethan had showed his changes to her, with a touch of comfort displayed in heavy, luscious fabrics and rustic detailing.

She sighed, working out a crease in the drape. She *had* tried to call Ethan. She had sent him a dozen messages. But, so far, he had yet to reply to any of them. It was as absolutely infuriating as it was upsetting. It seemed Ethan had simply decided to walk away with only the barest of facts and that hurt the most. All she had ever wanted was a chance to explain and it seemed he couldn't yet give that to her.

Keeley's phone began to ring and she stepped back from the curtains to remove it from the pocket of her jeans. It was her mum.

'Mum, hi.'

'Where are you, Keeley?' Lizzie asked, her voice on that very edge of frantic usually reserved for moments before curtain up on the latest book club meeting.

'I'm—'

Lizzie didn't give her the chance to reply. 'I will tell you where you're not, shall I?' she thundered on. 'You're not at the train station.'

Keeley closed her eyes and squeezed them up tight, the colour draining from her face. 'You're at St Pancras?'

'I'm at St Pancras,' Lizzie replied. 'And your father insisted on driving instead of getting on public transport so he is *still* looking for somewhere to park. *And* it's snowing.'

'It's snowing?' Keeley clarified. 'In London?'

'Keeley!' Lizzie exclaimed. 'That is not the most important part of what I'm trying to say to you. *Where* are you?!'

Keeley took a deep breath. She had only mooted to her mum in their last conversation that she and Rach *might* be back in London today. But since then she and Rach had talked at length. There was no rush to get back to London. Rach was managing her VIP client online and Keeley knew that they were both somehow wanting to stay a little longer to see what might transpire here before Christmas Day. Rach was taking things slower than she had ever taken things before with Antoine but Keeley knew her friend was hoping there might be a chance to spend the night together before she got on the Eurostar back home and was forced to think about a distance between them.

'I'm still in Paris,' Keeley told Lizzie.

'As if I hadn't guessed!'

'I didn't say I was *actually* coming back today, it was a thought, that's all.'

'You said you would let me know if you *weren't* coming back today. And you didn't.' Lizzie gasped. 'Tell me, honestly, is Silvie keeping you against your will?' she asked. 'And if she's there, blink twice if it's yes.'

'This… isn't FaceTime,' Keeley answered. 'How will you know if I'm blinking?'

'A code word then,' Lizzie whispered. 'Say "formaldehyde" if you're in trouble.'

'Are you still working at Mr Peterson's?' Keeley asked, mouth falling open.

'Roland and I have made tremendous headway with Mr Peterson. I'm confident we might get a sale of his place before Christmas.' Lizzie sniffed. 'There was one single lady who came round and said she actually liked the robins he'd stuffed for the church that he'd left on the dining room table.'

Keeley closed her eyes. That man was never going to change. But her mum actually sounded like she was enjoying the work. 'How is your squirrel injury?'

'Better. I don't need another vaccine for a year unless things take a turn.'

'That's good.'

'So, when are you coming home?' Lizzie asked. 'If it's not today.'

Keeley paused, listening in to the sound of London traffic and trying to imagine the city with snow. Suddenly her parents and everything she knew seemed so far away. Was staying longer really the right thing to do?

'Keeley?' Lizzie asked.

The sound of Rach's laughter rang out from behind her and she turned her head to see her friend kiss Antoine's cheek before he got back into professional mode and started to serve some new guests.

'I'll… let you know,' Keeley finally told her. 'I'll let you know for definite when we are back on the Eurostar and on our way. I promise.'

'And everything is OK?' Lizzie asked. 'With Silvie.'

'Yes,' Keeley reassured. 'Everything is fine, Mum. Please don't worry.'

Lizzie tutted. 'Asking me not to worry is like asking your father to take down Joan's infuriating decorations! Did you know I actually had bits of 1970s gossamer fairy wings in my sherry trifle last night! Luckily I spotted it before Juliet Honeydale dipped a spoon in. Those bloody awful outdated things!'

Keeley smiled. It sounded like things were exactly as they should be in England. 'Mum, I have to go now. I'll call you again soon. Bye.'

Sixty-Five

L'Hotel Perfect Paris, Opera District, Paris

'Good afternoon. Merry Christmas.'

Ethan was speaking and responding to guests and staff in the hotel, but it was as if his functions were being controlled by someone else. It was robotic. It was going through the motions. It was getting by. And that was what he had been doing for the past five days already. A replication of how he had been after Ferne's death.

He pushed the door to the boardroom and stepped inside. Today's mission, before he fled back into the anonymity of the city, was to ensure Noel was completely across the festive party bookings. Office workers, groups from construction, schoolteachers, they were all excited for the end of their working year and wanting to celebrate in style with dinner and dancing late into the night. It was a good money-maker as long as everything ran smoothly.

He entered, eyes to the floor, fingers clamped around a coffee he hadn't yet touched. 'Noel, can we make this quick so I can get back to other things?'

'Hello, Ethan,' Silvie's voice greeted.

He looked up then, the coffee cup falling out of his grasp. Around the boardroom table was Noel, Louis, Jeanne, Silvie and Bo-Bo was even sitting on his own chair looking like he might be about to start a presentation. 'What… is this?' Ethan gasped, hurriedly plucking the cup from the wood floor.

'This is a family meeting,' Silvie told him coolly. 'Please, sit down.'

'Family,' Ethan said shaking his head.

'Yes, Ethan,' Silvie said. 'Family. We are all here because we want the very same thing here. The best for our family. The Durand Family. And the best for Perfect Paris.'

Ethan's eyes went to Jeanne. How was she here? How was she sitting next to Silvie like she might be about to have lunch with a much-loved grandmother? Had he been so completely blinkered these past few days that he had missed significant developments. He was suddenly flooded with a worry that he hadn't left any food for Jeanne last night…

He put a hand on a chair and debated whether to drop into it or go running back out the door. What made him stay was the feeling of deep exhaustion he was carrying. He was so so tired.

'Ethan,' Louis said, appearing beside him and resting a hand on his shoulder. 'Come on, please, sit down.'

Ethan nodded, too tired to put up any sort of fight. If he didn't like what was about to be said he could always bury his head back in the snow later. He pulled out the seat and sat down, eyes dropping to the table. Bo-Bo let out a low whine.

'How are you feeling?' Silvie asked him.

'Like I am the subject of a social experiment right now,' he answered.

'I will... order some more coffees.'

Ethan raised his head at the sound of his assistant's voice and Noel offered him the smallest of smiles that very much said this meeting was not so much about business as it was about an intervention.

'Shall we start by talking about the hotels?' Silvie suggested.

Really? This was *about the hotels?* Then perhaps he could engage a little although... 'My assistant has left the room to make coffee. Perhaps we should...'

'I like the new concept for the hotels.'

Ethan turned a little in his seat at the sentence coming from Louis. The man was looking at him, a softness to his expression, the kind he had worn on the doorstep of Ethan's apartment before he dropped the bombshell that had altered the course of everything.

'I do not *like* the new concept,' Silvie said.

This was more like it. But Ethan had no fight left in him to counter.

'I *love* the new concept,' Silvie exclaimed in sheer excitement. 'Welcome Paris. Your home from home.'

His body responded before his brain could close it off. He was sitting more upright and he couldn't seem to settle his shoulders down again. It appeared his movement was no longer under his control.

'I think you have come up with an idea that will absolutely move the brand forward and it embraces everything a traveller needs as we look to a new year.' Silvie inhaled. 'The things we have missed most have been hugs. And I do not necessarily mean hugs from human contact, although, when we all had to be apart I *did* miss that. I mean the feeling of being supported… of being looked after and cherished…'

Comfortable. The word was in Ethan's mind immediately. Everything still ached from the revelation of five days ago. And still, every second of every day he was thinking only of Keeley.

'And… there are going to be more animals at the Tour Eiffel hotel,' Jeanne blurted out. Bo-Bo barked.

'The one thing we weren't quite sure about was rabbits in reception areas, despite the handwashing stations,' Silvie continued.

'Mother agreed,' Louis said, as if believing blame was likely to be levied in his direction. 'Even the animal shelter agreed.'

'So, there is now this cool barn in the garden!' Jeanne said, kneeling up on her chair and making pictures with her hands. 'There is a donkey and two sheep and the rabbits, plus some really cute little guinea pigs.'

'It is all being professionally overseen,' Louis continued. 'The animal association have helped with that – and they are hoping to raise awareness about animal kindness through the barn initiative. They will be giving out leaflets, collecting donations as the children staying at the hotel spend time in the petting zoo.'

'But grown-ups are allowed to hug too. Everyone needs something to cuddle sometimes,' Silvie added. She smiled like someone who had already had the pleasure of a guinea pig on their lap.

Ethan didn't know what to say. He was taking all this

in, but these people looking at him were different than they had been before. Altered from how they had been through the last twelve months. It was like while he had been hiding from the world they had all been reborn. And what had happened with Jeanne? Where had she really been while he had been turning back to Calvados? She was obviously here on the invitation of Silvie, or Louis, or both, and had been party to whatever had been happening over at the Tour Eiffel hotel. The one hotel he had made no attempt to visit at all.

'And the hotels are *all* getting a makeover,' Silvie stated. 'You have made a wonderful beginning with this hotel and a start has been made at Tour Eiffel. The other hotels will come on board in the new year.'

'It looks completely different!' Jeanne said, all eagerness. 'It looks like… a circus! With drapes and covers and lots of old stuff. Old stuff but nice stuff. Like we found at *Les Puces*.'

'We were going for a mix of log cabin and Bedouin tent with a Parisian twist,' Louis told him. 'I can… show you the drawings if you like.'

What did he say? It was now like all this information was on board an express train heading on a course straight for his heart. Somehow he knew now what this all was. It wasn't the Durands changing as people – not entirely anyhow – this was about someone else.

'The drawings do not do it justice, Louis,' Silvie insisted. 'Ethan needs to see it for himself.'

'Tonight!' Jeanne added, bouncing up higher on her knees and invigorating Bo-Bo. 'He should see it tonight!'

Ethan watched Silvie put a hand on Jeanne's shoulder

as if to quieten her and miraculously the girl complied. He rubbed his eyes with his fist. Jeanne's hair was pinned back from her face and set in a neat bun. He was just about getting used to her without the hat, but this neatness and care was brand new. And he had missed it. Because he had been only thinking of himself. How could he be that way if he was planning to provide a safe haven for the girl? He had to get himself together if he wanted to ensure a place with him was better for her health than living on the streets.

'What a wonderful suggestion, Jeanne,' Silvie said clapping her hands together. 'How about a family meal?'

Bo-Bo let out a bark and shook his head, drool landing on the polished boardroom table.

'Yes, and you too, Bo-Bo,' Silvie agreed.

And then something extraordinary happened. Silvie reached towards the dog and scratched the animal under its chin until it began licking her fingers and looked likely to try and mount the woman.

'I… cannot make it tonight,' Ethan found himself saying. 'I have other plans.'

'No, you do not,' Jeanne told him.

'Jeanne, I do.'

'You have been spending all your time drinking. You think I do not know the haunts of people from the street? I have spent time with Pierre from the secret bar in Montmartre.'

Ethan didn't know what to say. He had known Pierre for years. It hurt him that Jeanne was even acquainted with the barman who was known for helping those in need.

'Jeanne, Louis,' Silvie addressed them. 'Why don't you both see what Noel is doing about the coffee?'

Jeanne huffed a sigh and climbed down from her perch

on the chair, tugging Bo-Bo down with her. 'Perhaps he might respond if we had something stronger than coffee.'

'How about cake?' Louis suggested, shepherding Jeanne towards the door like a favourite uncle.

'And some for Bo-Bo?' she asked.

'Of course,' Louis replied.

As the door closed behind them Ethan got to his feet. 'What is going on here? How do you know Jeanne? What is happening with the hotels? And how did you get Louis to sign off on a barn?'

His agitation was the only thing driving him now, as he hadn't eaten properly in five days. That weakness was telling a tale on his attempt to appear together.

'Louis was happy to agree on animals. We did not agree on penguins.' She sighed. 'Sit back down, Ethan. We have some talking to do.'

'I do not want to talk,' he told her. 'I have nothing to say.'

'You have nothing to say?' Silvie asked. 'You do not want to say anything about how you decided to take in a street girl and her dog, inviting them to live with you! You do not want to say anything about the new idea you had to change the hotels so they cater completely for what customers *want* not what Ferne maybe thought our customers should aspire to?'

Ethan didn't know how to respond. Silvie was hitting the nail on the head with every breath. He sat back down.

'Or do you not want to say anything about Keeley?' Silvie asked. 'The woman you have fallen in love with but are too stupid to not take a chance with.'

Ethan bit his lip. The tears were in his eyes as soon as Silvie had said her name. 'I... cannot.'

'Why can't you?' Silvie asked him. 'I want to hear it in your words.'

He shook his head. 'She... and Ferne... it's too... crazy.'

'Crazy,' Silvie said with a nod. 'Yes, you are right. The situation is completely crazy. But, it is the kind of thing you read about all the time. Remember, the two people who found love in lockdown across their balconies. Or the cats that go missing, then walk hundreds of miles to get to their previous homes. Or how about... jetting into space... or that craziest of crazy men being in charge of the United States.' Silvie paused for a second. 'Crazy happens all the time, Ethan. It does not have to mean that crazy is wrong.'

He didn't have any more words. It was an unbelievable complication. Something that should not have been able to occur with no one knowing about it. If he had just paid a little more interest when Silvie had said the person who had received Ferne's kidney was here. If he had turned up at dinner...

'Look at it from Keeley's point of view,' Silvie carried on. 'I have asked her to come here. I have wanted to meet the woman who received Ferne's kidney. I wanted, very selfishly, to know who Keeley was and to also know that she was well. And to believe that some good was coming from the waste that was Ferne's death. Perhaps it was closure. Maybe, in truth, it was thinking that I might notice a little of Ferne about her. I know that sounds silly. Donating a kidney isn't some far-fetched kind of reincarnation, I realise that. I suppose, I wanted to know she was nice, and kind, or brave, or set to do remarkable things but what I found out was so much more than I could have anticipated.'

Ethan made no reply.

'I found out that she was the most beautiful soul in the simplest of ways. She *is* kind. And she *is* nice. And, my God, she has been so brave. Going through an accident, losing her sister, nearly losing her own life and having to pick up all those pieces afterwards. I can only imagine what she has had to go through.' Silvie shook her head. 'And to do all that and know that you are supposed to be living your best life each and every day, with the eyes of your overprotective mother on you, the hopes and dreams of a grieving French woman on you, and everyone else talking about second chances and making moments count. The poor *poor* girl hasn't been given a minute to even process what her new life means.' Silvie stood then, making her way around the table towards him. 'Until she met you.'

Ethan didn't dare look up. His heart was hammering against his rib cage and he felt rather like one of the rabbits from reception who got agitated if the children held them too long or too hard.

'Because Keeley met you with no precursor,' Silvie reminded him. 'She told me you literally ran into each other. With the penguin.'

He swallowed. 'Yes.'

'And, for a moment, for the very first time, Keeley was simply herself. A bright, intelligent, young woman in Paris, the person she was before these tragic events, the person she so wants to be if only fate would let her.'

Ethan shook his head, the tears coming then. 'I do not know what to do,' he sobbed. 'I cannot stop thinking about her. But every time I think about her I think about Ferne and how much I still miss her.'

Silvie slipped into the seat beside him then. 'We all still

miss her. And there is nothing wrong with that.' She sighed. 'I know that Louis thinks I have been spending too much time in Ferne's room, but there is a reason for that. I have decided... that it is time to clear a few things out. Not all of it. *Never* all of it. But there are deserving people who would appreciate almost a whole house of fashion that lives in her wardrobes.'

'She has more clothes than Givenchy,' Ethan answered.

Silvie laughed. 'She really does.'

Ethan smiled and rubbed at his eyes.

'Ethan,' Silvie said gently. 'The only body part that makes us who we are cannot be transplanted.' She sighed. 'Our soul.' She laid her hand on his. 'And... I believe that the soul dies altogether at exactly the same time we do.' Silvie smiled. 'Everything else about us is... simply machinery.'

'You really look at it like that?' Ethan asked her.

Silvie nodded. 'I also know that if Ferne had not been in the UK, in London, on that November night, Keeley would most likely not be here now.' She smiled at Ethan, patting his hand. 'Do not punish Keeley for being able to live because Ferne could not. I believe Keeley has been punishing herself for far too long already, with absolutely no grounds for it.'

'I don't know what to do,' Ethan said, watery eyes struggling to focus.

Silvie sighed. 'Yes, you do,' she told him sincerely. 'And you also know what Ferne would want you to do too.'

Suddenly, loud barking erupted from outside the door and, looking through the glass into the lobby area beyond, Ethan saw Bo-Bo was running off with a whole cake lodged in between his jaws.

'That dog!' Silvie said, shaking her head. 'It is a menace! And it needs a visit to the groomers.'

'So did Jeanne before I saw a bun in her hair today,' Ethan replied.

Silvie smiled. 'You liked my handiwork?'

'I knew you had done it. I just did not know why.'

'Jeanne was worried about you. She made sure we were introduced. And while you have been… absent… she has asked for some books from my library and some of Ferne's things to decorate her room.'

'I… do not know what I am doing with Jeanne either,' Ethan admitted. 'I did not think. I…'

'Oh no, Ethan,' Silvie interrupted. 'You *did* think. You thought very deeply with regard to Jeanne. Except you did not think with your head. You thought with your heart.' She squeezed his hand then. 'And that is what you should carry on doing. Come to the hotel tonight. Come and see what has changed.' A smile crossed her lips. 'I think you will be surprised.'

Sixty-Six

L'Hotel Paris Parfait, Tour Eiffel, Paris

'I'm quite nervous,' Keeley admitted. 'Almost as if this is my hotel.'

'Well,' Rach said, sheening a rather light-coloured lipstick for her over her mouth as they both looked at their reflections in the mirror of the ladies' toilets, 'you've designed all these changes and *made* some of the curtains. You made it all happen so it *is* your project really.'

'And it's your big date,' Keeley reminded. 'Tonight could be the night with Antoine, right?'

'I am counting on the romance in that yurt.'

Keeley smiled and touched a section of her hair, pulling it a little straighter. The yurt was a triumph even if she did say so herself. If the romantic or – as an alternative – intimate *family* dining experiences went well, she had suggested to Silvie and Louis that they purchase three more of the structures. Not only could they charge money for these extras, it also fitted very well with people's desire to still be a little socially distant. One table, one tent, one dinner to remember. 'Thank you for being my guinea pig. Not, you know, a guinea pig like they have in the petting zoo barn but—'

'Come on! I want to see the inside of the yurts with the elaborate drapes and the map of the sky and the Christmas trees with a gift to take home.' Rach grabbed Keeley's arm and pulled her towards the door.

Ethan couldn't believe the transformation. It wasn't like the small changes he had made in a corner of the hotel at Opera, this was a completely different dynamic. It was almost as if he were walking into someone else's establishment, one he did not know at all. But that lack of initial familiarity became a lead-in to a whole host of flashes from the past. With every footstep further into the bowels of his hotel he was bowled over by the Christmas décor – the real tree decorated with tiny gingerbread men, trains, wooden eggs, stars, toy soldiers, wrapped gifts with baskets of snow-topped logs at its base, bells and garlands of fir over picture frames and mirrors. Gentle festive music played but it wasn't an interference, it drew you in, made you feel as though you were part of a world that was going on undisturbed inside what was definitely going to be Welcome Paris. Stress was floating away, no one was without a smile, the traffic and inclement weather outside could be a mile away. Even if he hadn't known already, he could feel that this was all Keeley.

'Monsieur Bouchard,' Antoine greeted him as he headed towards the door to the restaurant.

Ethan cleared his throat. 'Good evening, Antoine.' It felt like it had been weeks since he had been here last.

'Your table is this way,' Antoine said, sticking out a hand and directing.

'I am meeting Madame Durand,' Ethan began.

'Yes,' Antoine answered with a nod.

'She is outside?' Ethan asked. 'Are we having dinner in this animal barn I have heard so much about?'

'You may laugh,' Antoine began. 'But for a moment, until the leaflets from the animal shelter began to arrive, Chef thought the sheep were for him. He was keen in creating lamb navarin.'

Ethan wasn't quite sure if Antoine was joking or not. He followed his directioning though, heading for the door to the garden.

A few paces later and they arrived in the area usually reserved for a few benches and racks to safely keep bicycles. The large wooden barn was at the very end, twinkling lights around his doorway, but here, now, in the foreground sat the most unusual tent he had ever seen. He paused, just looking, taking it all in. The garden was lit by flaming torches – far enough away from structures not to be a hazard – lanterns swung from the branches of the trees, illuminating the layer of crisp snow on the ground. And the tent itself – thick cream material in a circular shape, wooden struts poking out from its top – it looked like it was a dollop of thick clotted cream complete with chocolate flake that had been dropped into the centre of Paris.

'Please,' Antoine said. 'Come this way.'

'The tent?' Ethan asked, stepping onto the snow.

'For the brochure, it is intended to be called a "boutique boudoir".'

'I...' Ethan began.

'Very much can happen in five days,' Antoine said, smiling.

'So I am finding.'

Ethan stepped forward, moving up to the entrance, then tentatively he parted the curtain of fabric.

'Great!' Rach exclaimed. 'Right on time!'

Keeley span round to face the doorway and there was Ethan, standing on the coir matting a few short metres away. Her heart was in her throat before she could attempt to do anything to stop it and she felt like she didn't quite know what to do with herself. She drew her handbag towards her like it was a security blanket.

'Our work here is done,' Antoine stated, beckoning Rach towards him.

Suddenly, somehow, her best friend and her best friend's new boyfriend managed to leave the yurt and neither she nor Ethan had moved one centimetre.

'I… cannot believe it,' Ethan said finally. 'This… boutique boudoir.' He stepped closer then, his eyes roving over all the work she had put into it. 'It is phenomenal.'

That one word warmed Keeley all the way up and she took a step nearer to him. It was all billowing canvas above them, decorated with a map of the sky, tiny lights highlighting the constellations. There was a sofa to lounge on draped with thick fleecy throws, plaid blankets and furry cushions. From a small speaker, delicate music was gently rising into the air and there were trugs filled with wood around a roaring stove, Christmas stockings hung from the knobs of a sideboard sat next to a medium-sized Christmas tree. Perhaps, she wondered, if they started to talk about the décor, they could find their way back to a beginning.

'It's an idea I had when I was looking at fabric for the inside of the hotel. And then I did a little bit of research. Did you know that although most people say they wouldn't want to go camping, actually the being under canvas part, the simplicity and the rustic elements of it are not what they find unappealing?' Keeley said.

Ethan nodded. 'It is the cold and the rain and the holes in the canvas… or the hours that it takes to put up a tent in the cold and the rain with the holes in the canvas.'

'It sounds like you are speaking from experience,' Keeley ventured.

'The cold and the rain part comes from my few years living on the streets,' he admitted.

A pregnant pause followed until Keeley's self-preservation kicked in and she took another few steps towards him. 'There is insulation in the floor and… the wood burner. Anyone dining here has a choice whether to have someone tend the fire for them or to do it themselves. A home from home but with added touches if required.'

'It is amazing,' Ethan breathed. 'Truly amazing.'

Keeley was closer to him now and it reminded her of everything that had passed between them. The pure, wonderful times and the moment it had all gone wrong. Was there any way to move forward?

'I…'

'Do you…'

Keeley's cheeks flamed as they both started talking at exactly the same time. She closed her lips.

'Keeley, I need to say something to you,' Ethan began. 'Actually, I need to say a great many things to you.'

Keeley shook her head. 'Can I say something first?'

He nodded. 'Of course.'

She had always hoped she would see Ethan again. As soon as she had talked about staying in Paris longer than she and Rach had originally planned on, she knew it was because she wanted this chance to speak to him. But now, when he was stood right here, so close that even her defective smell receptors were definitely detecting a hint of musky pine, the words were threatening to come out in a different order than she wanted.

'I was going to tell you,' Keeley said. 'I would have told you. About... what happened to me. And about... Ferne. But I didn't know... until I knew for sure and...' She really was having trouble and her feelings were threatening to get the better of her.

'It is OK,' Ethan breathed.

'Is it?' she asked. She knew her expression was hopeful, but she couldn't help herself. She *wanted* to feel hope. She *wanted* to believe that two people who had become so connected could find a way through anything.

The canvas of the yurt was parted and Keeley took a step back from him, conscious that they were being interrupted.

'Monsieur, Madame.' It was a waiter wheeling in a trolley bearing rustic wooden domes.

'Shall we?' Ethan asked, indicating the beautifully set table in the middle of the room.

Keeley nodded. 'Yes.'

Sixty-Seven

The food was exquisite, but not in a scientific, planned feast for all senses kind of way. It was much more in a very humble, flavoursome, simply evocative kind of way. The starter had been wedges of fresh white bread accompanied by individual pots of a rich duck terrine. It was hearty, ideal winter food and a bottle of red wine had complemented it perfectly. Next was succulent chicken in a sauce that Ethan could taste each and every individual flavour of – onion, mushroom, garlic, a touch of bay leaf, the flavoursome stock holding it all together. It took him right back to one of the first meals he had shared with the Durand family.

'Silvie made this dish for us once, but with rabbit,' Ethan told Keeley as he paused in his eating. 'Silvie is a terrible cook by the way and she will be the first to admit it.'

Keeley smiled, nodding as she wiped her mouth with her napkin. 'The recipe is supposed to be with rabbit but, with the petting zoo barn, we didn't think it was appropriate.'

'*We*,' Ethan said. 'You are sounding like someone who is invested in the future of the hotels.'

'Oh,' Keeley said. 'Well, I really meant Silvie and Louis.

They have been making all the decisions. She asked me... *Silvie* asked me to continue with what you started and...'

'Keeley,' Ethan whispered. 'Why are you seeming to censor everything you say?'

'I'm not. I...' She paused and took a sip of her red wine before her eyes met his again. 'Tell me what you were going to say before the food arrived.'

Ethan put down his knife and fork and wiped his lips with his napkin. He sighed, holding her gaze and drinking her in. She was so beautiful, so gentle, just the thought of her made him smile a hundred times a day...

'I want to say that I am sorry,' Ethan finally said. 'I was a coward. A complete coward. I should have come to meet you at Passage Jouffroy. I should have kept my head and faced you but...'

'But?' Keeley asked.

'But... the noise was too loud.' He swallowed.

Why had he said that? It straightaway brought back every bad experience he had ever had. All the darkest memories from the orphanage and the loss he felt after Ferne.

'It means, in my head, everything was suddenly too much all at once. It was a cymbal... and a bass drum and... a high-pitched trumpet playing complicated jazz. And I did not know how to make it stop. Not at first.'

'I understand,' Keeley responded.

'No,' Ethan said. 'Do not understand. Do not be nice to me. I do not deserve it. I was stupid to hide away. I mean... I am twenty-eight years old. There is only so much hiding away from life you can do before it becomes more about how long you have before you die rather than embracing the living part.'

*

Keeley empathised absolutely. 'I know.'

She completely knew in relation to how her own life had been going and because of Bea and Erica.

'My friend Erica… the one we took a photo for…' Keeley started.

'I remember,' Ethan said. 'We got my best side.'

She forced a smile. 'Well… she passed away.' A knot of despair caught in her throat and it was taking everything not to let the tears drop.

'Oh, Keeley.'

She picked up her napkin at the very same moment he reached for her hand. She dabbed at her eyes and he retracted.

'We… knew it was going to happen. We met in the hospital during her treatment after all, but it just brings it home that… no one knows what's around the corner. Erica didn't. I didn't with my accident and losing Bea.' She took another breath. 'And neither did Ferne.'

Keeley watched Ethan look to the wood-burning stove then get to his feet. 'I think the fire requires another log.'

'It doesn't,' Keeley told him. 'Not yet.'

He stopped still, right by her chair now.

'Ethan, I'm only alive now because of Ferne and I can't apologise for that.'

'I know,' he answered. 'And, of course, why should you? As I have said, it is I who should be apologising.'

'I have to take tablets every day for the rest of my life,' Keeley continued. 'I have to check in with doctors all the time. I have to watch what I eat and drink and I should be exercising far more than I am. There is no guarantee that Ferne's kidney is going to be with me forever.' She sighed. 'There is going to come a time when I am going to need another transplant, maybe two. And each one is going to come at an enormous risk. Close matches aren't easy to find. My mum can't donate and my dad wasn't the best match so, if things got bad… the outcome might be quite different a second time around.'

'What are you trying to tell me?' Ethan asked, his eyes meeting hers.

'I'm trying to say that my life isn't as straightforward as it could be for you… with someone else.'

'Keeley,' he whispered. 'I—'

'No, don't say anything else yet. Let me finish.' She got to her feet too, moving over the matting to the gorgeous, thick and fluffy rug she had sourced for the room. Slipping off her shoes, she buried her stockinged feet into its depth, the heat from the stove warming right the way through her body. 'I have been tip-toeing though. Partly because my mother worries I am going to teleport to heaven if I eat more than the recommended daily fat intake of… I don't know… Bo-Bo.' She sighed. 'And also because I've been cautious. Too cautious. *I've* been the one *marking* time instead of *making* time. I don't want to do that anymore, Ethan. I want to *live* my life. Really live it.'

Her heart was thudding now. He was so close to her that if she reached out she could touch him. And she so wanted to touch him, more than anything else. But he had to want it too. He had to be sure. Because he knew everything now. Who she was. What her life had been like. Hopefully, what it could be.

'You think my life is straightforward?' Ethan asked, stepping away from her and heading to the basket of logs.

'No, of course not,' she answered. 'I didn't say it was.'

'I have a child living with me, Keeley. Me! Ethan Bouchard... has a child!' He quickly opened up the stove and threw another log into the flames. 'You know, people, they have sex without contraception and they ask themselves what happened when pregnancy occurs. Me, I find a girl taking chocolate from a Christmas tree and she moves in... with her dog! I do not even know her real name or how old she is! Am I completely mad?'

'Yes,' Keeley answered. 'But not when it comes to Jeanne.'

'Am I even the right person to be guiding her?'

'Ethan, she has been living on the streets for a reason. I suspect not just because there *is* no one else, but because she has never met anyone else who immediately cared like you did.'

Ethan turned around to face her, brushing his hands together. 'I barely know how to look after myself. Two days ago I ate something from the back of the fridge I could not even distinguish.'

'But you've been making meals for Jeanne and leaving them in boxes with her name on,' Keeley replied.

Ethan sighed. 'She told you that?'

'She has been worried about you. She cares about you almost as much as she cares for Bo-Bo.'

'I am surprised she has any care left the amount she gives to that *chien*.' He shook his head. 'I do not know what the future holds. I have never really known. Some of the very first things I do remember involve not knowing if I was going to survive the day. When you have felt like that it is hard to start doing any kind of planning but…'

'But?'

He sighed. '*Ma crevette*.'

It was that name again. The name of the person Ethan had talked about before. Who was she?

'Ferne,' he said. 'I called her "my shrimp". I have never known anyone be able to eat shrimp like she did.'

Keeley closed her eyes and shook her head. So much misunderstanding had gone on from the very beginning. But there was one thing she really needed to know if they were going to try to resolve things.

'I… care about you, Ethan,' she admitted. 'I haven't ever felt for anyone what I feel for you.' She swallowed, feeling exposed by that admission. 'But I know how my connection with Ferne might have made you feel.'

'Keeley…'

'No, I know it feels weird and it *is* weird I suppose. But I need to know that, when you look at me now, you still see the woman you met outside the hotel who chased a penguin down the street with you. That I'm still to you the woman who went running in her dad's darts jumper and whispered to an almost-dying dog, who somehow rose again, and laughed at the clowns at the circus and played very bad *petanque* and—'

The rest of her words never made it past her lips as her mouth was captured by Ethan's in a kiss that pulled her off her feet and into his embrace. It was as passionate as it was magical and it left her in no doubt that he had listened to every word she'd said. When Ethan broke off Keeley was out of breath and he was looking at her, gazing in wonder as if she were something precious that might evaporate if he took his eyes away.

'I only see you, Keeley,' he told her. 'I promise, I will always only see you.' He ran a thumb gently down her cheek to the curve of her lips. 'You are my "comfortable".'

This time it was Keeley who joined their lips together again. And as they kissed, she knew, whatever life had in store for them, she was going to be all in. Every time.

Sixty-Eight

L'Hotel Paris Parfait, Tour Eiffel, Paris

Christmas Day

'The children are touching everything!'

'Antoine, the children are meant to be touching everything. The touching is *making* their experience,' Rach said. She nudged him with her elbow. 'Touching always makes *my* experience.' She kissed the concierge in the kind of way that wasn't necessarily appropriate for a dining room full of street children.

'Rach, could you hand out some more crackers?' Keeley asked, presenting her friend with another box full. 'If you can leave Antoine alone for five minutes?'

'Just five minutes,' Rach said pinching Antoine's bum. 'No longer.' She took the box, turning around to blow her boyfriend a kiss on the way to the main table.

Keeley watched the children eating for all they were worth, some blowing up long sausage-shaped balloons and watching them fly around this dining area in the lobby she had constructed and decorated. There were fifty children, maybe more, the invitation to attend Perfect Paris on Christmas Day to be given a hot festive meal and a room for the night being passed by word of mouth, starting with Jeanne and the places she used to hang out. This year and every year after, it was going to be Christmas Day for everyone that needed it, as well as everyone who had paid for it. Seeing the delight in the children's faces now, Keeley could tell one meal, one day and night out of their normal lives, was going to mean everything.

'Juice, Keeley. They are going through juice like oranges are about to become a rarity. And one of them called Michael Bublé, Michael Booby! Sacrilege.'

Keeley smiled at her mum. Yes, Lizzie and Duncan were here for Christmas. A few FaceTime calls, an introduction to Silvie, Louis and Ethan and the Andrews had decided if Keeley was going to be staying in France for the festive season then they were going to make the journey too. And, Silvie and Lizzie had quite the sisterhood going, brought on by a conversation about all the recipes they had tried to make that hadn't quite gone to plan. Louis was still trying to beat Duncan at darts… What happened when the New Year arrived hadn't been decided yet, but Keeley had a feeling Rach might be more than open to looking for an apartment to share in Paris as opposed to London. In fact, Rach had already 'popped in to' a few Parisian estate agents to 'get a feel for the market'. Plus she had already mooted the idea of starting up a bespoke property search service with the help of the connections of the Bradburys she might be able to run alongside any other job with the hope it would take off.

And, as for Keeley, she had a position here if she wanted

it, making over all the Perfect Paris hotels. It would be helping Ethan, putting money in the bank and it would also be excellent for her interior design portfolio whether her business ended up being based in England or France.

'I'll get some more,' Keeley said, taking the jug from Lizzie's hands.

'Well,' Lizzie whispered, 'don't you have... you know... staff to do that for you?' She sniffed. 'I've never been to a hotel where the interior designer had to fetch drinks for guests.'

'The staff are all in the main restaurant serving the paying customers,' Keeley reminded her mum. 'This is for the children and... I want to do it.' She smiled at her mum. 'Ethan was one of these children once. And it was only through the kindness of others that his life changed. Maybe what we're doing today will change someone's life.'

'Oh, Keeley,' Lizzie said, her voice sounding a little teary. 'Bea would have loved this, wouldn't she?'

Keeley nodded. 'Bea would have been modelling those balloons and playing hide and seek and probably constructing a bridge made out of straws.'

'Ferne would have loved it also,' Silvie remarked, arriving next to the women. 'Particularly the Jeanne and Bo-Bo Puppet Show.'

Jeanne was in her element, showing the children around the new improved areas of the hotel and Ethan had fashioned her a puppet theatre style booth from which she was delivering timed performances of magic, plus dancing from Ferne's old puppet, Augusto. There were even doggy-tricks Bo-Bo was exceedingly bad at but no one seemed to mind. The girl was in trousers today, smart and black with a white shirt and bow tie, her hair slicked back from her face in a boyish avant-garde fashion that suited her so well.

Since their talk in the boutique boudoir, Keeley had spent nights at Ethan's apartment, curled up on the sofa between both him and Jeanne – plus Bo-Bo – toasting marshmallows, and for all intents and purposes being a family. It was all the proof anyone needed that family could come along when you least expected it and very rarely these days fitted with convention.

'Keeley!'

She turned to the sound of Ethan's voice and there he was, beckoning her to the outside, dressed in his three-piece suit looking as always, halfway between travelling conjuror and entrepreneur.

'I'll be back,' Keeley said to the two women. 'I'll come back with the juice.'

Silvie took the jug from Keeley's hands. 'I will get some more juice. Come, Lizzie, while we refill this, let us see if we can find a little adult juice in the kitchens.'

Ethan was nervous but his heart lifted as he saw Keeley walking towards him across the snow-covered garden. There were children all around, being taken into the barn to pet the animals by newly appointed Perfect Paris staff in charge of looking after the pets' welfare. It all really felt like a new dawn for the hotel brand. Welcome Paris would be ready to be everyone's home from home in 2021.

'What are you doing out here?' Keeley asked. 'We've got children to feed.'

'I know,' Ethan answered. 'Antoine says the hotel will never be the same.'

'Comfort, remember?' Keeley teased. 'Memories to treasure.'

'I remember,' Ethan breathed. 'And, trust me, I like it.' He kissed her lips. 'I really *really* like it.' He drew a wrapped gift from out of his pocket and held it out to her.

'Ethan, we said no gifts.'

'It was a stupid idea.'

'But I haven't got you anything.'

'Open it,' Ethan urged her.

Keeley smiled and began loosening the bow, before she tore at the edge of the paper, revealing a box beneath.

'Open it,' he urged her again.

He watched as she lifted the hinged lid then he smiled as she exhaled in delight.

'Oh, Ethan! I love it! It's so perfect!' She took the golden necklace out of its casing and held it out to him. 'Would you put it on for me?'

'*Absolument.*'

With trembling hands, he took the fine chain between his fingers and levelled it around her neck. 'Sorry,' he whispered as it took a few attempts to get the catch to fasten. 'There.'

Keeley turned around and put her fingers to the shiny penguin suspended from the necklace. 'It's… the best gift,' she said. 'Ever.'

'No,' Ethan told her. '*You* are the best gift.' He swallowed. 'And whoever I have to thank for bringing you to me – fate, Ferne… Pepe.' He sighed, happy tears forming in his eyes. 'I will be grateful for the rest of my days.'

Keeley put her arms around him, holding him close, and

as a children's chorus of 'Away in a Manger' drifted out of the barn and into the air, they both whispered to the afternoon sky.

'Merry Christmas.'

Dear Reader,

You've finished! Are you smiling, or crying, or maybe a bit of both?

I hope that Keeley and Ethan's love story, plus the stories of the Andrews and Durand families has left you feeling all warm, fuzzy and Christmassy. Who was your favourite character? Did you love feisty Erica? How about Jeanne? Or did the animals, Pepe and Bo-Bo, steal the show?

For me, Christmas is a time for reflection and counting blessings and that's truly what *A Perfect Paris Christmas* is all about. While I was researching organ donation and transplants I decided that I couldn't finish Keeley and Ferne's story without doing something personal to make a change. So, I signed up to the donor register. Now, if anything happens to me, someone can make use of my body parts just like Ferne's gift to Keeley. I know my decision isn't for everyone, but if you are interested in finding out more about being a donor after reading this book, why not visit the NHS Organ Donation website:

www.organdonation.nhs.uk/register-your-decision/

As always, I LOVE hearing your thoughts on my books! So, please, get in touch if something about *A Perfect Paris Christmas* has warmed your heart or made you smile, or you just want to tell me how HOT you thought Ethan was…

Lastly, thank you so so much for choosing to read my Christmas story and I hope you enjoyed your time in Paris! Here's to more happy-ever-afters in 2021!

Mandy xx

About the Author

MANDY BAGGOT is an international bestselling and award-winning romance writer. The winner of the Innovation in Romantic Fiction award at the UK's Festival of Romance, her romantic comedy novel, *One Wish in Manhattan*, was also shortlisted for the Romantic Novelists' Association Romantic Comedy Novel of the Year award in 2016. Mandy's books have so far been translated into German, Italian, Czech and Hungarian. Mandy loves the Greek island of Corfu, white wine, country music and handbags. Also a singer, she has taken part in ITV1's *Who Dares Sings* and *The X-Factor*. Mandy is a member of the Society of Authors and lives near Salisbury, Wiltshire, UK with her husband and two daughters.

Twitter: @mandybaggot
Facebook: @mandybaggotauthor
Instagram: @mandybaggot
Join the Mandy Baggot Book Club on Facebook
Website: www.mandybaggot.com